MURPH

UNEXPECTED

GRACE TURNER

Copyright © 2022 by Grace Turner

All rights reserved.

No part of this book may be reproduced in any form or by any electronic or mechanical means, including information storage and retrieval systems, without written permission from the author, except for the use of brief quotations in a book review.

CONTENTS

Content Warning	vii
Chapter 1	1
Chapter 2	9
Chapter 3	15
Chapter 4	21
Chapter 5	25
Chapter 6	41
Chapter 7	47
Chapter 8	53
Chapter 9	67
Chapter 10	73
Chapter 11	79
Chapter 12	89
Chapter 13	101
Chapter 14	113
Chapter 15	119
Chapter 16	125
Chapter 17	137
Chapter 18	151
Chapter 19	167
Chapter 20	173
Chapter 21	181
Chapter 22	195
Chapter 23	207
Chapter 24	217
Chapter 25	225
Chapter 26	235
Chapter 27	245
Chapter 28	255
Chapter 29	263
Chapter 30	273
Chapter 31	283
Chapter 32	291
Chapter 33	299

Chapter 34	313
Chapter 35	325
Chapter 36	335
Chapter 37	347
Chapter 38	361
Chapter 39	369
Chapter 40	385
Chapter 41	397
Chapter 42	407
Chapter 43	419
Chapter 44	429
Chapter 45	441
Chapter 46	459
Chapter 47	471
Chapter 48	477
Chapter 49	487
Chapter 50	497
Chapter 51	511
Chapter 52	517
Chapter 53	525
Chapter 54	535
Chapter 55	539
Chapter 56	549
Chapter 57	561
Epilogue	571
Acknowledgments	587
About the Author	589

To my younger self.

I'm so glad you kept writing.

CONTENT WARNING

This book is intended for adults and contains sexual situations. This book also mentions domestic violence and sexual assault.

Domestic violence resources

https://www.thehotline.org/

1-800-799-SAFE (7233)

ONE

Hazel

"I swear, I'm going to kill him this time," I mumbled as I looked from the car blocking my driveway to the illuminated house to my left. The thump of the music was obnoxious, and I was surprised no one had called the cops yet. There were a few partygoers congregating on the porch of the house, drinks in their hands and heads thrown back, laughing, but it looked like most of the party was happening inside.

I just needed whoever was parked behind me to move. Why anyone would intentionally park at the end of someone's driveway was beyond me, but if my neighbor's attitude and personality were any indications, I'm sure the people he hung around weren't all that great either.

I took a deep breath. The cool bite of the fall air felt good against my angry, flushed skin as I stomped toward his house. I marched down the sidewalk, my new black heels clicking against the concrete. The sound was satisfying and provided a needed boost of confidence. When I hit the bottom stair of the porch, I grabbed the rail to steady myself.

I drew the attention of every person outside while I gained

my balance. The closest person to me was a woman, roughly my age, with jet-black hair. Her red lips were a stark contrast to her extraordinarily white teeth. She gave me a slurred "hiiii" as I climbed the steps.

"Is Luke inside?" I asked, not missing a beat and hoping to get out unscathed and relatively unnoticed.

She gave me a curious look but eventually nodded and went back to talking to the guy hanging on her when I stepped through the front door.

For such a loud party, there weren't that many people in the house. It wasn't the first time I was party crashing, so I knew exactly where to go. I didn't stop as I scanned the faces of each person I passed. Most of them were drunk, or at least tipsy. A few were dancing, others were playing drinking games, and each person who noticed me gave me a look similar to the woman outside.

I found Luke in the kitchen, leaning back in front of the sink, with a beer in one hand and his phone in the other. I rounded the island, shimmied between a few people, and stood directly in front of him. That was mistake number one.

After fighting, arguing, bickering—whatever the hell you wanted to call it—with Luke for the previous two years, I learned it was better to keep my distance from him. He was a big guy. He was easily twice my size with a broad chest and biceps that were the size of my thighs. He was intimidating without trying to be, and although I wasn't scared of him, he did make me nervous when he looked down at me with dark, hooded eyes and an unbothered expression on his face. Without even trying, he made me feel small.

Then he opened his mouth and his deep voice, dripping with confidence and authority, added to my nerves. Thankfully, my three-inch heels helped—although not much—to decrease his height advantage. He was confident, brazen, and huge. A great combination.

"Hi, neighbor," I said between gritted teeth.

"Oh, look who it is!" Luke said as if he hadn't seen me standing right in front of him for several seconds. "Did you finally decide to come by and hang with us, neighbor?" He smirked. The guy standing next to him gave me a once-over and my skin began to crawl. I knew I looked hot in a formfitting black corset top that pushed my boobs up, a black blazer, skintight jeans, and black heels. But his leering made me want to turn and run.

Luke kept his eyes locked on my face, though.

"No. I'm trying to get out of my driveway, but one of your friends is parked directly behind me. I need them to move." I crossed my arms over my chest and lifted my chin. I refused to back down or seem small. I'd had enough of Luke and his bullshit.

He bought the house next door at approximately the same time Michael, my fiancé, and I moved in. Everything was fine until Luke's brother, Josh, also moved in almost two years later. Since then, they began having monthly parties that lasted all night and with music that vibrated our house, too. The parties were annoying, but what really pissed me off was that their dog, Sadie, got out all the time.

She was a sweet golden retriever that they couldn't seem to control. If I had a dollar for every time I had to return their damn dog...

"Why don't you stay? Maybe you'll understand why we always have people over if you meet a few of them." He sipped his beer and eyed me over the bottle, which looked too small for his oversized hand.

"I'm not staying. I'm meeting a friend, and I need my car," I said with as much conviction and confidence as I could muster. A few people had moved closer to witness our interaction and joined the crowd surrounding us.

Luke drained the last of his drink and set the empty bottle next to him on the counter. His forearms, covered in dark tattoos that eventually disappeared under his short sleeves, flexed as he mimicked my body language. He crossed his arms over his chest and leveled me with an uninterested look.

"Fine, we'll move the car because you asked so nicely," he relented, and I relaxed. "But..." I knew he wasn't going to let me off that easily. It seemed like Luke had a penchant for making me miserable whenever the opportunity presented itself.

"You can't just move the car to be a nice neighbor?" I asked, hoping for some grace.

"Now, why would I do that if we could have a little fun?" He used the collective *"we"* like whatever he had planned would actually be fun for me too. I highly doubted it.

I rolled my eyes. It was a habit I really needed to get under control, but that was difficult around that asshole. I raised my eyebrows in question.

"Just hurry up. What do you want me to do?"

"We were actually in the middle of a game when you marched your ass right on in, so play a round with us," Luke simply said.

I wasn't in the mood for games, and I was already late as it was. I had a short window of time I could spend with Stephanie, and I didn't want to waste it on a drinking game.

"Let's just get it over with. What's the stupid game?" I huffed, knowing it was easier to go along with it. Playing along would be the quickest way to get what I wanted: the car out of my way. I'd play a round and be on my way; otherwise, it would be at least another thirty minutes of arguing with Luke, and then I'd be extremely late for drinks and in an even worse mood.

He handed me his phone, which I took warily. "Just tap the screen," Luke instructed. "And you either have to do what the card asks you to do, answer the question, or take a shot if you want to forfeit the round."

"Can't I just take a shot and go?"

One corner of his mouth tipped up in a lopsided smile as he scrubbed a hand over his short, dark scruff along his chin. "Now, what would be the fun in that, neighbor?"

Next to me, Josh, Luke's brother, appeared and nudged me with his elbow. "Come on, Hazel," he said with a large smile. "Just one card and I'll make sure Luke moves the car." Josh's smile was contagious, and I gave him a small one in return.

He was easier to tolerate than Luke. He was at least apologetic most of the time, while Luke had an indifferent attitude toward all the issues that arose. Josh also had a boyish charm with his shaggy dirty-blond hair and tan skin. He and his laid-back personality were easier to deal with than Mr. Sarcastic And Hard To Read standing in front of me.

I leveled a stare at Luke and said, "Fine."

I tapped the screen, read the prompt, and shook my head.

Simulate an orgasm for 10 seconds.

Josh peered over my shoulder as I reread the prompt. I didn't want to do it, that was a given, but I also didn't want to give Luke the satisfaction of me backing down. I stared at the screen, willing it to somehow change and ask a stupid question instead. I could answer a ridiculous question but thinking about simulating an orgasm for ten seconds in front of a group of strangers, and my asshole neighbor, had my hands shaking. My mouth went dry, and I felt bile roll uncomfortably through my stomach as Josh blew out a breath next to me.

"Jeez, that's a rough one. I'll just go ahead and pour you a shot," he said, reaching for a small glass and filling it to the rim with whiskey.

"Wait, wait, wait. What is it, neighbor? What's it asking you to do?" Luke asked.

I narrowed my eyes as I looked up at him. That little lopsided smile was still plastered on his face as I threw daggers at him.

"Christ, if looks could kill…" Josh muttered, holding the shot glass.

Before I could stop him, Luke grabbed the phone from my

hands and read the screen. He raised his eyebrows and nodded. "You scared of showing us your orgasm face?"

Of course, he was challenging me to complete the stupid prompt. He didn't expect me to do it, and for some reason, that made me want to do it more. For a moment, we stared at each other as I contemplated which would give me the most satisfaction: taking the shot and getting the fuck out with no sweat off my back or seeing the shock on Luke's face when I completed the challenge.

I chose the latter.

Before I could lose my nerve, I took a deep breath, let my eyes fall closed, and let out my best breathy moan as I began counting to ten. I stuttered over another moan, trying to make it all realistic while also putting on the fucking show he seemed to want. My hands traveled up my body, over my chest, and wound up tangled in my hair as I turned up the volume on yet another moan before I finished it up with a throaty "fuck" for good measure.

Nine and ten.

I snapped my eyes open, immediately finding Luke, who was staring at me intently. The powerful, wanting look in his eyes was something I hadn't witnessed before and made my skin unbearably hot. But I stood there proving to him that I wasn't going to back down from his stupid taunting games. Neither of our glares wavered, although I could feel the blush fanning over my chest and up my neck.

"Okay, that was fucking hot," Josh murmured beside me. I appreciated Josh's compliment—I guess that was the point—but my eyes were still locked on Luke. It made me uncomfortable to be the center of his attention, but I couldn't help feeling a little triumphant that I obviously had some effect on him.

Trying to calm my nerves and give myself something else to focus on, I forcibly ripped my eyes away from Luke and grabbed the shot still in Josh's hands. Throwing it back quickly, I savored the burn of the liquor sliding down the back of my throat. Luke eyed my tongue as I licked around my lips, his usually vibrant green eyes seeming a little darker, and it wasn't until a sly smile pulled at the corners of my mouth that he finally pulled his eyes away.

He cleared his throat and glanced behind me. "James, I think it's your car in the way. Where are your keys? I'll move it." The guy tossed his keys to Luke, who grabbed them out of the air and started walking to the door without looking back.

"Score one for Hazel." Josh laughed, skimming his hand on the small of my back as I walked past. I tried not to cringe from the touch—it was friendly and nothing more—but I couldn't help that my skin felt hot and stung even from the soft touch over my clothes.

The party was already back in full swing as Luke hurried ahead of me.

Once I rounded the corner, I readjusted my clothes and ran my hand over my back where Josh's fingers touched, trying to replace the sensation with the feeling of my own hand.

Luke was already out the door by the time I made it to the entryway. The cool night air was a contradiction to the warmth of the party inside. Although it was October, it was still unseasonably chilly for Texas. With nights usually hovering in the eighties, I was surprised when I walked out my door that evening and wished I had worn something thicker.

Luke climbed into the driver's seat of the SUV and closed the door behind him without another word to me. I must have really gotten under his skin; it wasn't usual for him to be so quiet or without a sarcastic comment.

I could feel his eyes on me as I climbed into my own car and started the engine. I glanced at the time, only five minutes later than I was supposed to be. I could make it work. He pulled forward just enough for me to back my car out, and I gave him a wave and contemptuous grin as I passed.

Stopped at the stop sign at the end of our street, only two houses away from my own, I waited for the car coming the opposite direction to pass the intersection as I peeked into my rearview mirror. Luke was closing the car door and looking in the direction of my car.

He was illuminated by the streetlight directly above him; the warm light was soft around him and cast a dark shadow over his face. I could just barely make out his small smile as he ever so slightly shook his head before turning and walking back toward his house, leaving the car parked just past my driveway.

I assumed he was probably thinking how ridiculous that entire encounter was, and if that was the case, I couldn't have agreed more.

TWO

Hazel

The phone rang endlessly, and I thought it was going to go to voice mail when Michael abruptly answered and huffed out a "hello."

"Hey, babe. Good morning," I said as I settled into my favorite chair on our front porch. It was huge, with extra-soft cushions, and was my favorite place to curl up with a large cup of coffee in the morning. I threw the blanket over my legs and tried to hide from the chill in the air.

"Morning," Michael responded in a less than enthusiastic tone. It was early, but he told me to call.

"How'd you sleep?"

"Good."

"That's good. I never sleep well when you're gone."

"Seriously, Hazel? Is that how you want to start this conversation? With complaints? You know I can't control my schedule."

"Wait, that's not what I meant," I backpedaled and tried to explain before it turned into a full-fledged argument. "I just meant that I sleep better when you're next to me. It was meant to be a sweet comment. That's all."

"Sure, okay."

I waited for him to say something else, but when he didn't, I changed tactics. "What do you have planned for today?"

I heard what sounded like him chewing on the other end. "I'm trying to finish breakfast, and a couple of guys and I are going out. Not sure what we're doing."

"Oh, that'll be fun. Take lots of pictures. I've always wanted to go to Boston but haven't had the opportunity yet." I worried that my comment would incite a fight, so I added, "Maybe if you like it, we can go back together one day."

"Sure," he said with his mouth full. Translation: most likely not, but I didn't want to argue about it.

"So, I was discussing our wedding date with your mom and mine. They were both thinking this time next year, up in Nashville, would be great."

His several seconds of silence were heavy. "You know I wanted to be a part of this process, so don't make any unilateral decisions. What if that doesn't work for me?" he asked.

"I was asking. That's why I brought it up. If fall doesn't work for you, then we can figure something else out. I just want to set a date and get the planning process started."

Michael proposed when he began law school with the caveat that he wanted to wait until he was done and passed the bar exam to begin wedding planning. I agreed, of course, because I was smitten with my fiancé and was willing to wait. But the first year of his first job was rough. He traveled constantly while trying to move up and position himself well within the national law firm.

The wedding was put on the back burner until things slowed down, except they hadn't. I thought it was the traveling that was souring his mood. The longer he was gone, the quicker he was to anger until he came home, and we were in the same place once again. The cycle continued though, and I longed for the days that the traveling would cease and he would be in Austin full time, most of the time.

Our relationship seemed a big departure from where we began. After attending the same high school and running into each other at almost every social event because of our parents' growing friendship, Michael began pursuing me during our freshman year of college. The gifts were expensive. And although I never felt they were necessary, I loved the attention he paid me. No matter where we were or what we were doing, I was the only woman in the room.

I let him chase me for several months, testing his stamina and intentions before I gave in and let him take me on a proper date. The date was flawless, and he continued to be charming, lovable, and romantic as we fell in love.

But somewhere along the way—between graduating from college in Tennessee, getting engaged, and moving to Texas—everything had changed.

"Just don't set a date until you talk to me. Fall is fine."

"Perfect. I have a couple of venues in mind, but we can discuss it more when you get back. You'll be back on Halloween, right?"

"Mm-hmm," he said with what sounded like a mouthful of food. "Yeah, flight gets in that morning."

"Great! Just in time for my birthday. I'm thinking we can go to that Mexican restaurant we liked so much. The one just down the street."

"Of course, whatever you want to do. It's your birthday."

I had begun to respond when a new voice interrupted me. "Michael…" the voice—clearly a woman's—purred at the other end of the phone.

I stiffened in my chair and listened even more intently. She sounded far away—maybe across the room—and I waited for another sound or some tell of what was going on.

"Who was that?" I probed, unable to keep the hesitation from my voice.

"A coworker. We're leaving, so I gotta go. I'll talk to you later, baby."

He hung up abruptly, and I stared, gobsmacked, down at my phone. Overwhelming doubt slammed into me from all directions as I contemplated redialing his number to see if he would answer. I knew he wouldn't, though, and it would only make my panicking worse and him angry.

He could have been telling the truth, and it could have been a coworker in his room retrieving him for whatever outing they had planned. But I couldn't shake the suspicion twisting in my gut as the seductive sound of the woman's voice repeated in my head.

The lilt in her tone wasn't one that you used with a coworker. I chastised myself and began dissecting all our recent interactions. Was Michael cheating?

It couldn't be true. We had too much invested in this relationship for him to throw it all away like that. He loved me, and I focused on his sweet words and caring eyes that I wished I saw more often.

The distance didn't do us any favors.

My phone started vibrating in my hand, and a little hope blossomed in my chest that it was Michael calling back to apologize and continue our conversation. Maybe even eliminate some of my doubts.

But when I eagerly went to answer, it was my older sister's name scrolling across my screen. I didn't want to talk to Delilah, especially at that moment. She was Michael's biggest critic; she always believed and had no problem telling me that Michael was cheating and wasn't a good fit for me.

I couldn't talk to her. I needed to calm down and think rational thoughts, soothe my own doubts before she brought up the topic as she always did. My concern was always worse when Michael was out of town, but I was put at ease when he returned. He'd only left a few days before, but I was ready for him to be home.

I declined the call and tossed my phone on the chair next to me just as I spotted Sadie, Luke's dog, rolling around in my front yard. Her tongue hanging out, having the time of her life.

"Seriously? You've gotta be fucking kidding me…" I muttered before taking another sip of my coffee and tossing the blanket to the side.

THREE

Luke

I couldn't tell the difference between the pounding in my head and the pounding on my door until Josh's yelling pushed through the fog of sleep surrounding me.

"Dude, Hazel's at the door, and she's pissed," he said, opening my bedroom door just enough to peek inside.

I groaned against my pillow, damp with drool, and attempted to rub the sleep out of my eyes. "You can deal with her. It's your turn," I croaked, my voice still thick with sleep. My head was pounding before I even opened my eyes, and I instantly regretted the several shots I took after Hazel left last night.

"No can do. She's asking for you." Of course she fucking was. If I had to guess, the woman was trying to kill me or at least make my life miserable for the time she was in it.

I groaned again and popped a couple of pain relievers before I threw my legs over the side of the bed.

"Shit, dude. Do you ever sleep with clothes on?" Josh asked, his face twisted in disgust, before slamming the door.

"It's my fucking room. I can sleep naked if I want," I

bellowed and immediately regretted it when the pain in my head spiked.

I was not prepared for another Hazel confrontation after the previous night's showdown. She strutted into our kitchen, heels clicking, and tits pushed up, making demands, and after I was able to suppress my initial reaction to drag her to my bedroom, something in me wanted to knock her down a peg.

Apparently, I hadn't completely suppressed my attraction, though, because I was stupid enough to propose she play that stupid game. Watching her pretend to have an orgasm made me rock hard and curious if the faces she made and her little sounds were accurate.

"I swear he's coming. I just woke him up. Do you want to come inside?" I heard Josh inviting her in while I quickly pulled on the closest pair of sweats I could find.

Walking down the hallway, the sun was too damn bright, and it took a moment for my eyes to adjust. I swear I could smell the alcohol seeping from my skin.

After Hazel left, I took to drinking more than I usually would to dissolve the memories of her moans. It didn't work.

"There's the man. I'm gonna go," Josh said, patting me on the back before heading back to his room.

"What can I help you with?" I asked, leaning against the doorframe and still squinting against the morning light.

"I found Sadie in my yard again." I glanced behind me, and Sadie was curled up at the end of the sofa like usual.

"Well, thanks for bringing her back. You didn't have to get me out of bed for that, though. You could've just left her with Josh."

She shook her head and crossed her arms under her chest. My eyes, with a mind of their own, immediately darted lower. She wasn't wearing a bra and her nipples were hard from the cold morning air. Her look was also a complete contradiction to the one she donned last night. Last night, she looked like a domme or a sexy businesswoman in mostly black, high heels, and dark makeup. But standing at my door that morning, she was fresh faced and in thin pajamas that only left so much to the imagination.

"She's your dog, so I thought you would care to know that she got out again. I think that's the third time in the past week, Luke." Her accusatory tone reminded me that even though I found her fucking hot as hell, she could still be a little bit of a bitch sometimes.

I don't have the fight in me to tell her that it was likely someone from that night who left the back gate open. Sadie was also an expert escape artist, and Josh hadn't yet learned how to handle her.

"I'll work on it," was the best I could come up with.

"Seriously, you need to watch her. If something happens to her…" She trailed off, and I tensed.

"I said I'd work on it, Hazel. Are we done?"

She rolled her eyes and lifted her hand to touch her opposite arm. She pushed up the short sleeve to scratch just beneath it, her fucking massive engagement ring blinding me, but it wasn't the ring that had the hairs on the back of my neck standing up. She pushed her sleeve a little higher and a harsh, blue bruise was obvious on her upper arm.

Except it wasn't just one bruise. I examined the rest of her arm. Her skin was smooth but for the small goose bumps, and there, around her wrist, was another yellowed bruise. Another one, still slightly blue, was running along her collarbone. She was talking with her hands, but I didn't have a clue what the hell she was saying. I watched her wrist and sure enough, the yellow of the old bruise wrapped all the way around. I imagined that at one point when the bruise was fresh, it was a dark blue and purple.

I chanced another look at the dark-blue mark on her upper arm—it was new, maybe only a day or two old—before she tugged her sleeve back down and hugged her arms around her body. When her shirt settled back in place, the bruise on her collarbone was just barely visible.

The amount of force it would take to leave those kinds of bruises was disturbing. I felt the rage bubbling up, and my vision was beginning to blur. Something told me that the bruise around her wrist was not from bondage or handcuffs in bed and that the bruises on her upper arm and collarbone weren't accidental.

I quickly scanned the rest of her skin that was exposed—which wasn't much—but was relieved to not find any more bruises or signs of harm. Her other arm was only pale, soft skin.

"Hello? Luke?" Hazel peered up at me in question. God, had she always been so small?

"What?"

She rolled her eyes again and waved her hands dismissively. "Never mind."

"Hey, when will your fiancé get back? He's out of town, right? What's his name again?"

In the years I lived next door to Hazel, I'd only ever seen her fiancé a handful of times. Most of those were when we were leaving at the same time. I tried to be neighborly for a while by giving a quick wave when I saw him climbing into his fancy BMW, but he never returned the gesture, nor did he do anything more than glance my way. I affectionately referred to him as "douche," along with other similar names, because I couldn't remember his name. He didn't seem worth it.

And now, seeing the bruise on her arm, I thought even less of the piece of shit. I had no proof—it could be someone else or she could be accident prone—but I decided to keep a closer eye on her. No more new bruises or changes in attitude would go unnoticed by me. This wouldn't happen again.

"He'll be back on Halloween and his name is Michael." I carefully watched her demeanor and facial expression, but she showed no signs of wariness toward the subject.

"Mmm. See, I just call him douche because I can't ever seem

to remember his name." I had more than a week to figure out if it was him hitting her.

Her features morphed in anger, and her hands balled into fists. "Seriously, Luke? Why do you have to be such a dick? He's never done anything to you."

Her anger was palpable, but she wasn't very intimidating with her small stature. She lifted her chin and straightened her back to try to appear larger, but the determined look on her face was impressive.

"You're cute when you're angry," I said before thinking about the words leaving my mouth. I regretted them immediately, no matter how true the statement might have been.

She scoffed and began to turn away. "On that note, I hope I don't see you soon."

My comment was stupid, I knew that much, but her sarcastic reaction was well worth it. Arms still folded across her chest, braced against the chill, she hopped down the steps and started down the sidewalk.

I should have turned immediately and gone inside, but I was caught off guard by the bounce of her ass in her thin pajama pants as she walked away. My dick pulsed in my light sweatpants, and thankfully, the air was cool enough to keep it from making too much of an appearance. It would be hard to explain a seemingly random boner as she turned back to me.

"Oh, and just a pro-tip: don't call grown women cute. We don't appreciate it. Save that shit for puppies."

"What should I call you then?" I asked, unable to resist winding her up.

She waited until she was at her front door, about to step into her house, before she fired back, "I'd prefer if you didn't call me anything."

The woman was a firecracker, and I had to admit, it was kind of fun.

FOUR

Luke

I hadn't seen Hazel since she showed up at my door, returning Sadie a few days earlier. Michael still appeared to be out of town, and Hazel kept to herself in her house. But when I finally got home after a few after-work drinks with some coworkers, I caught a glimpse of her through my bedroom window.

The people who planned our neighborhood either had a sick sense of humor or were just shit at their jobs; all the homes were close together, but Hazel's house seemed closer than the neighbor on the other side. Not to mention, it was our bedroom windows that were only a couple of feet apart. If I wanted to, I likely could have reached out my window and touched hers.

I pushed my bedroom door open, but it caught on dirty laundry piled behind it. I scooped it up but paused before turning on the light. Through the window, a dull light streamed between the dark curtains and cast a warm glow over my cluttered space.

I pulled one curtain panel back and peered through the window. I expected to see an empty room, but with her curtains also open, I could easily see Hazel, perched on the edge of her bed, watching the TV near the window. Her legs, wrapped in tight black leggings, were swinging off the edge of the bed, and she cupped a bowl in her hand. She scooped a bite of whatever was in the bowl and licked the contents off the spoon.

Based on how she was dressed and the flush on her cheeks, I assumed she had just finished a workout. The woman was always running, and dear God did it show. Watching her lick what I believed to be ice cream off the spoon should not have affected me the way it did, but I unintentionally began envisioning that it was my dick she was licking so intently and not a damn spoon. Even if she was feisty sometimes, it was a lucky damn spoon.

I began to feel creepy, and with the steady tightening of my pants, I felt like a fucking perv, too. I was about to let the curtain fall as Hazel stood and set her bowl on the dresser near the TV. In one swift motion, she grabbed the hem of her top and lifted it over her head. She tossed it to the side and took another generous bite of ice cream.

I didn't make a move to back away from the window. I clearly had leaped over the line into being really fucking creepy when she turned in the direction of the window and I was given a front-row view of her tits pushed up in her sports bra. It was neon and the sweat covering her cleavage glistened in the dim light of the room and the TV.

She passed by the window and came back with a water bottle and her phone. She stared at her phone screen for a moment before shaking her head and setting it next to her bowl of ice cream. She yanked the hair tie from her hair and angrily scrubbed a hand through it. Her face was twisted in frustration.

What had she seen or read that made her so angry? She contemplated taking another bite, the spoon hovering just in front of her lips before she dropped it back in the bowl and pushed it away.

From what I could see of her bedroom, it was well decorated

with light colors, but I couldn't pull my eyes from her long enough to notice much more. The thought that her piece-of-shit fiancé shared the room with her made my fucking skin crawl. Although he was never home, which somehow made it better and worse.

She probably spent more nights alone than she did with him.

Speaking of the POS, I took the opportunity to try and look closer at her bruised arm. I squinted, and the bruise was still a deep blue close to her shoulder, but it was beginning to heal. The outside of it was fading to a light yellow. I couldn't see the one on her collarbone.

Lost in thought, I only caught a glimpse of Hazel's naked back as she shed her bra and stepped into her bathroom, out of view. A raw rage boiled through my veins. Her back was littered with black-and-blue bruises. They crawled up and down her spine, and although I couldn't get a good look, I knew it couldn't have been an accident.

I balled my fists and tried to tamp down the blinding anger. It was possible that even if I kept an eye on her, it wouldn't be enough. What had she gone through to get those bruises?

FIVE

Hazel

I DIDN'T WANT TO GO TO THE DAMN HALLOWEEN PARTY. BUT WHEN Becky sprinted out of her house as I was just beginning my nightly run the week before, I was too caught off guard to come up with a good enough excuse. I mean, I had plenty of excuses, but they were all ones that I'd already tried.

Then she threw in that her daughter, Emmy, was looking forward to seeing me, and I caved. I wasn't the biggest fan of Becky, but her daughter was incredibly sweet. In the years since we moved to Austin, I had become close to Emmy and occasionally babysat when needed. She also loved to show up at our door unannounced, requesting to go to the park just down the street or to bake cookies.

There were a number of times that we passed her house on our way to the park, and you could hear her parents bickering from inside. She came to see me when their arguing was relentless and she needed a break. And for that reason, I never turned Emmy away.

It had been a while since Emmy showed up at my door—which I took as a good sign. It had also been a while since Becky had invited me to a party. I realized that Becky was a stay-at-home mom whose hobby was being the best stay-at-home mom, which meant parties for every holiday or for no reason at all.

So, with Emmy on my mind, I threw on a tight, long-sleeve black top and my favorite high-waisted jeans. I went for a modest black chunky heel and some light makeup to complete the look. I felt like my clothes were my armor, shielding me from the outside world and everything in it.

I fidgeted in the mirror for a moment too long, eyeing my cleavage and wondering if it was too much for a neighborhood Halloween party when I got a panicked text from Becky.

If you don't get here right now, I think Emmy is going to have a fit! Where are you?

I knew what the text meant: I'm tired of dealing with my sometimes-unruly daughter. Please come relieve me of my motherly duties for at least a little while.

On that note, I decided my top would have to be fine, grabbed my small cross-body bag and headed out the door. I locked the door behind me and stepped down the front path. I wrapped my arms around my body, shielding as best I could from the chilly air, and set out at a quick pace toward Becky's. It was a short walk—they only lived on the other side of Luke and Josh—but the wind whipped furiously and unseasonably so for October in Texas.

I intentionally kept my gaze from lifting to Luke's house. There was something about him—although I'm not sure what—that threw me off balance. Each interaction was different with him. For a while, we didn't interact at all, then the parties began, and Sadie started showing up in my yard regularly, so most of our interactions were arguing. But as of recently, Luke seemed less inclined to argue with me as the arguing took on a flirty tone —on his part, not mine. I was beginning to believe he enjoyed our banter and our ridiculous arguments.

Most of our arguments were pointless. I would get angry that there were cars in our driveway or that the music from a party was too loud. He would tell me to get the stick out of my ass, and we would go back and forth with nothing resolved. If I was being honest with myself, it was kind of fun when the actual anger wore off. Would I ever admit that out loud? Absolutely not. But he kept me on my toes.

But for the last few weeks, his fight was slowly decreasing, and it was making me uncomfortable. His usual bored look was replaced by a heavy gaze. Like he was really trying to look at me. To see me.

I didn't want him to see me. I didn't think he'd like what he saw.

With this new dynamic also came more personal questions. I could count on one hand the number of personal questions he'd asked me before the past few weeks. Now, that's all he wanted to know. It was distressing, and I didn't understand the sudden change.

So, I tried to keep my eyes ahead and trudge past his house. But my self-control wavered, and my eyes lifted—of their own accord, of course—to the faint light emanating from his dining room. He was hunched over the table, intently staring at something. He was shirtless, and the tattoos I had only seen on his arms had, as I suspected, continued over his chest, down his back and almost to his neck.

"Hazellllll!"

I whipped my head toward the small yet high-pitched voice and saw Emmy sprinting toward me in a flashy princess costume.

"Emmy!" I laughed as she collided with my legs and almost knocked me off balance.

"You're late!" she whined. She pulled back and eyed my outfit. "You're pretty, but what are you supposed to be?"

"I'm just me," I said. I was me, but more specifically, I was an almost twenty-eight-year-old woman with a mostly absent fiancé, a career she didn't really care for, having a delayed quarter-life crisis and who was also upset because her neighbor was no longer arguing with her like he once did. Pretty terrifying. A monster would have been a more apt description.

"That's boring. You're supposed to be someone else on Halloween!" She tugged me along the sidewalk, eager to get back to the party.

"Well then, which princess are you?"

"I'm Princess Emmy. I'm the best princess." Touché.

The front porch was covered in faux spider webs and the entire house was reflected in purple-and-green lights. There was a smoke machine in the corner that was turned on full blast and made it difficult to actually see the door. Luckily, Emmy seemed to have memorized the path and helped me narrowly escape the clutches of a spider web.

The rest of the house was decorated just the same. All the food was Halloween-themed, including fake eyeball candy, spaghetti "brains," fingers, and blood punch. It was over the top and exactly what I expected from Becky.

"Hazel!" Becky cheered my name when I entered the kitchen with Emmy still tugging me. Like mother, like daughter.

"You have five minutes, then I'm coming back for you," Emmy instructed before running deeper into the house.

Becky's house was the largest on our street. Even from the outside, it seemed grander than the rest, and the inside was no different. Every finish was of the highest quality. Her marble countertops were immaculate, and the white cabinets were custom made—she made sure I knew that when we first met—and all the appliances were top of the line. But walking in for the party, you would never know. She had completely transformed the entire space into a dark, haunted house and every spare piece of counter space was covered by food, drinks, or decorations.

I spotted the alcohol right next to Becky, and as I stepped closer to her, I realized she was already more than a little tipsy.

"I'm so glad you're here," she slurred as she went in for a hug that turned into me catching her and spilling some of her drink on my shoulder.

"I'm so sorry," she apologized and leaned back, steadying herself against the part of the counter with the alcohol. Her costume of choice was an ostentatious and very unrealistic pirate getup that pushed her boobs up almost to her nose. The costume probably cost more than what I would spend on a normal outfit.

"This party has been stressful, and Chris has been absolutely no help," she continued. And as if he were summoned, I felt a hand swipe against my lower back and linger a touch too long. My skin crawled when I felt his hot liquor-coated breath against my ear.

"Look who it is. Hi, Brown." Chris thought he was funny calling me a synonym for my name. I shrugged his hand off the best I could and maneuvered around Becky to the alcohol.

Luckily, she was able to move just enough to let me pass while she argued in hushed tones with her husband. He was wearing a matching pirate costume complete with eyepatch and funny-looking hat.

Chris was a classically decent-looking guy and seemed harmless enough until you realized he had been staring at you far too long and made any excuse to touch you. He also made crude comments no matter who was around, including his daughter. After a not-so-great run-in with him while I was going for a run —when he all but ambushed me in front of their house—I did my best to stay as far away from him as possible. Never again did I want to be caught alone with him.

With the help of the immense amount of alcohol in both of their systems, their hushed arguing turned into actual arguing while I was pouring myself a hefty whiskey and Coke. Behind me, Becky was saying something about touching other women when she abruptly stopped the conversation and turned to the door.

"Luuuuke," she cried as our neighbor stepped into the

kitchen. Based on the look on his face, he could feel the tension in the room but did his best to smile.

"Hi," was all he said before he noticed me behind Becky and Chris. Even as Becky threw herself at him, spilling some of her drink once again, Luke's eyes stayed on me over her shoulder. My skin suddenly felt hot under his intense stare, and I downed my drink to give myself a little liquid courage and something else to do by making another. Refreshing my drink gave me a reason to look away from him as Becky began prattling on about her decorations and the time it took to set the entire place up.

Even while pouring my drink, I could still feel his eyes on me.

"Where's your brother? He wasn't able to make it?" I heard Becky ask him.

"No, he's working," Luke responded.

"Oh, right. The *bar*," Becky drawled. The way she said "bar" made it sound dirty or like she didn't approve of Josh's job choice. She probably didn't because everything in her life—at least on the surface—was perfect.

"I'm going to go find Emmy. I'll talk to you later," I said to Becky as I passed her and Luke. For Emmy, I would stay at least an hour, but I knew my ability to socialize for an extended period of time was lacking.

As I searched the house for Princess Emmy, I glanced at my phone for the millionth time. Michael promised he would call when he got back to his room, but I still hadn't received anything. He'd been difficult to reach since our conversation earlier in the week when I heard a woman's voice in his hotel room. I tried to steer my thoughts away from the possibility that he was cheating, but I'd spent more time considering it than I'd hoped. And the longer it took to reach him, the harder it became to forget the entire situation.

I found Emmy with her friends playing on the enclosed back porch. I didn't want to interrupt them, but when Emmy spotted me, she insisted I had to join in on the fun.

There were a few heaters on either end of the porch, which did a decent job of keeping the area warm.

I spent much longer with Emmy and her friends than I had originally planned, but she wouldn't let me leave until I told her I was going to pee my pants. She gave a hearty "ewww" and let me leave just as I was about to actually pee my pants.

I navigated my way through the maze of the haunted house and found the bathroom just in time. My ears were ringing from the mixture of six-year-olds screaming and the blaring music, so the bathroom was a nice moment to collect my thoughts and make sure my eardrums hadn't yet ruptured.

With my hands washed and my business finished, I plucked my phone out of my bag and was disappointed to find that Michael still hadn't called me. It was almost eleven and if he still wasn't back in his hotel room, I couldn't help but wonder what he was doing.

I stepped out of the bathroom and back into the loud hallway when I spotted Chris coming directly toward me from the end of the hall. The direction he came from was my only escape—the other end of the hall dead-ended to another room—so without any other options, I attempted to backpedal back into the bathroom. But before I got the door all the way closed, Chris's hand darted out and blocked it. It must've hurt his fingers—not that I cared—but he didn't even flinch when the door hit his knuckles.

Defeated and cornered, I tried to put on my best smile and find a way out of the situation. "Did you need to use the restroom? Here, let me get out of your way."

He laughed and pushed the door open. He walked in just as I slipped around him and into the hallway. I thought I'd outsmarted him until he grabbed my arm just at my elbow and pulled me back to him. My back hit his front and my stomach rolled. My skin crawled with the contact.

The liquor smell from earlier was even more potent and was mixed with his musty body odor. I could feel the bile clawing its way up my throat.

"Actually, I was looking for you." His voice was dark, and I could barely hear him over the music.

I tried to take another step, but that seemed to frustrate him, so he whipped around me and backed me up into the doorframe.

"Looks like my kid really likes you," he slurred, looking down at me.

My fight-or-flight response was triggered the moment I spotted Chris, but neither seemed like an option anymore. I didn't want to cause a scene by fighting, and my escape routes were blocked as he caged me in. My third option was to stay amicable and hope he lost interest. My hopes weren't high that it would work.

"Yeah, Emmy's really sweet. I like her, too." I nodded. He didn't make a move to let me by, and I tried to keep my breathing even. Although each breath was more difficult than the last, and the air was thick with his horrible odor, I knew he got off on scaring women. I wasn't going to let him see my fear if I had any say in the matter.

"So, is your husband still out of town?"

"He's actually getting back tonight. Thanks for asking." I paused as he scowled at me. I hoped he would take that as a reason to get the hell away from me, but of course, he didn't. I wasn't that lucky.

"I find you so interesting, Brown. How a man could leave you alone all the time is just crazy. If you were mine, I wouldn't let you go. Ever."

His right hand was planted on the wall beside my head while his left hand dropped to my hip. He roughly gripped me there and leaned in even closer. His eyes dropped to my cleavage, and he took the liberty of running his sweaty finger over the top of my shirt just above my boobs.

I started running through scenarios of how to get out of the situation with as little chaos as possible, but my mind was clouded and my judgment impaired. His hand moved lower, and I lifted my arms to push him away when a voice at the opposite end of the hallway caught both of our attention.

"Chris."

Luke was there. His body filling most of the opening, and he looked terrifying. The outline of him was illuminated by the flashing lights in the background.

He crossed the distance to us in only a few long strides, a menacing look creasing his forehead. Chris watched Luke stalk to us over his shoulder but didn't make to remove his hands from me. Whether it was the alcohol or downright stupidity, I didn't know. But when Luke's hand clamped down on his shoulder, Chris rolled his eyes and finally pulled back.

"I think you need to go find your wife," Luke said through clenched teeth.

He was at least several inches taller than Chris and should have been incredibly intimidating. But Chris's liquid courage (or lack of self-preservation) was strong, so he didn't immediately back down.

"The fuck are you talking about?" He shrugged Luke's hand off his shoulder and squared up to him. My exit was once again blocked—this time by Luke's hulking frame—and I didn't want to be caught in the middle of a fight.

Luke clenched his fists at his side and stepped closer to Chris. He had to stoop a little to get face-to-face with him, but when he did, he said again, "You need to go find your wife." He said it slowly and each word was etched in barely restrained anger.

Chris shook his head but cut his losses. He stepped around Luke and started down the hallway. Luke turned, arms folded over his chest, and watched him from in front of me.

"I'll see you later, Hazel." Chris turned to say, not being able to leave without the last word.

Before I even had time to register the threat, Luke added, "No, you won't." His tone was authoritative, and I almost laughed at the anger that passed across Chris's face.

I stayed behind Luke as Chris stumbled back down the hall

and paused at the end. I positioned myself even farther behind Luke—not hard when he was twice my size—so I was completely out of Chris's view. I thought he may argue again, but ultimately, he turned and left. I sighed with relief as he disappeared around the corner.

Once he was out of sight, Luke turned back to me.

"Are you okay?" he asked.

"I'm fine. I had it handled," I bit out. The concern on his face and in his words made me feel small, which made me defensive.

"I'm sure you did," he scoffed and rolled his eyes as his body relaxed.

"Don't say it like that."

"Seriously, Hazel?"

I fixed my top, pulling it up so less of my cleavage was showing, and yanked my purse over my shoulder. "Yes, seriously. I had it handled. He's a prick, and I know how to handle them."

"What were you going to do?" he asked, but I wasn't prepared for the question. I stuttered over my response because, in truth, I had no idea what I was planning on doing, but the smug look on his face fueled my need to win.

"I would've slapped his hands away and then told him if he touched me again, I'd chop his fingers off. Then I would have kneed him in the balls for good measure."

Luke nodded and chuckled. He scrubbed his mouth to wipe away his lopsided smile and leaned back against the wall on the opposite side of the hallway. "Well, I guess you did have it handled then."

"I did."

"But I'm not the kind of guy to just walk away when I see a woman being harassed by a man. Ever," he said. I swallowed down the thickness in my throat, unable to respond. The gravity of his words and the sincerity in which he said them made me feel uneasy and exposed.

He saw what was happening and inserted himself because he knew it was wrong. But the added "ever" at the end and the conviction in which he said it made me think he wasn't just talking about the hallway incident.

"That's very admirable. I..." The words get stuck, and I'm still not sure what I want to say. "I appreciate your help whether I had it under control or not. Okay?"

"Okay," he relented. I thought he would take the hint that he was dismissed, but he continued to lean against the wall and watch me.

For a moment or two, we stood there, staring at each other with only the sound of the music and the short width of the hallway between us. Only once did his eyes break from mine to sweep down my body. My reaction to his perusal couldn't be helped. It felt like my entire body was a live wire.

"Hazellllll!" Emmy called as she ran down the hallway. Only a six-year-old could make my two-syllable name eight syllables long.

"Here," she exclaimed as she shoved a headband in my hands. "It's for you since you didn't dress up."

I saw the amused expression on Luke's face—the lopsided smile back in place—before I looked at the headband in my hands. It was black with a white, fuzzy, sparkly halo attached to it.

Emmy noticed my hesitation and pulled me down to her as she ripped the headband from my hands. "You have to wear it!" she ordered.

"Okay, okay. I'll wear it," I conceded because I had no say in the matter.

"Do you know why I got this one for you?" she asked, and before I had a chance to respond, she added, "Because you're my angel."

She placed the headband on my head, and I felt my heart constrict in my chest. If the kid wanted me to wear the damn headband, then I'd wear the damn headband.

"Thank you, Princess Emmy," I said, and she wrapped her arms around me in the tightest hug. I caught a glimpse of Luke's facial expression, and it wasn't as hard as usual. His eyes were softer and his broad shoulders relaxed.

Feeling too much in the moment, I asked Emmy, "Well, what about Luke? He's not dressed up either, so maybe he needs a headband, too."

He scowled down at me as I grinned up at him.

"Mommy said Luke is moody and that I should leave him alone." She shrugged. I barked out a laugh, and Emmy smiled, although she didn't really understand the hilarity of her comment.

"Your mommy's right. Luke is a little moody sometimes," I agreed.

"Hey now," he finally spoke up. "I'm not moody."

Emmy looked from Luke to me, where I still squatted in front of her. She wore a mischievous grin as she leaned forward, cupped her hand around her mouth, and attempted to whisper in my ear. The volume of the music had been turned down slightly, and Emmy hadn't exactly gotten the hang of whispering yet, so Luke could hear, too, when she said, "He's looking at you with googly eyes."

She saw the confusion on my face, so she clarified, "Mommy said that when a boy does googly eyes at a girl, it means he likes her."

"Is that so?" I asked, deciding to play along for a moment.

She nodded and glanced back up at Luke one last time before sprinting back down the hallway.

"Well, she's something," Luke muttered. His relaxed demeanor from just a moment ago was once again replaced with a hard exterior.

"She is, and on that note, I think I'm going home. Thanks again for being my knight in shining armor." I turned and expected Luke to argue, but he didn't. I made my way back down the hallway without looking back. I wanted to know if he was following or watching me. I felt like he was watching me because I swore I could feel his eyes on my back. For some reason, Luke watching me didn't seem to bother me like most men watching me did. Maybe because I'd never witnessed ill-intent in his eyes the number of times I'd encountered him.

I made a right and swerved around decorations until I was almost to the front door. As I reached for the knob, another hand got to it before me and twisted it. Startled, I looked up to my left and found Luke ushering me out of the door with his hand lightly on the small of my back. I let him lead me out of the house and into the cold.

With the door closed behind us, I faced him. "What the hell are you doing?"

"Chris was tracking you through the house and was about to follow you out the door. I thought I'd be the lesser of two evils in this situation."

He was looking out for me. But it wasn't only that, Luke was looking out for me and was willing to jump in.

"Okay, well, thanks. Good night." I waved and walked down the front steps, almost stepping in a spider web once again.

"I'd feel better if I walked you home," Luke said as he jogged up next to me.

"I think I can manage to get from here to my house without a chaperone," I said, but I didn't actually tell him no. I knew I should have fought harder and asked that he leave me alone, but I didn't want to. He was right, he was the lesser of two evils and I wouldn't put it past Chris to follow me home.

I didn't argue, and we walked the short distance to my house in comfortable silence. Whether it was intentional or not, I appreciated the several inches he kept between us. I was still very much on edge after dealing with Chris and was already thinking about the shower I would take to remove the lingering feeling of his hands on me.

Luke walked me all the way to the bottom of my porch, and we both paused at the stairs.

"Okay, well, I'm home now, so—"

"Do you have your phone?" Luke asked abruptly.

Not knowing where he was going with the line of questioning and curious to know what he needed with my phone, I pulled it out of my purse. He held out his hand, and I hesitated.

"I promise I'm not going to scroll through your photos or your texts," he said as he pushed his hand closer. My curiosity won over my hesitation, so I unlocked my phone and placed it in his palm.

My regular-sized phone looked so tiny in his large hands. As he tapped the screen, I watched his face partially illuminated by my dim porch light. His dark brows furrowed, and the deep green of his eyes danced in the phone screen light. He tapped the screen a few times and handed it back to me.

"Now you have my number if ever you need it."

"You didn't have to do that. I don't need to be rescued all the time," I joked, but when I looked back up at him after putting my phone away, his expression was deadly serious.

"Look, I hope you don't have to use it, but it's also good to have your neighbors' phone numbers," he sighed. "Why are you always so difficult? I'm trying to be nice and do the right thing."

"Since when?"

"Since when what?" he questioned.

I nervously shifted my weight on my feet and wished I could have darted inside. "Since when are you trying to be nice and do the right thing? We've been arguing for years. What changed?"

He laughed humorlessly and shook his head. "I'm actually a nice person, Hazel. Maybe you just haven't given me a chance."

I contemplated his response. I could see his argument—I was probably more of a pain in the ass than necessary—but he drove me fucking crazy most of the time.

"Fine. Thank you," I gritted out.

"Was that so hard?" he asked, cocking his head to one side and giving me that damn lopsided smile and showing off his one little dimple that was only slightly visible under his facial hair. His condescending look made me want to take it all back and start another argument, but I decided to be the bigger person for once.

"Good night, neighbor," I said as I started up the stairs. I was the bigger person, but I couldn't help calling him neighbor since I knew he hated it. I wasn't going to let him off that easily.

"Good night, Angel." He smiled in response. I turned around, halfway through the front door, to ask what that was supposed to mean when I remembered the damn halo on my head.

I knew I was never going to hear the end of that one.

Inside, I threw my purse on the small entry table but not before retrieving my phone from the inside pocket. When I unlocked the screen, the contact Luke had entered was still up. Or at least I'd assumed that's what it was since he'd entered his phone number under the name "Neighbor" instead of his actual name.

If he hadn't already done it, I would've changed it immediately. Why he felt the need to use a code name, I didn't know.

SIX

Luke

I was fucking pathetic. Since the Halloween party, I found myself looking for Hazel. When I was in my bedroom, I constantly peeked out my window, hoping to catch a glimpse of her. When I pulled into the driveway from work, I looked to her driveway to see if her car was there.

She hadn't texted me—which I assumed was a good thing—but I also found myself wanting to hear from her.

Like I said, fucking pathetic. But I was never going to get the picture of her face while Chris had her cornered out of my head.

One of his arms caged her in while the other touched her, obviously without her permission. Her eyes were blazing with a rage that directly contradicted the quickness of her breaths and her quivering chin. She was frightened but didn't want him to see that. Whether she thought she had it handled or not, I wasn't going to leave without the asshole knowing I had her back.

I was close to flying into a rage and beating the ever-loving shit out of the guy, but I didn't want to scare Hazel more than she already was. I'm sure watching me almost kill him in his own home wasn't going to help her.

And then watching her easily slip from nervous and defensive to cheerful when Emmy came up with that silly little headband was eye opening. The woman could expertly switch her emotions and let you see only what she wanted you to see. Like she always had a mask at the ready.

But once Emmy left and I walked her home, all I could think about were the marks under her clothes. She was beautiful in a way that any man—or woman—would appreciate. But I was less concerned about what she looked like. It was hard not to imagine that her body was covered in black-and-blue bruises. There were likely other marks, scars, and untreated injuries that no one could see.

Having seen the marks on her skin, I felt like I understood her better. Especially her behavior. There had been a few times when she'd encountered men that I'd noticed she was, for lack of a better word, uncomfortable with the situation. Even friendly touches or an accidental graze of an arm when they passed by her made her face drop and threw up all of her walls.

That, combined with the bruises, was telling. There was something more behind her pained expressions, fake smiles, and her ability to slyly peel herself from a situation without being noticed.

I needed her to know that I could be trusted. I was one of the good ones, and to do that, I needed to prove myself. I couldn't be sure what she had experienced but if it was even half as bad as I imagined it was, it would take time to become her friend and earn her trust. Especially since she despised me. But I would make sure it happened.

And after two days of not seeing Hazel even once, I was beginning to get concerned. Until I pulled into my driveway and spotted Josh, Becky and Hazel standing in front of my house, deep in conversation.

I hesitated before getting out of my truck. Hazel looked like she was about to go on her nightly run when she stopped to talk. She was wearing teal leggings that hugged every one of her curves. They were high waisted, and she paired them with a short, cropped top that showed only a sliver of her midriff.

She would have made a paper bag look fucking hot, and I quickly averted my eyes before my dick got any harder than it already was. Josh waved me over to them when I hopped out of the truck and tried to readjust my tighter than usual jeans.

"What's going on?" I asked. Josh narrowed his eyes at my funky walk while Becky's face split into a huge, very toothy smile. I dropped my eyes to Hazel, who appeared restless as she tossed her wireless headphones from one hand to the other. She glanced up at me and gave a tight smile before averting her attention back to Becky.

"Becky, tell Luke what happened."

"Sure, sure. Of course," she said with a sigh. "I got back from picking Emmy up from school this afternoon to find one of our windows smashed in. It looks like whoever it was stole a few electronics and some of my jewelry. We just all need to be extra vigilant."

"Did the cops tell you anything? Any idea who it might have been?"

She shook her head. "Not yet. But I'll let you know when I hear anything."

"That's fucking crazy," Josh murmured next to me. "Glad y'all weren't home."

Becky nodded and put her hand over her chest. "Dear goodness, me too! You would've heard me scream all the way over at your house, Hazel, if someone would've broken in while I was home."

She covered the hand on her chest with the other and shook her head in disbelief.

"But Hazel, you really should be extra careful running at night and with your fiancé being gone all the time. You don't want to make yourself an easy target." Although I assumed Becky was actually trying to watch out for Hazel, her Southern drawl and usual condescending tone made it sound like she was singling her out.

"She can handle it," I said before Hazel had an opportunity to respond.

"I can," she agreed, this time letting her eyes stay on me for a second longer. She was the first to look away when Becky began speaking once more about the safety of everyone in the neighborhood. I didn't hear what she was saying because I was too focused on her husband coming down his stairs and staring intently at Hazel.

"Hi, honey," Becky cooed when he stepped into our little circle. Josh gave him a tight-lipped nod, and I couldn't make myself greet him by doing anything other than taking half a step closer to Hazel when his eyes lazily perused her body.

Chris noticed my movement and stared at me for a beat before turning to his wife. "You telling them about the break-in?" I could have been making it up, but it sounded like there was something more in Chris's voice—a threatening lilt to his words.

Becky had begun prattling again, and I tuned her out. Chris constantly stared at Hazel, who hadn't moved away from me when I got closer as I thought she would. I took that as a small win.

"Well, I need to get to work. Let us know if you hear anything," Josh said just as I was imagining the several creative ways I could rip Chris's eyes out.

"Yeah, we have dinner reservations," Becky added. "Good night, everyone. Stay safe!" she added while tugging her husband along behind her. Chris winked at Hazel, and I tensed. I clenched my fist, and I felt the anger as it began to boil in my stomach. The asshole just couldn't quit.

I hadn't realized I'd taken a step toward him until I felt a small hand grip my wrist from behind and pull me back to reality.

Behind me, Hazel flicked me a cautious look followed by a

slight shake of her head. "Don't," is all she said before she let go of my wrist and we were the only two left.

"He has a death wish," I muttered under my breath.

"He'll get what's coming to him. I believe in karma."

I wished I could serve the karma, but I was hoping she was right.

"Wonder if his wife noticed him staring at your tits the entire time," I asked seriously.

She threw her head back and laughed. It was a sweet sound that immediately unsoured my mood. She should laugh more often.

"Probably not since she was staring at you the entire time."

That surprised me. I gave her a questioning look, and she raised her eyebrows at me.

"It's true. She didn't look at Josh or me after you walked up. Woman has a serious crush on you."

I wouldn't have noticed because I was too concerned about the way Chris was eye fucking Hazel. Recently, with Hazel around, I had a tough time focusing on anything besides her.

"See you later, neighbor," she called as she put in one headphone and pulled out her phone.

"Bye, Angel," I yelled after her just before she put in the other earpiece. She shook her head, and I watched her ass bounce as she jogged off.

SEVEN

Hazel

Huddled under the thick blankets on my bed, I flipped on the TV at the same time my phone began vibrating next to me. Delilah's name flashed across the screen, and I hurried to answer it.

"What's up, sis?"

"Hazel Grace, I swear I have to call you ten times before you answer the phone once."

I laughed, but she was right. She called at the most inopportune times.

"I'm sorry. How's it going?"

"I need a damn vacation is how it's going…" Delilah began. Although she had always been my overdramatic older sister, I could understand why she would need a vacation. She and her husband, Tony, had been together for more than ten years and had two beautiful, hellion children: Miles and Amber. I loved them so much, but they were a handful, as was Delilah when she was a child. She didn't like to be reminded of that fact, but it didn't make it less true.

I was lucky to have a good relationship with my older sister, but she did tend to mother me at times. I knew she couldn't help it, though. She had a structured life that was scheduled almost down to the second, but her children were free spirits, which made it harder and harder to keep the schedule.

She owned her own boutique marketing firm in Nashville while Tony was a full-time stay-at-home dad. His hobbies included woodworking, fishing, and making my sister crazy yet insanely happy.

Delilah, as usual, talked on and on about what trouble Miles and Amber had gotten into this time. (Stealing the three bags of Halloween candy my sister bought, refusing to give them back and proceeding to eat them over the past two days.)

"So, what's been going on with you?" she asked after she sighed and reassured me that she really did love them.

"Same ol' same ol'."

"Okay, you know that response is not going to work for me. I need the details of your life."

I sighed audibly, and she started to nag again before I cut her off. "Everything is good. I'm writing more, and I feel like it's really coming along well." Partly a lie, but it was something to say.

"The book, right?"

"Yes, the book." My sister was the only person that knew I was writing a book. After years of technical writing experience, I needed a better creative outlet. I loved writing in high school, so when Michael started traveling more, it was an enjoyable way to fill my time.

I hoped it would eventually turn into a full-length novel, but lately, each time I sat down to write, it became more and more difficult to put words down on the page. It seemed I was never in the right headspace to write my chosen romance novel.

"Can I know what it's about yet?"

"Nope."

"When do I get to know?"

"When it's done." To be honest, I wasn't completely confident that I could write a romance novel like I was envisioning. I didn't want to tell anyone until I knew for certain I could do it.

"How long until it's done?"

"D, is this twenty questions about my damn book or what?"

"Fine, fine," she conceded. "Tell me about Michael then. Let me guess, he's traveling?"

And like clockwork, the Michael bashing began. When I didn't respond, she continued, "I'm sorry. I won't say anything else besides the fact that he's always gone, and it's a red flag. I don't want to see my little sister hurt. Also, if you need me, I will be there faster than you can say, 'get on a plane and come see me,' okay? Just say okay, so I know you heard me."

"Okay, D." I was not going to argue with her. It was a moot point and would only end in us hanging up on each other and being angry the rest of the day.

A part of me, that kept growing and was slowly taking over every other part of me, had begun to believe that her comments and concerns were warranted. After hearing the woman in the background purring my fiancé's name in his hotel room, I couldn't scrub the doubt from my mind. I couldn't allow myself to be cheated on and not do anything about it.

I needed to see him in person. That usually made it better. When I got in my own head, seeing his face light up when he saw me made it all make sense.

"I can't believe you're going to be twenty-eight. I can't be old enough to have a twenty-eight-year-old little sister," Delilah said, expertly changing the subject.

I chuckled. "You're only five years older than me. It wasn't long ago you were twenty-eight."

"I guess you're right," she said before screaming erupted in the background, and a string of creative names for her children, including *shit munchers, Neanderthals, and demon spawns,* flew out of her mouth.

"One second, Hazel. Oh my god, one second," she cried into the phone before I heard stomping and even more yelling on the other end of the line. As I listened to my sister chase her children around the house—or so it sounded—I peered through my bedroom window to see Luke peeling off a light-blue shirt before stepping into his bathroom.

With no one around, I let myself stare at his heavily tattooed upper body. The dark hair over his chest ran down between his abs and continued until it disappeared beneath his shorts. When he walked into his bathroom, I got an eyeful of his toned back and the intricate ink there. I felt my cheeks heat when I thought about what it might be like to outline his tattoos and see the details up close. Thoughts an engaged woman should definitely not be having about anyone besides her fiancé. My face flushed deeper just at the thought.

Michael had clean, unmarked skin and very little body hair. I was amazed that the sight of Luke—Michael's opposite in so many ways—had any effect on me.

There was the faint sound of slamming that knocked me back just before she said, out of breath, "I'm back."

"What the hell happened, or do I even want to know?"

"You probably don't want to know, but I'm going to tell you anyway. The little pests brought a little pest inside my damn house. They brought a freaking rodent in here and tried to show it to me like they had just won the damn lottery. I swear these are not my children. I'm beginning to believe that they were switched at the hospital," she decided.

"Right. Both of your children? What are the odds that the children you had two years apart were both switched at birth?"

"Oh, hell, I don't know," she said, exasperated. "But it's a lot more likely than them being related to me."

"Whatever you say, sis."

"Maybe I'll just ship them to you for a week and see what you think."

"That's quite alright," I began to argue, but she cut me off.

"Actually, I think that's a great idea. What do you think about the week after—"

I started to make noises with my mouth, mimicking the line breaking up. "I'm going through a tunnel. I can't hear—call you —bye."

I hung up the phone as she was attempting to persuade me that sending her hellions to me was a good idea. I loved them, but I was not ready to care for children full time.

I was going to slip back under the covers, but I glanced at the clock next to the TV on our dresser and saw it was already well past eight in the morning. I had a video meeting at nine, for which I had to look at least a little presentable. So, I begrudgingly flung my legs over the side of the bed and walked to the bathroom. I whipped my sleep shirt over my head and tossed it in the basket right inside the bathroom when something in my peripheral caught my eye.

Just out my window, I saw Luke, a towel hung loosely around his waist, hair soaked from his shower, staring wide eyed at me and my completely topless upper body. It took us both more than a second to comprehend the entire scene, but when we did, I sprinted forward into my bathroom as Luke jogged farther into his room.

I sank down onto the floor against my sink to try to calm my breathing and my sporadic heartbeat.

Well, my hot neighbor saw me naked. Or naked on the top, as I liked to call it as a child. Hopefully he enjoyed the freaking peep show. But as worried as I was about him seeing my boobs, there were other more revealing and telling parts of me that I was more concerned he had seen.

EIGHT

Hazel

My desk was littered with papers of handwritten outlines, ideas for character development, and interesting dialogue that I could use in my book. I had a lot of decent ideas, but I couldn't seem to bring any of them to fruition. I couldn't get the dots to connect, and I sure as hell lacked the creativity and imagination needed to make the characters come alive and appear to be more than just words on a page.

I manifested my frustration by furiously scribbling through bad ideas with a red pen and aggressively backspacing through the entire two-thousand-word chapter I had written.

After my actual technical writing work—drafting documentation for manufacturing equipment—was done a little past lunchtime, I was excited to have time to sit down and write. I was sorely disappointed in myself.

For the most part, I enjoyed my position as a technical writer for an engineering company—it provided me the ability to work from home and set my own schedule, which was vital when I decided to relocate to Austin with Michael. I wanted a flexible schedule and opportunities to achieve goals outside of work.

It was especially important when we decided to have kids, because I wanted the ability to stay at home.

That wasn't happening anytime soon, though, and until then, I hadn't realized how much I would miss going into an office every day and getting to see someone else's face. Working from home, I'd go days without seeing anyone. And my only friend I'd made at work, Stephanie, had her own family and friends and life. So, without much else going for me, I was at least thankful that my job afforded me the ability to write creatively and often.

As I stewed in my self-pity and questioned my life choices, my phone buzzed with a new text message. Eager for distraction, I clicked on the new message.

Michael: I'll be there tomorrow afternoon. Flight was already delayed. Did you get your exercise bike fixed?

Me: No, I've been running in the evenings instead. I like to be outside while the weather is so nice.

His texts had been short and sporadic the entire day, but the dots indicating that he was typing a response immediately appeared.

Michael: I gave you the guy's number to have it fixed. Why haven't you texted him yet? Also, the bike is a better workout, and I spent a fuckton on it.

Michael: Get it fixed and use it.

Michael: Please.

The damn exercise bike had been broken for weeks, and as evidenced by my lack of trying to have it repaired, I didn't really want to. I preferred outdoor activities. My nightly run was something I looked forward to every evening just before dinner and after I had completed work. It was a nice way to get out of the house and was my time to unwind, throw my headphones in, and leave the rest of the world behind me.

The bike had been a surprise gift from Michael at the beginning of the year. It was top of the line, and he said it was to help improve my overall physical health and fitness. When he was home, I used it frequently, but when he was traveling, I went back to my preferred method of exercise.

My time outside was sacred, but Michael was more concerned that I use my exercising time wisely. And I had to admit, my ass looked rounder the longer I used the bike. Michael took notice of it as well.

Me: I will. I can't wait to see you tomorrow!

I stared at my phone for a few minutes, hoping for a quick response, but when one didn't come, I locked my phone and set it screen-side down on my desk. I had renewed hope that I would find my muse and write something actually worth reading. Maybe I would include an exercise bike in the next chapter.

I poised my hands above the keyboard, pushing my worthless notes to the side, but before I struck any keys, my attention was pulled to the front yard.

Directly in front of my desk was a picture window looking into the front yard and street beyond. When setting up my office, I decided it would be nice to stare outside instead of at a wall. The idea was fine, except I had grossly misjudged my own ability to focus and found myself distracted by people, cars, and whatever else.

That time I was distracted by a dog, but not just any dog. Sadie, my wonderful neighbor's dog, was sunbathing in my front yard. I let a second or two pass, scanned the rest of the yard, and when I decided that sure enough, she had gotten out once again, I got up from my desk.

I opened the front door, and rather than dart off like most dogs would, Sadie rolled onto her back with her tongue hanging out of the side of her mouth.

"Hi, sweet girl," I cooed as I approached her slowly, still hoping she wouldn't dart off into the street.

She pawed at the air and stretched to show me more of her stomach. I ran my fingers through her blonde coat and gave her the tummy rubs she was after. Just to be sure, I checked her collar and confirmed that it was Sadie and that Luke's phone number was on the reverse side along with his address.

I stood and began walking toward his house while patting my thigh. "Come on. Let's go home," I said in a high-pitched voice I reserved only for cute dogs and babies.

She slowly rolled onto her stomach and stood up. She looked a little uneasy, and when she began walking to me, she refused to put any weight on her front right paw. She held it tucked to her side as she tried to move as quickly as her injured body would take her.

Shit. Not only had I found Luke's dog in my yard, but I had found her injured in my yard.

Luke and Josh always parked in the driveway, and when I turned to find that neither of their trucks was there, I decided just to bite the bullet and call Luke.

I sat down in the grass and Sadie followed. I rubbed between her ears as her eyes drooped close.

"Luke Shepherd's phone," a bright, unexpected voice answered.

"Umm, yes. Is Luke available?" I asked after gathering my thoughts.

"He's actually busy at the moment. Can I help with something?"

"I'm his neighbor, and I found his dog in my front yard. It looks like her front paw or leg is hurt."

"Oh, no. Hold on one second," she said before I heard shuffling and low whispers in the background. "Are you there?"

"Yes."

"Could you bring her to the Forest Vet Clinic? I can give you the address if you need it."

She provided the address as I typed it into my phone, and I was happy to see it was only five-ish minutes away. She said she would meet me out front to take Sadie. She instructed me to park in one of the reserved spots near the door, and she would wait there.

Thankfully, we were seated in the grass fairly close to my car, and Sadie didn't appear to really want to go anywhere. So, I rushed into the house, grabbed my purse, and locked the door. Sadie was able to slowly amble to my car, but I had to lift her to get her in the back seat. It probably took longer than it should have, but the last thing I wanted to do was hurt her even more.

Sadie looked sad on the way to the vet, so I talked to her and assured her that I would beat her daddy's ass for letting her escape again.

Just as she said she would be, a woman was outside waiting for me when I pulled into the closest spot to the door. She whipped the back door open before saying anything to me and scooped all seventy pounds of Sadie into her arms like it was no big deal.

"I'm just going to take her inside. You don't have to stay," she said over her shoulder while walking to the door. I turned the car off and grabbed my purse off of the passenger seat.

"Actually, I thought I'd sit and wait with her," I said and ran ahead to open the door for the veterinary technician.

For some reason, she seemed hesitant to let me stay but led me through the lobby and into an examination room at the back of the building. She told me I could wait in the small room while she took Sadie back for some X-rays. Her long, blonde ponytail swung as she walked through a separate door in the room that appeared to lead to the back of the clinic.

I plopped into one of the black plastic chairs on the opposite wall and shivered when the air conditioning kicked on and blew directly on me. The only decorations in the room were funny pictures of dogs hanging on the walls. But the can of treats and bottle of squeeze cheese on the counter were also nice touches.

Without a better way to pass the time, I pulled out my phone. My mom had sent me several text messages with names of wedding venues along with their availability. Other messages were pictures of wedding dresses that were more extravagant than what I was wanting but were beautiful, nonetheless.

I clicked the links she sent for the venues and gawked at the absolutely insane price tags. I was typing out my thoughts on one venue when the door leading to the back opened again.

I expected to see the petite blonde but was surprised when six-foot-something Luke stepped inside.

He was wearing dark-blue scrubs that hugged his biceps, his chest, his thighs, and suddenly the room felt even smaller than it had a few moments before. I chastised myself for finding him attractive. I mean, I was a woman, and just because I was engaged didn't mean I turned off my hormones or was exempt from feeling a certain way sometimes. Then I realized the last time he'd seen me, I'd been accidentally topless and flushed at the memory.

"Hey, thanks for bringing her by," Luke said as he approached the opposite side of the exam table. He was casual and definitely not thinking about me topless. Good.

"Umm, yes, of course," I stuttered over the words, my mouth dry and unable to focus on anything except for how good he looked in navy blue. I stood from the chair, threw my phone in my purse without finishing the text to my mom, and approached the other side of the exam table. "Is she okay?"

He chuckled. "Yes, she'll be okay. It doesn't look like anything is broken, so I think she's just being a little dramatic."

I nodded in response. "Did I know that you're a vet?"

He laughed again, but this time it was a little louder. He crossed his arms over his chest, and the sleeves of his scrub top constricted even tighter around the tattoos on his arms. "I'm not sure. Based on your expression, I'd say probably not."

"I feel like I should have known that."

He shrugged and began to say something until the door opened and interrupted us. The blonde came in with Sadie on a leash. She seemed to be walking better and at least putting a little weight on her injured leg.

"Hi," the blonde greeted me flatly before turning to Luke with a bright smile. "She's ready to go unless there's anything else you need me to do." Her words sounded like she was hoping he'd give her something to do.

"No, do I have any other patients?" I quietly chuckled at him calling the animals patients, but I couldn't think of a better word that fit either. Still sounded funny whether it was correct or not.

"No, you're done. Do you need me to drive you home?"

"Actually," Luke said as he turned back to me, holding Sadie's leash firmly in his hand. "Hazel, would you mind if I catch a ride with you? I was going to have Crystal take me, but since you're here, it'd be more convenient if I could just go with you."

"Sure, that's fine," I agreed and didn't miss the contempt and disappointment on Crystal's face at the change of plans.

"Okay, let's go home," he said more to Sadie than me as he led us out of the room. As we entered the lobby, he said his goodbyes to the receptionists and the vet techs at the front. He also stopped to talk to an older woman who carried an older dog close to her chest. Each woman, and one of the men, seemed to ogle Luke in almost the same way Crystal had. Crystal's ogling, however, was tremendously more transparent.

I opened the back door for Luke, and he effortlessly lifted Sadie into the back seat.

"I'll pay to have your car vacuumed sometime soon. She sheds like crazy," he commented while squeezing into the passenger seat. My car was not small, but I imagined Luke, being the size he was, had an issue fitting into a lot of cars. His driving a spacious truck made sense.

"It's not a big deal. Tan seats, tan dog. No one will know." I pulled out of the parking lot and headed toward home.

I loved the fall, but the time of year was always weird to me. It was just after five o'clock and the sun was already beginning to set in the distance. Luke was quiet in the passenger seat, looking at the setting sun and tapping his thigh to the beat of the Guns N' Roses song on the radio.

I was focused on the road, but I was yet again in a small space with the large man. It was difficult to focus, which was not a good sign since I was the one driving.

Luke was gripping the handle above the window, but it wasn't because my driving warranted it as much as it allowed him to spread out a little more. His arm tensed and the veins running up and down his forearm bulged.

I felt the blush as it began to bloom over my neck and face even though he hadn't caught me staring at his toned arms and muscular jaw. My embarrassment was probably a good sign that my thoughts and subsequent feelings were encroaching on a territory that was highly inappropriate.

"Let's go to dinner," Luke stated out of the blue.

I jerked my head to the side and tried not to jerk the wheel as well.

"I—uh. What?"

Only around him did words not seem to come out of my mouth well at all. I sounded like I didn't know the English language. Like I hadn't studied it in college nor spoken it since birth.

"Let me take you to dinner as repayment for rescuing Sadie."

I considered the invitation for a moment but hesitated too long.

"Are you really going to pass up some free food?" he argued, sensing my hesitation.

His point was valid; I didn't usually pass up free anything, but I didn't want to cross a line. But Luke seemed casual about the invitation and didn't insinuate that he was looking for anything more than a friendly dinner. Could I be friendly with the neighbor I had grown to loathe? That was another question entirely, but an innocent dinner was just that: innocent.

"No, I'm not going to pass up free food. Where do you wanna go?" I asked, making my decision.

"Turn right at the next light, and then make a right into the first parking lot." I did as he instructed, and we pulled into the parking lot of a small burger joint. Literally, the place was called Burger Joint, according to the sign above the door.

"I hope you eat meat because they don't have any vegetarian options here."

"I like meat," I responded, and the words leaving my mouth sounded too dirty. Luke chuckled, and I willed my cheeks not to blush. When that didn't work, I hurried and hopped out of the car and into the chilly evening air.

Luke retrieved Sadie from the back, who had made a miraculous recovery after our short drive to the restaurant.

"Told you she was being dramatic," Luke announced. He led us into the patio area, and we took a table near the back corner and a giant heater. I was thankful for the warmth and after I sat down, I scooted my metal chair closer to the heat source.

Luke tied Sadie's leash around the table, but I didn't think she was going to go anywhere. She plopped comfortably on the concrete floor and laid her head on her paws the moment we sat down. It wasn't even a second later before her eyelids grew heavy and I thought I heard her snoring even over the sound of the other restaurant patrons.

Luke took the chair next to me—I noted that he didn't try to sit across from me—and pulled out his phone. A few moments later, he passed it to me. "Look over the menu and let me know what you want. I'll go in and order if you can stay with Sadie."

It didn't take me long, and I was all too aware of Luke watching me as I scanned the short menu. "Just a regular cheeseburger, but with no onions. And sweet potato fries instead of regular fries."

"Really? Sweet potato fries instead of regular fries? They have the best fries in Austin. You're going to be disappointed if you don't get them."

I rolled my eyes. "If you were going to argue with what I ordered, then why did you let me look at the menu in the first place?"

"Okay, okay. Sweet potato fries it is, but I'm getting you a beer."

Before I could argue, he was striding into the restaurant and out of sight. I took the opportunity while he was gone to check my phone. I still hadn't received a response from Michael and prayed he wasn't upset that I hadn't fixed the damn bike. He'd been gone for so long, and I wanted a happy Michael when he got back.

"I don't even want to know what happened to make you make that face," Luke commented while placing a beer in front of me and a number tent on the table.

"It's nothing," I said before taking a sip of the beer to have something else to do.

Luke nodded, but his eyes inspected my face like he didn't believe me. He shouldn't, because it was something, but I didn't give him any reason to doubt me.

He continued to study my face as I took a longer-than-necessary sip of the fruity beer. I felt exposed with his eyes on me, like a large neon sign—similar to the one above the door—was hanging above my head, alerting him that I was worried about my fiancé's return home.

"So, I made a promise to Sadie while we were on our way to the vet," I began, trying to change the subject and interrupt his perusal of my face.

"You're promising my dog things?"

"Yes," I said. The wind picked up around us, so I huddled closer to the heater and, subsequently, closer to Luke. "I promised her that I would kick your ass for letting her get out again."

He threw his head back and laughed heartily. "I would like to see you try to kick my ass. Actually, I would pay to see you try."

I scoffed. "I could give you a run for your money. Just because I'm small doesn't mean that I can't pack a punch."

"I believe you," he said, then paused like he had more to add. "You know I don't intentionally let Sadie get out, right? I'm a good dog owner."

"I'm sure you don't intentionally do it, but she's either Houdini reincarnate, or you slip up often enough that she winds up rolling around in my front yard at least once a week."

He took a long sip of his beer, and I found myself watching his Adam's apple bob as he swallowed. The dark scruff along his jaw was too long to be called a shadow but too short to be called a beard and was trimmed neatly along his neck.

"It's Josh."

I tried to connect the dots and how that comment made sense in our conversation. Luke must have noticed the confusion on my face, so he clarified, "Not sure if you remember, but the first year or two we lived next door to each other, Sadie didn't get out once. But when my brother moved in, that's when she began escaping. He's a little careless with doors and gates. But he also doesn't check before letting her out. Someone left the gate open the other night, and she took the opportunity. She is also a little escape artist, but I'm beginning to think it's because she likes you."

For my sanity, I ignored his final comment. But the time line added up, and I guess I probably should have also blamed the other Shepherd brother living in the house. But since she was Luke's dog, I just blamed him.

"Wait, so you let me just blame you and give you crap about it for the past almost two years without once telling me it wasn't true?"

His only response was a shrug.

"Hmm," is all I could come up with at the moment.

"What does that mean? 'Hmm'?" he mimicked in a higher pitch.

Our food arrived before I had a chance to respond. When the young waiter pushed my food in front of me, wafting the freshly grilled burger scent toward me, I realized how hungry I was. It was my first meal of the day, and I had to hold myself back from scarfing it down like a starving animal.

Instead of going straight for the burger, I picked up a sweet potato fry covered in freshly grated parmesan cheese and popped it into my mouth. Luke reached for his fries first as well, but instead of eating one, his hand disappeared under the table. I felt Sadie stir from her place up against my foot to grab the fry from his hand.

I chuckled and couldn't wait any longer to try the burger. My first bite was too large, and juice squirted across the table in front of me. I didn't have a moment to be embarrassed, though, because I was totally consumed by the delicious taste of the food.

Without my permission, a groan escaped my full mouth, and I barely had the willpower to keep my eyes from slipping closed. Luke stared at me intently with a lopsided smile and a full mouth while I lost myself in food bliss.

"Told you it was the best," Luke said confidently.

"It's so good," I agreed. I decided that I didn't mind his company when he wasn't thoroughly pissing me off.

"Only the best for dog rescuers that are willing to kick anyone's ass in the name of their neighbor's dog."

"Better not forget it. I will make good on my promise if need be." Sadie put her head on my thigh and innocently begged for any of my table scraps. I gave in and let her have a sweet potato fry. Not that I needed them all anyway. "And next time—which I hope there isn't, by the way—I'll yell at Josh, too, if Sadie gets out."

Luke laughed again, and I thought it was a good laugh. Not

too loud or boisterous, but just enough to let the person know that he appreciated whatever they said.

"I appreciate that, but Josh is a little sensitive. He probably wouldn't take your constructive criticism very well. I think you should continue to file your grievances with me."

I shook my head. "Fine by me."

Conversation tapered off as we both enjoyed our food. I was in the perfect location—the back corner of the patio—to see everyone going in and out of the restaurant, along with every person on the patio. There were a few couples that appeared to be on dates, a young family with unruly children and an older couple sharing a burger and a milkshake. The older man was constantly doing things to make the woman—who I assumed was his wife—laugh. Each time she threw her head back or closed her eyes and shook her head at his nonsense, he glowed with pride.

"What do you say we start over?" Luke asked.

"We as in us?" I questioned, motioning between the two of us, startled by the sudden question.

"Yes, since we're the only two people sitting at this table." I didn't appreciate his sarcasm, but I guess it was somewhat warranted. I rolled my eyes.

"Start over, how? Why?"

"We've been neighbors for years and you just learned today that I'm a vet. Don't you think neighbors should at least know the basics of each other's lives? That way, when I come over to borrow an egg or two, maybe a cup of flour, it doesn't seem so random or strange."

"Do you plan on baking lots of cakes in the future, Luke?" He eyed me like he didn't appreciate my sarcasm. "What? It's an honest question. I need to know, so I can keep an extra carton of eggs in the fridge. Make sure I have extra flour, too. Butter is also usually required for baking a cake, so I'll make sure to buy an extra stick or two."

He leaned back in his chair and scooted farther to the edge, pushing his empty basket closer to the center of the table. The sun was almost past the horizon and the streetlights, along with the lights around the restaurant, flicked on.

"I think you know what I mean."

"Yeah," I conceded, then shrugged. "So, let's start over."

NINE

Hazel

He stuck his hand out across the table and said, "Hi, I'm Luke. I live next door."

I giggled at his formality but took his hand anyway. "Hi, I'm Hazel." I gave his hand a firm shake, but neither of us pulled away immediately. His hand enveloped mine completely and his calloused, worn palm was an interesting contradiction to my smooth hands. I wondered if he ever worked with his hands.

He was the first to finally, yet slowly, let go, and I followed his lead. "Tell me about yourself, Hazel."

"Well," I said, then stopped to think for a moment. "I'm twenty-seven, almost twenty-eight. I'm a technical writer for an engineering company, and I like to read and run in my free time. Your turn."

He scrubbed his hand, the one that was just holding mine, over his jaw. "I'm thirty-one, and I'm a vet. I have a dog named Sadie, and my brother, Josh, lives with me."

"I already knew all of that," I argued. "You have to tell me something new."

The waiter cleared our plates and Luke ordered us two more

beers. I guess he was enjoying our dinner enough to want to extend it. Or he needed more alcohol if we were going to stay. Not that I cared.

"I already knew most of that stuff about you, too," he countered.

"Umm, you know what I do for a living?"

"Okay, fine. I didn't know that one thing. I knew the rest, though."

"How do you know that I like to read and run in my free time or how old I am?"

He shrugged. "Even if you don't tell me things, you tell other people on our street things. And people like to talk about you."

"What does that mean?" I questioned defensively. What kinds of things were people saying?

As if reading my mind, Luke said, "It's nothing bad. People like you, so you come up in conversation sometimes."

I nodded, hoping that he was telling the truth.

"So, since we already know the basics, tell me something about yourself that you don't usually tell other people. Something that I can't find on social media or wherever else. I don't know. Be creative. Just something interesting about yourself."

I'm not interesting, I wanted to say, but I didn't. Instead, I contemplated and dug down deep to find a fact that maybe not necessarily everyone would know about me.

"I'm writing a book." The words came out like vomit and before I could even think about what I was going to say. He wanted an interesting fact, but my life was boring. The word *creative* had me thinking of my creative outlet, and apparently, it was the best I had.

"Very interesting, go on," he urged me to tell him more, but I didn't have any more to tell.

"That's all. I'm writing a book. I haven't gotten very far, and the writer's block has been fierce lately, but I've started."

He leaned forward, elbows propped up on the edge of the

table, giving me another eyeful of his thick, veiny forearms. He grabbed his new, full beer glass and asked, "What's it about?"

I shook my head, reaching for my own beer. "I'm not telling anyone that. Only you and my sister now know that it's even happening, but I'm not telling what it's about just yet."

He gave me a fake pouty face, and I laughed. "Why not?"

"Because one of the authors I admire the most had some really good advice on the subject: if you tell what your story is about, people will be less interested once it's down on paper and then less inclined to read it. If I want people to read my book, I need them to be interested."

"Do you want me to read your book?"

The question was a genuine one, and I was taken off guard by the sincerity in his voice. I felt, for some reason, like my answer was important.

"I want to have as many readers as possible, so yes, I'd want you to read it if you felt so inclined." He nodded, and I continued, "Your turn. Give me something interesting about you that not everyone would know."

He paused for a long minute like he was thoroughly debating the same question he asked of me. "I used to fight."

"Like MMA or… boxing?" I asked for clarification on his broad statement.

He laughed without humor and rubbed the back of his head. "I wish. But no. I was an angry kid, and I took my anger out on other people. It was mostly underground fighting throughout high school and some of college."

I was surprised that he was so candid in his admission. Although my admitting that I was writing a book was as deeply personal to me, it seemed like that really was something most wouldn't know about him.

Pain from those memories made themselves apparent on the lines and the few small scars on his face. His past was obvious in the slight bump in his nose where it had likely been broken and was clearly written on the scars along his knuckles. But knowing his past made it hard to miss.

Some scars are hard to see unless you know what to look for.

"So, you fought out of anger as a way to channel it? What made you so angry?"

He was deep in thought when I posed my question, and he waited for a moment before answering. "That's a subject for another time," he said as he tipped his beer up and finished it off.

Usually, I would push for more information, but the look on his face, combined with his already heavy confession, told me not to.

"I think I misjudged you," I said instead. He quirked an eyebrow at me in surprise.

"Did you?" he asked as if he wasn't surprised by my admission.

"Yes. You're not what I expected; actually, you're wholly unexpected," I said, without the intention of expanding. Maybe another time, I would. I finished off the rest of my beer, and we both stood and headed back to the car.

I helped him get Sadie in the back seat, and he opened the driver's side door and closed it behind me after I slid inside. The small act sent butterflies fluttering through me. I couldn't remember the last time a man had voluntarily opened the door for me.

Most of the drive home was silent until "Highway to Hell" came on the radio, and Luke proclaimed it was one of his favorite classic rock songs. He turned it up and proceeded to play the air guitar and air drums for the four-minute-long song.

After I got over my fear of him hearing my tone-deaf voice, I began to sing along, which granted me an unusually large smile from him. Seeing him smile at me made the muscles in my stomach tighten and my mouth go dry.

At the end of the song, the screen on the dashboard lit up and announced I had a new text from Michael.

"You can listen to it if you need to," Luke said as we turned down our street.

"No, that's okay. It can wait a few minutes." As I said it, I attempted to press the ignore button, but as luck would have it, my finger slipped, and I inadvertently hit the listen button instead.

"I don't want to have to remind you about the fucking bike again. I spent a lot of money on that, so get it fixed. Also, don't forget to clean up before I get home. I'm excited to see you too."

I was mortified. I was used to Michael's angry messages when he was stressed with work. I could handle it, but I didn't want anyone else to hear it. I knew the way it sounded.

I silently cursed the slow speed limit in our neighborhood and the several children playing in the street. I wanted to rush home and hide in the house for the rest of eternity, but I continued to crawl at a snail's pace as I weaved through the children and toys.

"I'm sorry." It was barely above a whisper, but I knew Luke could hear it in the silent car.

I didn't want to look at him, but when he didn't respond, I snuck a quick glance in his direction. His hand was back to holding the handle above the door, and he was staring straight ahead. The muscles in his jaw were ticcing, and a new vein I hadn't noticed before in the side of his neck was very pronounced.

"You have nothing to apologize for," is all he said before I *finally* pulled into my driveway.

My will to hide was pulling me to the front door, and I could hear the new bottle of wine I bought yesterday calling my name. "Well, thank you for dinner, and—"

"Does he always talk to you like that?"

The question startled me, and I wasn't sure how to respond after I unintentionally flinched at his tone. I could feel the tension, even anger rolling off him in waves as I searched my mind for the simplest answer.

"No, he's just stressed with work, and he's been gone awhile. Being gone, being away from me, is hard on him."

He nodded but didn't respond. He was still tense, but the vein in his neck was less pronounced. Without another word, he opened his door and let Sadie out of the back. This time she easily bounced out of the open door and headed to their house.

"Thank you again for helping Sadie, and..." He trailed off, lost in thought, before he finally said, "If you ever need me, I'm right next door."

"Same to you," I said and he gave me a smile that didn't reach anywhere near his emerald-green eyes. Eyes a color that I didn't fully appreciate until that moment when they were full of so many questions, I knew he wanted to ask but thankfully didn't.

Once at my front door, I felt guilty for how poorly a rather good night ended, so I called out, "Did you remember your Halloween candy? Or do you need to borrow some?"

I got a chuckle out of him, but not the laugh I was hoping for.

"I got some, but thanks."

"OK, good. Good night, neighbor."

He let Sadie inside, but before stepping in, he said, "Good night, Angel."

TEN

Luke

I HAD LIVED IN TEXAS MY WHOLE LIFE. MY MOM AND DAD WERE also born in Texas and raised Josh and me in a suburb of Austin until they died when we were in high school. I tried not to think about them often—they didn't die from natural causes and their deaths were completely preventable—but when it was hot as it was even at the end of October, it was hard not to think about them.

My childhood was not very joyful, and I couldn't remember many times of laughter or serenity except when we went to the lake. After school started every year, my parents would load Josh and me up in the car and make the hour drive to Lake Travis. We would only go once school started because it was too busy any other time, yet it was still warm enough to enjoy.

One year Josh begged my dad to buy us a float or two so we could float around the water. For once, my dad agreed and bought each of us a float of our choosing, within reason. We didn't have money for a lot, but that was a big-ass win in our book.

Josh and I would fuck around in the water, usually pissing

off my dad, who sat on the water's edge, drinking as many beers as he could until he passed out in the sun. My mom would read an entire book every time we went to the lake. She loved to read, but she didn't have much time to do it with the way my dad liked the house run. She took full advantage of his drunken state. She read and then jumped in the water with us.

Even in the afternoon on Halloween, the temperature was in the mideighties, although a cold front was due later. It would've been a good day to go to the lake.

I was mowing the yard in the heat. It had gotten out of hand, and I'd already received two notices from our hoity-toity homeowners' association, letting me know that the next notice would include a two-hundred-dollar fine. So, I braved the stupid heat and mowed the front and backyard.

I was about to put the lawn mower away and begin the cleanup process when I noticed Hazel's yard was also looking a little—better yet, a lot—out of sorts. Since we'd decided to start over, I thought I'd do the neighborly thing and knock on her door to ask if she wanted me to at least mow her front yard. It had nothing to do with the fact that I was still stewing over that fucking text message I heard from her fiancé last night.

Luke from several years ago would have demanded his number and set up a time to "talk" about the way he spoke to his fiancée—future wife. But I had moved past the anger and would continue my plan of attack: get in Hazel's good graces and watch her back like a fucking hawk.

I stood at her door for a minute after knocking, thinking that maybe she wasn't home. I raised my fist to knock again when she swung the door open, looking disheveled and a little sweaty.

"Hi," she said, out of breath.

"Hey, I was just mowing my yard and was wondering if you wanted me to do yours too."

She smiled and leaned against the door. "That's really nice of you, but the guys who usually do it should be here a little later. I started paying the high school kid down the street twenty bucks a week to do it."

As she spoke, I tried to slyly take in her outfit. She was dressed for the heat in small workout shorts that showed off the curve of her legs and a fitted tank top. There was a sheen covering her skin, her cheeks were flushed from exertion, and the ponytail her hair was in was a little mussed. I wasn't sure what she had been doing, but my mind immediately began wondering if that's what she may look like after sex.

Not necessarily where my mind needed to be going, but I had little control over it.

When I finally pulled my mind out of the gutter, I realized she was waiting for me to respond or leave or something. I stopped staring at her and caught a glimpse of the interesting arrangement of her living room furniture.

"Doing some redecorating?"

She laughed—God, it was a good sound—and looked over her shoulder. "Yeah, I needed a change. I was cleaning and then decided that I wanted the couch over by the windows, so I cleaned under it and moved the rug. The stupid leg fell off the coffee table, though. I'm just having trouble getting it back on. I can't find the damn screwdriver anywhere."

"What kind of screwdriver do you need? I can grab one from the garage."

She bit her bottom lip as if contemplating if she really wanted to take my help. With another glance over her shoulder, she said, "Phillips."

"I'll be back." I jogged over to the garage, grabbed the screwdriver from the top drawer of my toolbox and let myself in her front door that was left slightly ajar.

Hazel was kneeling over the upturned coffee table, trying to shove the leg back on with a murderous look in her eye.

"I swear I'm about to just buy a new damn table," she muttered as I stooped and inspected the table. Within a minute, I had the leg in place and the table upright once again.

"Yeah, the screwdriver was necessary."

She nodded and began arranging the rest of the furniture the way she wanted it. "Since you're here…" she began as she lifted one side of the couch and eyed the other.

I picked up the other side as she instructed me where it should go. We had it in position, and I took it upon myself to place the couch cushions that were thrown on the other side of the room back in their rightful places.

Hazel was busying herself with decorations on one of the end tables while I placed the pillows. "Women and their damn decorative pillows. Is this right?"

She whipped around and inspected my work. The corners of her mouth tilted in a small smile. "No, but I'll fix it." She turned back to continue rearranging the books on the table for the tenth time when her ponytail landed over her shoulder, and I noticed the top of the bruises I had seen the week before.

From the little skin of her back that I could see, it looked like the bruises—now more yellow and green and less black and blue—followed the length of her spine. I tried to tell myself that it could've been an accident or a fall, but I couldn't believe it. Without thinking, I closed the distance between us and ran my thumb along her spine and along the bruised area.

Hazel immediately tensed and gasped when my hand touched her exposed skin.

"Hazel," I said her name in a low whisper. She wouldn't have known, but I was begging for her to let me help her. To tell me what the fuck was going on.

I expected her to jerk away from me immediately, but her reaction was delayed. She didn't relax, but for a few seconds, she let me touch the bruised skin. I'm not sure why I felt a pull to touch her. Maybe to make sure the bruises were real? Or to try to erase the brutality of it with a softer touch?

She finally stepped away from me and replaced my hand with her own at the base of her neck. She faced me, and I tried to decipher the unreadable expression on her face.

"Hazel," I said her name again, hoping to elicit a vocal response.

"What? I fell trying to replace a light bulb outside last week. I landed straight on my back on the concrete." It sounded a lot like an excuse, but what proof did I have that it wasn't actually an accident as she said? I had none, that was the problem.

I had my suspicions, odd bruises on her body and shitty texts from her fiancé. Sadly, none of it amounted to much compared to what I was on the verge of alleging.

"When does he get back?" As soon as the words left my mouth, I regretted them, and then heard what sounded like the garage door opening behind me.

Hazel's eyes went wide, and I could finally clearly read her expression: full-fledged fear. "Fuck," she all but whimpered. Her eyes darted around in a panic, and she tried to shove me toward the back door. It was the closest exit that didn't require passing the garage to leave.

But it was too late. The door leading from the garage into the house closed and her fiancé called her name. He rounded the corner into the living room where I stood just behind Hazel and a large armchair missing the cushions.

"What's going on?" The accusation was clear in his voice.

"Michael, you're home!" Hazel said cheerfully, replacing any trace of the fear from just a moment ago.

She crossed the room and flung her arms around his neck. Michael accepted the hug but didn't return it. His eyes were still locked on me as they had been since he first walked in.

For the first time in the years we'd lived next to each other, I saw him up close. He was the blond-haired asshole I was expecting and not much else.

Finally, he hugged Hazel back, running his hand down her bruised spine. I narrowed my eyes at him as a smile split his smug fucking face. I ran the odds of me beating his ass in my head as he kissed her cheek. Even after a flight, he was wearing an expensive suit and his hair was perfectly styled. I decided my odds were good.

"Hi, baby," he whispered. "Who's this?"

Hazel pulled back from him and looked my way. She didn't make eye contact, but said, "This is Luke, our neighbor. He came by to ask if he needed to mow our yard and ended up helping me fix the coffee table." Her words were sweet but measured, like she was choosing them carefully.

"Mm-hmm. How neighborly of you," Michael said with a sly grin still plastered to his face, narrowing his eyes at me.

"No problem," I responded, looking back to Hazel, hoping she'd finally look at me. She looked everywhere except at me.

"Well, if you don't mind," Michael began before kissing the top of Hazel's head and pulling her closer. The movement was too aggressive, and I tensed. "I haven't seen my fiancé in more than a week, and I'd like to greet her *properly*."

What he was suggesting was clear, but I was hesitant to leave. To leave her there alone with him. Finally, Hazel looked me in the eyes. "Thanks for your help, Luke." She dismissed me and her eyes were as steadfast as her words.

A mask firmly back in place. Or was I seeing something that wasn't there? Did I see abuse in every relationship now?

I knew I couldn't stay but leaving was harder than expected. In my experience, if she left her situation, it had to be her idea. It wasn't the time to confront either of them, so I balled my fist and headed to the door.

"Bye, Hazel," I said before closing the door behind me and praying there were no new bruises the next time I saw her.

ELEVEN

Luke

Like the psycho I had apparently become, I cleaned up the front yard and sat in my room waiting to see something of Hazel or her fiancé, but the blinds were closed. If they were in there, I wouldn't have seen it anyway.

The trick-or-treaters began ringing the doorbell just after five that night, so I sulked into the living room, where I planted my ass on the couch with a beer.

I did my best to not think about fuckface (which was his actual name in my book and an upgrade from douche) or the fact that I had no other choice than to trust Hazel and leave her alone with him. Every part of me wanted to rush over there and pull her out of that house. His grip on her was aggressive as he tried to mark her as his territory earlier. He might as well have pissed on her instead.

I needed to do something, but I knew if I did anything in that moment, I would likely make it worse for her. I hoped he'd be careful with his actions, knowing I was right next door. There was no way he'd missed the warning on my face. But the last thing I wanted was to make it worse, so in the interim, I needed to find a distraction.

The constant trick-or-treaters were enough of a distraction for a while, but by nine p.m., most of them were high schoolers who were probably too old for the shit anyway. After I answered the door to find the third kid, who was about as tall as me, wearing street clothes and a boring-ass "scary" mask, I flipped my porch light off and hunkered down with Sadie.

I searched for a scary movie, but nothing sounded like it would hold my attention. I went back to *The Exorcist* and turned it on for my hundredth viewing. During the movie, I declined three calls from an unknown number which served as another distraction. They left no voice mails, so I chalked it up to kids playing games, prank calling people on Halloween. Normally, I would've answered and fucked with them a little, but I wasn't in the mood.

My phone began buzzing again, and I was about to chuck it across the room when, to my surprise, Hazel's name began scrolling across my phone screen. It was past eleven, and my pulse began racing as I hit the green button as quickly as I could.

"Hello?"

"Hey, it's Josh." My brother's voice bellowed on the other end of the phone. I did a double take, looking back at my phone to make sure it was Hazel's number. He was obviously calling from the bar based on the loud thumping music in the background.

"What the hell are you doing with Hazel's phone?"

He sighed. "Hazel showed up at Murphy's tonight. I was working in the back bar, so I didn't see her until just now, and dude, she's shit-faced. Apparently, she mentioned your name, and one of the bartenders came and grabbed me. I think she's about ready to go, but there's no way in hell she's driving, and I'm not about to put her in an Uber by herself. Think you can come get her? I would bring her, but I've got another two hours left in my shift." My mind could not keep up with the rate at which he was talking as I strained to hear him over the thumping music.

"Umm…yeah, yeah, I'll be right there."

"Okay, I'll see you in a few," he said before the line disconnected.

Luckily, I was too lazy to change my clothes earlier, so I simply patted Sadie on the head, grabbed my shit and headed out the door. As I walked to my truck parked in the driveway, I glanced over to Hazel's house. Her jeep was gone, but Michael's car was still there.

Fuck. I was going to kill the fuckface if something happened to her. I knew it was his fault, whatever had happened.

I sped to the bar, Murphy's Law or Murphy's, sometimes, and peeled into the parking lot going much faster than I should have been. But I didn't want to waste any time going the speed limit.

I found the one empty space near the front and was throwing the door open as I turned off the engine.

I passed beneath the glowing neon sign positioned above the front door, *"Expect the Unexpected,"* and part of me felt nostalgic while the other half of me wanted to get out as soon as possible.

Inside, the bar was loud and full of people wearing costumes and colorful makeup. Murphy's Law was a large, older home that the owner, Rhonda, had renovated almost fifteen years before. She'd knocked down several walls and removed the entire second floor to make room for high ceilings. The third floor was only used for storage, and walking into the familiar space, a shiver shifted down my spine.

To call my memories of the place bad was an understatement. Which was unfortunate since, in college and afterward, it was where our group of friends hung out every weekend. It took one night, one stupid fucking night to ruin all the good.

I navigated through the ocean of people and with each face I passed, I double-checked that I hadn't missed Hazel among them. I waved to Rhonda, who was tucked in a corner dealing with an unruly customer, and she gave me a knowing look that warned me not to fuck around.

One girl grabbed my arm and pushed herself up against me. Her tits were pushed up to her chin in a tight, black corset, and once I noticed her pointy cat ears, I rolled my eyes, pushed her off and moved on.

With cat lady stomping off, I looked up to find Hazel at the other side of the bar laughing with Josh.

She was wearing a tight red top and had that silly halo headband on. She was smiling the biggest, brightest smile I had seen from her, but I could also tell she was fucking hammered.

I pushed the rest of the way through the crowd and plopped down in the barstool next to her.

"She's all yours, man. I've gotta get back to the back bar," Josh sighed and raised his eyebrows at me as he walked away.

"You're drunk, Angel."

"Hi, Luuuke," the way she said my name was almost a purr, and fuck if I didn't already love the way my name sounded coming out of her mouth.

"Ready to go?" I asked, but I was just being polite. I was getting her the hell out of this place as soon as possible. My skin was crawling with old memories.

"I—" She didn't finish her sentence as "Bad Girlfriend" by Theory of a Deadman boomed over the speakers. "I *love* this song!" she proclaimed and was off the barstool and heading for the dance floor before I even had a chance to comprehend what happened. I battled with what to do: grab her ass and, if necessary, carry her over my shoulder out of the bar or let her have one last dance. I decided on the latter and leaned back in my barstool.

Luckily, she stayed toward the perimeter of the mass of dancing people where I could see her. She found a group of girls all dressed like Harley Quinn and joined them. She whipped her curled, dark-brown hair back and forth as she danced and sang.

She was completely free and without a care in the world for at least a moment.

As the chorus began, she moved her hips, rolling them to the beat. Her hands tangled in her hair as she glanced back and smiled at me watching her. Her hips circled and one of the women she was dancing with placed her hands there. The woman tried to move her hips in sync with Hazel but couldn't quite match the motion.

She looked back at me again, biting her plump lower lip, and if it were any other time, I would be on her in a minute. Hazel looking at me like that made it feel like she was performing her own little seductive dance just for me.

She jumped with the beat and spun as the music crescendoed. As she danced, the smile on her face never faltered, and that was by far the best part. That was until a completely unaware Hazel was approached from behind by a guy that grabbed her waist and spun her to face him. She was small, and he easily whipped her around as she was enveloped in the music.

I didn't think as I shot off the barstool and got to Hazel and the stupid guy before anything more could happen. I stuck my arm between them and pulled Hazel into me. She was tense and shaking when her back hit my stomach. I rubbed my hand down her arm, keeping the other wrapped around her stomach, as I whispered in her ear, "You're okay. It's me."

She didn't completely relax as I'd hoped, but her shoulders dropped a little and she acknowledged what I said with a quick nod. She was still drunk, and it was the best I was going to get from her. I slowly counted to ten in my head as the guy tried to protest. Rhonda would ban me forever if I fought in Murphy's again. And Blakely, who was our friend and the manager, would seriously have my balls along with Josh. But when the guy had to tilt his head up to look me in the eye, he backed off quickly. I was still fuming, but it was easier to walk away when they weren't also ready to fight.

I tucked Hazel into my side, grabbed her purse from the barstool and hurried us out the door. My mind immediately circled back to the last time I was in the bar—wasted and begging for someone like that douche to make a move. Quickly exiting the bar was what I should have done the first time, too.

Once we hit the cool fall air—several degrees cooler from the cold front—Hazel immediately began to shiver, and I pulled her closer.

I clicked the lock button on her keys and saw the lights flash on her jeep at the end of the row. I tucked her keys back into her purse and opened the passenger door of my truck. She managed to pull herself up and into the truck and plop herself in the seat. I handed her the seat belt and helped her guide it to her left. I leaned around her, and even with the alcohol on her breath and the sweat sticking to her skin, she still smelled sweet. I buckled her and moved out of her space. Her eyes fluttered closed, and she ran her hand down my arm before I was able to pull it away.

"Thank you," she whispered.

I smiled to myself, closed her door carefully, and jumped into the driver's side. I turned the air a little higher and prayed we could make it without her vomiting all over my truck.

"Hazel, where do you want me to take you?" There was only one place I felt confident enough that she'd be safe, especially in her drunken state, but I resisted the urge to be a demanding alpha dick and asked politely instead.

"Nearest hotel," she murmured, half-awake.

"Yeah, that's not happening. Try again."

She opened her eyes enough to attempt to glare at me. It was a weak attempt, but she tried. "Well," she began as she sat up straighter and cleared her throat. "You can't take me home, so a hotel it is."

"You're being difficult. I said no. Now, try again." For the moment, I ignored the comment about her not being able to go home. That would be a conversation for tomorrow when she wasn't drunk.

"There's nowhere else for me to go, and I just want to sleep. A hotel is my best bet." Her head lolled to the side as she struggled to keep her eyes open.

"I'm not going to just dump you at a hotel when you're shit-faced. If you choke on your vomit and die, it'll forever be on my conscience."

She sighed deeply and finally conceded. "Fine. Take me wherever."

My house it was. We were already pulling down our street anyway, and of course, fuckface was planted in a chair on their front porch. He was smoking a cigar and twirling a tumbler full of amber-colored liquor in his other hand. He eyed my truck as I silently prayed that the garage was clean enough for me to pull straight in.

I pressed the garage door button and carefully maneuvered my truck inside. It was a tight fit, but I eased in until my bumper almost touched the back wall, and I was able to close the garage door behind us. I held my breath until the door closed. When the light from the streetlights disappeared behind the closed door, I hopped from the truck.

Hazel was semicoherent and was able to unbuckle her own belt as I opened the door. She swung her legs around and set her bare feet on the running board. Her heels were discarded on the passenger floorboard, and as I went to grab them, she tried to step down out of the truck only to fall into me. Her face hit my chest, and she groaned at the impact.

Hazel did not seem like the type of person to get absolutely shit-faced without a proper plan of getting home in place. As I wrapped my arms around her and lifted her, I knew there was only one person that could have done something bad enough to elicit this reaction from her. Whatever he had done—and even if it wasn't him, I decided, although it was unlikely to be anyone but him—I was going to beat his ass for it. Fuck being the nice guy if it meant she got hurt.

Hazel was light, and I was able to easily grab her bag, shut the door and get us inside while she wrapped her arms around my neck and settled into my chest. Her hair had fallen over her face, but she sighed against my neck. Through the short hallway, I passed the living room and opened the door to the guest bedroom.

"Fuck." Josh had decided to clean out the closet that was filled with most of his shit earlier in the day. The contents of the closet had been scattered over the guest bed, and I didn't have the time nor the desire to clean it up.

Since I sure as hell wasn't just going to leave her on the couch, I continued down the hall to my bedroom. I laid her on the edge of the bed, and she released her arms from around my neck with a groan.

Sadie entered the room behind me and promptly jumped on the bed to snuggle right next to Hazel.

I grabbed the comforter I discarded at the end of the bed that morning but paused before I pulled it around her. Hazel's shirt had fallen in the front and exposed her black lacy bra. Her tits were straining against the fabric and were begging to be released. Even in her drunken stupor, the woman was a fucking siren and my dick stirred to life.

She looked peaceful in my bed, and I had to admit, I'd thought about that before. Although Hazel wasn't blackout drunk the way I'd imagined it, I had given the idea of her in my bed more thought than I'd ever admit aloud. Her little spitfire personality and smart mouth—whether I acted like it pissed me off or not—made her even more desirable.

I pulled her top up slightly until at least her bra was covered before I laid the comforter over her. It had been ages since I had taken care of a drunk woman, and I would've preferred to never think about the time before, so it took me a minute to remember what else I needed to do.

I retrieved the trash can from the bathroom and placed the bottle of pain reliever and a cup of water on the nightstand. Content with my setup, I whispered for Sadie to follow me out of the room. I figured I'd grab the couch, although the thought of kicking Josh out of his bed since he'd left a big-ass mess on the guest room bed was enough to make me chuckle.

Sadie eyed me and gave me a look that said she wasn't leaving, so dejected and kind of interested that my dog picked Hazel over me, I cracked the door and headed to the living room.

It was well past midnight when my head finally hit the pillow. I was pissed that something happened to make Hazel drink herself into oblivion, but a part of me was also at peace knowing that at least for one night, she was under my roof where I knew nothing bad would happen to her.

TWELVE

Hazel

I'M DEAD, WAS MY FIRST THOUGHT WHEN I WOKE UP THE NEXT morning—on my birthday, no less—with the worst, world-shattering headache I'd ever had. But then I realized death would have been peaceful with (hopefully) no pain and would have been a million times better than the torture I was being subjected to in that moment.

These were all my thoughts before I even opened my eyes, which I realized was going to be much more difficult than usual when I tried to peel my eyelids apart and my stomach rolled with nausea.

With the option of opening my eyes to puke up the entire contents of my stomach *or* keep them closed in the soft, comfortable bed, the choice was easy as I snuggled back in.

I lay as still as I could manage while I tried to force my headache to go away. I was able to lay there for a couple of minutes and compose myself, believing I could manage to move when something licked my face. Right up my cheek, from my jaw to my hairline, leaving behind a wet mess.

I darted up and immediately regretted it when the room

spun, and the outside of my vision darkened. But I found the culprit next to me on top of the pillow on the other side of the bed. Sadie's tail, no, actually, her entire butt was wagging as I squinted at her.

I scanned the rest of the room and quickly realized that none of it looked familiar. Panic began to set in immediately as I raced to mentally retrace my steps and the events of the night before. I was still wearing my clothes—a red top and jeans—and my shoes were placed on the floor next to me. My breath smelled rancid but other than the hangover trying to kill me, I seemed fine.

I knew I was in Luke's house. Well, Luke and Josh's house, judging by his dog that lay next to me and the picture of who appeared to be Luke, Josh, and a woman on the bedside table. I was in Luke's house, and based on the rich, clean, manly scent that I recognized covering his sheets, I was in his bed.

Next to the photo on the table was a bottle of pain reliever, a cup of water, and a folded piece of plain white paper. I popped three of the pain relievers and chugged as much water as I could, then I unfolded the paper.

Went to get hangover food. Take the meds and drink some water. And don't leave before I get back.
  Luke

Whatever Luke had in mind for hangover food sounded amazing, and I smiled at his chicken scratch handwriting.

Since I knew where I was, some of the panic had subsided, and bits and pieces from the night before were falling into place.

I remembered finding the bar, taking shots, and then being surprised yet thrilled to see Josh behind the bar. I recalled Luke arriving at the bar, talking to Josh for a few minutes, and some of the dancing—although the memories of dancing were foggy. I also had a vague memory of Harley Quinn in triplicate.

I remembered seeing Luke close the door behind him as he

left his room. I didn't think he came back after that, and judging by the other side of the bed, which was still in pristine condition, I assumed that was true.

I remembered that stupid *"Expect the Unexpected"* sign that I stared at before I walked in and then glanced at again when I left with Luke. It was hazier the second time, the words were blurred by my drunken stupor, but I remembered it. And how well it fit my current situation.

I was beyond embarrassed. Getting drunk at a bar by myself was very uncharacteristic of me. But panic washed over me anew when I remembered the events that led to me seeking out the bar in the first place. The events leading up to me getting drunk alone on Halloween flooded my mind. Sweat beaded on my upper lip and around my hairline.

Michael got home when Luke was there. Not only when Luke was there but while Luke was sweaty and shirtless in my living room. After he fixed the coffee table, I should have asked him to leave, but I couldn't find the strength to do it.

I had been cleaning all day. I had moved every piece of furniture, washed all the sheets, and even climbed on top of the counters to dust the top of the kitchen cabinets. I was exhausted, and when Luke offered his help with the table, I took advantage of his kindness, eagerness to help, and, well, his large muscles.

The house was supposed to be spotless when Michael got home, but instead, he arrived before I could fix everything—including my appearance—and before I could hide our neighbor. Our neighbor who was sweaty, big, and concerned. The one who made my whole body hot and made it miserably difficult to breathe when we were in the same room.

I knew immediately when I heard the garage door that it wasn't going to end well. The scraping and grinding of the gears and the metal door creaking higher and higher echoed through our little house.

Luke had touched the back of my neck, where I knew the

bruise was visible. The way he said my name was like a soft plea, but what did he want me to do?

No one understood.

And I couldn't comprehend the intense reaction my body had when his fingertips touched my skin. His touch was so soft against my tender spine, and his thumb brushing back and forth over the spot felt like he was trying to wipe it away.

Then I did what I always did: I explained away the marks with an accident. Maybe slightly unbelievable at times, but no one really pried further. Luke looked like he wanted to, though, and that scared me even more.

Then he hesitated, with determination and another silent plea in his eyes, but ultimately left when Michael insinuated he wanted alone time with me. Michael was concerned that I was in the house alone with a man we barely knew. He was upset, and he was concerned.

I understood.

After reasoning with him that Luke was our friend—both of ours and our neighbor—I thought the topic was dropped. But when I stepped out of the bathroom, freshly showered, dressed and ready to go to my early birthday dinner, I could smell the alcohol on Michael's breath and felt the frustration in his fingers as he kneaded my upper arm.

His doubt was palpable. He yelled, and I raised my voice back, although it couldn't be called a yell. I didn't want to yell at him. And when I realized I could no longer reason with him, I ran.

I never ran. I always stayed and tried to find a way to make peace. But something in me told me I needed to leave, so for once, I listened to the voice in the back of my head and let it lead me to that damn bar.

I felt at peace for a minute of the car ride before I realized he'd be even angrier when I returned. Because I had to return. He was my fiancé, and he had a right to be mad that his partner ran out on him.

So, during my panic attack sitting in the bar parking lot, I sent him a text that said I'd be back soon and I needed a moment to myself. Much to my dismay, he never responded, and a moment turned into several margaritas, which turned into Luke picking me up and bringing me back to his house.

I needed to find my phone and my purse, I decided. I also needed to figure out how to get my car which I assumed was still at the bar.

I gave Sadie a few final head scratches and walked into the bathroom to inspect my appearance in the mirror. I was surprised that I didn't look as deathly as I felt, thanks to the expensive makeup Michael convinced me to buy a few weeks ago.

I was also surprised that for a bachelor pad, Luke's room was clean and mostly tidy. For a man with thick, dark facial hair, there weren't any hairs in the sink or the counter and the few bottles in his shower were organized. There were still clothes around the laundry hamper instead of inside, but I wouldn't expect any different.

Back in his room, the same was true. Everything was relatively tidy but for a few clothes and shoes here and there.

As quietly as I could, I opened the bedroom door and peeked down the hallway. There was faint music coming from the kitchen and I was thankful that his house had the same layout—with almost the same finishes—as mine so I didn't have to wander around trying to find the front door.

I opened the door farther but didn't take a step before Sadie darted past me and into the main living area. Over the music, I could hear Luke's deep voice when he greeted Sadie. As the back door opened, I softly padded down the hardwood floors of the hallway and into the living room.

"You're up," Luke said as he left the door slightly ajar for Sadie to come back in.

"Mostly," I said with a smile. I could smell something greasy and fried, and my stomach rumbled at the array of fast-food breakfast options on the kitchen island.

"Well, I got one of everything. The lady at the window looked like she was going to quit over my order, but to me, there's nothing better than this when dealing with a hangover." He fanned his arms out over the island.

"My stomach agrees," I said as I rounded the island and stood next to him. My earlier plan of leaving immediately was easily forgotten as I grabbed a sandwich and a hash brown. I also wanted to delay the inevitable as long as possible. Luke slid a coffee across the counter and into my waiting hand. Our fingers brushed for a moment, and I was thrust back to the day before and his tender touch on my neck.

He was a larger man, and his presence took up an entire room, but his touch was light. The contradiction was fascinating.

He pointed to one of the wooden barstools at the island, so I sat as he took the seat next to me. "So, how do you feel?"

"Like warmed up shit, but I think the pain meds are kicking in, so that's a good sign," I said around a way too large bite of my breakfast sandwich.

He chuckled, but it sounded like a pity laugh at best. Out of the corner of my eye, I watched his face fall and the skin between his brow furrow slightly before he took a sip of his coffee. I didn't necessarily know why he was concerned, but I figured it had to do with me. I wanted to scoot closer, feel his calming presence wash over me and tell him I was okay.

It probably would have been a lie, though, so I settled for the next best thing. "Thank you for last night. I don't usually need to be rescued from bars, but I appreciate it." I was sure getting a call late at night that his crazy neighbor was drunk at a bar wasn't what he expected.

He nodded. "Not a problem. Glad Josh called me."

"I didn't know that's the bar Josh worked at," I commented, trying to make small talk.

"Yeah, we used to go to Murphy's all the time—us and our group of friends."

"That's cool. I liked it."

"Do you remember much from last night?" he asked around a bite of sandwich.

I nodded, finishing a bite of my own food. "I remember drinking, some of the dancing, I think I wanted to do karaoke, but your brother talked me out of it. I like all the paraphernalia and signs they have on the wall, I remember going around and reading them after maybe my sixth or seventh shot of tequila," I chuckled, and so did Luke. I was trying to cover my embarrassment for the situation in humor, but it wasn't working. I could still feel the gnawing in my gut.

"What was that sign above the door about?"

Luke tensed beside me and glanced at me out of the corner of his eye. "Which one?"

"*Expect the Unexpected.*"

He shrugged. "Rhonda, the owner, thought it was fitting with the name of the bar—Murphy's Law says that anything that can go wrong, will go wrong, so she said you should expect the unexpected."

I nodded, remembering Murphy's Law and all its rules. "Seems pessimistic," I murmured. But it also felt truer than anything I'd heard lately. It was odd, though, to put it right above the front door.

"Or realistic," he said back. His whole body was tense, his jaw tight as he robotically chewed his food without sparing me a glance.

"Well, when you say it like that, it makes it sound like all unexpected things are bad. That the unexpected thing means something's gone wrong, but I won't believe that. Some unexpected things are good."

"Sure," he responded and continued eating. For some reason, he seemed to really despise the subject, so I let it drop.

He didn't say anything else, and we ate our breakfast in

silence—I was too occupied with settling my nausea and hunger with the greasy food—but occasionally, I would catch him looking at me out of the corner of his eye. He seemed upset by more than just the earlier conversation topic, and I realized I was probably a burden having to be picked up from the bar drunk off my ass in the middle of the night. He didn't sign up for that when he moved in next door or gave me his number.

"Okay, well, I'm going to go get my car. I really do appreciate your help, and umm... I don't plan on this happening again," I said as I slid from the barstool and chunked my trash in the bin.

"Wait," Luke said just as he gripped my wrist, keeping me from going anywhere. I tried not to flinch away from his touch. "I'll take you to your car."

"You don't have to do that, Luke. You've already done more than enough," I argued.

"It's not a problem. Let me take you."

"Luke."

"Hazel."

"Fine. Okay," I reluctantly agreed only to get him to stop arguing with me.

"But I need to ask..." Luke began as I stared at his hand that had slid down my wrist and was gripping my hand. "What the hell is going on, Hazel?" I wanted to entwine our fingers—his thick fingers wrapped around mine. But his question was the one question I was hoping he wouldn't ask (okay, maybe not the only one).

"What do you mean?"

He huffed and laughed humorlessly. "You don't strike me as the type of person to get drunk alone at a bar and need a ride for no reason. I know we don't know each other that well, but I have eyes and I know you well enough that I have a good feeling something is up. So, that being said, what the hell happened yesterday after I left?"

My whole body tensed as my mind was screaming at me to *lie, lie, lie, LIE!*

"Nothing happened. I just wanted a drink but got carried away, it happens to the best of us."

The lies used to sour on my tongue. Each time I would find myself in a situation where it was necessary, I would taste it for days afterward. Getting physically sick was also an awful side effect, but I had become so good at half-truths and omitting information that it no longer tasted off but felt more comfortable than the truth.

Luke didn't respond. His eyes held mine, and as much as I wanted to, I couldn't look away. He had his ideas about what might be happening, I could see it written on his face: doubt, confusion, concern and judgment. His touch that just seconds ago felt somewhat comforting had begun to spoil, and I felt the unshed tears gathering in the corner of my eyes.

"Was it because of me?" he said in a quiet voice. His grip on my hand tightened and he began rubbing small circles on the back of my hand. Goose bumps appeared over my arms at the intimacy in the motion of his finger. I wanted to believe him holding my hand was an act of care or concern, but the doubt that it was all a farce was overwhelming and a tactic to keep me in that spot.

A deep pit in my stomach opened as he neared closer to the truth. His eyes urged me to talk.

"I'm not sure what you're talking about." My voice was small and pathetic and by the look on Luke's face, he didn't believe me. I had let him get too close—I got too close to him—and he was beginning to piece it together. I didn't know when that had happened, but it was my life to live. This was on me.

"Hazel, I've seen..." He trailed off and looked away from me, finally freeing me from his intense gaze and judgment-laden eyes. "I've seen the bruises; I've heard how he speaks to you. Just... did me being there cause an argument?"

I wished that pit in my stomach would open even wider so I would also fall in. My mind raced, my eyes flicking back and forth between Luke's as I tried to come up with a way out of the situation. I didn't want to talk about my homelife, and it was none of his business.

More lies. I would have to lie, and I knew the best lies contained most of the truth.

"Yes," I stated simply.

"What happened?" he persisted.

Lie. "Seriously, Luke? Does it matter? I'm fine, it wasn't a big deal."

"It was a big enough deal that you left without him and called *me* to come pick you up. So, please..." he pleaded.

I sighed. "Josh actually called you, but yes, we argued. He was upset because he came home to a shirtless man in his home alone with his soon-to-be wife. If you were in his shoes, wouldn't you be mad, too?"

He didn't respond so I took that as a yes. "I'm fine and just needed some time to cool off and got carried away at the bar. Couples fight, it's normal, and that's all."

I finally found the strength to free my hand from his hold and was thankful that he didn't try to hang on, although he did attempt to grab it again.

"I know couples fight, Hazel. I've been in my fair share of relationships." He took a deep breath, evening out his tone. "I was married." His confession threw me. At only thirty-one, I couldn't imagine what happened to end a marriage so early in life. I also couldn't imagine Luke with another woman, let alone with a wife, and I was pissed that the thought even angered me. He was sitting there passing judgment on me and my relationship, and all I could think about was what kind of husband he had been. "But arguing is as far as it should go, it should never—"

"I know. I know," I cut him off before he could say anything more. If the words left his mouth, I don't think I could control my reaction. This conversation was becoming dangerous and my whole body began to vibrate with anxiety.

He didn't respond, although I knew he wanted to—that he

probably had a million things to say—as his jaw twitched and his fists clenched. His deep-green eyes held me hostage in the middle of his kitchen, surrounded by his clean scent, and I hoped I was wrong. That the judgment I thought I saw in his eyes and felt in his words was all my head playing tricks with me.

With a deep breath, and without looking away, I said, "I'm going to order an Uber to drive me to go get my car."

"No," he argued immediately, darting up from his barstool. "I'll drive you, just let me take a shower first, okay?"

When I didn't answer, he continued, "Please? I'll only be five minutes. Or if you'd prefer, I can have Josh drive you."

"Fine," I conceded, only to finish the conversation quickly.

I didn't move when he stood and began to walk past me. Shoulder to shoulder, he stopped, and I could see the struggle on his face. What he was struggling with, I wasn't sure, but he reached his hand out and ran his fingers down the length of my arm from just below my shoulder, across my elbow to where the sleeve of my shirt stopped at my wrist.

His touch—one I wished so badly I could feel on my skin and not through the fabric of my shirt—didn't feel judgmental as I thought it might. But I felt the pity within him almost boil over.

He didn't linger but a second more before he continued out of the kitchen, down the hallway and into his bedroom. I followed behind him for a moment and paused just out of sight until I heard the shower turn on.

Once I knew he wouldn't hear me, I grabbed my purse from the entry table where I spotted it walking past earlier and located my phone and wallet inside. Without another thought, I pulled the strap over my head and across my body. My heart was pounding in my chest, and I held my breath as I sneaked out the back door. In a rush to flee Luke's house and his suspicions, I didn't even pause to say goodbye to Sadie as she sunbathed in the middle of the backyard.

Either Luke or the previous homeowners had built a small,

raised garden in the back corner of the yard. A few leaves were sprouting out of the soil, but most of it was dirt. I hopped up on it, and when the rough wood cut into the bottoms of my feet, I realized that in my rush to leave, I forgot my damn shoes in his room.

It was too late, and I couldn't turn back with the possibility of him stopping me, so I pushed through the mild pain and scaled the back fence. Again, saying a silent thank-you that our houses backed up to a greenbelt, I started walking. The grass wasn't too tall, but I still paid as close attention as I could as I trudged along, all while pulling out my phone—ignoring the few dozen unread texts and missed calls from Michael—and ordered an Uber to pick me up around the corner.

Happy birthday to me.

THIRTEEN

Hazel

The driver dropped me off at my car a little after nine a.m., but I didn't make it back to our house until almost an hour later.

I sat in my car in front of the bar for several minutes before I gathered enough strength to look at the several missed texts from Michael. I ignored the third call from Luke, as well as the several texts wishing me a happy birthday from various friends and relatives, as I opened the messages between me and Michael. Many of them were paragraph length and ran the spectrum of emotions. He was furious when I left, which turned into disgust and then he began to apologize for his part. The apologies morphed into worry, and it appeared that as of this morning, he was getting angry again.

Before I left the bar, I texted him that I was on my way home. And sure enough, when I pulled into the driveway, a tired and disheveled Michael was standing on our front porch waiting for me.

I'd never done a walk of shame before, but I knew that's what it would've felt like as Michael watched me step out of my car, close the door, and make my way toward him. I couldn't read the expression on his face, and his squinted eyes could have been relief or anger or a whole host of other emotions. I couldn't have guessed what he may have been feeling.

"Glad you're alive. I was about an hour from calling the police and reporting you missing," he said as I stopped at the bottom of the porch stairs. My phone was buzzing relentlessly in my purse, and I knew it was Luke.

"I'm sorry, Michael," I whispered just loud enough for him to hear. To my right, Luke's front door banged open and out stepped a very large, pissed-off man. With his phone still to his ear—probably listening to my voice mail since my phone was no longer vibrating—he immediately looked at me and then Michael.

He appeared relieved to see me, but when he saw Michael, with his arms crossed, staring down at me, Luke's eyes narrowed. I swear I saw a vein in his forehead bulge when their eyes met.

The stare down between the two was intense. Luke turned to us, arms rigid at his sides and shoulders taut just below his ears. He wasn't just angry that I left, he was livid. Michael, although still staring at Luke, didn't seem fazed by him at all. If Luke was looking at me with murder in his eyes, I would have been fazed, and maybe a wiser and less cocky man would have been, too.

Without breaking eye contact with Luke, Michael said, "Get in the house, Hazel." It wasn't a request; it was a demand that I would be stupid not to obey.

I couldn't look at Luke. I wanted to, but Michael quickly flicked his eyes back to me, and I knew that if I even acknowledged Luke's presence, it would only end badly.

Michael kept his emotions close to the vest until the last second, and Luke usually played the same game. But in the morning light, Luke's emotions were evident in his eyes and his facial expressions. I saw the rage, but I wanted to see if the pity I noticed before was still there.

I gripped my purse tighter in my hands and hurried up the

stairs, not pausing for a minute until I was through the door. I took a deep, relieved breath until I heard Michael slam the door behind me—the walls around it vibrating on impact. My breath was stuck, and my relief was gone.

"Would you like to tell me where you've been, Hazel?" I was suddenly very aware of him directly behind me, his body less than an inch from my own. His breath was hot on my neck and my ear, and I could still smell the alcohol on him. It was the smell of the extra expensive bourbon he had to buy. I didn't want to hope that he had started drinking already that morning, but the smell was too potent to be left over from last night. It was either he just started drinking, or he'd never stopped.

When I didn't answer, my voice cut off by fear of his next move, he chuckled. "Why don't you put your purse down, and let's talk." He lifted my purse from my hands and took my hand. "We have a lot to discuss and fix after you ran out last night."

He led me to the couch, urging me forward by pulling my hand. His grip tightened when I didn't move immediately, and I knew it was a warning. My fear carried me forward and kept my mouth shut when Michael told me to sit on the couch. He sat on the coffee table across from me, legs spread and elbows propped on his knees.

We were mere inches apart, but I had never felt further away from him.

He was disheveled, still wearing the same white shirt and slacks he'd worn yesterday, except his jacket and lavender tie were nowhere to be seen. The dark circles under his eyes closely resembled my own, and uncharacteristically, his hair was sticking out in every direction as though he'd been pulling his fingers through it all night.

"I'm going to ask this once, and I want the truth: where have you been?" His voice was a low rumble and was laced with disdain.

"I went to a bar, and then I went to a hotel."

He nodded and peered up at me under hooded eyes. "I saw

the charges for the bar, but there wasn't a charge for a hotel room, Hazel."

The room was suddenly spinning as my panic bubbled to the surface. I wanted to release it in the sobs I felt at the base of my throat—it was the only way to release it completely—but I couldn't cry.

"I used my other card," I said in a small voice. Years of training taught me how to keep my composure while every part of me inside was in turmoil; however, I never could keep my voice level. The panic seeped through my words.

"I'm sure you did, baby." Michael reached out his hand and patted my knee. It took all of my strength not to flinch when his hand softly landed on me, rubbing back and forth over my skin through a rip in my jeans. "Everything went so wrong last night, and I think we need to start over."

I nodded, but when I didn't say anything, he squeezed my knee, fingers digging into my flesh. "Yes, let's start over," I responded in a gasp.

"Good, good." He relaxed his hand. "I know you said Luke, or whatever the fuck his name is, was just here by coincidence, and fine, I'll give you that one. But I need to know, Hazel, has anything happened with him?"

"No, Michael. Absolutely not," I said exasperatedly. The words came out in a rush, like I couldn't get them out quick enough.

"Let me rephrase: have you kissed him?" I shook my head. "Fucked him?"

I shook my head again while simultaneously I pleaded, *"No."*

"Did you let him touch you at all?" *Yes.* But it wasn't how he was implying, so I answered honestly.

"No."

Michael seemed to believe me. He wrapped his hands around my own as his knee bounced. He was lost in thought, and I was scared to imagine what was going on inside his head.

"Okay, I believe you, baby. I do." Once the words left his mouth, I felt a hesitant wave of relief wash over me.

"I would never do anything to jeopardize us."

He nodded in agreement, but when his eyes met mine, there was something behind the normal baby blue that made me think there was more to it than what he was letting on.

"I'm sure, baby. You would never do anything intentionally to jeopardize us, but..."

I sucked in a breath.

"What you do, or what you could do, may be unintentional. I just want to make sure you understand that your actions could have consequences for our relationship. You should stay away from men like him. Honestly, you should stay away from men in general."

"Men like him?" I asked and immediately regretted it when I saw the anger flash across his face.

"Men that obviously want something more from you, Hazel. And I'm not talking about friendship," he sneered.

"Michael, I don't think—"

"You don't think what, Hazel? That he doesn't fantasize about what you'd look like spread out on his bed? Or on your knees with his cock shoved down your throat?" I winced as spit flew from his mouth. Each consonant was harsher than the last and drove home his point. "I can tell by the way he looked at you that he wants more than friendship, so don't give me that shit unless you're even more blind than I thought you were. Are you really that ignorant that you can't see what's going on right in front of you?"

Nothing was making sense anymore. Whether Michael was right or wrong, I didn't know. But all I knew was that he was getting even angrier, and I had to do something to change the trajectory of the conversation.

Small beads of sweat had formed above his eyebrows, and his face was growing redder by the second as I sat silent in front of him. He was waiting on me to respond, but I needed to carefully craft my answer. That took time I knew I didn't have. He squeezed his hands together in his lap before shooting out and gripping my upper arm.

"I'm so sorry. I really didn't know anything. I won't see him again," I said in a hurry.

It must have been the correct response because his grip loosened once my words set in. The hand that had been gripping my arm wiped the sweat from his brow and then continued stroking my knee. My stomach rolled at the thought that his sweat-covered hand was touching me. Sweat that was only present because he was drunk and mad and unfathomably out of control.

"Good, baby. Do you understand now?"

I nodded, but thought better of it and said, "Yes."

He scooted closer to the very edge of the coffee table that Luke fixed and took hold of my hips. Thinking of Luke for even a second made my heart hurt. For that one moment I thought maybe I had overreacted earlier and the emotion in his eyes wasn't pity but worry. The thought was fleeting though. Only a few inches from my face, the reek of the alcohol even stronger combined with Michael's body odor as he continued, "Everything I do, I do for us. I work so hard so that we can have the life we want and the life we always talked about. Do you remember when we were about to graduate, and we were sitting in the library studying for finals..."

Before he even started, I knew the moment he was going to implore me to remember. The peak of our happiness was in that moment, right before we realized—or I realized—that we had been jaded by the luxury of our childhoods.

"... and you had the best concentration face. I think you were studying for one of your literature class finals..."

He knew which final it was—women writers—he just didn't think it was an actual class. I recall a moment when he told me if there was a class about women writers, then there should be a mandatory class about men writers. I didn't argue the topic then, but sometimes I wish I had. Maybe I would have learned the truth sooner if I had.

I don't interrupt him now, either.

"... and I thought to myself, 'I'm going to marry this woman.' So, I told you right then, in the middle of the silent library, that I wanted to marry you..."

He proclaimed his intentions so loudly that there were a few gasps and several hushed shushes throughout the floor. We had discussed the topic before but not at length until that day.

"... I couldn't hold back anymore. I knew I wanted to marry you from the moment I saw you at orientation before freshman year. You seemed so different than the girl I'd grown up with. Then you told me, 'I want to marry you, too.' That was one of the best days of my entire life..."

If only I had known then what I did now, sitting on the couch under his dominating, constricting hold.

"... then do you remember what we talked about?"

I nodded as I tried to simultaneously push the memory away. We were so damn happy. I was deliriously happy to know that the boy I had loved so fully, that had turned into a gorgeous, charming man, wanted me.

Not once during this entire story did Michael's eyes move from my own. He knew he had a powerful pull over me. He would look at me with a fondness I didn't usually see and drag us back to those happy times and try to conjure those feelings once again. He would use it to erase all the bad and start fresh with the old feelings leading the way.

Except it was temporary every time. Every single time we would revert to our new normal. A normal that didn't include abundant happiness and jaded hope for the future.

He brushed a few pieces of hair that had fallen into my face behind my ear and cupped my cheek. "We talked about what we wanted from the future and what that would look like. We agreed that we wanted a big house with three kids and a backyard for a dog. We wanted barbecues in the summer and a pool.

We dreamed up our own happily ever after, and I'm trying to make that a reality for us."

I finally pulled my eyes from his, but he used his grip on my face to pull them back once again. Like he always did.

"I don't want anything to stand in our way of having what we want. That's why I do what I do," he finished and searched my eyes for my understanding.

"You forgot one thing," I said before I could even think about the words. They just tumbled out of my mouth like I was going to die unless I said it.

When he didn't respond, only continued searching my eyes and raised his eyebrows like he was curious about what I had to say, I said, "Our vision for our future included happiness, but I don't think you're happy with me anymore."

His eyes dropped to my mouth and his jaw ticced. A new sheen of sweat covered his forehead and just under his nose as his lip quirked up on one side. "What makes you say that, baby?"

The question was a test. It was a test I had grown ever more familiar with, and it was a test I had begun to fail more and more. It was also a side effect of our new normal.

When I didn't respond immediately, the tips of his fingers dug into my cheek and my lip, where he held my face. His opposite hand was still wrapped around my much too boney hip, and its grip also tightened. He hated it when I went quiet, especially when he expected an answer.

A small yelp escaped through my clenched teeth and my eyes widened when I caught the small upturn of his lips. My pain was his pleasure.

"Tell me, baby..." His voice was low. "Why don't you think I'm happy?" As he spoke, he used his thumb to pull down my jaw and aggressively rub my lower lip.

Worried that he'd inflict more pain, I said, "You don't act like you're happy with me."

I failed the test. I failed it miserably, and I knew I had when his smile widened and his hand flexed around my jaw. He inched closer, sweat dripping from his forehead down his cheek and through his short stubble at his chin.

I tried not to react to his proximity and the rage and excitement billowing off him, but I knew he could feel my rapidly building pulse underneath the pressure of his fingers.

"Baby, if I'm not happy, then that's your fault," he said simply.

I didn't believe that. I was the best fiancé I could be. I was understanding, doted on him, and gave it up every time he asked. I couldn't be the problem. I knew I wasn't. Each breath I took before responding resulted in his grasp tightening.

"No." I knew he was wrong and that I couldn't be the reason for his unhappiness. It couldn't be my fault when I tried to be perfect for him, but as his hand pulled back, I knew he didn't agree.

I think I heard the impact of his palm against my cheek before I felt the sting of the slap. My head whipped to the right, but I didn't have time to recover as he wrapped his fingers around my jaw and yanked me closer to him. His hand was a flame against my sensitive skin.

Our faces were only an inch apart, and he was seething between clenched teeth. "If I'm unhappy, then it's your fault, Hazel. And you damn well fucking know it."

He released me with a push but didn't pull back. The cushion behind me had slid down a little and my head hit the hard back of the couch. The sting of my cheek and now the dull ache in the back of my head were painful yet not unusual.

I thought he'd be done, that he made his point that I was the problem, but he didn't leave. I thought he'd get up, look at me with disgust in his eyes and make himself another drink. I'd then apologize profusely and try to mend the broken situation before it broke us. After I'd taken the blame for everything, he'd agree to give me another chance.

But that didn't happen.

"Do you want to make me happy?" he asked but didn't give me time to respond before he stood. He kicked the coffee table away to give more room between it and the couch. He fisted the back of my hair, still loosely held together at the top of my head by a hair band and forced me to my knees in front of him. My knees hit the unforgiving floor with a thud that vibrated through my body. My face, my head, and my knees were all in pain.

I couldn't wrap my head around his intention until I heard the telltale sign of his belt unfastening. My eyes were on the ground, but I immediately jerked my gaze up to him.

The grin was still plastered to his face as he fumbled with his belt. As he yanked it from the belt loops and tossed it behind me, he said, "Oh, baby, you look scared. Don't be scared of me. You want to make me happy? This is how."

I couldn't make my body move. Fear kept me frozen to the spot as his face contorted in pleasure, and each word he spoke pushed me further to an edge I didn't think I'd ever find. The sound of his zipper slowly descending and the understanding of what he was about to do made me move.

His phone buzzed from where it lay on the coffee table. He cursed under his breath at the interruption, but he couldn't let it go unanswered. While he was distracted, I took the opportunity to run.

I scrambled to my feet and ran. I didn't know where I was going or what I was doing, but I let my newfound strength propel my legs forward and away from Michael. Somewhere in the distance—he sounded so far away—I could hear him yelling and fumbling with his pants as he pursued me. His steps were loud on our hardwood floors, but I only focused on where I was going instead of where he was.

I took a sharp right into my office and slammed the door shut just before I felt him run into it. I flipped the lock and backed away from the door as he rammed against it. The solid wood door bowed inward on impact. One sob broke free and instinctively, my hands flew to my mouth to cover the sound of my weakness.

"What the fuck, Hazel? Get the fuck out here NOW!" he bellowed as he continued to beat against the door.

"No!" I found my voice and strength knowing it would take more effort than he could probably put forth to get through the door. For more assurance, I pushed a dresser in front of it.

At the sound of the scraping of a large piece of furniture against the floor, Michael paused his attack.

"I don't know what the fuck has gotten into you, but it's not wise to deny your future husband when he wants a fucking blow job!"

"That isn't going to help anything!" I yelled back.

"Yes, it will. You want to make me happy?" His voice was eerily calm. "This is the beginning of making me happy. It would also make me happy if I had a fiancé that was faithful and didn't go behind my back with our neighbor. Is that why you won't suck my dick? You've been too busy sucking his while I've been gone?"

I shook my head as an aggravated yell bubbled up from my chest. "I have always been faithful to you! Can you say the same thing about me?" My newfound confidence felt good pulsing through my veins, although I was frustrated that it took a locked door and heavy furniture between us to find it. Nevertheless, I wanted it to stay.

Michael continued pounding on the door. I covered my ears, trying to hide from the noise in the far corner of the room, when suddenly, with a frustrated growl, he stopped.

"You know what, fine! You're right, baby. I've been with plenty of other women. But don't think for a fucking second that you aren't mine. You will always be mine, and you eventually have to come out of that fucking room. And when you do come out, I'll be right here."

I slipped down the wall on the far side of the room and let the tears finally fall as he confirmed what, deep in my soul, I already knew was true. He thought I was the root of our issues when he was the one that couldn't keep it in his pants. Each tear was silent yet heavy against my skin.

Not more than a minute later, I heard the door slamming. I crawled to the window and peered over my desk. Michael had his suit jacket in one hand with his phone pressed to his ear. He unlocked his car and got in hastily. In another second, he peeled out of the driveway and sped off.

He was gone. I waited for relief to wash over me, but it didn't. He was right, after all, and he would be back eventually. With the sinking feeling returning, I sank to the floor, curled up and cried myself to sleep on my multicolored rug.

FOURTEEN

Luke

"Are you sure there's nothing else I need to do before I leave? You look stressed and I'm happy to stay and help as long as you need," Crystal said as she waved goodbye to our last client of the day. She was standing too close to me, and I wasn't in the mood to try to fight off her advances.

"No, I'm fine. You can go," I said dismissively. For the millionth time that day, I reached into my pocket and checked my phone. Still nothing from Hazel.

"Okay, if you say so. But let me know if anything changes and—"

"It won't change. Enjoy your evening." I knew my tone was too harsh, but she was barking up the wrong damn tree.

I hadn't been able to keep my mind from Hazel for too long since she disappeared the morning before and popped up on her front porch with her fiancé. A fiancé that looked like he wanted to kill me for nothing more than looking at Hazel.

She might have told me that they only had a fight, but I didn't believe her, especially after she skipped out while I was in the shower. She wouldn't have run if she didn't have something to hide.

I'd texted her a few times and called twice when I got out of the shower and couldn't find her. Like the fucking creep I turned into, when I heard a car door shut outside, I hurried out to the porch and found her cowering in front of fuckface. He looked all high and mighty on his porch, looking over her. I couldn't imagine Hazel had done anything to warrant the kind of look he gave her.

The dumbfuck didn't even flinch when I returned the look he gave her with my own murderous glare.

Replaying the scene in my head and the terrified way she scurried inside their house, I unlocked my phone. My thumb hovered over her name, ready to dial her number, but I waited.

I didn't want to make this worse. I didn't know what happened, but I knew hearing from me—or God forbid, if Michael saw "Neighbor" flash across her phone screen—would do just the opposite of what I was hoping to accomplish.

I quickly gathered my belongings, said "fuck it" to the work I planned to finish, and sped home. Pulling into the driveway, I felt some relief when I saw that Michael's car was still gone. He'd left after I'd gone to work the day before, and I didn't think he'd returned.

Hazel's white jeep sat alone in the driveway and with the knowledge that they didn't ever use their garage that was packed to the brim with old furniture, I didn't give it a second thought before jumping out of the truck and striding over to her front door.

I rang the bell, then felt the need to knock as well against the wood door. I nervously shuffled my weight from one foot to the other and peered through the glass in the door, waiting to see her. I wasn't leaving until I saw that she was okay with my own eyes.

After thirty seconds passed with no answer, I knocked even more urgently a second time. I prepared myself for the possibility that Michael may have answered the door even though his car was gone. It wasn't out of the realm of possibility, so I decided, if he did answer the door, I'd do whatever was necessary to make sure Hazel was safe.

I raised my hand to ring the doorbell again when Hazel stepped into view. At the end of the entryway, she stood frozen, staring at me with a deer in headlights look. My eyes roamed over her face, down her exposed arms, and although I couldn't see much from a distance, it didn't look like she had suffered any new injuries. When she didn't move, I waved and smiled.

She shook her head. Confused by her response, I nodded. This happened twice more before she rolled her eyes, folded her arms over her stomach and opened the door.

"What are you doing here?" she whispered.

Finally able to inspect her closely, I noticed her red-rimmed-and-swollen eyes, but that appeared to be the only issue. She was still beautiful, but I couldn't get past the obvious outward signs of her sadness.

"Luke," she said my name harshly. "You need to go."

"I just wanted to check on you. You haven't responded to me, and I've been worried since you disappeared yesterday morning."

"Okay, well, here I am. I'm fine. You can go now." She tried to shut the door, but I stuck my hand out and stopped it.

"You don't look fine."

She scoffed, "Thanks for that, but I am fine. Now, leave." Her words were harsh, but I saw her chin quiver slightly as she backed away.

"I don't think you're actually fine. Hazel, please tell me. Did he hurt you?"

Her eyes went wide once again when I bluntly asked the question that had been stewing for the past few weeks. She softly, ever so slightly, shook her head, but it wasn't believable.

"Don't lie to me, Hazel. I can't help you if you lie to me."

She peered over my shoulder and glanced around for a

moment. I thought she was going to say something before she reached in her pocket and pulled out her phone. She groaned and the quivering of her chin became more prominent.

"You have to leave. Please, Luke." She was at the point of begging, which was alarming since I'd never heard Hazel do anything close to begging.

"Angel…" The pet name I had started calling her slipped and she shook her head violently.

"Do you want to help?"

"Yes."

"Then I need you to leave."

"No. That's not going to help you. I—"

She opened the door wider and stepped toward me. One of her shaking hands landed on my chest. It was the first time she'd voluntarily touched me, and her hand felt so tiny against me. She had to have felt my heart attempting to beat out of my chest as she crowded me.

Reflexively, my hand found her hip, urging her not to move away too soon.

"Do you…" She trailed off for a moment, lost in thought. "Do you want to help? Do you… really care?"

I swallowed around the lump in my throat. "Yes," I whispered.

I watched her mouth as she bit her bottom lip, hard. "Then please, if you care about me, leave."

In her eyes, I saw her determination. She wasn't going to back down, and I didn't want to either. We could stand in a stalemate all day for all I cared.

Apparently, she also saw the determination on my face. She glanced down at her phone one more time and cursed under her breath.

"*Shit.*" When she looked back up at me, her eyes were brimming with tears. One fell and I quickly swiped it away. I let my hand linger on her cheek, her skin was so soft beneath my calloused and worn palm, and she leaned into my touch for a second before she caught herself.

"I will text you later, I promise. But for now, you have to go." She used her hand on my chest to push me back. I was too caught up in the way she surrendered to my touch that I didn't react quick enough to catch her before she was back inside and had locked the door.

Defeated and with no other plan up my sleeve, I lumbered back home. Sadie was in the front yard, and I sighed. I patted my thigh and whistled so she'd follow me into the house. Once I stepped inside, I texted Hazel.

If you need me, I'm here.

FIFTEEN

Luke

Her toned, bare legs make my mouth water as I run my hands down her thighs and lift her into my arms. She giggles, and the sound is contagious. Her hair tickles the top of my arms as it falls down her back. I bury my face in her neck and begin kissing and licking up to her ear. Her skin is smooth beneath my lips, and she tastes so sweet.

"Mmm… Luke," she mewls as she grasps the back of my head, pulling me to her mouth. Her tongue peeks out between her lips and she hungrily licks my bottom lip.

"Fuck you, you little cunt!" I jerk my head away and try to look in the direction of the yelling, but my little Angel in my arms won't be deterred. I close my eyes and cherish the way her warm mouth feels on mine. I release one of my arms from around her, easily holding her with only one, and grip her face.

"Ouch," she whines, and I peel my eyes open to see what I could have done. Her eyes that were perfectly clear a moment ago are now rimmed with darkness and ripe, red blood is trickling from between her lips. The taste of her blood is metallic on my tongue as more blood runs down her chin and her chest. In a panic, I try to move and find her help, *but I can't. My feet won't move no matter how hard I try. She moans in pain and coughs, spitting more blood all over my face...*

I jolted out of bed and quickly realized that it was just a dream. A very graphic and real dream, but just a dream, nonetheless. I took a moment to calm my breathing and steady my pounding heart. Once my heart rate was relatively normal and I could fully fill my lungs with air, I patted Sadie's head as she continued to sleep undisturbed next to me.

"You're such a fucking bitch!" I jerked my head to where I believed the sound was coming from. Sadie popped up next to me and let out a low warning growl.

I swung my legs over the side of the bed and looked out the window into Hazel's room. I left the curtains open—deciding her safety was more important than my semi-creepy behavior—so I could see if anything happened in the middle of the night.

All the lights were on in her house, but there was no one in her room. I grabbed my phone from the bedside table. At almost three in the morning, there was no good reason why all of the lights may be on.

I took one final look through the window, and when I didn't hear anything or see fuckface or Hazel, I made for the door.

With Sadie on my heels, I quickly jerked open Josh's door in search of backup but found his bed empty. Dude was probably passed out at the bar again after another late-night shift.

Luckily, I fell asleep with my clothes on, so I wasn't slowed down by having to change. I pulled up Hazel's number and wedged my phone between my shoulder and ear as I slipped my shoes on at the front door. When her phone went straight to voice mail, my heart plummeted.

I whipped the front door open as Michael's car peeled out of the driveway and sped off down the street. He flew through the stop sign and made a quick right turn out of the neighborhood.

Sadie sprinted out the door just as I stepped outside. She barked as she ran to Hazel's house, up the porch and inside. Realizing the front door was still open, I took off after Sadie.

I took her porch stairs two at a time but stopped at the open door. The heat emanating from inside the house was welcome against my cold face and hands. I went to close the door but paused with my hand midair. There was blood smeared on the door handle, and I prayed it was his blood, not hers. If it wasn't his blood, I knew I'd make him bleed.

"Hazel?" I called out, pushing the door closed and locking it behind me, careful not to disturb the blood. The house was eerily quiet, and I fumed. I knew I shouldn't have left her alone. I might have made the situation worse, but he wouldn't have had the fucking chance to touch her with me around.

When there was no response, I peeked in the dining room and continued down the entryway. The living room was empty, although the coffee table was out of place and the cushions on the couch were tossed on the floor. The decorations on the side table that Hazel took so much effort to place only a few days before were scattered over the floor. A frame holding a picture of her family was cracked. Pieces of glass crunched under my shoes.

The kitchen also looked somewhat normal. A half-eaten pizza was still in the box on the kitchen island. Next to the trash can on the opposite side of the island sat an empty bottle of wine along with two empty liquor bottles.

"Hazel?" I called again and paused to listen for any sound. Still nothing.

I tried not to disturb anything but tripped over more pillows on the ground near the hallway. Near the side of the house, I heard Sadie's faint whining. Sadie was not one to whine about anything, and pure panic set in. I tore down the hallway flinging one door open after the next. One was an office, the next the bathroom, a guest bedroom and all were completely empty. Finally, I made it to the main bedroom.

The door was slightly ajar, unlike the rest of the rooms. All of the lights—each one on the nightstands, the one on her dresser and the overhead light—were on. The curtains were open, and I could see directly into my bedroom through the slats of the blinds.

The bed was unmade, and it was there that I found the only other blood in the house. I fisted the white comforter as I inspected the lines and drops of blood over the corner that seemed to be closest to Hazel's side of the bed. On her clean nightstand sat an empty, stained wineglass, her engagement ring, and a hundred-dollar bill. I looked at the picture there and my stomach rolled. Michael had his arm wrapped around Hazel as he smiled at her, and she smiled at the camera.

I wanted to wipe that fucking smile off his face, and I imagined the ways I could do that as the panic turned to rage and continued to course through my body. The situation warranted anger and I wanted to rip off the tight lid I had on the emotion, but first, I had to find Hazel.

Sadie let out another low whine from just outside of their bathroom door. She pawed at the closed door and stuck her nose into the small crack at the bottom. I could hear the exhaust fan whirring behind the door and light seeped around the doorframe.

"Hazel?" I said at the same time I rapped my knuckles softly on the door. The house was silent, and I didn't hear anything behind the door. Unless she hadn't been in the house this entire time or was outside, she had to be in the bathroom.

I took one breath, trying to steady my shaking hand and my hammering heart before I opened the door. I was terrified of what state I'd find her in.

I tried to turn the knob, but it was locked. I tried once more, but the knob stuck.

No. No, this couldn't be happening again.

"Hazel, can you hear me? Can you open the door?"

Nothing.

"Angel, I know you're in there. Michael's gone; can you please open the door?"

Nothing but the sound of the whirring fan came from inside

the bathroom. I pulled out my phone and dialed her number. The vibrating came from the bed, and I found her phone abandoned underneath the bloody comforter.

Fuck. I was going to have to kick the door down because picking the lock was going to take too damn long. I wasn't going to wait any longer.

I prayed that she wasn't near the door. It had been years, approximately fifteen years since I'd kicked down a door. The similarities of the two situations were too much for my mind to handle. If I let myself go there, I wasn't going to make it through getting her help.

I shook off the memories and cleared the chaos they created in my head. I took one step back, lined up, and remembered where I needed to hit. I stepped and kicked my leg out just as the door swung open.

SIXTEEN

Luke

On the other side, Hazel stood on shaking legs, blood covering her face and her hands. Behind the blood staining her skin, I could tell she was weak and pale. The blue beneath her eyes was almost black. Her eyes were heavy, but they were opened wide as she swayed.

"He's gone?" she asked softly. Pain: that's what was in her eyes and appeared in the unshed tears.

"Angel," I gasped as I walked to her and said, "Yes, he's gone." Her relief was immediate as her legs gave out and a strangled sob escaped her lips. I caught her before she hit the ground, hoping she didn't have any major injuries as I scooped her up into my arms. In a fireman's carry, I whistled for Sadie to follow, walked out of her fucking hell of a house, across the yard and into my own.

She wasn't wearing very many clothes, but she didn't even shiver against the cold early morning air. She was tiny and limp in my arms. I jostled her to make sure she stayed awake when I got to my front door. In the kitchen, I pushed away the dirty dishes, and as they fell into the sink, I set Hazel on the counter.

"Hazel, can you tell me what hurts?"

She moaned when I ran my thumbs over her cheeks, careful not to pull at her skin. Her eyes were only half open, but she was conscious. "Can you sit up on your own?"

She gave a weak nod that I took as a maybe. With one hand, I held her to keep her upright and with the other, I grabbed the closest clean dish towel, ran it under lukewarm water and began to clean the blood from her neck and lower half of her face. Quickly I realized most of the blood had come from her nose, but the active bleeding had stopped.

She winced when I cleaned around her nose, but I kept my touch light around the sensitive area. The blood stained her porcelain skin, but she looked less like Carrie after I was done. The entire time she sat still and only sucked in a breath when I got too close to her nose.

As I cleaned her, I whispered assurances.

"You're safe."

"He's gone."

"I've got you."

"No one will ever hurt you again."

I tossed the dish towel, now covered in blood and likely stained beyond repair, in the sink. I ran my hands down her arms and when I gripped her hands in mine, I realized they also needed to be washed. The fingers were painted in her blood. More memories surged forward of my younger, less worn hands covered in blood. I grabbed the towel and turned on the water to wet it again.

"I can do it," she said. I didn't argue when she slowly squirted the soap in her hands and meticulously scrubbed every inch of her hands—under her nails, her palms, between her fingers, her cuticles—and her wrists. She rinsed the pink soap and let her wet hands fall back into her lap. She was wearing only a big T-shirt with small boy shorts underneath. In my rush to get her out of the house, I hadn't noticed how little she was wearing.

I pulled another dish towel from the drawer to our right and dried her hands.

"I'm okay." Her words were strained, but she looked me in the eye when she said them. The terror I saw earlier had subsided, and her shoulders seemed to relax. I didn't let go of her hands after I chucked the towel in the sink as well.

"Thank you."

"You don't need to thank me, Angel." I wanted to know so badly what happened, but I knew I shouldn't press her for details. "I don't think your nose is broken, thankfully. What else hurts?"

I didn't want to fucking ask because I was worried if she was hurt anywhere else, I might go on a rampage. The broken woman in front of me, beaten, bloodied, and bruised, didn't deserve such violence. Her hands were still shaking, but each moment I held them, it felt like the intensity of the shaking lessened. I needed to keep her calm and show her I wasn't him.

She finally shook her head, but it was slow.

"Angel, if you don't tell me, then I can't help."

"I'm not hurt anywhere else..." She sat for a moment and, after a breath, finally said, "Physically."

The statement stopped me like I'd run into a fucking brick wall. Red blurred along the outside of my vision, and my head pounded as my imagination ran wild. *What the fuck had he done?*

"I'll kill him," I said in a voice so low that it was almost a growl.

I expected Hazel to say something along the lines of "no, you can't," but she didn't. Her hands were still shaking, and her eyes were miles away, but she stayed silent as I fumed.

Once I had calmed myself down enough, I peered up at her beaten face, stained with her blood. "What happened?"

I was amazed by the way she had kept from crying through the entire cleanup, even with my not-so-gentle hands around her face, but once I asked about it, a tear slipped free. Then another and another until she was silently crying like she didn't even realize the tears had fallen.

I reached up to brush away a tear, but she flinched away from my hand. It broke my already decimated heart.

"*Fuck, Angel,*" I whispered as I pulled back. "I'm so sorry. I swear I will never, *never* hurt you," I stated firmly but hopefully convincingly. Slowly, I reached up once again and kept my touch light as she let me brush away her tears. I couldn't resist and placed a kiss on the center of her forehead.

She sighed, and I felt maybe I had gained a little more of her trust. The fucker had done a number on her, but I'd do my best to mend what he'd broken.

"That's what Michael said, too." The words were so soft I almost missed them. Gone was the confident, sassy voice I'd grown used to and expected from her.

"What?"

She cleared her throat and pulled her hands from mine to wipe her face. I was itching to get the rest of the blood off her and remove any sign of this fucking night, but I needed to make sure she was really okay first.

"Michael said he wouldn't hurt me either," she clarified and gave an unamused laugh.

"I would rather die than ever hurt you." I carefully placed my hands on either side of her face and urged her to look me in the eye, hoping to convey how fucking serious I was. She fought for a moment, looking everywhere besides at me, but finally gave in. I watched as her eyes flickered with understanding as she took in a sharp breath.

Even smeared in blood and beginning to bruise, she was breathtaking. Going about half of the speed I would normally move, I let one hand fall from her face and wrap around her waist while I gripped the back of her neck with the other. Carefully, I urged her closer to the edge of the counter. She scooted forward and hesitated for only a moment before wrapping her arms around me.

I breathed a sigh of relief in feeling her safe in my arms. I kissed the top of her head and reveled in the smell of her clean hair.

I held her against me until her breathing evened out, her shaking subsided, and I felt the tears stop.

"Do you know where he went?" I asked into the top of her head.

She shook her head, not letting go of me.

"Can you tell me what happened?" She tensed against me, and I smoothed my hands down her back, rubbing back and forth to ease the new tension. "I just want to help."

"Shit, I got blood on your shirt," she said as she tried to pull away.

"Don't you dare move. I'm not worried about the stupid shirt."

She nodded and settled back against my chest. "He got home a few hours ago. He'd left yesterday, or whatever day that was and didn't come back until now. It was right after I got home from staying the night here..." She paused and took a breath as I closed my eyes and braced for a story I didn't know if I was ready to hear.

"He was so drunk. I think he went to work and then out, and he was so drunk and so mad. I really thought he would have calmed down, but it was like he couldn't contain his anger and he just decided to—" She was speaking faster and faster until she stopped completely. She sniffled and groaned in pain from her busted nose. "I locked myself in the bathroom when I was able to get away and when I realized it wasn't going to stop. He left after that, and you found me only a few minutes later."

"I'm so sorry, Angel," I whispered into her hair. I was torn between wanting to comfort the woman in my arms and hunting down the son of a bitch to make good on my threat from earlier. I wanted to kill him. Actually, I wanted to torture him and let him feel the pain he had inflicted on her a hundred times over before I ended him.

"We should call the cops."

I didn't think my statement was unwarranted, but the way Hazel looked at me—her face contorted in panic and terror—I began questioning what the right way was to handle the situation.

"We can't," she said just above a whisper. "I—I can't, Luke, please don't." A few tears rolled down her cheeks, and I couldn't stand to see her absolutely terrified.

"Okay, we can talk about it later," I conceded.

She nodded and, after a moment, asked, "Is there still blood on my face?" She pulled back and looked up at me, large hazel eyes shiny with tears.

I smoothed down the sides of her hair and nodded. "Yeah, you're going to have to wash it off. Is your nose okay?"

Her fingers ran over the bridge of her nose and along the outside. It was swollen, and I couldn't tell if the blue under her eyes was from exhaustion or if they were already bruising. "Yeah. I don't know if it's broken."

"I don't believe it is. I think it's just bruised."

"How do you know?" she asked.

"I used to fight a lot. You figure out when something's actually broken and needs attention or when you can hold off." I shrugged.

The fact that he hit her at all, or even raised his voice to her, had my blood boiling, but knowing he hit her hard enough to cause bleeding and a bruised nose had me teetering on the edge of insanity.

"Why don't you stay here tonight?"

"Luke, you've already done enough. I don't think Michael will be back tonight, and—"

"I'm not letting you out of my sight. If you want to stay at your house, I'm staying with you."

She huffed but didn't try to argue further. "It would make me feel a lot better if I knew you were safe," I said, giving her a reason to not feel so bad about taking me up on my offer.

"Okay." She placed both of her hands on my chest and gave me a soft smile before she scooted off the counter. She grimaced when her feet hit the cold tile but recovered quickly as her big shirt fell over her underwear. She tugged it down a little farther. "I probably need a change of clothes. And I should lock up the house…"

She peered over her shoulder and turned to the front door. She looked like she was going to take a step in that direction but hesitated as she bit her bottom lip. She scrubbed a hand through her hair and groaned in frustration.

"Could you come with me?" she asked, looking back at me with wide eyes. It was evident she was scared to go back by herself, and I couldn't blame her, nor could I tell her no.

"Of course. I'm not letting you out of my sight, remember?" The relief on her face knowing I was going to be close, combined with the hint of a smile pulling at the corners of her mouth, brought forth feelings I had forgotten I was capable of.

"Do you want a jacket or some, um… pants before we walk over there?" I asked once we got to the front door, and I found myself staring at her bare legs.

"I can make it next door. Let's just hope that no one is out at almost four in the morning to see me run from your house back to mine half naked. Don't need the neighborhood rumor mill getting a hold of that gold." She rolled her eyes and tried to laugh as she opened the door. It only sounded sad.

That time she shivered when the cold breeze whipped around us, which I took as a sign that her earlier shock was subsiding. I couldn't let her fight against the cold by herself—even if it was for a short walk—so I wrapped an arm around her, pulling her into my side. She tensed when my hand landed on her shoulder but quickly relaxed into me.

We hurried to her house and once I shut and locked the front door, I could see and feel her anxiety begin to creep back in. She moved farther into the house, down the entryway, cautiously peeking around corners like she was waiting for him to jump out. She had one hand absentmindedly wrapped around her throat while the other hugged her stomach.

After such a long time, I'd mastered keeping a lid on my anger and violent thoughts, but knowing Hazel was terrified of her own home made it impossible not to want to right this wrong for her. My heart roared with a fierce protectiveness.

"Maybe I should clean up a little. Shit, did that frame break?" She stepped toward the frame, broken and discarded next to the table.

"Wait, don't worry about it. You don't have any shoes on." She looked down at her feet in surprise, like she forgot they were bare. "Just go grab your stuff, and I'll take care of this."

For a long second, she stared at the broken frame and the photo in it: her family—including Michael—smiling at the camera. It looked like they were all crowded together, just barely in the frame to take the photo.

"Hazel?"

She glanced up at me and nodded. "Yes, thanks."

I cleaned the broken glass and reassembled the cushions on the couch. The coffee table was broken yet again, and I made a mental note to come over another time and make sure it was fixed.

After I stuffed the leftover pizza into the fridge and double-checked that I hadn't missed any glass, I went to find Hazel. She hadn't reappeared from her bedroom, and I began to worry.

"Hazel? You ready?" I asked as I knocked on the bedroom door. It was slightly ajar and when I knocked, it opened wider. The comforter had been stripped from the bed and lay in a pile next to the door. On top of it were what looked like bathroom rugs and towels also stained with blood.

I opened the door farther and spotted Hazel on her hands and knees in the middle of her bathroom. The entire bathroom was pristinely white aside from the streaks of red on the floor and the counter. The odor of bleach was noxious in the small space. I flipped on the exhaust fan as I walked into the bathroom.

"There was blood everywhere. I couldn't just leave it like this," Hazel said. She didn't look up from where she was intently and viciously scrubbing the grout between the tiles.

It seemed like something she needed to do—clean the tiles, clean the sink and wash away the evidence. I would have preferred she leave it for the cops to see, but she was already more than halfway done by the time I found her.

When she finally stood, the tiles were whiter than I could have imagined. She tossed the sponge into the sink and used a towel to wipe up the excess bleach. She was still wearing her large T-shirt, and she hadn't yet washed her bloodstained face.

"Umm... okay. Let me just grab a few things," she said, mostly to herself as she grabbed a bag and chucked in pants, a shirt, and toiletries. She nervously flitted around her closet and the bathroom.

"Could I—" She started as I took a step out of the bathroom to give her privacy. She cleared her throat and started again, swiping a hand through her hair. "Could I shower at your house? I don't want to be here longer than necessary."

"Yeah, of course. Just grab what you need, and we can head back now."

Hazel nodded, her eyes still far away, as she pulled on a pair of joggers and zipped her bag. I grabbed her small duffel before she had a chance to and tossed it over my shoulder. When she smiled up at me, peering through tear-soaked lashes and still lost in her own head, I wanted nothing more than to console her, comfort her and do whatever I needed to do to make her realize not all men were like him.

She stepped next to me and was about to walk out of the bedroom when I reached for her hand and intertwined our fingers. My hand swallowed hers, but she didn't pull back.

· · ·

Thankfully, I had taken the time to bitch at Josh about leaving the huge mess in the guest bedroom, so it was clean when I set Hazel up in there. She finally showered and washed her face, clearing off the final remnants of blood. The dark circles under her eyes were morphing into black eyes, but she hadn't begun shaking again and seemed more in touch with reality.

I was in the kitchen, grabbing a beer and contemplating what Hazel may want, if anything, when the water turned off in the shower and I heard her walk into the guest bedroom. She was in the bathroom for almost half an hour. When I walked past to throw extra blankets on the bed, I thought I heard her crying.

Sadie was snoring at my feet in one of her favorite spots on the kitchen rug when she also heard Hazel shuffling down the hallway. She perked up, tilted her head to one side, then the other, ears flopping before she bounced up and followed the sound.

"Sadie, hey, leave her alone," I said as I approached the door hot on her tail. Sadie jumped up and used her paws to push down on the door handle to open it with an expertise she had honed in the few years we had lived in the house. I reminded myself for the millionth time that I needed to replace the damn door handles.

"Sadie, come," I said in a stern voice and turned the corner into the room before I knew what I was doing. My only intent was to give Hazel some privacy, but I ended up walking in on her changing.

She was wearing black athletic shorts that hugged her thighs and using the towel to dry her wet hair.

"Sadie—" I began again, but I couldn't finish the command. Hazel hadn't yet put on a shirt and quickly covered her chest with the towel when she realized I had also stepped into the room.

Sadie hopped on the bed, sniffing inside of Hazel's small duffel bag, as I whipped my head, looking back down the hall. As quick as I was, I still got an eyeful of Hazel's bare back. Her skin was pale and appeared smooth, almost without imperfection but for the angry blue bruise plastered to her side. From my short glance, it appeared the bruise began just under her right breast and wrapped around her side, ending just underneath her shoulder blade.

The bruises I noticed on her neck were too faint for me to see anymore, especially from where I stood several feet away, but the bruise on her side was fresh, new.

I was serious when I told Hazel that I wanted to kill him.

I turned back into the room once I heard Hazel saying something to Sadie. "So, your dog knows how to open doors?" she asked, smiling at Sadie before glancing at me.

Relief flooded over me when she smiled. "Yes," I said with a laugh. "I usually tell people to lock the door, but I totally forgot this time. My bad…"

"That's okay. At least I like you, right, Sadie?" she cooed at Sadie as she flopped over on the bed, begging for Hazel to rub her stomach. Hazel giggled when Sadie pawed at her and obliged the very needy dog.

"I was maybe going to throw on a movie if you want to watch it with me. I'm not sure I'm going to be able to sleep anyway," I offered.

Hazel's smile immediately dropped. "I'm so sorry, Luke, for putting you out like this…"

"No, no. You have nothing to apologize for." I crossed the room and stopped just in front of where she sat on the edge of the bed.

She seemed to believe me that time, so she nodded and continued stroking Sadie, who had begun to fall asleep on the bed. "I think I'm going to try to get some rest. I'm not sure I'll be able to, but…"

"Sounds good. I work in the morning, but you're more than welcome to stay here as long as you need. You're not putting me out, and I'll let Josh know you're here so he doesn't freak out when he does eventually come home."

I wanted to cross the foot or two of space between us, wrap my arms around her and hold her until all the pain disappeared. It was especially taunting since she smelled like my body wash that I had also thrown in the guest bathroom. But I refrained, knowing any comfort I could give her would likely only be welcome in the form of staying the fuck away.

"Good night," I murmured as I let Sadie lead us out and closed the door.

"Wait." Hazel hurried to the door just before I closed it completely and pulled it open once again. "Seriously, thank you." She was so close I could smell her mint toothpaste and almost feel how clean her skin was.

"Anytime, Angel," I said.

Much to my surprise, Hazel pressed up on her toes as high as she could go and brushed her lips against my cheek, just above my beard. She lingered there for a moment, and I clenched my fists at my sides in an attempt not to ambush her with affection.

"Good night," she whispered against my skin, and I stepped back so she could close the door.

SEVENTEEN

Hazel

I slept no more than an hour that night with Sadie curled in the crook of my legs. Every time I closed my eyes, I saw Michael, eyes filled with rage, hurling a fist toward my face. I even heard the crack and felt the spray of blood. No matter how hard I tried, I couldn't close my eyes and push through the terrible memories. Sleep finally washed over me in the early hours of the morning, and when I awoke no more than an hour later, I was covered in a thin layer of sweat with my heart racing.

The sheets were drenched around me, and the lingering scent of Luke's body wash was gone and replaced by my own body odor.

For a moment, I felt the panic start to set in once again. It started low in my stomach as a clenching, tightening, then clawed its way up until I could feel the sobs sitting at the base of my throat. I knew if I let it, the panic would overwhelm all my senses, and I'd be lost.

So instead of letting it in, letting it win, I swung my feet over the edge of the bed, grabbed a change of clothes, and headed to the bathroom.

The hot water running over me felt like it was doing more than washing my skin; it was ridding my body of the memories of my nightmares and the sweaty remnants of them as well. I lathered the Luke-scented soap in my hands and let it wash it all away.

I couldn't pinpoint when it happened, but at some point in the past few weeks, Luke's presence morphed from annoying the ever-loving shit out of me to something else entirely. He made me feel safe and calm, but along with his words and actions, I'd come to find the way he smelled—all manly and a little rough—calming, too. It was a little bit of everything.

After I stood in the shower for longer than I should have, smelling the body wash, I realized I had fallen off the crazy train and hurried to rinse off and finish up before all the hot water was gone.

When I stepped out of the bathroom, my mouth immediately began watering at the smell of fresh coffee. With only a few hours of sleep, coffee was the only thing on my mind as I tossed my old, sweaty clothes onto my duffel bag and urged Sadie—who was still curled up at the foot of the bed—to get moving.

She hurried down the hallway in front of me. And I forgot in my haste that Josh also lived there. I stopped at the end of the hallway when I saw him on the couch. Luke was nowhere in sight, but my hand reflexively reached for one of my eyes as I remembered the bruising beneath them. I glanced quickly in the mirror earlier in the bathroom, and upon finding the beginning of two bruises beneath my eyes, I recoiled from the sight. Seeing the bruises—the physical manifestation of Michael's abuse—made it too real.

Before I had time to slither back down the hallway, Josh turned from the TV to me.

"Good morn—" he began but stopped as he took in the state of my face. He jumped from the couch and hurried to me with arms outstretched. "What the hell happened? Whose ass am I beating? Luke!"

His eyes combed over my face as he put his hands on each of my shoulders. I tried not to flinch when he touched me. At least he didn't grab me like it appeared he might, and his eyes were kind and brimming with concern.

"Josh, give her some room." Luke's voice came from behind me, and I turned just enough to see him walking down the hallway from his bedroom. His hair was still wet from what I assumed was his morning shower, and he was wearing his dark-blue scrubs that hugged his arms, chest, thighs, and other areas…

"Dude, you told me she was here, but look at her," Josh said over my head. "Seriously," he continued, now speaking to me, "tell me whose ass I need to kick, and no questions asked, we will do it."

As he spoke, his grip became tighter, and I could feel each of his fingers individually as they began digging into my arms through my long-sleeve T-shirt. Luke stopped to my right; the opening of the hallway was just barely large enough to fit us both.

I could feel his eyes on me, also appraising the damage in the new light of the morning. I wanted to look up at him and meet his soft-green eyes, but I was too focused on not screaming at Josh to please stop touching me.

"Josh, take a breather." Luke's voice held an authority that conveyed to Josh it was absolutely not a request but an order.

After glancing between Luke and me, Josh dropped his hands, fingers brushing down my arms as he apologized. He continued talking and asking questions about what happened, but I didn't pay him any attention. Especially not when Luke's fingers gently ran down the length of my spine and goose bumps erupted over my skin. Silently I breathed in a sharp breath that would have been imperceptible if Luke hadn't been watching me, gauging my reaction so intently. When my chest expanded slightly, he flattened his hand on my lower back in a purposefully steadying way.

Standing so close, I realized his body wash smelled so much better on him.

"I would ask you how you slept, but I'm assuming you didn't," he said only loud enough for me to hear. I shook my head.

"Coffee then?"

I nodded enthusiastically, and he chuckled. I couldn't help but try to return his smile when the sound of his laugh seemed to lighten the sinking feeling I couldn't otherwise shake.

He sauntered past the living room and into the kitchen. I immediately missed the warmth of his hand, and I tried not to stare at his perfectly rounded ass that was also put on further display from the tight scrubs.

"I'll bring it to you," Luke said as he motioned to the couch where Josh was trying to watch us out of the corner of his eyes. His gaze followed me as I rounded the couch and sat next to Sadie, folding my legs underneath me.

"Do you want to talk about it?" Josh asked.

"Not exactly."

He released a breath. "Well, are you okay at least?"

I thought for a moment, unsure what the answer was. The physical bruises on my skin, the ones everyone could see, didn't hurt as bad nor penetrate as deep as the internal ones that no one knew were there.

"I'm working on it," I said just as Luke lowered a cup of coffee in front of my face. I cupped the warm mug with both hands and took a generous sip.

"Thanks," I said before taking another sip.

"Did Sadie sleep with you last night?" Luke asked as he leaned against the wall next to the TV.

"Yeah, she didn't leave my side all night." I laughed and patted her head. She was already fast asleep next to me. Apparently, the walk from the bedroom to the living room tired her out.

"Hmm..." was Luke's only response. I watched as he cut his eyes quickly at Josh and then back to me, sipping his coffee intently. Watching him carefully, through narrowed eyes, I could have sworn I saw a glint of something in his eyes. His facial expressions were usually composed—as opposed to my own, wherein anyone could read my thoughts by looking at my face—but his eyes were the gateway into his head.

"What?" I needed to know if he'd explain the glint I saw.

"Sadie has never not slept with me, no matter who stays over. She won't even sleep with Josh and trust me, he's tried."

The fact that Sadie liked me warmed my heart. Having her warmth curled against me all night long was like a weighted blanket for my anxiety.

"Stole your dog's attention while you cleaned me up and gave me a place to crash when my life is falling apart—didn't think being nice to me was going to get you all this, am I right?" I laughed, but it sounded hollow and forced. Thankfully, Luke gave me a pity laugh while Josh grunted on the other end of the sectional.

"Mmm. Do you know where my phone is?" I asked, quickly changing the subject. By the time I got into bed last night, curled into the soft sheets and hoping that sleep would come easily, the last thing I wanted to do was search Luke's house for it.

"Yeah. You left it in the kitchen last night. It's sitting on the counter by the coffee maker," he said as I stood, taking my coffee with me.

I topped off my cup, which I had already slurped down, probably too quickly to be deemed normal and took a deep breath before I unlocked my phone. I hadn't known what to expect from Michael—there were times when he was apologetic and remorseful and other times, he was angry and rested the blame solely on my shoulders. At that moment, I didn't know what I wanted to see. I couldn't let my wishful thinking get the better of me, but I hoped he wouldn't have sent anything at all.

When he apologized, he did it so well, making me feel like he really meant it with tears in his eyes, hands shaking. And when he was angry, there was usually an eerie calmness about him that was followed by accusations and yelling. So much yelling.

Neither was easy to handle and there usually wasn't much between them. I couldn't handle either in my already fragile state.

There was a text from him, though.

I'm coming by the house to pack for a trip. I don't want to see you when I get there. I'll be there in an hour.

My reaction surprised me as relief had my shoulders falling and my fists unclenching. I tipped my head to the side and rolled it along my shoulders from one side to the other.

He was leaving. Which meant I didn't have to go anywhere right then.

"You okay?" Once again, Luke appeared behind me. For such a large man, he had an uncanny ability to sneak up on me, especially since I'd become very adept at not allowing men an opening to approach me when I was unaware.

He didn't touch me, but he was standing so close behind me that I could feel a whisper of his earlier touch. If I didn't know any better, I might have begun hoping he would touch me again.

"Umm, yeah. Michael's leaving town, so he let me know he'll be getting stuff from the house. Make sure I'm not there…" The text said it was sent thirty minutes ago, so in another thirty minutes we'd only be a house apart. Air burned when it entered my lungs, and my breath shook a little at the tightening in my chest.

"We should call the police, Hazel. This isn't okay. What he did…" he ground out the words in a low voice. "What he did is absolutely not okay."

My head began shaking before I realized I was doing it.

"I can't." Yet again, my voice sounded small and unlike the person I once was.

"Hazel, we can't—"

"I'm serious. I can't do this." I whipped around and peered up at Luke so he could see the seriousness on my face while hearing the conviction in my voice.

I knew I should call the police and report him, but every time I thought about turning him in, the only thing that ran through my mind were memories of each good time we spent together. Because there were good times. And I imagined what it would do to his family and how much it would crush his parents, who were my parents' best friends. Our lives were inexplicably intertwined and after spending so many years with him and growing up beside him, I couldn't fathom ruining his life.

The frustration was evident in Luke's eyes. His lips were a sharp, set line, and I could tell he was holding back as he clenched his jaw.

"I understand, but I just can't do it right now. Okay?"

He nodded and crossed his arms over his chest right in front of my face. I had the urge to run my fingers over the intricate black tattoos and trace each individual line and follow the shading over his skin.

"Maybe I should go speak to him then," he seethed.

His words were like a bucket of cold water unexpectedly being poured over my head. "Absolutely not."

It wasn't an option. I flashed back to Luke threatening to kill Michael the night before—there was a gravity to his voice that made each word sound like a promise, not a veiled threat of violence. I knew what would happen if they met once again.

"I will not let him hurt you again, Hazel. And if that means that I step in, then I will without hesitation." He took a half step closer to me, watching my face intently. I had to tilt my head up even higher to maintain eye contact.

Another promise.

"I didn't mean to put you in the middle of this."

He shook his head and said, his tone suddenly softer. "You didn't put me in the middle of anything, Angel." I couldn't breathe when the term of endearment slipped between his plump lips. He uncrossed his arms and slipped one of his hands into mine. His brow furrowed and his voice was tight as he said, "I have to go to work, but I need you to do one thing for me."

I watched him, wanting to swipe a finger between his eyebrows and erase the concern, the tension.

"Stay here. Don't go over there no matter what." I heard and felt the protectiveness in his voice and through the way he squeezed my hand. I tried to hide the emotion I felt at hearing the unrestrained urgency in his voice. I knew it wasn't an act, and for his own reasons—whether it be because I had endured what I had or for his own personal qualms—he wanted me to be safe.

"Okay," I said. I didn't think it was necessary to tell him that I hadn't planned on going home until I knew Michael would be gone for a good long while.

Some of the concern on his face was scrubbed away by my compliance. "Okay," he said as well before running his thumb in a circle on the back of my hand, giving me a tight smile and letting Josh know that he'd be home later.

Thirty minutes later, Luke had left for work and Josh was dozing on the couch while I was pacing the length of the kitchen. The tile was cool on my bare feet, and the house was a comfortable temperature, however, the sweat I had washed off from my nightmares that morning had returned. It dripped down my back and pooled underneath my breasts.

Sadie strode by my side, her nails tapping the tiles back and forth for a while until she got tired and curled up next to Josh.

Ten a.m., Michael was supposed to be at our house then, and with each minute that ticked by, the deeper I had to dig to keep the panic at bay. My eyes darted to the clock on the oven across the room as I heard an engine rev outside.

Right on time. He was always so punctual.

I stole a quick glance toward the couch to make sure Josh was still asleep before I padded into the front room. I hid just next to the window as Michael climbed out of his car wearing the same outfit from yesterday—tan joggers and a green T-shirt, except the hoodie he was also wearing was tied around his waist. Probably to cover the blood I knew was smeared on the side of those pristine pants.

Getting his pants dirty had earned me another slap for "good measure," he'd said.

He stomped through the grass, completely bypassing the walkway. His eyes darted around as he approached the house, and I tucked myself farther into the corner I was in, making sure I wasn't visible in the slightest.

He disappeared onto the porch, and I immediately headed toward the other side of Luke's house. Sadie saw me heading to Luke's bedroom and jumped off the couch to follow me. She panted softly and nudged me with her nose on my calf as we hurried down the hallway. I stepped into Luke's room just as Michael stepped into ours.

I dropped to the floor before he could see me, directly in front of the window, and I reached to open the blinds just a little more. He'd moved through the house so quickly that I wasn't prepared.

I was barely able to grab the cord with my fingertips but yanked it down. The blinds opened, and I peeked over the edge of the window. I felt ridiculous.

Michael must have left the room, so I took the opportunity to find a better vantage point. To my left was Luke's bathroom—still as clean as it was the other night—and I hurried in that direction. I stopped at the doorframe and crouched a little. From that position, there was no way Michael could see me unless he walked to the window and looked closely.

Just as I got into position, Michael strode out of the bathroom in different clothes and holding a suitcase. He dug through the drawers, chucking stuff over his shoulder before going back into the bathroom and returning with dress shirts on hangers and a plethora of slacks. He carefully folded each piece of clothing and arranged it in the suitcase. The suit jackets he stuffed into the hanging bag I bought him only a few weeks ago when I noticed his old one was worn down.

The suitcase open on our bed was the one Michael bought for me when we moved to Austin. I was excited about our new chapter, but I was nervous about leaving the only place I'd ever called home. He bought me the suitcase—it was dark blue with a built-in charger—and told me, with the sweetest smile, that he'd pay for any plane ticket back to Nashville whenever I wanted.

While I was immersed in the memories, Michael left the room and reappeared with his toiletries bag stuffed to the brim. With the amount he was packing, it looked like he didn't expect to return for a while.

I wondered if he could smell the bleach in the bathroom. I had used almost the entire gallon jug just on the bathroom floor where it had splattered and then on the counter where I had gripped to keep from falling to the floor where I ended up anyway. He had to have smelled it.

Stuffing his toiletries into my suitcase, he zipped it and surveyed the room. He must've noticed the pile of bloody towels and our bloody comforter in the corner, but if he did, he didn't react. He didn't react to the uncharacteristically unkempt room. He didn't seem to notice anything, or care, until he saw my discarded engagement ring on our dresser.

His eyes narrowed at the ring, and he crossed the large room in only a few strides. He carefully picked it up like it was a bomb that would detonate at any moment. I could see the wheels in his head turning as he tried to understand what it meant that I left the house without it on—I didn't usually take my ring off for any reason, which was an explicit request from Michael when he first put it on my finger.

"This looks too good on you, so I don't want you to ever take it off," he'd said years earlier.

Truthfully, I hadn't meant to leave it, especially in such a conspicuous location. But when I got to Luke's last night and realized I had forgotten it, I didn't go back for it. It felt wrong wearing a ring Michael had so gently slipped onto my finger all those years ago while that same hand, that same man, had given me black eyes and a busted nose.

Still hidden halfway in Luke's bathroom, I watched as Michael shook his head at the large diamond in his hand. He twisted it back and forth, glinting slightly in the small ray of light that peeked through the blinds. Without a second thought, he ripped the lamp from the dresser right in front of him and heaved it across the room at the opposite wall. I could hear it shatter from where I stood and flinched as if he had actually thrown it at me.

I knew in my bones that if I had been there, he would've aimed the lamp at me.

He heaved a few more breaths, took one final look at the ring and shoved it in the front pocket of his jeans. He scrubbed both hands down his face before he grabbed the suitcase and left the room.

That should have been my cue to also leave Luke's room, but I couldn't move. He had taken my engagement ring and the overabundance of emotions storming through me kept me frozen in place.

I knew last night was a turning point. After years of gaslighting, torment, narcissism, and anger, I needed to be done. When he made me truly bleed, something in me snapped. For a while, I had been planning what I would do if I wanted to leave: where I would go, what I would say to my family, how much money I needed.

I had the fundamental aspects of an elementary plan, and I

would put it into action to the best of my ability. I knew it was for the best. I couldn't do this for one more day, one more minute, and my life was quite literally on the line. But it still hurt, watching him scowl at my engagement ring and stuff it into his pocket. I would never wear it again, I told myself.

Whether it was for the best or not, when a part of your life comes to such a violent, tragic end, it still hurts.

I hadn't realized I started crying until I heard Josh say my name when he came into Luke's room. I quickly tried to right myself, wiping the tears from my cheeks and sniffling quietly.

"Hey, what's going on?" he asked with a tentative hand on my shoulder.

I cleared my throat. "Umm, Michael was getting his stuff," I said, pointing toward the window.

Josh nodded. "How long will he be gone?"

"I'm not sure. Probably a week, at least."

For a moment, we stood there in silence as I stared out the window at the few broken shards of the lamp I could see on our bedroom floor. Josh didn't move his hand from my shoulder, and although it could have been awkward, it was oddly comforting. He didn't seem to expect me to say anything, and I didn't expect him to have words of wisdom for me either.

"I was going to watch a movie. Want to join?" he asked, finally breaking the silence.

In the few seconds it took me to respond, I contemplated going back to my own house. Every square inch of it was in serious need of cleaning, and I needed to set my plan in motion. Step one: clean up, step two: get my shit together, and step three: get the fuck out. But the thought of going back into the house just after Michael was there, walking in and out of the same rooms where less than twelve hours ago, I thought my life was going to possibly end, didn't sound good. It made me sick to my stomach thinking about it.

"Yeah, that sounds good."

It could all wait until later. I suddenly realized that I had my entire life to figure out once again since the life I thought I was going to have disintegrated right before my eyes. It could all wait.

So, I curled up on the couch with Sadie, Josh plopped on the other end, and we watched movie after movie until my lack of sleep the night before caught up to me.

EIGHTEEN

Luke

I SHUT OFF THE CLINIC LIGHTS AND WAITED WITH THE DOOR OPEN for the few stragglers to follow me out. Our receptionist and two of the vet techs waved goodbye as they all headed toward their cars.

As usual, Crystal was the last one out the door so she could catch me alone. I had made the mistake once, right after I began working at the clinic and right after I moved, of acting interested in Crystal for a moment.

She was pretty, had a nice smile and was quite obviously interested in me, her new boss. After one conversation with her in which she insinuated that her sexual appetite was insatiable, I knew she could be a good distraction from my recent chaotic divorce. I was desperate to move on and get Valerie out of my head once and for all.

But after one coffee date, I realized the error of my ways. Dating my staff was not going to bode well, and Crystal wanted so much more than I was willing to give. I made it clear then that I didn't believe we were compatible for a number of reasons, but I had to give it to her, the woman didn't give up. Even three years later, she continued taking any opportunity to ask me out or flirt.

"Have a good night," I said hurriedly, trying to leave before Crystal began what I knew was coming.

"Actually," she started, and I paused because I was trying not to be rude, although I wanted to run away in the middle of her sentence. "I'm going to grab drinks with a couple of friends tonight. You should join us."

I saw the hope in her eyes, and as much as I wanted to be a good guy, I knew I needed to end this once and for all. She wasn't going to stop otherwise.

"Thanks for the invite, but I can't tonight. I actually have someone waiting on me at home."

Her face dropped immediately. I could see hurt replace the hope that was there only a second ago before she could school her features. It wasn't an all-out lie; Hazel was waiting on me, just not in the way I had insinuated.

"Oh, well, sure. Have a good night," she said with a half-hearted smile. She spun on her heels and hightailed it to her little silver Kia.

I jumped in my own truck and checked my phone one last time before I headed home and to Hazel. My phone had been attached to my hip the better part of the day, and I had texted back and forth with Josh about how Hazel was doing. He let me know that he'd found Hazel in my bedroom watching Michael pack his shit. Otherwise, they had been watching movies all day.

He got tired of my constant need for updates about an hour before and told me I was obsessed along with a few other colorful phrases.

I wasn't obsessed, I was concerned and with good reason. My concern for Hazel had me driving faster than usual and stepping on the gas to make sure I made it through yellow lights.

Michael's white BMW wasn't in the driveway when I pulled up, and I prayed I never saw it in their driveway again.

Sadie greeted me at the door, tail wagging and dog hair flying all over the place, as usual. She promptly flipped onto her back in the middle of the entryway, and I scratched her stomach for a few seconds before I asked her, "Where's Hazel? Let's go find her."

Sadie hopped up and bounded back into the living room.

"Hey, man, how's—"

"Shhh..." Josh cut me off with his finger to his lips. He pointed to the other end of the sectional, directly in front of me. I took a step forward and curled up under my favorite thick red blanket was Hazel.

Josh hopped off the couch and motioned for me to follow him into the kitchen.

"How's she doing?" I whispered and grabbed a beer out of the fridge.

Josh rolled his eyes and gave me a disbelieving look. "For the millionth fucking time today, she is okay. She's not great, but she's okay. We watched movies all day, and she slept."

"Did she say anything about last night?"

He shook his head and took the beer I offered to him.

"You going to tell me what happened or am I going to be left in the dark forever?"

I sighed and scrubbed a hand through my hair. "Her fiancé beat the shit out of her." Saying the words out loud hurt just as much as I thought they would, like my own punch to the gut. My anger flared.

"Fuck, I knew it. You've gotta be fucking kidding me!" he said too loud, and we both peeked over the island to make sure he hadn't disturbed Hazel.

"Yeah, I had suspected something was going on for a couple of weeks, but the prick was out of town. He came back into town on Halloween when I was over at her house trying to help her fix some shit. When he walked in and saw us there alone together, he practically pissed all over her, marking his territory. She was insistent that everything was fine and wouldn't let me help.

Long story short, he beat the crap out of her last night and I'm sure that wasn't the first time. Hopefully it's the last, though."

Josh stood wide eyed, shaking his head at me. I downed the rest of my beer, chucked it in the trash and took another one from the fridge.

"That's why she ended up at Murphy's... Makes sense why you're overly protective then. Y'know, because of what happened with Mom..."

I cut my eyes at him as I popped the top off of the bottle. He threw his hands up. "I'm just saying..." He trailed off and I knew he was right. That didn't mean he had to say it out loud, though.

"I found her in her bathroom covered in blood last night. Almost had to kick down the door..."

"Sounds familiar..." Josh's face dropped, and I knew the memories were ambushing him, too.

Memories I had forced myself to forget so many years ago began frequenting my thoughts the morning I saw the first bruises on Hazel's arm. Bruises, blood, tears—each memory contained it all.

"Anyway, I just want to make sure she's safe. He's not touching a hair on her fucking head again." My whole body was buzzing with newfound adrenaline, thanks in part to the old memories the entire situation had drawn up along with the woman that lay on my couch. I felt a fierce protectiveness for her.

"Hey, I'm right there with you. We'll get her through this. Her family's out of town, right?"

I nodded. "Yeah, they're in Nashville. I'm going to try to talk to her tonight and see what she's thinking."

Josh finished his beer and immediately yawned. My little brother was looking older by the day. The circles under his eyes were darker than usual, and he looked altogether worn down.

"You doing okay?" I asked.

"Yeah, yeah, I'm great. Just lots going on between work and

Zach."

My nephew was nearly five going on fifty if you asked me. The kid was wise beyond his years and sweet as hell, which was surprising since his dad was, well, my brother and his mom was. . . his mom.

When Josh and his ex-girlfriend, Samantha, began dating six years earlier, he told me it was just a fling. They were casually dating until she found out she was pregnant a few months in.

Sam made life shit for Josh. She always held Zach over his head—nothing was ever good enough. And he always gave her however much money she needed. When it got to be too much—rent, child support, work—he moved in with me. I never charged him rent as long as he saved and saw his kid as much as he could.

"She still giving you shit?"

He laughed. "Always, bro. But Zach's fifth birthday is coming up, and I was hoping to throw his birthday party here, if that's okay?"

"Absolutely. Whatever you want to do. I'll bring the cake."

He smiled, although it didn't seem entirely genuine. I'm not sure I had seen a genuine smile from him since everything happened with our parents. He became good at putting on a front, but that's all it was—his cheery and lively personality was a front for all the pain, and it was his way of dealing with the fucking trauma. He made jokes and made everyone else feel great while my coping mechanism became beating the shit out of people. We made it work.

He patted me on the arm and hiked his thumb over his shoulder. "I gotta get ready for work but let me know if you need any help with Hazel."

"Hey," I asked before he could leave the room, remembering something he had told me the other day. "Did you ever find your phone?" Guy was always losing his phone, but usually it would turn up in a random spot at the bar or somewhere around the house.

He shook his head and rolled his eyes. "Nah, must've fallen out when I was at work or something. Halloween was a fucking crazy night, so I couldn't find it at the bar. But I got a new one. Same number and all that."

"Okay, cool. And thanks for hanging out with her today."

He shrugged. "Not a problem. She's good company."

Yes, she was.

The house was dark, and I swore I could smell the tangy, metallic odor of blood when I walked in the door. The door was unlocked, the house was dark, and I smelled blood. All bad signs, but I continued through the hallway into the living room.

The coffee table was overturned in the middle of the room. The books my mom kept there were discarded beside it, along with the empty beer bottles my dad had most likely collected throughout the day.

Where was Josh?

Dad's recliner was tipped back and that's the first place I found blood. The tan arm of his chair that was dirty from years of sweat was now smeared with blood. But who's blood?

Where was Josh? Where was Mom?

I wanted to call out to them, but fear kept me quiet. Fear had me tiptoeing around the contents of the side table that usually stood by Dad's chair. Picture frames were shattered, and his house shoes were there and so was the remote.

The kitchen appeared the same as it was the day before when I left for the night. I shouldn't have left for the night, but there was a party, and I told my parents I was going to spend the night at a friend's house. I woke up that afternoon still drunk from the night before and left for home only after I shoveled down a cheeseburger and some fries. I could still taste the grease on my tongue.

Through the kitchen and around the corner was the hallway that contained all the bedrooms and the guest bathroom that Josh and I shared. The smell of blood became stronger the deeper I went into the house.

I bypassed our bedrooms and instead paused at my parents' bedroom door. I waited for a moment and stared at it. More blood covered the brass doorknob and was smudged around it.

They were in there. Behind the bedroom door, covered in blood, were my parents, maybe my brother. I knew it with my entire being as the hallway spun and my fear turned into terror, which turned into absolute horror when I finally found the strength to push open the door. I didn't touch the knob or the blood. My mother's blood.

I lurched myself out of the dream and in a state of semiconsciousness, I peered around the living room to gather myself.

It was the same dream I'd had since it happened: I'd walk into the house and make it to the bedroom door. I would always wake myself up before I saw what was inside, though. I think it was a tiny portion of my brain trying to protect me from seeing the scene once again.

I hadn't had the dream in years, replaced by other nightmares of new memories, but I knew finding Hazel covered in blood, the same smell from before, had them back in full force.

When I read the time on my phone, I realized I had only been out for an hour, and Hazel was still asleep next to me.

The house was quiet around us. I turned on the fire after Josh left and sat down next to her before I also passed out.

I scanned Hazel's face. There was no panic there, and her forehead wasn't creased in worry as she slept. Her eyelashes fell atop her bruised eyes and her nose was slightly swollen, but she was still beautiful. Seeing her beaten yet still beautiful and strong pulled at a place in my heart that I'd forgotten about. The feeling, the tugging, was foreign to me.

As I stared down at her, her eyes fluttered open, and before I knew it, a sleepy smile spread across her face. Her pink lips upturned and for a moment, she seemed content staring at me.

"Hi there, Angel," I said as I pushed a few stray pieces of hair off her forehead.

"Hi," she said in a cute voice laced with sleep. She pushed

herself up and winced as she stretched her arms at her sides. "How long was I asleep?"

I didn't register her question immediately because I was too enthralled with the blush of her cheeks and the sound of her voice.

"Umm... a couple of hours at least."

"Where's Josh?"

"Work."

Her eyes widened. "It's that late? Shit. I swear it was two when I fell asleep. I told him to wake me up."

I laughed. "I think you needed the rest. Are you hungry?"

The very loud growl of her stomach was all the answer I needed as I pulled up the food delivery app. "Chinese?"

"Yeah, sure, that sounds good," she said as she stood and padded down the hallway. I heard the bathroom door open and close, then the water running.

I ordered a little bit of everything before she returned. She paused at the archway between the living room and the hallway with a concerned look on her face. The lines between her brows were too deep compared to the peace I saw on her face only moments before.

"What's wrong?"

"I think I should go home. I've way overstayed my welcome at this point," she said as she nervously knotted her shirt between her hands. The gray material rose just above the waist of her athletic shorts, and I saw what appeared to be another bruise at her hip. I hoped it was a shadow.

Slowly, I stood and closed the short distance between us. I unraveled her hands from her shirt and held them in both of mine. "You haven't overstayed your welcome. Actually, I don't think you've been here long enough. You should stay longer."

She laughed and shook her head. "I'm being serious, Luke."

"I know you are, and so am I. I just ordered a shit ton of Chinese food, so we're going to eat and maybe drink and be fucking merry. How 'bout that?"

She sighed. "Fine, I just don't want you to think I'm some sort of charity case or that you have to do this. I'm not expecting anything, and I can find my own way."

"I have no doubt that you can more than manage, but is it such a bad thing that I want to help you?"

She thought for a moment, staring at our hands clasped together. She bit her bottom lip, and I wanted to pull it free and then press my lips to hers. But I wouldn't. I'd only kiss her when she told me she wanted me to.

"I guess it's not a bad thing. I think I need a drink."

"That's my girl. What do you want?"

She laughed again, and with each laugh and smile, I could see a little bit of the woman I knew coming back to life.

"Whiskey."

"So, you're a whiskey girl, huh?" I asked over my shoulder as I grabbed the bottle and two tumblers from the bar cart in the dining room. Out the large picture window facing the front of the house, I saw Emmy running down the sidewalk, blonde pigtails waving behind her in a mismatched outfit of sparkles and different patterns. I pulled one of the blue curtains closed as I spotted Chris begrudgingly following his kid.

Like he could feel me watching, he jerked his head to the right and held my stare. His overall demeanor—arms crossed over his chest, hood covering most of his face—appeared disinterested and at odds with his lively daughter, now skipping under the streetlights.

His glare was cold, and I was sure that without the window between us or his daughter, who had begun grabbing his hand, urging him to continue walking, he would have had more than a few words for me. I didn't give a fuck, though; he was another abuser that needed to be put in his place.

It looked like he was about to give me an obscene gesture just as Becky came jogging up. She followed her husband's eyes and saw me standing in the window. I would have thought I looked a little creepy, but she smiled at me and waved eagerly.

I quickly closed the curtains, plunging the dining room into darkness, after giving her a tight-lipped smile of my own.

I found Hazel seated in the middle of the kitchen floor, Sadie sprawled out in front of her, graciously accepting all the belly rubs she could get. I couldn't help the smile that spread across my face and the twinge of emotion in my chest at the two of them. I watched them for a minute before Hazel caught me as I leaned against the counter, whiskey and tumblers still in my hands.

"What is that look for?" she asked as she pushed herself off the floor with another cringe.

"What do you mean? What look?" I asked, grabbing a bottle of painkillers from the cabinet and filling a clean glass with water. I pushed both toward her and she smiled gratefully. I wanted to take away her pain, and what better way to start than Advil and alcohol?

She downed the water, narrowed her eyes at me and leaned on the counter. "I don't know, it was just an interesting look. Anyway... you found whiskey." She pointed at the bottle in my hand.

"Yes," I said, shrugging off her comment about my odd facial expression. "Is diet Coke okay, or do you want it straight?"

"Diet Coke is good. If I drink it straight, I could be drunk before the food gets here and that's not necessarily how I was planning for this night to go."

"So is whiskey usually your drink of choice?"

"I'm not very picky, but whiskey, tequila and red wine are my go-tos. Well," she thought for a moment. "I might be done with tequila for a while after Halloween, but..." She trailed off, not finishing her sentence.

Sensing her hesitation, I quickly changed the subject. "How was Josh today? Hopefully not a total dick."

She laughed as I handed her the drink, making herself comfortable on one of the barstools. "No, I actually really like Josh."

The way she said it—hesitant and quiet—made me question the meaning behind it. I raised my eyebrows and peered over the rim of the glass as I took a sip. The whiskey was a welcome burn at the back of my throat.

She recognized the look and question in my eyes. She rolled her own, in a gesture I found endearing, and shook her head. "Not like that," she scoffed before taking a long sip. "I just mean he's not what I thought."

"And what did you think he'd be like?"

She tilted her head to one side in contemplation. "I'm going to sound like a bitch, but... I thought he was irresponsible and lazy, maybe? I just didn't think he took life that seriously, or at least that's the way he seemed. But after spending today with him, I can tell that is definitely not the case."

I nodded in agreement. I wasn't surprised by Hazel's admission—most people, when first meeting Josh, had the same impression, when in reality, it couldn't be further from the truth. He let the nonchalant, carefree parts of his personality cover up the crazy shit going on in his life.

"I didn't know he had a son and a crazy ex-girlfriend, or baby mama, as he so affectionately calls her," she continued. "He's still pretty easygoing, but there's more there than just that."

"Yeah, he's easygoing and loves life, but he also cares about Zach more than anything and would do anything for him. He would even put up with Sam's shit. I can't believe he told you that much—he usually likes to keep everything involving them very under wraps. He only discusses it with our friends who were there and witnessed most of it happening."

She took another long sip of her drink, more than half of it gone already, and ran her tongue along her plump lower lip. The move wasn't meant to be sexual, but my thoughts had a mind of their own when around Hazel. Watching her tongue lick up the tiny remnants of her drink on her lower lip made me wonder if she tasted as sweet as she always smelled. I felt a twinge of regret about my dirty thoughts when I looked at her eyes once again, sad and rimmed with black.

"I mean, after a while, I kind of figured out what he was doing—I think he was telling me about his personal life, so I'd feel more comfortable..." She cleared her throat as her shoulders tensed. "So, I'd feel more comfortable talking about everything if I wanted to."

One of Josh's skills was connecting with people; he really did care about people on a level I never understood hence why I found myself more drawn to animals. Also, being a bartender, Josh was used to listening to people and giving feedback and sometimes feigning interest.

"Did you talk to him about it?" I asked, although I already knew the answer. I wanted her to talk to me, and it seemed like a good way to begin the conversation.

She only shook her head and finished her drink, the ice clinking loudly against the empty glass. Maybe not a good way to start the conversation, so I tried again.

"Do you want to talk about it?"

She stared up at me as I leaned forward, my elbows resting on top of the cold, granite surface of the island across from her. I tried to convey through my body language that she could talk to me and that I was ready to listen to whatever she had to say. She didn't tense at my proximity, and there was a flicker of softness in her hazel eyes.

Her chest rose slowly as she took in a deep breath. "I'm not sure. I think I'm still... processing?"

"I understand," I said softly. I waited for a moment, giving her the opportunity to say something else, but she didn't. "Refill?"

She looked at her empty glass, nodded and pushed it toward me. I dumped the old ice and after I finished putting new ice in her glass, and as I popped the top of the whiskey bottle, she began talking.

"I knew what was happening wasn't okay... I knew it wasn't

okay when he started jerking me around and when it escalated, and he hit me for the first time." My back was to her as I downed the rest of my drink, needing the liquid courage to hear about what she'd been through. I kept my back to her as I slowly refilled both of our drinks. I worried that if I turned my attention to her at that moment, she would have stopped talking.

"But it wasn't all bad, you know? At the beginning, God." She sighed. "He was the sweetest boyfriend. No matter what, I had all of his attention and he said all the right things at all the right moments. I seriously believed that I was the lucky one, and I questioned every day what I did to deserve him."

With our glasses refilled, I turned back to her. I placed her drink in front of her, where she was fidgeting with her chipped nail polish as she spoke. She whispered a quiet "thanks" but didn't look up at me. I realized why she wouldn't meet my eyes when one lone tear slid down her cheek.

"It wasn't until we moved here that things seemed to change. It was slow at first, and I realize now, only after seeing everything with new eyes, that there were a few red flags that I should have noticed beforehand that I thought nothing of at the time." She was silent for a long minute, lost in the memories, and I could see by the twist of her face that she was just barely hanging on.

"What were the red flags?"

"Umm… he liked to tell me who I could and couldn't hang out with. He liked to comment on what I ate and how it would affect how I looked. He only wanted me to wear certain things. Now looking back, he also wasn't just affectionate, he became aggressively possessive. And all of that became worse when we moved here and away from our families. He began dictating almost every part of my life, including who I hung out with, what food we kept in the house, when I could go places, anything and everything had to be his way."

Her hand was shaking as she lifted her glass to her mouth. Cautiously, and unable to hold back the need to touch her any longer, I reached out and placed my hand on top of hers that still lay on the counter. In a move I wasn't anticipating, she wrapped her fingers around my hand and squeezed.

"He isolated me. I don't exactly have any friends here because he wanted to keep me to himself. Then he wanted to make sure I looked a certain way, so he kept me *accountable* to a specific diet and workouts," she said with disdain. I could feel and see her shift from sadness to contempt. Her shoulders tensed, along with her grip on my hand as her face pinched. "Did you know he cheated on me?"

I kept my facial expression subtle, only narrowing my eyes and shaking my head. I mumbled, "Fucking idiot," under my breath, but I didn't let her see the fucking rage boiling in my veins as I tried to keep a lid on my anger. Each detail made it all the worse.

"That's what pushed me over the edge. When he told me he'd been cheating on me for a while, I—I realized that I couldn't do it any longer. For so long, I thought if I tried hard enough, maybe I could fix things and if he saw how much I wanted to be with him, then he'd revert back to his old self. Which I know sounds stupid—"

"No, it's not stupid."

Her eyes jumped to mine, and I could see the doubt there. I couldn't let her blame herself for any of it; no one was by any means perfect, but none of what she had been through was even remotely her fault.

"Well, I feel stupid. I should have left after the first time he hit me. I should have left before that, but I had invested too much at that point. I mean, our families are best friends, I've known him since I was a kid and I moved across the country for him. The worst part was he was always so apologetic. He was so good at getting me to believe that it was just a one-time mistake and that he wouldn't do it again. And for a while, he wouldn't." She was speaking quicker—each word seeming to flow a little easier than the previous—but she still wavered over certain parts and shook her head at her recollection. She stuttered over the good parts, and from experience, I knew those were the worst. Relationships end and when they do, thinking of the good times seemed to sometimes outweigh the bad. Even if the bad was horrible.

"He would stop, and all would seem right in the world until I would fuck up again. And slowly, as time went on, his outbursts became more frequent—" The doorbell rang, and she whipped her head to the front of the house, her eyes wide with fear.

"Shit, I forgot about the food. Let me get it and we can eat in the living room." I gave her hand a final squeeze before I retrieved the bags of hot Chinese food from the shivering delivery guy. I tipped him generously, feeling like I needed to put a little extra good out into the world after hearing Hazel's story.

I arranged the cartons of food on the coffee table while Hazel got comfortable on the couch under the blanket. The room was chilly from the unusually cold evening, so I turned the fireplace higher and turned the heat up a degree or two. I settled in next to her after making sure we had anything else we may need.

We made our plates, and I switched on the TV for background noise. I didn't know if she wanted to continue talking or if she had more to say. I was caught between pressing her for more information and bringing up a new topic.

We both ate in silence. I watched her from my peripheral—trying not to look like I was actually watching her—and was immediately impressed with her ability to eat rice with the cheap wooden chopsticks they provided. She watched the TV intently when she wasn't looking at the food on her plate, and not once did she look toward me in the few minutes we sat together.

Before long, she had cleared her plate and set it on the coffee table in front of us. She sipped her drink and settled back into the couch cushions. She looked so at home in my home and on my couch with my dog settled in next to her. I decided that I liked her being there.

"I didn't mean to unload all of my stuff on you like that," she said. Her knees were tucked up against her chest and she seemed so small again.

"It might make you feel better to talk about it, and I'm more than willing to listen. I know I like having someone to talk to when shit goes down."

"I do kind of feel better. Like I said, I don't have many friends here, and telling my family anything is going to be a nightmare I'm not exactly ready for, so I appreciate you listening. You did not sign up for any of this."

She was right. I hadn't signed up for it, but neither had she. She didn't sign up for the abuse and manipulation, especially from someone who was supposed to love her. The least I could do was be there when she needed me and however she needed me—I wanted to do it.

"I'm here for whatever you need. We're friends—" The words sounded weird and inaccurate when I spoke them, but I didn't have a better word for our relationship. It felt like more than that.

She nodded but didn't say anything else. From experience, I knew talking had to be on your own time, but I waited too long after my parents to talk to anyone and it did damage that was hard to undo—damage that was still evident each and every day. After Valerie and I divorced, I learned from my experience and confided in Josh, along with my therapist. I couldn't let Hazel endure what I did after my parents.

"You said the other night that you'd... you'd kill him." Her statement caught me off guard as I placed my empty plate on top of hers. I leaned back and turned toward her, wanting to see her face before responding. Her glass was propped up on her knees just in front of her face with her eyes wide and curious. In the dim light, the fire cast shadows that danced across her face. Her black eyes didn't seem as dark in the faint light.

"I did."

NINETEEN

Luke

My throat was tight as I waited for her reaction. Seriously threatening to kill someone wasn't something to gawk at or take lightly.

"You weren't being serious, though. It was just the adrenaline or whatever talking?"

Hearing the question in her voice, I waited until her eyes met mine so she had access to all the emotion tumbling through me and saw my intention. I reached out slowly and grasped the side of her neck, my fingers tangling in her hair. She bit her lip, waiting for me to respond, and I used my thumb to pull it free.

She had no reason to be nervous.

Her skin was extraordinarily soft under my calloused palm, and my hand looked huge against her face. We were closer than we'd ever been, and even in the faint light of the fireplace and the glow of the TV, I scanned her face. I noticed the freckles along her nose and forehead, the faint scar above her lip, and the way her lip was quivering ever so slightly as my thumb rested on her chin.

"If I knew it would take away even an ounce of your pain," I said with conviction. "I wouldn't hesitate to do it."

Her lips parted at my admission, and she sucked in a breath. I felt her pulse quicken under my palm, and I swore I could hear her heart thudding in her chest. Or maybe it was my own as the blood whooshed behind my ears.

Almost imperceptibly quick, her eyes darted from mine to my lips and then back. I wanted to lean in and finally confirm how well I knew we'd fit together and do something about this aggressive chemistry between us, but I didn't for fear of her reaction to any move I made. So instead, I stayed still and watched her. Her brow furrowed slightly as she watched my mouth, and under her gaze, my lips went dry. I stuck my tongue out to wet them, and before I had a chance to realize it, she closed the distance between us, and her lips were on mine.

For a moment, I still didn't move as she kissed me. There was a war brewing in my mind: kiss her and claim her like I wanted to or put a stop to it all because her actions could only be a reaction to her emotional few days. A bigger, better man may have stopped it or wouldn't have touched her in the first place, knowing that she was trying not to fall apart as her life crumbled around her. But I realized I wasn't a better man, and my need for her, to feel her in my arms, to keep her safe and help her come back from it all, won out.

Once I made the decision, I couldn't hold back a moment longer. I heard the ice rattling in her glass, still gripped in one of her hands, as her kiss grew more urgent. I responded in kind, grabbing the glass from her and placing it on the table without breaking our connection. I gripped the other side of her face with my free hand and pulled her toward me. She pressed her hands on my chest, still allowing a little room between us, but leaned forward.

I slipped my tongue against her already slightly parted lips, and she immediately opened for me. She was as sweet as I knew she'd be, and the whiskey on her tongue amplified it all. My hand trailed down her back, and I gripped her hip; I wanted to explore her entire body with my hands, my mouth.

She grunted in pain, and in the fog of the passion swirling around us, I had forgotten about the bruises just beneath my hands, on both of her hips.

I tensed, ready to pull back, but her hands covered my own, urging me to tighten my grip on her. "I'm okay," she muttered against my mouth.

She pressed up onto her knees next to me and wrapped her hands around my neck and through my short hair. The teasing scrape of her fingernails against my neck raised goose bumps down my arms and stoked the fire in me. Her chest pressed up against mine as a breathy moan escaped her lips, and I swallowed it down. All restraint lost, I pulled her hips, eager to have her straddling me and as close as she could get. With each swipe of her tongue against mine, each illicit sound, and each time she pressed into me harder, the more I craved her. I was never going to get enough.

My actions, though, were suddenly met with resistance. Immediately, I loosened my grip on her hips but kept my kiss eager. I would let her set our pace, let her be in control, but I needed her to know I wanted this. Without warning, she pulled her mouth from mine and unraveled her hands from where they were twisted through my hair.

She fell back against the couch, her fingers tracing over her swollen lips. Around her mouth and her chin, her skin was red and slightly raw from my short beard, and she looked absolutely beautiful. I immediately missed her mouth, her hands, her noises.

My dick was uncomfortably hard against the zipper of my pants as we both tried to calm our breathing, and I tried to slow my pounding pulse. She stared at me for a moment, seemingly shocked by her actions, before her eyes trailed over me and grew wider when she saw the evidence of my arousal straining against the material of my jeans.

"Shit..." she muttered under her breath. She looked like she was about to leap off the couch, and I wanted her to do anything but that. "I don't—I didn't... that's not... shit." She pushed herself up and was off the couch before I could totally wrap my head around the situation. Too much of the blood was being forced to my smaller head, and it was hindering my ability to think clearly.

"Wait," I said, reaching for her hand. She quickly yanked it away, and I watched the fear tear across her face. My heart sank as she flinched, but she didn't continue her retreat. I rose from the couch and reached for the hand she yanked away before. She let me hold it as I said, "Everything's fine."

She shook her head and released a breath. "I'm embarrassed," she admitted, not meeting my eyes. "I didn't mean to jump you like that, I'm just all over the place and don't know what I'm feeling right now. With everything that's happened, especially the timing of it all, I can't seem to get my head straight."

"Well, couple things about that: one, you shouldn't be embarrassed when, as you can tell, I enjoyed you jumping me..." I paused, and she blushed as she caught on to my meaning. "Two, it's normal that your feelings are all over the place right now. Just don't run. When I said I'm here, I meant it."

She finally met my eyes, and some of the embarrassment and uncertainty that I saw before were gone.

"Okay."

I pulled her back down on the couch, and she sat down next to me, our movement only slightly disturbing Sadie, who stopped snoring for a moment to look at us before she let her head fall back to the couch. I slung my arm on the cushion behind Hazel, giving her the option to sit as close as she wanted without touching me. She readjusted until she was close but not touching me. She felt a mile away.

"What did you mean about the timing of everything?"

"Umm... well, my birthday was the first," she said. "I woke

up on my birthday here, I—" She cleared her throat. "I snuck out of your house and went home to find Michael, who was extremely angry. It was just a really shitty way to spend my birthday."

"I think that's the understatement of the year. Why didn't you say anything about it being your birthday?"

"Because I didn't want to make a big deal out of it, and I already had enough stuff going on. It's fine, I'll have another birthday next year, and I'll celebrate twice as much or something."

I settled farther back into the couch and with my arm still thrown over the cushion, I let my fingers trace circles over Hazel's shoulder. When she was so close, I found it hard not to touch her. "No, that's not going to work for me. Let's do something on Friday. How about I cook, and we can celebrate your birthday a week late?"

"You're going to cook for me?"

"Of course. Don't sound so surprised."

She looked at me out of the corner of her eye. "You're not going to let me say no, are you?"

"I'll never force you to do anything." After everything she'd told me earlier, I felt it necessary to clarify that. "But you deserve to be properly celebrated."

Slowly, she turned her head. I watched as her eyes first landed on my hand gripping my leg before she continued up my arm, pausing on the dark tattoos there until her eyes finally reached my face. The corners of her lips were upturned in a soft smile, and she leaned into my side before looking back to the TV once again.

"You're such a fucking sweet talker. How the hell am I supposed to argue with that?"

I threw my head back laughing. When I looked back down, her eyebrows were raised in question.

"There's the spitfire I was missing." Her smile broadened and my chest tightened. "I do have to say something, though." I couldn't move on until I got it off my chest.

"The fight between the two of you on Halloween... I'm sorry I made it harder for you. I didn't know what to do in that moment. I knew you were terrified, and..."

She tensed against my side and started fidgeting with her hands again as she seemed to do when she was nervous.

"He was already in a shitty mood." I was thankful she spoke up, because I honestly had no idea what else to say. Nothing would have made it better, but I wanted her to know I was sorry. "He had been gone a while, and so when he saw you there, it definitely set him off a little more. But..." She peered up at me through her dark lashes. "I don't want you to think it's your fault. He would've found something to argue about and you were just an easy out."

I nodded, and although she said it wasn't my fault, I did feel guilty. I wanted to help her and find a way into her life to keep her safe, but instead, I made the situation worse for her. My plan royally backfired.

"I'm sorry I made it worse for you, that wasn't my intention."

"I know," she said, the small smile back on her face. "Can we not talk about it anymore?"

"Of course." I turned up the volume of the cooking show that was on the TV. As we settled back into the couch, fire roaring in the corner, Hazel draped the blanket over us both and let her head fall onto my chest.

Something had been shifting between us—as arguing turned into quick, stolen looks and cautious flirting. Kissing her, Hazel kissing me with a sincerity and passion I had never felt, had changed everything. This was our turning point, and I couldn't remember the last time I had been so content or felt so at peace. I'd do whatever I needed to do to protect our peace. I'd protect her from her past and from my own.

TWENTY

Hazel

EVEN DAYS LATER, THE FEELING OF LUKE'S LIPS ON MINE CONTINUED to linger. I found myself replaying our kiss over and over again as I attempted to figure out the rest of my life. It was a huge distraction. Especially since I knew he was right next door.

Until I logged into the account I used for work on Monday morning, I had forgotten that my coworker, Stephanie, was on vacation and had all her emails forwarded to me. I spent the week working on her projects as well as my own while trying to stay on top of both of our emails. It didn't help that with the end of the year right around the corner, there were several projects that I needed to close out.

I could have worked faster and been more efficient, but for some reason, my creativity was in overdrive. I found it difficult to complete my actual work when writing my novel was coming so naturally.

Since I'd decided I wanted to write a book, my creativity was stagnant, and the tangible ideas were few and far between. But since Halloween, and what I deemed as the day my life restarted, I couldn't stop writing. I found that I was negotiating with myself: if you send this email or finish this proof, you can write another five hundred words.

When I wasn't near my computer—which wasn't often—I jotted notes on my phone or any piece of paper available. Who knew that breaking off your several-year-long engagement was the key to begin writing your first romance novel?

In four days, I had an outline of the major plot points, a deep dive into each of my main characters and their relationships along with the first six chapters.

I felt unstoppable. That was until I received the first text from Michael in the middle of the week.

Three days with no communication after I'd watched him pack up and take my engagement ring. A few days after he almost broke my nose, gave me two black eyes and shoved my face in the bloody mess I made, and the first text I got was: **I miss you.**

Seeing his name on my home screen made me sick, and when I opened the text to see those three little words, I emptied the rest of my stomach contents.

I didn't respond but that didn't stop him. The back and forth of his emotions gave me whiplash. Eventually, he let me know that he'd be gone for two weeks total, giving me only that much time to get the hell out of the house.

After he gave me his time line, I blocked him. When I hit that red button, I felt like a weight was lifted off my shoulders. Even more weight was lifted when I began searching for apartments nearby and had the dreaded conversation with my sister and mom.

"Wait, wait, wait, Hazel. Michael told his mother that you were just taking some time apart," my mom said loudly over my sister, who hadn't stopped talking since I told them that our engagement was off.

I sighed audibly into the phone and both my sister and mom stopped talking. "Okay, look, I know this is a surprise, but I don't want to have a long-winded discussion about it. I've made my decision, and whether Michael knows it right now or not, this is the best thing for us both."

"I say good riddance," Delilah chirped.

"Delilah Cooper, do not say that. Hazel, you and Michael have been together forever. You really don't think this is a misunderstanding?" Mom pleaded.

"No, it's not a misunderstanding."

"Mom, if Hazel says it's over, then let her make that decision. It's her life," Delilah said.

"I just don't want to see her make a mistake, Delilah," Mom countered.

"It's not a mistake, Mom. We've had this talk before. He's not good for her, and quite honestly, he's a piece of shit."

"Delilah!" Mom said, enunciating every syllable like she did when we were children. "That's just not right. We've known Michael for forever. He's so sweet and would do anything for Hazel."

They went back and forth for a while, arguing over my relationship and whether I was making a mistake. Finally, I reached my limit and said the one thing that I never thought I would say to my mom or my sister.

I cut Delilah off, raising my voice just enough that she shut up, and said, "If by doing anything for me means beating the crap out of me for about a year now, then you're right, Mom. He'd do anything for me."

For a long time neither of them said a word. The silence on the other end of the line was all the confirmation I needed that neither of them had expected me to say anything like that.

"I'll kill him," Delilah seethed.

"Yeah, get in line." Remembering Luke saying those exact same words made me smile. I knew both he and my sister were as serious as a person could be.

"Hazel, I don't know what to say." My mom's voice was soft, and I heard her sniffle a few times.

"You don't have to say anything, Mom. I didn't think I was

going to tell y'all because, honestly, I don't want to talk about it. I just want to move on and keep moving forward. Right now, I'm just worried about finding an apartment and moving out."

"You should come back home, honey. We have more than enough room here."

I knew it was coming: my parents did have more than enough room. They still lived in the large, seven-bedroom house we grew up in, right outside of Nashville, and if I went back, I would have my own wing that at one point was for guests, but my mom promised it would be mine if I ever returned.

But I couldn't go back home. Even though Michael had prevented me from seeing most of Austin, I wanted to give it a fighting chance before I turned tail and headed back up north. I thought I might actually grow to like the city.

"I'm not going to come home," I said, and when she began to argue, along with my sister, I added, "at least not yet. I need to stand on my own for a while and staying here is how I want to do that. All I need from y'all is support. Just support me as my big sister and my mom."

"I'm always here for you, Haze. When you're ready to talk about it, let me know. I'll come visit soon."

"Thanks, D." As rough as my sister was around the edges sometimes, she always had my back as a sister should.

"I don't think Michael's parents know the extent of it all. What—what should I say? If she asks if I've talked to you about it."

I never believed our breakup would be easy; I knew it would be messy at best but knowing my mom would have to figure out how to move forward with her best friend of thirty years, who also happened to be Michael's mom, was awful.

"You can say whatever you need to say, Mom. I know you disagree, but I'm not sure Michael's mom ever liked me very much, so I don't think she'll believe you if you tell her about the —" I couldn't say the word *abuse* without it making my skin crawl. "If you tell her about everything. If she asks if you talked to me, I would just tell her that you have and that Michael took the ring back. That we're done."

"I can do that. And just so you know, Hazel, I'm always on your side. I love you so much."

"I love you too, Mom. I have a lot of packing and cleaning to do, so I'm going to go. I'll keep y'all updated on everything."

They both said they loved me again, and when I hung up the phone, I cried for such a long time. I felt like a failure, although I knew I shouldn't. I didn't want my family to be caught up in our mess, but it was going to happen.

While I cleaned the house and organized all our things into three different categories: Michael's shit, my shit, and shit to throw away, I attempted to listen to a few podcasts Delilah sent my way about life after breakups and domestic abuse. A few of them I couldn't get through—the ones with survivor's stories—without having flashbacks to specific times as they related to my own experiences. But of the ones I could get through, I found them somewhat helpful.

I told Delilah that they made a world of difference, though I don't think she believed me but pretended like she did.

I was deep in our guest bedroom closet, trying to block out the memories of us discussing how we would decorate it as a nursery as well as trying—and failing—to hold back tears, when my phone buzzed from the bedside table.

I huffed at the inconvenient timing as I stepped over a box of Michael's high school trophies, around a lawn statue of St. Peter his parents gifted us as a housewarming gift and finally, tripped over our old comforter before I made it out of the closet. I looked back at the shit piled a mile high and slammed the door shut—it was Michael's mess to deal with.

Our once pristinely clean, all-white guest bedroom—white by Michael's request—was now littered with everything from under the bed and a few of the items I did want to keep from the closet. When I looked around, it didn't look like I had made a ton of progress, but it was the second-to-last room that I needed to clean out.

I could see the finish line, and it looked like there was an expensive bottle of red wine and a ton of fucking independence on the other side.

I grabbed my phone and couldn't help the smile that crossed my face when I saw Luke's name appear.

Luke: No, I don't think I need a statue of St. Peter. Sadie has an issue with statues. I bought a garden gnome once and learned my lesson really quick.

I laughed and imagined Sadie growling at a little, innocent garden gnome.

Me: Well, if Sadie says no, then it's a definite no.

I hadn't seen Luke since earlier that week when I stayed at his house. Between trying to work, clean out the house, and find a new place to live, among other things, I didn't have much free time. Although I did always find time to text him.

With everything else going on, I didn't know if I also wanted to add on top of that trying to navigate my new feelings for him. Feelings that I also hadn't felt since Michael and I started dating, but even then, it was hard to compare. It seemed different. It was different.

Without knowing too much about him, I already trusted Luke. But I felt guilty for flirting—even if it was just innocent and over text—when I was going through a breakup. I didn't even know if I could see myself in another relationship, nor did I know if that's what he wanted.

I kept myself awake at night, trying to figure out what the hell I was doing or what he was thinking. I compared how I was healing and recovering—words I found myself using more often after the stupid podcasts—to others and then felt bad for appearing to be okay when I didn't always feel okay.

I was a mess.

Luke: She is in charge.

When I didn't respond right away, another text came through.

Luke: Steak or chicken?

Me: Steak.

Luke: I was hoping you'd say that ;)

I peered around the room once more and tried to come up with a game plan. I had two hours until I was supposed to meet Luke at his house for my late birthday dinner that I had already tried to get out of a few times over the week.

Not that I didn't want to spend time with Luke. It was the exact opposite... I was nervous about how much I did want to spend more time with him and how excited I was at the prospect of him making me dinner.

I knew I needed to shower and shave—just in case—as well as pick out an acceptable outfit and do my hair. I decided to leave the room in the chaotic state it was in and get ready as my heart pounded in anticipation.

TWENTY-ONE

Hazel

I was fifteen minutes late. Even though I lived next door, I was still late, because I changed my outfit six times and had to redo my makeup. It took me a while to figure out how best to apply the makeup to cover up the dull blue and yellow under my eyes. My nose was also still sore, so I did what I could to be careful when applying the concealer and powder to the center of my face.

I hurried up the porch stairs and knocked on Luke's front door. The only upside to being late was that I was too concerned about how late I was, and I didn't have time to psych myself out. It wasn't until I saw Sadie running toward the door and Luke turning around the corner from the kitchen that the nerves really set in.

"Hey, come in," Luke said as he waved me inside. It took me a moment to register that he had invited me in. I fought the nerves and attempted to remind myself that it was just a casual dinner with my neighbor. My neighbor that I hadn't stopped thinking about over the past week. I hadn't stopped thinking about him or the desperate kiss we shared.

Silently, I stepped inside and hoped I could keep my shit together for the night.

As Luke shut and locked the door, I greeted Sadie, who proceeded to weave in and out between my legs and cover my black sweater dress in golden dog fur. I couldn't help but laugh at her tongue hanging out of the side of her mouth.

Once I was thoroughly coated in dog hair and a little slobber, Sadie trotted away. I brushed off what I could of the fur but figured it would happen again anyway.

I caught Luke watching me with a curious look in his eyes as I stood up. He brazenly raked his eyes over my body, and goose bumps appeared over my skin and under his gaze. He paused, for the smallest second, on my hips and my chest, that were snuggly wrapped in the material of the dress, before meeting my stare and giving me a lopsided smile with his signature dimple. A dimple that was sometimes hidden by the scruff of his short beard, and I suddenly so desperately wanted to kiss.

He didn't seem to care at all that he had been caught checking me out, and I honestly didn't care that he had. The dress was a strategic choice since it showed off all my best assets.

And my strategy was working.

To return the favor, I also let my eyes wander over his body. He'd neatly trimmed his dark facial hair and wore a long-sleeved green shirt that closely matched his eyes. It was just tight enough across his chest and stomach that I could imagine the strength beneath it and could faintly make out the hard planes of his body. Like usual, his jeans were dark, and if I looked close enough, I swore I could see the outline of something hard below his belt.

A blush quickly heated my cheeks when the thought crossed my mind. "Something smells amazing," I said, frantically trying to move things along and change the direction of my thoughts.

"It's almost done," he said before placing his hand lightly on the small of my back and leading me into the kitchen.

"Wine okay?" Luke asked as I took a deep breath, smelling the herbs and spices that filled the spotless kitchen.

"Always," I said with a smile.

While he popped the bottle and poured two healthy glasses of wine, I peered into the pot on the stove and peeked into the oven.

"We're having steak, garlic and rosemary potatoes, and this salad that I've never made before that I hope turns out at least decent." He handed me my glass as my mouth watered for the wine and the food.

"That sounds amazing." I took a large sip of the wine and immediately realized it was much more expensive than the usual ten-dollar bottle I got once—or maybe twice—a week. "Thank you so much for doing this," I said, waving my free hand around and gesturing to the food and the wine and everything.

"I told you I would," he said as he threw a few carrots into a large salad bowl and took a generous gulp of his wine.

"Properly celebrated…" I murmured as I glanced around the kitchen and into the living room. The fire was roaring in the fireplace, and there was a '90s alternative music station quietly playing from the TV. I couldn't help the appreciative smile that creeped across my face at the music selection—also one of my favorites.

"Yes, properly celebrated," Luke said. I glanced back to find him directly in front of me, the two of us standing between the kitchen island and the sink on the opposite wall. We were close enough that I could almost smell his body wash over the other delectable scents swirling around us.

"Is this your version of how to properly celebrate someone?" I asked, hoping I appeared confident while inside, my heart was beating overtime. I tilted my glass up to my mouth—to give me something else to do besides saying more inane things—and realized my hand was shaking when the glass almost collided with my front teeth.

Luke quirked a dark brow as I held his eyes. His lopsided

smile was back in place, and he seemed too laid back with the look on his face and his arms crossed over his chest. He looked good in green, but I wished I could see the tattoos hiding beneath his sleeves and along his chest, his stomach.

"Well…" he began and for a moment, I'd forgotten that I had asked a question. "It depends on the person really, but this is a version of celebrating someone, yes."

I nodded, ready to move on when he continued, "But if I'm being honest, there are…" He paused like he was contemplating his next words then his voice dropped a little lower, "there are other ways I would like to properly celebrate you."

The innuendo didn't escape me as he licked his bottom lip, and an insane heat rushed over my neck and face. He watched me for a moment, squirming under his gaze, while I tried to find the right words. But I couldn't focus on speaking when my mind was overcome with images of what Luke's version of celebrating me might have looked like. As generous as he had been with his time, and his home, it was easy to imagine that he would also be generous in other ways.

I shifted my weight from one foot to the other as heat invaded other areas of my body—specifically pulsing between my legs—and I seriously couldn't focus on much else besides what to do next and the onslaught of dirty, amazing thoughts.

My body had a mind of its own around the tall, burly man in front of me, and much to my surprise, I was not mad about it at all.

The timer on the oven beeped, and Luke turned his attention to it, thus allowing me to take a deep breath and finish off my glass of wine.

Before I could ask, Luke appeared in front of me with the bottle of red and refilled my glass. "Want to come outside while I cook these? It won't take too long and there's a heater out there," he asked, grabbing a tray with two seasoned steaks.

"You have a heater?" I questioned as I followed him outside. Sure enough, there was a heater perfectly placed next to the patio table. I pulled out one of the chairs next to it and was immediately bathed in its warmth.

As Luke put the steaks on the grill—after politely asking me how I would like mine cooked—I took the time to glance around the patio. There was a small gray couch and ottoman in one corner closest to the door, along with a firepit that looked like it had been used often. The entire patio was softly illuminated by the string lights hung on the pergola.

I hadn't noticed when I escaped out the backyard after being rescued from the bar on my birthday.

"This is one of my favorite places," Luke said, taking the seat next to me instead of the one across the table and next to the heater. His leg accidentally brushed mine as he sat down, and I hoped it wasn't the last time he'd touch me that night.

"It is really cozy. I like the lights and the heater makes it bearable even when it's cold."

"That's exactly what I was going for. It seems to be where everyone gathers when they come over, too."

"Oh, I know." I cut my eyes at him, catching a glimpse of his sly smile as he chuckled.

"How many times do you think you've stormed into one of our parties over the past few years? It has to be over a dozen at this point."

His voice was light with laughter, and I didn't sense any hostility, but I still cringed at the reminder of my actions.

"Easily a dozen. God… I was such a bitch."

Luke tossed his head back and laughed at my comment.

"I wouldn't say you were a bitch. That's a little harsh, and we were pretty fucking loud. You had a right to be upset, and damn, you were. You came in here guns blazing."

"Ugh," I groaned, sinking lower into my chair. "Don't remind me."

"Don't beat yourself up about it. I honestly kind of enjoyed our little arguments. You were so fucking sarcastic and witty."

"You enjoyed our arguments?" I asked in shock as Luke

stood from his seat to flip the steaks, giving me the perfect view of his ass. I didn't know that men could have such a perfectly rounded ass, but there he was, proving me wrong.

"I didn't necessarily enjoy the fact that you were absolutely livid with me, but you were always ready to throw my bullshit right back at me."

"My mom just tells me I'm sassy and hardheaded."

He closed the lid to the grill, the smell wafted toward me, and my mouth watered once again. If the food tasted half as good as it smelled, I'd be thoroughly impressed.

"Sassy, huh? Well, then I guess I like that you're sassy and hardheaded," he stated simply before heading back into the house.

In the few moments he was gone, I found that I couldn't stop smiling to myself. Knowing that he had gone through all of the trouble of cooking me dinner, buying me nice wine, and whatever else he may have planned had butterflies annihilating my freaking stomach.

Being celebrated, as he liked to call it, was not something I was used to. It wasn't something that Michael did often, even on my birthday. As quickly as the thought popped into my head, I shut it down. I wouldn't compare the two, because I knew that it would quickly snowball into comparing everything.

I knew I was getting ahead of myself anyway. One kiss—no matter how mind blowing—didn't make a relationship; neither did flirting, texting or him making me dinner. None of that meant that we were in a relationship or even dating or, better yet, even thinking about it, no matter how real the sexual tension was.

It felt bizarre to be comparing my almost decade-long relationship with Michael to my friendship with Luke—a man who used to make my blood boil.

I was sure I'd lost my fucking mind, but Luke was a good type of unexpected.

"I was thinking we could eat out here. It's not too bad with the heater," Luke said. Balanced in his hands were two plates, silverware, the potatoes from the oven and the salad.

"Yeah, that sounds great."

In front of me, he set a white porcelain plate along with a knife and fork before he placed the bowl of potatoes and salad in the center of the table.

"Go ahead and start. I'm just going to grab the steaks and the rest of the wine." He didn't have to ask me twice. I grabbed the tongs for the salad, and as my stomach ached, I realized it was my first meal of the day.

It also made sense why the one glass of wine was already going to my head.

Luke laid the plate with our steaks next to the potatoes and pointed mine out. I quickly speared it with my fork before taking a large bite of the potatoes. They were buttery and fluffy and perfect. Carbs had been a big no-no for Michael; he said they would only accentuate my love handles.

I couldn't give a shit about the effect of the food on my body as the flavor bloomed on my tongue.

Similarly, the steak was perfectly cooked and seasoned. Midbite, I unintentionally let out a groan of pleasure, eliciting a chuckle from Luke across from me. I realized then that I had closed my eyes and probably looked nuts while enjoying my food. When I looked over at him, he was eyeing me suspiciously, taking a bite of his own.

"Good?"

"*So* good," I said before taking a bite of salad, making sure that each ingredient was on my fork.

"I'm glad you like it."

"So, you can cook?"

He nodded as I watched him take a bite of steak. Even the fork and knife in his hands appeared so much smaller than the ones I was holding. Everything about him seemed larger than life.

"Where'd you learn how to cook?"

He shrugged. "Just kind of picked it up. I cooked for Josh a lot and just got better with more practice. Don't think I'm a chef or anything, though. I never cook anything too complicated. If I stick to the basics, then I usually don't mess it up."

"Did your mom or dad teach you? My dad is the cook in our family most of the time. But my mom can bake anything."

His body language changed instantly. The moment the words left my mouth Luke's shoulders tensed and his grip on his fork tightened. Even in the dim glow of the string lights, I could see the white around his knuckles and the usually soft lines on his forehead deepen.

I tried to backtrack and figure out how my question could have caused such a visceral reaction. Parents were a relatively safe topic of conversation.

"No, they didn't." His response was surprisingly clipped and strained.

I gulped back more wine. "I'm sorry, I was just trying to ask questions, you know? Get to know you... like you said the other day, we've been neighbors for years and don't know each other at all, so I just wanted to make conversation. I didn't mean to—"

"Hazel," he cut me off midramble with an authoritative tone. I liked the way my name sounded when he said it like that, and it immediately shut me up. I watched a little smile creep across his face, pulling at one corner of his mouth but not touching his eyes. "Don't worry about it. My parents are just a tough subject."

"Hmm... I see," I said, trying to not ramble and give my nerves time to settle back down. "Strained relationship with parents, got it."

"I guess you could say that. They actually died when Josh and I were teenagers."

"Oh, wow, Luke. I'm so sorry. I can't even imagine losing your parents at such a young age." I struggled to find the right words and imagined little Luke, maybe just old enough to drive, losing his parents and consoling his younger brother. Because I knew he would have. Because that's the kind of person Luke was, and I had sorely misjudged him.

"Yeah, it was hard, but Josh and I stuck together, and we lived with my mom's brother for a while. He was a..." He stumbled for a moment before blowing out a breath like he was carefully choosing his words. "He was a decent person. He took Josh and me in when we had nowhere else to go. He passed away a few years ago."

He cleared his throat and refilled his wineglass. The pain of the memories seemed to still be raw based on the twisted expression on his face. The usually calm, neutral facade was long gone.

"Shit, Luke. I'm so—"

"No need to be sorry. You didn't kill them, so don't apologize," he said with a slight smile. "I just haven't talked to anyone about it in a while. Most of my friends know the story already, and since Josh and Zach are my only family left, we don't bring it up often. I thought it would be harder to talk about, but this wasn't too painful."

"I understand," I simply stated before refilling both of our wineglasses and finishing off the bottle. "I'm always happy to listen."

"Well, the details aren't exactly ones I like to relive, at least about my parents. My uncle just passed away from a heart attack. Natural causes or whatever."

I read between the lines of that statement—his parents did not die from natural causes and therefore, it was probably painful for him to relive.

"So, how's the book going?" Luke asked, changing the subject completely. I was so caught off guard by the question that I almost choked on my last bite of potato.

With food still in my mouth, I froze and stared up at him, shocked that he remembered my confession from our post-saving-Sadie dinner.

"It's going well," I said, finishing my food.

He chuckled and smiled a genuine smile this time, showing

off his gorgeous, straight teeth. "Come on, Angel, you've got to give me more than that. Will you tell me what it's about? What genre?"

Although I didn't believe Luke would make fun of me for my genre of choice, I didn't want to chance it. Even the slightest look of disappointment or dissatisfaction would have plummeted my self-esteem. It was partially why I decided not to tell anyone that I was writing besides my sister and Luke, accidentally.

"It's a book, or it will be when I'm done. I don't want to give away all the details yet."

"Yes, I remember you saying that, but I don't see how that prevents you from telling me what genre it is or how it's going."

"Do you really care to know that?" The question came off a little dismissive and the tone of my voice was sharp. Luke didn't seem to care, though.

He leaned forward in his chair, bracing his elbows on the metal table in front of him, and with his right hand, reached out and carefully gripped my left. Even the small touch of our fingertips pressed together sent my body buzzing and my heart racing. I also leaned forward—eager to be closer to him—until the cold metal of the table began seeping through my dress and into my arms.

"Hazel, I want to know everything about you. Even the smallest detail. I also don't ask questions I don't want to know the answer to. So, please tell me about your book."

When he put it like that—looking me directly in the eye, voice unwavering and so honest—how could a woman possibly say no to fucking anything?

"It's a romance novel." Like the man was a truth serum, the words came tumbling out of my mouth. I braced myself for the reaction I knew was coming.

"I love romance novels."

What? "Wait. What?"

I pushed a few strands of hair out of my face as the wind

picked up, blowing chilled air around us and overpowering the heater for a moment.

"Yeah, I like romance novels. I used to read a few in high school and college. My mom read them all the time growing up, and they remind me of her. Haven't read one in a while, though." As he spoke, he began rubbing the back of my hand with his thumb in soft, even strokes. The action was familiar, and for a moment, I hoped he wouldn't ever stop.

"I would have never guessed that."

"Why, because I'm a man?"

"Well... yeah, actually. Men don't usually read romance, right? I think romance is for anyone, but it's just usually women."

"I think men should especially read romance novels. It gives you really good insight into a woman's mind, and who the hell doesn't like a happily ever after?"

I laughed, because he was right, and I couldn't agree more. "You're right. The happily ever after is one of my favorite parts."

He reached over our joined hands with his opposite arm to grab his wineglass. The decision, although subtle, was very telling—he didn't want to let go of my hand and a little thrill pulsed through me.

"So, you'll write a happy ending?"

"Yes. I went back and forth for a while, because as I've recently found out, not every love story has a happy ending in real life."

He nodded, setting his empty glass back down on the metal table with a tiny clink. "True. I think everyone knows that but that's the great thing about reading those books: you can live the happy ending through someone else. Makes you believe that it could still be out there."

"I sincerely hope it is."

"It is," he said with a soft smile. The lights hanging above us twinkled in his emerald eyes. "So, otherwise, how far along are you with it? I don't know much about writing a book, but it seems time consuming."

I chuckled because that was a freaking understatement if I'd ever heard one. "It's definitely time consuming, but it's flowing a lot easier now, actually. I have an outline done, character development and the first few chapters. I realized that when your love life is shit, it's harder to write about happy people. I've actually written more this past week since Michael's left than I did for the past year."

"I'm glad to hear that it's going so well. Now that you know I like reading romance, let me know if you need me to proofread anything. I'd be happy to help."

"Umm... I'm not sure about that." I laughed and pushed away my empty plate after contemplating a third helping of potatoes. "I'm still a little unsure about sharing my writing before I've gone through and edited it. But maybe after that..."

He smiled.

"But that's a big maybe," I clarified as a strong gust of wind whirled around us, sending a powerful shiver down my back. The later it got, the less the heater was working.

"Let's go inside. I have a surprise for you," Luke said as he reluctantly let go of my hand to scoop up our plates and the almost empty food dishes.

"A surprise?" I questioned, grabbing the empty wineglasses and bottle of wine. I flicked off the heater and hustled inside behind Luke.

He popped open another bottle and instructed me to make myself comfortable on the couch, so I did just that. Sadie was curled up at one end of the sectional closest to the fire on top of the thick red blanket I'd used when I stayed over there. She barely stirred when I sat down next to her after kicking off my short booties and tucking my feet underneath her warm body.

"Okay, close your eyes," Luke yelled from the kitchen.

Nervously, I obeyed and closed my eyes. I heard the telling shuffle of Luke walking across the rug in the living room and then the clink of what I believed were wineglasses on the coffee table. A second later, the couch shifted beneath me as Luke took the spot next to me. His hand slid up my back and lightly grasped the back of my neck beneath my hair, brushing his fingers against my skin. His touch didn't feel possessive, rather, it felt protective in a way I wasn't expecting. My eyelids fluttered at the skin-to-skin contact, and I struggled to keep them closed.

"Okay, open."

TWENTY-TWO

Hazel

In front of me, perfectly placed on the glass table, was a small pink cake with one candle lit in the very center. Light-pink frosting was smoothed around the entirety of the cake while small, magenta swirls were strategically placed on the top and around the base. My favorite parts were the small rainbow sprinkles dusted over it.

"Happy birthday," Luke said as I turned to look at him. "I got the cake but forgot candles, of course. I found this one in a drawer in the kitchen. I think it was left over from Zach's last birthday party we had here."

"You bought me a cake?" I was already gobsmacked that he would put the effort into cooking me dinner but thinking of buying me a birthday cake seemed way above and beyond what I was expecting.

"Of course. It's your birthday, so you have to have a cake."

I didn't respond. Rather, I covered my mouth with my hand and for some reason had to force myself to hold back tears. Michael would have never thought to buy me a cake, and I chastised myself for the thought. Was I really going to cry over a man buying me a cake?

"I can't tell if you like it or not," Luke said while his thumb began running over the skin on my neck, sending a shiver down my back. "Your face could go either way, I think."

I cleared my throat and smiled. "I love it."

"Good, now make a wish and blow out the candle so we can eat it."

"You're not going to sing to me? Isn't that the point: you sing, I sit here awkwardly, and then I blow out the candle?"

"You do not want to hear me sing."

"I heard you sing in the car the other day. You're not that bad."

He shrugged. "That was with very loud music. If I have something drowning me out, I sound better."

I rolled my eyes but licked my lips, eyeing the cake again. "Fine," I conceded.

For a moment, I pondered my wish, wanting to make sure it was really good and something important for this new stage of my life. It was also a pretty cake, so I felt it needed to be an equally good wish.

With my wish firmly at the front of my mind, I closed my eyes and blew out the candles, hoping that Luke's pink cake had some magical powers that might make the wish come true. I needed all the help I could get.

"Well, now that you've heard my story, tell me about your family," Luke said, heading to the kitchen and returning with two forks.

"There's not much to tell. We're all pretty normal, to be honest." Luke raised a dark eyebrow at me as I stabbed my fork into the cake and took a bite that was much too large.

"Strawberry cake is my favorite," I mumbled around the sweet cake and creamy frosting.

"Good guess on my part, then."

"Or you're a stalker."

"Do you think I'm a stalker?"

I paused, cutting my eyes at him and taking another generous bite as he did the same. "That question sounded suspicious." I shrugged. "But I don't think you're a stalker, although I do catch you looking into my bedroom window quite often."

He froze with his fork in his mouth, brows raised and a terrified look in his eye. I had to laugh at his stunned expression and the realization that he'd been caught.

"But…" I began, setting my fork down on the table and settling back into the couch. "I guess if I saw you looking through my window, that would mean that I was looking at you through mine."

The wine coursing through me gave me a confidence I wasn't expecting.

"Although it was completely unintentional, I—" He cleared his throat and laughed. "I did enjoy that peep show not too long ago. I think we were both caught in compromising positions."

I felt the blush creep up my neck and bloom over my cheeks. The wine apparently didn't keep me from getting embarrassed.

"It's amazing that it's the first time that's happened. Whoever built these damn houses was insane, I swear. Why do the houses have to be so close together, and why our bedroom windows of all things?"

Luke tossed his fork on the table next to mine and the already half-eaten cake before he leaned back into the couch and threw his arm behind me. With his arm resting on the top of the couch behind my head, his fingers lazily ran through my hair and then skimmed over my neck.

It seemed like he constantly wanted to touch me, and I didn't want to shy away from the affection.

"I agree. I promise, though, I've never intentionally watched you. That would be fucking creepy." His words said one thing, but the sly smile playing on his lips said another.

"If you say so. However, if I catch you watching again, I may just give you something to watch." As soon as the words left my mouth, I couldn't believe I had actually said them. Quickly, I schooled my expression, keeping it neutral and unbothered, while inside, I tried to sober up. I wasn't that drunk. It was just something about Luke that made words fly out of my mouth or kept me from speaking coherently at all.

"Oh, really? Well, then you might catch me looking through your window more often if that's on the table." His green eyes were brilliant in the light coming from the fireplace, and his face was partially obscured by shadows cast around us. Even in the dim light, I couldn't miss the desire that danced behind his eyes and in the slight tic of his jaw.

After years of being his neighbor, I thought that he was always so stoic and unbothered, but after getting to know him and watching him up close, I realized he was rather expressive. It was just all in the minute changes in his expression, body language and word choice.

He was pretty easy to read when you knew what to look for.

When I didn't say anything, Luke changed the subject. "So, your family's pretty normal?"

"Yes, my parents have been together since college. My mom drives me crazy, but I love her nonetheless. My dad works so much that I honestly don't have much of a relationship with him. I have an older sister, Delilah. She's married with two kids, Miles and Amber. They're freaking great. I seriously think I miss them the most."

"When's the last time you went back to Nashville?"

It had been so long that it took me a moment to remember my last trip to Nashville. "I went in March while Miles and Amber were on spring break from school. We did a little mini vacation in the Smoky Mountains. They were planning on coming here for Thanksgiving, but I don't think that's going to happen anymore."

Sadie stirred beside me as Luke's phone began vibrating on the coffee table in front of us. Before he scooped it up, I glanced at the screen as the words "Unknown Caller" rolled across it. He silenced it with a shake of his head and tossed it on the couch beside him, once again giving me his full attention.

"Spam?" I asked.

He shrugged. "No idea. There's been a shit ton lately from either an unknown number or blocked caller, but whatever."

Next to him, his phone began vibrating again. That time, he not only declined the call, but turned his phone off altogether.

"It's always at the worst damn times, too. So, have you decided if you're moving back to Nashville?"

"I decided I'm going to stay here for now at least."

I leaned forward to pick up my fork again, only scraping off some of the magenta frosting from the top and savoring the extra sweet taste on my tongue. I'd missed sweets so much.

"Really?"

"Yeah, I think I want to give the city a chance before I run back home. Why do you sound so surprised?"

He held up his left hand in defense as his right sat idle at the back of my neck. "Maybe I am a little surprised, but I don't mean anything by it. It just seems like you're close to your family and may want to be near them since you're done with fuckface."

I rolled my eyes at the derogatory name for my ex-fiancé, but he could have honestly called him whatever he wanted to. I probably would have agreed with whatever he came up with.

"I thought about it, and of course, my mom was the first one to tell me to come home. But I moved here for Michael, and…" Saying his name was more difficult than I was prepared for. My voice caught at the back of my throat before I could continue and both good and terrifyingly awful memories flooded back to me. "Because our relationship was the way it was, I didn't get a chance to really know what it's like to live here. I think I would like it, so I want to give it a chance."

Nervous energy pounded through me at even the smallest mention of Michael's name and my previous life. Needing something to do with my hands, I took another bite of cake.

"I understand. Are you keeping the house?"

"No, I can't do it. There are too many bad memories there, I would feel like my every step was haunted by them or something. It's also in Michael's name—the mortgage is—so I can't. I'm going tomorrow to look at a few apartments not too far away. I'm excited to have my own space, or that's at least what I've been telling myself."

I went to pick up my wineglass, but still feeling the effects of the previous three glasses, I opted for more cake instead to soak up the alcohol.

"You have icing all over your mouth and chin." Luke laughed as I turned back to him. I quickly licked my lips and used my fingers to wipe around my mouth and over my chin.

Laughing again, Luke shook his head and swiped his thumb just below my bottom lip, collecting the icing I had missed. Without missing a beat and without taking his eyes off of me, he put his thumb to his mouth and licked the pink remnants from his finger. The way my body reacted you would have thought he licked me instead of his own damn finger.

I stared at his lips—plump, slightly wet and parted—long after it was appropriate to do so as I remembered how his tongue felt against mine not so long ago.

When a faint smile hooked his lips, I was pulled from my thoughts and readjusted on the couch.

"I'll come with you," he said.

"Come with me?"

"To look at apartments. It's always nice to have an extra set of eyes."

"Yeah, that'd actually be nice," I said. It would be nice to not have to walk through apartments all day by myself, but I was also excited about the prospect of spending an entire day with Luke. To get to see him outside of his house.

He also seemed excited that I wasn't leaving Austin, and I needed his excited energy to get me through the process of finding a new place to live.

"Great. You have some places picked out?" he asked before

picking up the cake and pointing at it, silently asking if I wanted more. I waved him off—I was more full than I had been in what felt like years.

"Yeah, they're nothing special, but I'm sure I'll find something."

"I guess you have to start somewhere."

He shut off the kitchen light before fishing the red blanket out from underneath Sadie, who just groaned softly before readjusting on the couch.

"Those are all of my surprises for tonight."

"It was all perfect and freaking delicious. Thank you again," I said honestly while he settled next to me, tossing the blanket over my legs. I hadn't realized I was cold until the warmth of the blanket settled over me.

Luke turned on a movie. It was supposedly new and really great, but neither of us watched it. Instead, we spent the duration of the movie talking about anything that came to mind, making up for the years we knew each other but never actually spoke, while the movie played in the background.

As we talked, we slowly migrated closer to each other. Our knees pressed together under the warmth of the blanket as Luke discussed how he got through college without the support of his parents and with the little support his uncle could offer. It seemed mostly due to his friends, whom I was eager to meet. Our thighs brushed against each other's as I described how bossy Delilah was when we were younger, and we ended up both laughing hysterically when I told the story about falling off the kitchen counter and getting stuck on the drawer pull. Luke snorted when I described the look on D's face, her carefree shrug she had already mastered at ten, and the way I hung there until my parents got home half an hour later.

He finally told me that fighting was a release for him after his parents died—a way to rid himself of the overwhelming anger flooding through him. Anger that was actually grief he hadn't worked through. But he didn't offer too many details about his parents or the fighting other than he made a decent amount of money and was undefeated for a while. He quietly confessed that he had taken strides to control his angry beginning after he had suffered a brutal loss in the makeshift ring they'd used. It was the fight immediately after his first loss. He was hotheaded and too fucking cocky (his words). He went into the ring too soon after his previous loss and against a man with much more experience. He was lucky to walk away.

Then he had to reevaluate everything once again after he was nearly arrested for fighting. On that topic, he didn't expand.

In a soft whisper, he confessed this. He told me that he had put a firm lid on the anger that once ruled his life. Or at least he thought he had until I showed up blooded and bruised and impossibly broken. He said it was the first time he saw red again in so many years. When his voice broke slightly under the immense weight of the memories, I cautiously slid my hand over his jean-clad thigh and squeezed.

I didn't press for details about his parents, although I could sense that there was so much more to the story that maybe I would know eventually.

Luke asked about how Michael and I met and the beginning of our relationship.

I gave him the short version, not wanting to relive those now sickly sweet memories from another life.

Before I knew it, I was curled into his side, my legs slung over his lap as his fingers traced light lines up and down my shins. His fingers only barely touched the hem of my dress at midthigh, but each time he did, I had to forcefully hold back the desire to urge him higher.

We moved on to lighter topics: movies, music, secret hobbies. Although I already knew Luke's old hobby included erotic romance novels—preferably cowboy ones.

The last thing I remembered before my eyes fluttered closed

with Luke's clean, manly scent surrounding me was discussing our favorite comfort TV shows. I must have fallen asleep after conceding that *The Office* was also one of my favorites but only behind *Friends* and *Gilmore Girls*.

I rubbed the sleep from my eyes, then winced when I remembered too late that I had makeup on, hoping I hadn't disturbed it too much. Luke's right arm was banded around me as I lay on his chest, which steadily rose and fell with each even breath. My arm was wrapped around his stomach, and I could feel the shallow indentations of his abdominal muscles under my hand. Each time he breathed out, I could feel his breath on the top of my head.

I peered up at Luke, who lay back on the sofa, his head fallen to the side on the couch cushion. His face was calm and blank, aside from a soft smile playing just at the corners of his lips.

I felt stupid, but I hoped maybe he was dreaming of me.

Although we had just begun a friendship after several years of being neighbors, it didn't feel like we had just met or that we were new friends. Being in his arms, cuddling on his way too damn comfy couch that I always ended up falling asleep on when I was there, felt perfectly normal. It scared me how normal it all seemed.

I needed to find my phone and check the time. I was sure it was late, but I didn't want to move and risk disturbing the peaceful giant under me. So instead, I laid my head back on his shoulder and let my eyes drift closed to the sound of the fire crackling in the background and Sadie snoring on the other side of Luke.

It only seemed like minutes before Luke stirred awake beside me. I didn't open my eyes though, as I felt him stretch and yawn quietly. The pads of his fingers brushed over my cheek as he pushed a stray hair out of my face, tucking it behind my ear. My eyelashes fluttered of their own accord, and he laughed a low, throaty chuckle when I didn't open my eyes or stir.

"I can tell that you're awake." He brushed his thumb over my cheek as I opened my eyes.

"I was just enjoying a few more seconds of... of this."

He made a sound of approval from the back of his throat and pushed my hair out of the way to grip the side of my neck. "You're more than welcome to stay."

At his statement, my eyes popped open. I didn't know what scared me more: the fact that he wanted me to stay or that I sincerely wanted to. But it was all too soon, and everything was moving too quickly. It hadn't been more than a week since I decided to call off the engagement, and Michael had left.

The panic tightened in my chest and felt heavy in my stomach as I stared at Luke's midnight-green eyes. I could tell he was trying to read my facial expression as he squinted in concentration, and even if he asked, I probably wouldn't have been able to tell him what I was feeling. I could barely comprehend my own emotions.

"I can't. This is..." I trailed off as I suddenly needed distance, pulling myself from the couch and finding my phone on the coffee table.

It was almost one in the morning. Luke made like he was going to grab my arm as I moved around the coffee table, but thankfully, he thought better of it and let his hand fall to rest on his thigh.

"I'll walk you out," Luke said instead, rising to his full six-and-a-half-foot height. He straightened his clothes as I did the same before slipping on my boots.

My panic subsided as I realized he wouldn't put up a fight about letting me go home. I kept forgetting that I had my own free will and could do as I pleased. Something I had given up with Michael and was confused about finding again.

I slowly padded through the entryway with Luke next to me. He reached for the door handle before I could, but he paused.

Before he could say anything, I spoke up. "I'm sorry. I'm just a little—"

"Hazel, don't apologize," Luke said, removing his hand from the doorknob and lightly gripping my upper arm. "I understand it. All of it, so you don't have to apologize to me. And I'm going to break you of that habit. You don't need to constantly apologize."

He grasped my chin, urging me to look up at him as he stepped forward. I stayed still as he ran his thumb along my lower lip. "We're on your time line, Angel. But I'd be lying to both of us if I didn't say that I want to see where this goes. I want to see so fucking bad." My eyelids closed as his words washed over me. The panic from just a moment ago was easily appeased when he confirmed he was going to follow my time line. I wasn't sure what my time line looked like since I hadn't given it much thought but knowing that it could be happening with Luke was exciting.

When I opened my eyes again, I immediately found a spark of hunger behind his own that wasn't there before. It lit something in me as well, watching him watch my mouth as his thumb traced just below my bottom lip.

I placed my hands on his chest, pushed up on my toes, and let my mind and the thoughts of how crazy fast we were moving take a back seat as I let my body lead. Luke watched me for a moment before he stooped to press his lips to mine.

Unlike our kiss before, this one was soft yet eager as I tilted my head and ran my tongue against his lips. As his hand shifted to grip the back of my neck—what seemed to be his favorite spot —I let mine reach around his midsection, pulling him closer to me.

It took some serious self-control to not deepen the kiss even further as my entire body thrummed with excitement. When I felt his erection press against my stomach, I knew if I didn't stop then, I would never stop. So reluctantly, and for my own mental health, I pulled away with one last peck on his now wet lips.

He groaned as I planted my feet back on the floor, thus unintentionally sliding myself down his hard-on. I loved the sound so much that it was a miracle I only pressed my face into his chest as he wrapped his arms around me.

"Thank you for tonight. Thank you for everything."

"Anytime, Angel," he murmured against my hair.

And I left. Wrapping my arms around myself in the early morning air and hustled back to my house. Luke watched me with a half smile on his face until I disappeared through the door.

TWENTY-THREE

Hazel

When I stepped up into Luke's truck and out of the cold, rainy morning, I was ecstatic that he insisted on driving. My butt hit the warm passenger seat and I think I might have audibly moaned.

"I thought when I moved to Texas that it would be warm all year around. This weather is miserable," I complained as I buckled and curled up onto the seat, my rain jacket draped over my lap.

Luke chuckled and shook his head, flashing me a wide grin that released butterflies in my stomach. "Well, we do have all four seasons. It's just that they're usually short lived and happen sometimes in the same day or the same week."

He backed out of his driveway—after I insisted that he did not need to drive to my driveway to pick me up—and followed the GPS to the first apartment complex. It was the farthest away—still only twenty minutes from our neighborhood—and the cheapest of the three. It was also the lowest on my list; I wanted to save the best for last, which was the one with an updated fitness center, pool and free Starbucks coffee.

"Well, I don't like this season."

"You look cute all bundled up, though," he said as he glanced at me from the corner of his eye before turning onto the main road.

"What did I tell you about calling grown women cute?"

He laughed but didn't respond.

"I am cozy, but that doesn't mean I like the weather. I like the clothes, but not how cold it is." I was wearing dark jeans, a thick, off-white cable-knit sweater, and a beanie. I layered a white long-sleeved shirt under the sweater to ensure that no cold breeze would slip through the tiny holes in the fabric. I wasn't playing around with being cold.

"I like the hat." Luke smirked as he playfully flicked the maroon pom-pom on top of my beanie. "Although I prefer the halo, I think."

I rolled my eyes. He was never going to let me forget about that damn halo. "You're going to be sorely disappointed when you realize I'm not actually an angel, and the nickname doesn't fit well at all."

He chuckled and scooted farther down in his seat. His right arm was slung over the center console, fingers idly tapping the gearshift as his left elbow perched on the window. He only steered with the first two fingers of his left hand.

There was something about the way he drove with the same relaxed confidence he exuded every time I was near him that made me uncross and recross my legs. He was also freshly showered, and I remembered the way the scent of him—his body wash and whatever else he used—clung to me after I got home the night before. I contemplated sleeping in the dress I wore to dinner just to be able to smell him throughout the night but thought better of it. So, I settled for sleeping with my face in my hair which I splayed out across the pillow. His clean, manly scent and the floral shampoo I used complemented each other well.

"Hmm…" he mused. "I don't think I'd mind at all if you don't turn out to be an angel."

My brows shot to my hairline and I jerked my head at the innuendo-laced comment. I expected him to be laughing at either himself or the shocked expression I knew I wore, but he sat perfectly still and stoned face, staring out the windshield.

"Wait, that's not what I meant."

"I know." He shrugged.

My phone dinged from inside my purse, and I begrudgingly fished it out of the bottom of my bag. I already knew it was my mom, and if it were anyone but her, I would probably ignore it.

Sure enough, it was another plea for me to *see all of the benefits* of moving back to Nashville. For the umpteenth time, I responded by telling her the same thing: no thanks.

"Who is it?" Luke asked as I rolled the tense muscles of my shoulders.

"Just my mom."

He made a sound of understanding.

"She's asking me for the millionth time to move back, and then when I tell her for the millionth time that I'm not going to, she asks why. Every reason I give her, she doesn't understand."

"What does your sister have to say about it?"

I laughed and chucked my phone back in my bag. "Since we moved here, my sister has been the loudest and proudest member of the *I Hate Michael* fan club. She said as long as I'm not going back to him and am making smart decisions, she's going to stay out of it."

"Sounds like a good sisterly stance to take," he agreed, pulling down a street flanked by colorful homes and storefronts. It would have been pretty—pastels and bright colors seemed to be the colors of choice—had it not been for the haunting mist dancing over the roofs and pristine gardens.

"She's usually pretty good about that. She only gives explicit advice when I ask for it, unless she thinks I'm in trouble." It wasn't always like that growing up—she was the typical bossy and nosy sister for most of our lives—but when she met Tony and they began their own family, I was no longer top priority for her worrying. She slowly realized I was a capable adult.

"Well, you can tell her that I'm also now a member of the *I Hate Michael* fan club. Maybe the new loudest and proudest member."

"I'm not sure about that. It would take a lot to beat my sister."

Luke shook his head, eyes darting over to me before he scrubbed his hand across his jaw. He was wearing a gray pullover with the sleeves pulled up around his thick, tattooed forearms, dark jeans, and boots. It was a good look on him.

"I don't know, sweetheart. Finding you in the bathroom and having to fix you up almost broke me. Like I said before, I wanted to kill him."

It almost broke him? I wanted to ask him what he meant and how something happening to me could have possibly affected him so much. But I didn't. The conviction and sincerity in his words kept me silent as we pulled into the small parking lot of apartment complex number one.

"And here we are," Luke said less than enthusiastically.

As I peered around at the two-story buildings surrounding the dilapidated leasing office, I realized I had been catfished. Nothing was as it appeared on the website. I could see the pool through the fence just beyond the leasing office and what had appeared to be a pristine, relaxing area perfect for a summer afternoon was actually a pool closer to the size of a hot tub surrounded by rusty pool chairs.

They had slapped a fresh coat of off-white paint over each building's exterior, but it hadn't covered up the old stucco finish. Sadly, their idea of curb appeal consisted of "Beware of Dog" signs, trash overflowing out of the nearby dumpsters and an old Hyundai with its door falling off.

Next to me, Luke was leaning forward in his seat, squinting into the rearview mirror with an incredulous look on his face.

"What are you looking at?"

He squinted harder. "I think that guy behind us is doing drugs."

I scoffed and whipped around in my seat. "No, he isn't!"

But I was wrong. He was, in fact, doing drugs.

I turned back around in my seat and straightened my beanie, taking one last look around. I spotted a small man behind the desk in the leasing office, and he perked up when we made eye contact through the windshield.

"Well, maybe it'll be better—"

Luke laughed once and put the truck in reverse, leaving no room for argument. "Not happening, Angel. Where's the next stop?"

I plugged the address into his truck's GPS and sat back. It was only a couple of minutes away, and as we drove back the way we came, the sun began to peek out from behind the clouds.

"What's the name of this place?"

I pulled up the website on my phone. "Ella Apartments. The reviews are really good. No mention of tenants doing drugs."

"Yeah, I've heard of that place. Should probably be a good option. One of my friends, James, or maybe it was Devon. Either way, one of them used to live there, I think."

We turned into the parking lot, and my spirits immediately lifted. Everything was the exact opposite of the previous place—neat, trim, kept up. I was worried the entire day would be a bust, and when I spotted the relieved look on Luke's face as he backed into the spot, I knew he had been thinking the same thing.

"Let's go," I said, hopping out of the truck and leaving my rain jacket in the car as the sun evaporated most of the mist. Luke met me on the passenger side of the truck as I slung my purse across my body.

Like it was something he'd always done, he grabbed my hand and led us both inside.

"Pool looks nice," he commented before opening the door for me to step into the well-decorated leasing office.

"Good morning!" a chipper voice greeted us as the click of heels followed. "How are y'all doing? I'm Savannah." The woman appeared through a door at our left and stuck out her hand. Her Southern drawl was thick and made each word a little longer than necessary. Her long blonde hair was perfectly curled, and her ruffled blue blouse matched the blue in the pattern of her pencil skirt. With her heels, she was a few inches taller than me.

"Hi, I'm Hazel," I introduced myself first, shaking her hand and then motioning to Luke just behind me. "And this is Luke."

Quickly, she shifted from me, removing her hand midshake to offer it to Luke. "It's so nice to meet you... both." She added the last part like an afterthought, like she had already forgotten I was there.

Luke pulled his hand back quickly and placed it on his favorite spot at the back of my neck. A gesture that did not go unnoticed by Savannah, who straightened, only letting her beaming white smile slip for a moment.

"So, what can I help y'all with today?"

I cleared my throat, drawing her attention away from Luke and to me. "I'm looking for an apartment."

"Perfect, I'd love to help you. Let's go into the office, and I'll have you fill out some paperwork just so I can get some more information."

We sat down in the office, which was unnecessarily warm and smelled like burned vanilla.

The blonde shuffled a few papers around on her desk, scattering a few on the floor, but she scooped them up quicker than I could even help being the closest to her. She was frazzled and I couldn't imagine it was because I was inquiring about apartment availability. I had a feeling it was because of the man now gripping my thigh as we waited for the necessary paperwork.

"I'm sorry, I'm a little out of sorts this morning. Y'all came on in before I had a chance to grab my coffee. Here it is," she said, sliding a piece of paper and a pen to me. "Just fill this out while I go grab that coffee. Can I get y'all anything?"

"We're fine, thanks," Luke answered for us both, and I could feel the warmth of his hand seeping through my jeans and to my thigh. His hand had migrated up just enough that I suddenly forgot my birth date and most of the other information required on the stupid form.

I shifted in my chair and nudged him. "I can't think straight when you're grabbing me like that."

He chuckled but moved his hand closer to my knee, still keeping his grip tight. "Sorry, I have a hard time not touching you, and I get a little carried away sometimes."

I bit my lower lip as I tried to contain the smile that threatened to split my face at his words. "I like it when you touch me," I said while throwing him a face that warned him not to make a sexual joke before continuing, "but it makes me lose focus."

"I'll try to behave," he said through a lopsided grin, showing off that dimple again.

"Good."

By the time Savannah returned with a large "Don't Mess with Texas" mug full of coffee, I had finished the form and was nervously waiting to get started. Luke had already asked me to quit fidgeting twice and moved his hand back up my thigh. His fingers were encroaching awfully close to a place that I had longed for him to be for a while. With his hand there, it was the only thing I could focus on, and the nerves dissipated. He laughed, gauging my reaction.

"Okay, great. So, you're looking for a one-bedroom apartment for an immediate move-in." She pulled out another paper with a few different one-bedroom floor plan options and was relatively professional throughout her presentation. I only caught her batting her lashes at Luke twice.

"Which one do you think you're interested in?" she asked.

I glanced at each. "They're all fine. I just need something that's available as soon as possible."

"Got it. If that's the case, then this one will be available in two weeks." I cringed because even two weeks was pushing my time line—I wanted to be out of the house in no more than a week. I couldn't risk Michael coming back with me still living in the house.

Even with the possibility that it might be too far off, I asked to see that floor plan. We were already there anyway.

As we walked to the model, she showed us all the amenities and discussed the perks in depth. There was an upgraded twenty-four-hour gym, an Olympic-sized pool, two hot tubs, and anything else my heart could desire.

The model was nice, with quartz countertops and dark cabinets. The fixtures were new, and I made sure to confirm with Savannah—who, might I add, was gawking at Luke from across the room—that it was exactly what the apartment coming available would look like.

"Yes, it will be identical to this, except there will be carpet in the bedroom."

I nodded and crossed the living room and out onto the balcony where Luke was inspecting the outside. "What do you think?"

He tossed his head from side to side for a second, then shrugged. "It's nice. You can tell that they used cheap materials and cut corners on quite a few things, but it's not the worst I've seen, especially for the price."

"That's what I was thinking," I said.

"Will two weeks work though? When do you need to be out?" he said carefully, running a hand down my arm.

"Ideally, by the end of this week, but I'm not sure I have much of an option if I want something decent. I mean, I'm sure the last place would lease me an apartment today," I laughed, but Luke didn't return it.

"That's never happening, but you're right. If anything, you can just stay with me until you can move in here."

"Luke, I could—"

"We have one more place to see, right?" he cut me off as I began to argue. If we were going along with my time line that absolutely didn't include moving in with him so soon.

"Yes, one more on the list."

He nodded. "Then let's go see that one and go from there, okay?"

I mumbled my agreement before heading back inside and letting Savannah know that I would keep it on the list and that I really needed an earlier move-in date. She said exactly what I expected her to say—a week move-in would be hard to come by anywhere.

She led us back to the leasing office, where she gave me her card and a folder with all of the information. I waved goodbye and thanked her for her help as Luke warmed up the truck outside.

"What are you doing?" I asked, finding him leaned up against the passenger side door with the truck still running. He pushed off the truck and opened the door, waving at me to jump in.

I threw my head back and laughed but hopped up. He rounded the front of the truck, keeping his eyes on me the entire time before he also got in.

"You look shocked that I'd open the door for you," he said, like my reaction was crazy.

I plugged the last address into the GPS and warmed my hands up close to the vents. "I kind of am."

"Well, you should get used to it," he said as he placed his hand on my thigh.

"Hmm... that address sounds familiar."

"It's right by our neighborhood, maybe that's why," I said, but as we got closer to our third stop, Luke's grip on my thigh became increasingly tight. The muscles in his shoulders stiffened and his brow furrowed into deep set lines. Whatever he was feeling was palpable and made the air in the cabin of the truck thick.

"What's wrong?" I finally asked as we pulled to an abrupt stop just on the other side of the gate and in a spot with a *"future resident"* sign in front of it.

When Luke pulled his hand away, lifting to grip the wheel, I noticed he was shaking and breathing hard.

"Luke, you're scaring me," I said, unbuckling and poising myself over the center console. "What's going on?"

TWENTY-FOUR

Hazel

Luke took one deep breath, closing his eyes and letting his head fall back onto the headrest. "This is the apartment I lived in during and after my divorce. I have some… shitty memories from when I was living here."

"Okay, well, we do not need to go inside. Just give me a minute, and let me look at this app. There're a few other places I liked." I reached to pull out my phone, but Luke's hand wrapped around my wrist, stilling me.

"No, we should go in. This apartment was really nice, and you need something sooner rather than later. I'll be fine, just give me a second."

He rolled his head along his shoulders and took one final deep breath before giving me a steady, serious look. The nosiest parts of me wanted to immediately ask what the hell could have happened to make him react that way, but I bit my tongue. There were certain things I wasn't ready to talk about either but seeing him get upset had me buzzing to fix it all.

Luke must've seen the question in my face because he huffed out a breath and instead of turning to exit the truck, he settled back in the seat. "I got divorced not long before I moved in next door to you. For about a year, and while I was going through all of that, I lived here. Our divorce was not… easy." His tone was robotic, like he was reading off a script in his head and memorized all the details earlier. "There were some very important irreconcilable differences."

I nodded, trying to keep my expression unreadable.

"We had a few incidents that happened here, and they were not exactly good memories. I didn't realize this place would still be an issue for me all these years later."

I could feel my stomach roll and my mouth was suddenly dry. "Incidents?" I asked in a small voice, hoping that their incidents were nothing like mine.

"Hazel, no," he said, reading my expression and the tone of my voice. "I absolutely never touched her like that. I swear to you I would never hit a woman." He wrapped my hands together in his and looked me directly in the eye. If he was lying, I saw no trace of it. All his actions up until that point also told me he was telling the truth.

"I believe you."

"Good, good. God," he sighed. "This is not how I was hoping today would go. Just… Valerie was very upset about the divorce. She created a lot of problems for me, and I was eventually able to get a protective order before the divorce was finalized."

"Shit," I murmured. *Valerie.* I knew after having done my own research that the evidence required to get a protective order had to be detailed and obvious. I couldn't imagine—nor did I want to imagine—what likely occurred to enable him to get the order.

"Luke, I'm serious, we don't need to go in. I had other options…" Before I even finished the sentence, he was shaking his head.

"Nope, let's go. I'm going to be fine," he said as he hopped out of the car, effectively ending the conversation and giving me no choice but to follow him.

. . .

Not surprisingly, it wasn't exactly fine.

Just as Luke said, though, the complex was pretty amazing. Each space was renovated and there were more amenities than I could ever need.

The one-bedroom apartment the leasing agent showed us was larger than the second place and had nicer finishes. Luke agreed that it was a better deal, even if it was more expensive.

But his reaction to walking around the complex—especially the way his entire body tensed when we walked past his old apartment and the way he shuddered slightly when he looked at the small balcony for a second too long—made it obvious that it wasn't actually fine.

Back in the truck, Luke seemed to visibly relax when he shut the door and cranked the heat in the cabin. He rolled his shoulders and let out a long breath.

The leasing agent said they wouldn't have a one-bedroom available for more than a month. However, they had several two-bedroom options available immediately. I could have probably afforded the two-bedroom if I had cut down on other expenses—fewer books each month or less eating out—but I didn't want to have to cut back on all of the little things I enjoyed. Coffee and books were two things I enjoyed immensely.

It was also more than obvious that the apartment complex would likely never be an okay place for Luke. He had too many ghosts lurking around that place, and it was scary to admit to myself—even if it was just in my own head—but he had just entered my life and was making himself at home. I knew if I moved in there, he would suffer through visiting me or I would see less of him.

The idea of seeing less of him was... not my favorite.

"So, the two-bedroom sounds like a good deal," Luke said. Although a lot of the tension had left his body, his leg still bounced as he clicked his seat belt.

I also buckled and made a sound of disagreement. "It does

sound like a good deal, but I'd have to rework my budget. I'm not sure I can swing it without cutting out a few things."

He nodded and began to say something, but the ringing of his phone over the truck's Bluetooth cut him off. His brow furrowed when the "Unknown Number" caller ID popped up on the screen between us. He immediately declined the call with a quick shake of his head.

"Spam calls on a Saturday? That should be illegal. I mean, they deserve a few days off, too, right?" I laughed.

My joke fell flat, although I wasn't expecting a full belly laugh or anything. Just a pity laugh would have sufficed, and I could tell that going back there had ruined his whole mood.

I wanted to know what the hell happened. And it was on the tip of my tongue to ask until my phone ringing interrupted my thoughts.

A familiar number with an Austin area code scrolled across the screen.

"Hello?" I answered as Luke shot me a curious look.

"Hi, is this Hazel?" a sweet, Southern drawl asked on the other line.

"Yes, this is she."

"Hi, sweetie, this is Savannah from the leasing office at Ella Apartments."

"Hi, Savannah," I said. I glanced at Luke, who gave me a questioning look as I shrugged.

"I just wanted to let you know that I was mistaken earlier. We will have a one-bedroom unit available by the end of this week if it's something you're interested in. I know the time line was important to you."

"Yes, I'm interested!" I all but yelled down the phone and quickly settled down when Luke began to laugh next to me.

"I figured you would say that. I will say, though, that if you want to lease this unit, y'all should come back and fill out this paperwork immediately. There're a few things to take care of in the office here, and then the rest can be done online."

"Okay, we'll head back that way now. Thank you so much for letting me know."

She laughed over the line as Luke pulled into a left-hand turn lane to go back toward Ella Apartments, the second spot we looked at.

I disconnected the call and did a small happy dance in my seat, which consisted of me wiggling back and forth and punching the air. I didn't care if I looked like an idiot. I was too freaking excited.

"They have a unit available at the end of the week," I relayed to Luke as he stopped at the light right outside of the complex.

"Sweet. I think that place will work out well for you."

I nodded. I hoped it would work out well. "Maybe Savannah pulled some strings to be able to see you again. It wouldn't surprise me the way she was staring at you the entire time."

Luke laughed and rolled his eyes. "What are you talking about?"

"You can't tell me you didn't notice her gawking and obnoxiously flirting the entire time we were there. Or that her boobs are huge and pushed up to her nose."

He narrowed his eyes and rubbed his hand over his chin. "Yeah, her boobs were pretty hard to miss, especially in such a low-cut top."

I jerked my head forward and tried not to react to his comment. It wasn't what I was expecting in the least, but I didn't have a say in the women he found interest in or where he looked. Even though I knew I didn't have a right to feel those things, it didn't make the feelings of disappointment any less real.

Luke pulled into the same parking spot we had stopped in a few hours earlier and chuckled. I couldn't look at him though, otherwise I knew he'd see my emotions clearly written on my face. I needed to get my reactions under control.

When the truck was in park, Luke reached over the center

console to grip the back of my neck and urged me to look at him. His thumb softly rubbed back and forth over my cheek while he held my eyes with his own. Humor danced playfully behind his emerald-green gaze as a sly smile pulled at one corner of his mouth.

"I'm kidding, Angel. I seriously didn't notice much about her past shaking her hand. I had other things on my mind." He chuckled.

I shrugged and tried to seem nonchalant. "That's fine. You're a single guy, and you can look at whoever you want, whenever you want."

He quirked a brow and opened his mouth to respond before shutting it again. He shook his head and then said, "I'm a little preoccupied with this beautiful brunette. Seems like I can't focus on anything else at the fucking moment. If you must know."

I wanted him to kiss me. The words coming out of his mouth were as sweet as his lips actually were, and I needed to feel them on mine again. His constant contact all day long—holding my hand, gripping my thighs, grasping the back of my neck—had me wound tight.

For a moment, it looked like he wouldn't kiss me as he hesitated. His eyes flitted back and forth from holding my gaze to my lips and back again. I didn't know what it was that was causing his hesitation, but I was ready for good things in my life, and he seemed to be one of the good things. So, I closed the gap between us.

I pushed against the center console with my forearms and pressed a soft kiss to his lips. I didn't mean to let the kiss linger for more than a moment, but Luke had other ideas. He used his grip on the back of my neck to deepen our kiss and hold me to him.

The kiss still wasn't long and only lasted a few seconds before we both pulled back. I had to bite my lip to keep the cheesy grin from splitting my face, but I couldn't do anything about the flush spreading over my cheeks.

With another kiss to my forehead, Luke released me and hopped out of the truck. I fixed my beanie before I also jumped out of the truck—literally, I had to jump—and tangled my fingers with Luke's as he reached out his hand from where he stood.

"Looks like it's all working out," Luke said.

I smiled. "Looks like it."

TWENTY-FIVE

Luke

For the twentieth time that day, my phone buzzed with a call from an unknown number.

I had tried to ignore them for as long as I could, but I eventually got fed up and answered one of the calls two days earlier. I had some colorful words for the person on the other line who only breathed deeply as I berated their attempts to get ahold of me. I made veiled threats toward them if they didn't stop, and the following day, there were no calls.

My relief was short lived, though, because the calls had begun again.

Josh had witnessed me almost chuck my phone across the fucking living room while he was leaving to go to Murphy's and as I was finally getting home from a long day at the clinic.

"Dude, just answer and don't say anything. They'll think they've got a wrong number or something and will take your name off the list. It's worked for me a few times in the past," Josh instructed.

It was the first time I'd seen him in several days. I worked long days, and he worked from evening until well past two in the morning at the bar. It was lucky if I saw him at all.

"Thanks. I'll try that the next time they call, which will probably be in the next ten minutes," I said as Josh put his empty dinner plate in the dishwasher and rinsed off his hands. "Everything good with you?" I asked before he could sprint out of the house. Based on the time, I knew he was running behind, but I wanted to check in.

"Yeah, man. All good on this front. Actually, I was going to ask, are we still doing Friendsgiving here this year?"

The annual Friendsgiving celebration had completely slipped my mind. It seemed since that stupid fucking Halloween party, Hazel had held most of my attention and thoughts whether she was around or not.

"Yeah, of course. I'll send out a text to everyone with details soon."

"You bringing Hazel?" Josh asked and waggled his eyebrows suggestively.

I rolled my eyes and playfully shoved him in the arm. "Dude, seriously? Why do you have to say it like that?"

Josh shrugged as he tossed on his jacket and grabbed his keys. "I know you've got a thing going, so it was just a simple question. Don't get all bent out of shape about it."

"I don't know if we have a thing going…" I muttered.

"Have you slept with her?"

I shook my head.

"There's no way you haven't at least kissed her though, right?"

I nodded my confirmation. Somehow words were escaping me.

"So, it's definitely a *thing*," he said, using his fingers as air quotes. "Only a matter of time."

He waved and was gone before I had a chance to roll my eyes again. But who was I kidding? The possibility of sex with Hazel was a thought that crossed my mind way too often and always at the absolute worst times.

I shook off the arousal and let Sadie out the back door. She happily trotted to the center of the yard, did her business, and then plopped in a spot where the last of the day's sun was shining on the grass.

I refilled Sadie's water bowl and filled her food bowl for when she decided to come back inside. I was watching her through the back window, moving as the sun moved around the yard and just finishing the rest of the dishes left in the sink, when my phone rang again with a call from the fucking unknown number.

It took effort to tamp down my anger and not go off on the prick again, but I successfully answered the phone and immediately hit the mute button.

I waited, irritated and tapping my foot on the tile floor in the kitchen as I stared at the phone on the counter. After thirty seconds had elapsed and I heard nothing on the line, I reached for the disconnect button just as a voice quietly said, "Shit, seriously?" before the call dropped.

My hand hovered over my phone, the screen going black, and a strange feeling washed over me. A feeling like I'd heard that damn voice before, but I couldn't place it. The words were whispered and muffled, so it was possible that I had misheard the voice. But it didn't feel likely.

Sadie pulled me from my thoughts as she pushed in through the back door. I shut and locked it behind her and started toward my bedroom for a shower when I noticed Hazel outside, walking back to her house. Chris watched her go with an unwavering intensity.

Hazel was wearing a long-sleeve workout top that only barely brushed the top of her high-waisted leggings. I stepped up to the front window and glared at Chris, whose stare was glued on Hazel's ass.

Yes, the leggings hugged her muscular legs in all the right

ways, but he didn't need to openly gawk. He glanced around for a moment as Hazel got to the bottom of her porch and suddenly started walking toward her.

I couldn't deal with any more fuckers fucking with Hazel. Without thinking past my immediate anger, I ripped my front door open, which effectively stopped Chris in his tracks. I stepped onto the porch and casually pushed my hands into the pockets of my scrubs. He was just past the end of my walkway, and I let him see the fire his behavior was stoking inside of me. The flames were lapping and ready to be released if he even took one more fucking step.

When I knew he wasn't continuing his approach, I turned to give Hazel a small smile as she paused on her front porch.

"Good run?" I asked, keeping my voice light and friendly. And the exact opposite of what I was feeling at that moment.

She darted her eyes back and forth from me to Chris, who was still frozen midstep on the sidewalk.

"Yup," she responded.

"Good. Have a good night, babe." I added the pet name at the end for Chris's benefit and it was worth it to see the hostility cross his face. I would have loved to beat the shit out of the fucker if he'd only given me another opportunity. The nice guy with zero anger issues didn't have a chance when Hazel was around.

"You too," Hazel said before throwing one last glance at Chris over her shoulder and walking inside her house. I couldn't hear the click of her front door locking, but I didn't doubt she'd immediately moved the dead bolt into place just as she stepped inside.

With Hazel safe, I turned my attention back to Chris, who was outwardly fuming. He shifted and opened his mouth like he was going to say something, but smartly thought better of it.

He stomped back to his house like a two-year-old throwing a tantrum. I walked back inside with a smug grin as my phone vibrated in my pocket.

Hazel: THANK YOU

Me: Anytime, Angel. Guy's a fucking creep.

As I waited for her response, I grabbed my Bluetooth speaker from the kitchen and headed to take a shower that I so desperately needed. Not one but two dogs pooped directly on me, and even changing my scrubs and scrubbing my arms didn't make me feel any cleaner. I needed a long, hot shower.

I flipped on the Bluetooth speaker, turned the water in the shower to a skin-melting temperature and read Hazel's response.

Hazel: 100%. When a guy says that his wife is cockblocking him...

Me: What a piece of shit. Want me to beat his ass?

Hazel: I think you staring him down worked for now at least. You can look seriously mean and intimidating when you want to

Me: What do you mean when I want to? I always look mean and intimidating.

Hazel: Sure. You keep telling yourself that, tough guy

I rolled my eyes at her sassy reply but was secretly excited the more and more she seemed to return to her snarky self. I had missed her witty comebacks and our verbal sparring matches.

We had been texting back and forth since we went our separate ways after a long day spent apartment hunting. I sincerely believed that my reaction to the third apartment complex we toured—the one where my divorce became nasty and violent—would dissuade Hazel from wanting anything to do with me.

She had just left a fucked-up relationship, the last thing she needed was some guy who couldn't keep his emotions in check because of shit that had happened several years before.

But I was nonetheless happy—fucking ecstatic—that Hazel took my emotions in stride. She listened to what I had to say and didn't press for too much more information than I was willing to fork over.

I had to worry about the present, though, because the idea of telling her much more than I already had about my fucked-up past had me an anxious and stressed-out mess. Some of it I knew could be a deal breaker, especially for her.

And I wasn't ready to risk telling her at that point—the selfish part of me wanted to keep our good thing going. Before we got too serious—if it ever came to that—I would tell her.

We both deserved some happy shit in our lives.

The long shower I thought I wanted to take didn't seem so nice when I knew I could be talking to Hazel. *Fuck*, yeah, I knew I had it bad.

I did, however, make sure to scrub all of the possibly lingering fecal matter from my body and stood with my head bowed under the warm spray, slowly walking the temperature of the water higher until it couldn't go any warmer.

I stepped out of the shower with relaxed muscles as the steam wafted through the air and fogged up the mirror. All my large towels were dirty—courtesy of Josh—so I wrapped a regular-sized towel around my waist the best I could. A regular person would have done fine with the towel, but there was a good almost two-inch gap where you could see most of my right thigh and part of my dick if you were looking closely.

I retrieved my phone from the counter, thought for a minute and then shot a text back to my neighbor.

Me: What are you up to tonight?

I stepped out of the bathroom, hoping the towel would stay

around my waist for a moment until I could find a pair of sweatpants and dry off properly, when I spotted the lights on in Hazel's bedroom. The warm light of her room was inviting—or at least that's what I told myself—as I stopped to peer through the curtains.

Her blinds were open, so I had a clear line of sight into her bedroom. I could tell, based on the pictures she had removed from the walls, the piles of clothes on the floor and a few boxes stacked in the corner, that she was in full packing swing. With her lease signed and a plan in place, I could tell she was feeling better. It also helped that the bruises were fading—or at least the ones on the outside.

Hazel was perched on the end of their king-size bed, the white comforter pulled up and the pillows placed perfectly at the top of the bed. She was still wearing her black leggings, but it looked like she had already shed her long-sleeved top from earlier and was now only in a dark-green sports bra. Her legs were dangling off the end of the bed, swinging as she drank from her water bottle and typed on her phone.

She dropped her phone to her side and held her large water with two hands before she returned her attention to the TV in front of her. My phone buzzed right on cue.

Hazel: Packing, packing and more packing. May try to write some, too.

Me: How is the packing going? I'll come over soon to help out. Also, glad to see you haven't lost your writing muse.

I sent the text and immediately watched through the window to see her response. My chest tightened when she picked up her phone and a huge smile spread across her face. She squeezed her water bottle between her legs so she could type using both hands.

Hazel: I would never turn down free packing help, and yes, the muse is still around. He's actually making it hard to focus on anything else at this point. I can't write fast enough.

She gave me an update on her writing every day. She was writing thousands of words a day and had already begun outlining her next book. Even over the phone and through texts, her excitement about what she was creating was palpable. She still wouldn't tell me anything about the plot or any other details besides how it was going, but I was supportive of anything that kept the fucking breathtaking smile on her face.

Before I had a chance to respond, she texted again.

Hazel: What are your plans for the night?

I contemplated my response only for a second before I began typing.

Me: Well, I'm currently enjoying the view outside of my bedroom window.

It was a ballsy text and could have sounded incredibly creepy. But that's not how I meant it. I didn't intentionally leave my curtains open and I'm sure she didn't either.

She reached for her phone, another smile pulling at the corners of her mouth before it suddenly dropped, and she slowly swiveled her head to peer out of her window.

Okay, yeah, it was a little fucking creepy.

I gave her my best noncreepy smile and waved. For a long moment, she didn't move. She was frozen with her water bottle held to her perfectly pouty lips and her phone in her other hand. She held my stare without moving for far too long, I started to believe I had genuinely fucked up.

I typed out a quick message and hit send.

Me: I wasn't trying to be creepy. I swear. I was just getting out of the shower and saw you.

My text had her attention, and she finally pulled her eyes away from my own. She hopped off of her bed and set her water bottle on the dresser across from her. Her head was tilted down as she read my message and typed what I hoped would be a response back. I wanted to read her facial expression, but she kept her face averted.

I anxiously watched my phone, my eyes flitting back and forth from Hazel to my dark screen. When the text finally came through, I let out a deep breath and opened it.

Hazel: If it were anyone else, it might have been creepy... and not sure you know or not, but your towel is WAY too small for you. I can see a lot even from over here

I read the text once and then a second time before looking up to find Hazel staring at me with her bottom lip pulled between her teeth. And although I wasn't as close as I wanted to be, I believed it was barely restrained desire flaming in her eyes.

And *God*, did I want to burn in it.

TWENTY-SIX

Luke

Hazel's long brown hair was pulled back at the top of her head, and the sheen of sweat still lingering on her skin—especially over her chest that was close to spilling out of her damn bra—was mesmerizing. I wanted to taste the salty tang of her sweat mixed with the sweetness of her skin as I memorized every curve and dip of her body with my tongue.

I inched closer to the window, not worrying too much when the towel separated a little more. Just another half an inch and she would see exactly how hard she made me by doing almost nothing.

Her eyes stayed locked on my face for an extra second before they ran down my naked chest and towel-clad waist.

I craved to be closer to her. I wanted to know if her breath quickened when she saw the way my cock tented the towel or if her heart was beating out of her fucking chest like mine felt like it was about to.

I needed to see the desire flare behind her eyes—I'd only had a little taste of it before. My only sign that I was affecting her was the quickened rise and fall of her chest. There was also the way she twisted her legs together to relieve some of the pressure likely growing there and how she couldn't look away from me.

Me: Glad to know I'm not the only one staring. You look so good right now. I could lick the sweat right off you.

Once I sent the text, I anxiously waited to watch her response and read her reply. A mischievous grin spread across her face, and I couldn't help but mimic it with my own.

Hazel: I think I'd like that.

Me: Angel, I know you would like everything I can do with my tongue.

Her hand went to her mouth, trying to hide her reaction and proving that I'd hit my intended mark. I could have immediately thrown up the window and climbed into her bedroom to make good on my promise. I could have even found the sweatpants I had initially been searching for and actually walked out the front door. I could have done a number of things to actually be able to touch her and feel her, which sounded more and more like a good idea as the seconds ticked by. But I didn't think she was ready.

After what she had gone through with fuckface, her bruises were healing, but the scars were deep. Each interaction we'd had proved that it would be better for her to take it slow. No matter how much it killed me or gave me the bluest fucking balls known to man, I'd wait until she was ready.

Hazel: You know for a fact, huh? Well, maybe one day we can test that theory. But for now…

Me: I promise one day we will test that theory, because we'd both thoroughly enjoy it. But, for now?

Her response was immediate, and I let out a pained groan when I read the short text.

Hazel: Take off the towel and show me what I'm missing.

All reason had already gone out the fucking window where she was concerned. *No pun intended.*

So, I set my phone on the windowsill and made sure Hazel's eyes were on me before I untucked the small piece of towel still hanging on and let it drop at my feet in a damp pile.

I had nothing to be ashamed of, and I craved her reaction. Unlike what I thought would happen, her eyes didn't immediately dart to my dick that bobbed long and seriously fucking hard in front of me.

Her eyes began a slow perusal from my face, down my tattooed chest and torso and continued until the tattoos ended just past my waistline. When she saw me in all my glory, I witnessed her sharp intake of breath as she bit her lip.

I gripped the base of myself, squeezing as a drop of precum beaded at the tip. Watching her watch me as I pumped my hand up and down my shaft made me delirious. It took all my self-control not to beckon her over to me as I thought about what her soft, little hands would feel like wrapped around my length. She'd probably have no problem using two hands to work me over, and my dick throbbed with the mental images that appeared behind my eyes.

Before I could let what little of my self-control I still possessed shatter, I had another idea that may have comfortably inched her in the direction I knew we both wanted to go. The end result we both wanted: my cock buried deep inside her tight, warm cunt. But we would get there on her time line.

Her time line, not mine, because mine would have had me already in her bedroom with my mouth between her legs. So, option two it was.

I grabbed my phone, still slowly stroking myself, and dialed

Hazel's number. When I put my phone to my ear, her brow furrowed, and she reluctantly answered her own phone.

"Yes?" she asked in a soft voice.

"Hi, Angel."

"Hi."

"Are you enjoying your view?"

She laughed but didn't tear her eyes away from me. "Yes," she said breathlessly.

"It looks like you're a little overdressed for this party, don't you think?"

Her eyebrows shot up as she glanced down at her sports bra and leggings. She nervously crossed an arm in front of herself as she recrossed her legs.

"Am I?" Her voice was reluctant, but I pressed on.

"Yes, you most definitely are. But that can be easily remedied."

I continued the slow strokes up and down my dick as I held the phone to my ear. If this continued in the direction I was hoping it would go, it was going to be difficult to stay standing.

"Luke, I—" she began to protest.

"Angel, do you trust me?" I saw her eyes flutter as she rolled them, and I scoffed. "Have I ever given you a reason not to trust me?" I reworded the question.

She shook her head, but I needed more than that. "Answer me."

"No, you've never given me a reason not to trust you."

Just the sound of her voice made my balls tighten and whatever blood was still in the rest of my body made its way to my dick.

"Okay, so take your clothes off." I could see the gears turning in her head as she contemplated my demand and probably wondered how far I would take it.

It wasn't until she set the phone down on the dresser, with her hip still pressed against the drawers, and turned on the speakerphone that a victorious smile crossed my face. Her movements became rushed and awkward as she toed off her sneakers and yanked off her neon socks.

"Slowly, please," I said, and then added, "there's no need to rush when we have all night."

She stopped with her hands poised at the top of her leggings. Her fingers had barely breached the fabric there when her eyes darted back to me. With a shake of her head, she said, "So you're going to demand that I undress and then tell me how to?"

I laughed. "It's like opening a present that I've been waiting years for. I want to take my time peeling back each layer and appreciate it fully as I unwrap it."

"Sounds like you're getting a lot of pleasure out of this."

"Mmm... I am, and I will. But don't worry, beautiful girl, I'll make sure you do, too."

She continued undressing just the way I wanted her to, by dipping her hands teasingly under her leggings and running her fingers across her stomach to her hips. She pushed them down her legs, revealing each inch of her pale legs with a teasingly unhurried pace.

She used her foot to kick them to the side and stood confidently with only her sports bra and a black thong left.

"What next?" she asked with a small grin, licking her lower lip as her eyes watched me continue to tease the shit out of myself. "You want to make the rules, so what do you want me to take off next?"

A sound erupted from the back of my throat that resembled a growl. It was a sound I'd never made before, but she was playing along, and it was doing things to me that I couldn't control.

"Take your hair down," I requested through clenched teeth.

She immediately did so, letting her dark-brown locks fall over her shoulders before she ran a hand through it.

I loosened my grip, just holding the base of myself because at the rate we were going, I would have blown my load long before she'd even been completely undressed.

"Bra next."

She ran her fingers over her collarbones and pushed the hair that had fallen forward back over her shoulders. Her touch looked featherlight over her skin, and I wondered if she had goose bumps. She pushed a strap down on one side and touched the skin of her shoulder. Her hands lightly trailed down until she rubbed back and forth over the lower band of the bra.

I was about to lose my mind. "Angel..." I groaned, "please."

She laughed and it was a bright, playful sound. "Since you asked so nicely." As she pulled off the fabric of the bra, I heard it over the phone and watched her breasts spring free. They were perfect handfuls, and her nipples were already hard.

She tossed her bra over to where she had already discarded her leggings and cupped both her breasts in her hands.

"Better?" she asked as she tweaked her nipples and let out her first soft moan. It was the most beautiful sound I'd ever heard.

"You're so fucking beautiful," I said when I was finally able to get myself together again. "Keep going."

I didn't have to ask twice and was pleasantly surprised when she didn't tease me with her thong. Instead, she simply slipped her hand beneath the small piece of fabric and pushed it down her legs. Once she stood up after throwing her thong into the small pile of clothes behind her, and I saw the neat triangle of dark hair between her hips, the rest of my self-control snapped.

I pulled a chair from the other side of my dresser and positioned it directly in front of the window before I plopped down into it. I set my phone on the windowsill, turned on the speaker, and leaned back. At that point, I couldn't not grab myself, so I roughly gripped the base of my dick.

Hazel hadn't moved in the few seconds I took to retrieve the chair, but she seemed slightly more nervous now that she was completely nude.

"You still with me, beautiful?"

She nodded tentatively and then said, "Yes," in a shaky voice.

"There's no reason to be nervous. Do you see what you're doing to me?" Her eyes darted down to my dick, which was standing at full attention and harder than ever before.

"Yes." Her voice was still soft, but not nearly as nervous.

"You do this to me, beautiful. You're so perfect."

She scoffed and twirled her fingers through her hair, bringing a few strands in front of her and over her shoulder.

"I'm serious. You're absolutely perfect, and if you think anything less than that, then you're wrong."

"I'm wrong?" she asked, still twirling her damn hair, but I had a better plan for her hands.

"Yes, now, do you still trust me?"

"Yes."

"Get on top of your dresser, as close to the window as you can."

Her eyes widened slightly, and after a moment's hesitation, she did. She moved closer to the window, turned her back to the dresser and effortlessly pushed herself up. Her butt landed on the smooth wood top, and she reached to move her phone closer before she turned her head back to me, waiting for further instruction.

"Turn toward me and open your legs."

She nervously bit her bottom lip and twisted her hands in her lap.

"I need to see you," I added, and after a deep breath that raised her shoulders high, she turned. She propped one foot on the edge of the dresser and let the other hang off the side. Besides the small triangle of dark hair, she was bare, and I could see her wetness already glistening. She scooted her hips closer to the edge of the dresser without me having to ask, and I had a decent view of her. But nothing would ever be enough until I could run my fingers through every fold, circle her clit with my tongue and plunge my fingers inside of her. Even then, I didn't know if I'd ever get enough.

"That's such a good girl," I said, and her eyes fluttered shut for a second before they lazily opened again.

I chuckled darkly. "Do you like it when I call you a good girl?"

"Yes. Yes, I do," she said with renewed confidence.

"You are such a good girl. Now, I want you to play with yourself. I want to see you come."

I thought we were past the nerves, but I should have known better. It was one thing to be naked in front of someone else, but it was something else to bare everything by touching your most private areas with the intent of completely coming undone.

"Don't be nervous," I said when I noticed her grip on her thighs tighten and her breathing stopped. "You've touched yourself before, right?"

She nodded, and I wasn't going to force her to confirm out loud.

"Good, so just do whatever you usually do to get yourself off. I'm going to love anything you do to yourself, Angel. I need to see you come apart, and I'm going to be right there with you."

She didn't move, and I stopped stroking myself, although my whole body hated the lack of friction.

"Do you want to stop?" I asked, giving her a clear out.

"No," she said resolutely, meeting my eyes and relaxing her grip on her thighs.

"Then touch yourself."

When she flipped her hair over her shoulder and leaned back on one hand while slowly bringing the other toward where I wanted to see it most, I replaced my hand around my cock, willing myself to hang on for at least a few minutes.

She pushed her hand lower and spread her fingers so they ran down both of her lower lips. She teased herself, touching everywhere except where I knew she probably wanted to the most.

For being so nervous only a minute ago, her hand was confident.

She reached her hand up to her mouth and sucked her two middle fingers into her mouth.

"Dear God, Angel," I groaned, watching her wet her fingers before pressing them to her clit. She tossed back her head, letting it fall between her shoulders and a moan, so much louder than any of the ones before, clawed its way up her throat.

Her motions became more hurried as she rubbed circles over her clit before dipping a finger into her pussy. She gasped at the intrusion but pushed her middle finger all the way in as her hips pushed to meet it.

"Look at me," I growled, needing to see her face as she finger fucked herself. She raised her head, eyes hooded with pleasure and her lips parted. I could hear her little pants through the phone but wanted more. I imagined that I could feel each little breath on my lips or my neck as I fingered her wet heat.

"Are you going to come like a good girl?" Now that I knew she liked it, I wanted her to be my good girl.

"Yes, I'm already close," she pleaded.

"Add another finger," I instructed, and she did with a low groan.

She rubbed her clit against the heel of her palm as she pushed the two fingers deeper. As her movements intensified, the quicker my strokes became, but I wasn't going to come until she did.

"That's so good. When you come, when you clench around your fingers," I said with my jaw tight, desire clouding my vision. "I want you to imagine it's my fingers inside of you. Show me how bad you want my fingers in you, Angel. How bad you want my cock."

As the last words left my mouth, she cried out her blissful release. She kept her head forward so I could see the contortion of her features as her movements mostly stopped besides the short thrusts of her hips as she rode out each wave.

She moaned out a broken "yes," followed by my name, and then I was done. The orgasm I had kept on a short leash the entire time reared back and crashed over me. Two more hard strokes were all it took as my balls drew up, and I groaned my release.

It took me a minute to recover and for the post-orgasm fog to lift. My hand and stomach were coated in my release, and I seriously needed another shower.

Hazel was still perched on the edge of the dresser, heaving deep breaths and watching me through hooded eyes. A lazy smile tugged at the corners of her mouth as she enjoyed her own post-O joy.

"That was fun," she said before dropping her legs together and scooting carefully onto the floor. Her legs buckled slightly, but she quickly recovered, pulling her phone to her ear. I did the same, taking the phone off speaker and settling back into my chair while using my towel to wipe off my hand and stomach.

"Agreed." I chuckled.

"I guess I should go pack. You did give me some good ideas about a scene I should add to my book, though. I think I might have to put my thoughts down first, otherwise, I won't get any packing done." She wiggled her eyebrows up and down before scooping her clothes from the floor.

"If you need more inspiration, just remember, I'm right next door."

"How could I forget?"

I laughed. "I'll be over soon to help you pack."

"Okay. Good night, Luke."

I loved the way my name rolled off her tongue. "Good night, Hazel."

I didn't think I was ever going to wipe the smile off my face. The woman was perfect, just like I had told her, and I was still fucking flying preparing for another shower as my phone rang with a call from an unknown number.

I declined the call. Fuckers couldn't take a hint.

TWENTY-SEVEN

Hazel

I had a pre-moving checklist. It could also have been called a postbreakup checklist since many of the items related to my recent split, but the list was my lifeline in the days leading up to moving.

I had already cleaned out most of the house and donated several bags and boxes full of items to the local women's shelter, both of which were items on my list. I rearranged the old furniture in the garage, moving all the pieces I wanted to take to one side of the garage and shoving Michael's shit to the other.

Most of the furniture inside the house would stay whether I wanted it to or not; I didn't have room for most of it in my small six-hundred-square-foot, one-bedroom apartment.

Each time I completed a task, I was relieved to check it off my never-ending list. With the way my life had fallen into chaos, it was a simple lifeline that kept me moving forward.

The one item on my list that I dreaded more than anything was STD testing.

After Michael copped to cheating on me, I knew I had to get tested. We hadn't used condoms for most of our relationship;

once we were official, it didn't seem necessary. I'd been on some form of birth control since college, and since we were only sleeping with each other—or so I thought—it was optional.

I went to my normal OB-GYN for the testing and was lucky enough that it fell around the time that I was due for my annual exam, so it didn't seem out of the ordinary to test for STDs. My results were emailed to me a few days later: all clear. And I cried.

The piece of shit had beaten me, cheated and completely controlled my life for years, but at least he hadn't given me a disease.

Word had also begun to spread around the tight-knit community my parents and Michael's parents were still actively part of in Nashville. Rumors began that I had been unfaithful or had a secret child with another man. I was sure all of the nasty rumors were courtesy of my ex-future mother-in-law, who had also taken to social media to covertly begin the *Hazel Hate Campaign*.

None of her posts or comments were about me explicitly—she still had a reputation to maintain, of course—but with the way those old women gossiped, it didn't take a rocket scientist to figure out who she was alluding to.

My sister, and always my defender, took every opportunity to tear down the rumors and tell anyone who would listen in no uncertain terms that our split was Michael's fault. After I told her that I didn't want the entire world knowing about our situation, she kept the reasons quiet and simply just called Michael a manipulative, lying, cheating piece of shit.

Although it wasn't the whole truth, it was still completely accurate.

My mom continued to provide her support via daily phone calls and text reminders that my room looked the same as it did when I left for college too many years prior. She even went as far as to send me job listings for technical writing positions in and around Nashville.

Each time I told her that I appreciated the thought, but I wasn't going back.

The most surprising was the call I received from my dad a few days after I told my mom and sister the few details I could share about the years of abuse.

My dad and I had a strained relationship for no other reason besides him constantly working when I was a kid. His work as an engineer took him to different countries every month and when he was in the U.S., he still spent more hours at the office than he did at home.

My parents' marriage didn't seem to suffer, at least from what we could tell, but his relationship with me and D was rocky. I still loved him, but it was always from a distance. Thankfully, I never felt uncared for or unloved, especially since my mom smothered both my sister and me.

But the call from my dad, even in those circumstances, was a surprise. When my phone rang, I was preparing to receive bad news about my STD test, but my dad's name scrolling across the screen had even more anxiety slicing through me.

"Hi, Dad," I said quietly while packing up another box of clothes. It was my fourth and I regretted not donating more because I knew I wouldn't have room.

"Hi, honey." I hadn't heard his voice in a while. It seemed gruffer and more aged. "How's it goin'?"

"Umm... it's going fine, I guess. How are you?"

"Not too bad."

There was a short silence where it sounded like we both took deep breaths and prepared for the conversation ahead.

He was the first to speak again. "Your mom told me," he said, and then added, "actually your mom told me and then Delilah berated me for not calling sooner. I'm sorry about that."

"Don't worry about it, Dad. I wasn't expecting a phone call." It wasn't meant to come across as dismissive, but I think it might have been based on the way he grunted in response.

"I'm sorry, kid." His voice cracked, and the emotion in just the short apology made the muscles around my heart clench.

I had to clear the emotion from my own throat to respond. "Thanks, Dad. But you don't need to be sorry. None of this was your fault. The blame solely lies on Michael's shoulders."

"I know, but still..." He trailed off. My dad was always a well-spoken, articulate man; he never stumbled over his words and commanded attention when he spoke. For him to trail off, lost in thought, I knew he had to be struggling.

"Situations like these are difficult on everyone involved. I understand it's a lot."

I heard him take another deep breath over the line and then I thought I could make out a sniffle. The sound was quick, barely even a sound so I couldn't be sure. I'd never seen my father cry.

"I should have done more."

"Dad, there's nothing you could have done. We were here and y'all were there..."

"I should have seen this coming. I never liked the prick all that much," he said with clear disdain in his voice.

That was news to me. He never outwardly showed signs that he disliked Michael in the years we had been together.

I chuckled. "It's becoming clear that a lot of people didn't like him and just never told me."

"I should have told you. I was trying to protect your feelings because it looked like the two of you were so in love, but I should have pushed all of that to the side and protected you. A father never wants something like this for their daughter. I don't want to make this about me, because it damn well isn't about me, but I feel like I've failed you. You've grown up to be a beautiful, caring, selfless woman, and you never deserved this."

A single tear slid down my cheek as I let his words wash over me. I slumped on my closet floor, leaning against the wall between two full boxes of clothes, as I pressed the phone harder to my ear. It was probably the most my father had ever said to me at once.

"It means a lot to hear you say that, Dad. But I don't blame you, so you should try not to blame yourself. I'm going to be okay."

We were both silent for another long moment, but I swear I felt something shift between us. I hoped it would be a new opportunity for something so much better between us.

"Just know that the next person to come into your life is going to have a hell of a test to pass before they get the okay from any of us."

I laughed, and surprisingly he also chuckled down the phone. My mind immediately thought about Luke and if he would pass my dad's new tests. I'm sure he would, although I knew we had a long way to go before those tests would be necessary. Either way, the idea made me happy.

"I'm sure they'll understand."

"I love you, honey," my dad said, and more emotion swept over me.

"I love you, too, Dad."

We said our goodbyes, and I stayed situated between those two boxes of clothes for a while after I ended the call. Something about hearing those words from my dad and knowing he didn't fault me for my failed engagement healed a small part of me.

The backyard was flooding, and the rain hadn't paused for even a second since I woke up that morning.

In the background, the news was on and there were reports of flooding throughout the city. The water standing in the backyard wasn't nearly as bad as the video footage constantly looping on the local channel.

"And it doesn't look like it's going to be letting up anytime soon. These storms will be moving through the area until late into this evening…" The reporter was intently staring through the TV, asking that all city residents heed the warnings to stay off the roads.

Luckily, I had nowhere to be and a ton of writing to catch up on. It was inconvenient timing that I finally had the drive to write while trying to move. The two did not work well together.

I was trying not to worry about the couple of inches of water in the backyard that was creeping closer and closer to the back door and up the patio when someone knocked on my front door.

I hesitated, peeking my head around the corner to see through the glass on the door. Although partially obscured by the viscous rain beating down, I could make out the very identifiable bleach-blonde hair.

With a gust of cold November wind, I opened the door to reveal a soaking wet Becky and Emmy. A small, broken umbrella hung from Becky's hand with her impeccably painted nails.

"Hazel!" Emmy squealed before she lunged toward me, her clothes hanging limply over her.

"Hi, Em. It's so good to see you," I said, letting her wrap her wet arms around my hips.

"Can I go get my coloring books?"

"Yeah, sure, honey. But grab a towel out of the laundry room first."

She hurried toward the laundry room at the back of the house with a squeak of her wet tennis shoes against the clean wood floors.

"Be careful!" Becky warned as a peel of giggles erupted from around the corner.

"I am, Mom!" Emmy said back as I heard my office door open and quickly slam shut behind us.

Becky wrung her drenched hands in front of her but didn't make a move to come inside. Her usually flawless eye makeup was dripping down her face in long black streaks, but it was her bloodshot eyes that clued me into the possibility that it wasn't just the rain that had messed it up.

She scrubbed a hand through her unkempt hair and took a

low, deep breath. "I'm so sorry to spring this on you, Hazel, but could you watch Emmy for a few hours?"

I nodded before she finished talking. "Of course. It's no problem."

She nodded and mumbled a thanks as she tucked a stray piece of blonde hair behind her ear. "I'll pick her up around dinner. I should be done by then..." Her voice trailed off like she was lost in thought. Her eyes wouldn't meet mine, and I was growing more and more worried as the seconds passed.

"I'll just feed her tonight. I have some chicken nuggets in the freezer that I would love an excuse to eat," I chuckled, and she gave me a sad smile in return.

I cautiously took a step forward and placed my hand on her forearm that was wrapped around her midsection.

"Is everything okay?"

Her eyes were wide and seemed extra blue as tears readied to fall. As I watched the emotion drift over her face, warping her sharp features, a knowing unease settled over me. It was even more intense when her facial expression quickly morphed again into an ungenuine lopsided grin.

"Oh, everything's fine," she said with a chuckle and patted my hand, which I took as a cue to remove it from her arm. "Just a lot going on at home, you know? It's easier to not have to entertain my crazy child for a few hours."

"I see..." I murmured. Everything about Becky—her demeanor, sloppy clothing, and overall disheveled appearance—was screaming the opposite of her words.

As I searched for the right words, hoping to make her talk, her eyes locked on something behind me. I turned just enough to see she had noticed the large stack of boxes behind me labeled with the respective rooms they would go in.

"Y'all are moving?" she asked in a flat tone.

"Actually," I began after a much-needed calming breath, "I'm moving. I'm not sure what Michael's plan is."

Her eyes widened in surprise and her brows shot almost to her hairline. "You've broken up?"

I nodded.

She shook her head as her jaw hung open. "I'm so surprised."

I shrugged because I knew she was telling the truth. I was beginning to believe that the only reason anyone was surprised by our breakup was because they didn't really know our relationship. I wasn't that good of a liar.

"Are you..." she began and then darted her eyes around the porch like she was confirming we were alone. "Are you happy? Are you glad you broke off the engagement?"

It was the last question I was expecting, although the answer was simple. "Yes," I said, wanting to leave it at that.

For the second time, she nodded and looked past me like her mind was wandering somewhere else.

"I'll give you my new apartment address—it's about ten minutes from here—so you can still bring Emmy by whenever."

"I really appreciate that, Hazel. You don't know what it means to me."

I smiled and tried to make my expression warm and welcoming. She said she had to leave and quickly declined my offer of a new, not broken, umbrella to use on her way home.

She jogged back to her own house which required trudging through the water accumulating on the sidewalk and charging against the stifling chilly wind. I watched her from the somewhat safety of my own porch as she climbed her porch stairs and slid into her home.

As I closed and locked the door, I said a silent prayer that she was okay. My mind immediately summoned the worst possibility I could think of: that Chris was as abusive as Michael, and Emmy would find herself without a mom.

I couldn't shake the terrifying thought even when I sat down to color with Emmy, or when I made her hot chocolate with extra chocolate. Or when Luke sent me a picture of the cutest dog.

When the thought wouldn't disappear, even with no evidence of abuse besides Chris's behavior toward me, I shot a quick text to Becky, letting her know that Emmy was great and that I'd drop her off around seven p.m.

I would check everything out for myself when I dropped her off, evaluate the situation, and plan accordingly.

I hoped my own situation had just made me paranoid, and I wasn't just seeing abuse when it was only normal relationship disagreements and issues. But I couldn't shake the feeling that something more was going on.

TWENTY-EIGHT

Hazel

I gained no clarity when I dropped Emmy at her house later that night. There was no sign of Chris anywhere, and Becky had returned to her normal self—she was perfectly primped with her hair and each swipe of makeup in the exact place it was meant to be.

She thanked me profusely for watching Emmy and apologized just the same for her untidy appearance earlier. To anyone else, she would have seemed fine, but I knew that fake smile all too well. It was the same one I wore for more than a year.

In our short conversation, and as she all but pushed me out of the front door, I repeated that I was always around the corner and texted her my new address.

Without her cooperation, I had to hope that I'd done everything I could, and she would heed my advice to let me know if she needed anything at all, ever.

As my luck would have it, the rain had slowed as Becky and I stood awkwardly in her entryway but began to pick up again as I stepped off the porch steps and headed back to my place.

By the time I peeled my rain jacket off, slung it over the arm of a patio chair and hurried into the warmth of the house, I was thoroughly freezing. My leggings were soaked, as my jacket didn't provide much protection for my legs, especially when the wind was whipping violently. My rain boots were also filled with water which I made a point to slip off carefully, dump on the porch and leave outside with my jacket.

I changed into a white T-shirt, joggers, and fuzzy socks before I wrapped a blanket around my shoulders for an extra layer of warmth. I slid into the kitchen and hopped up onto the island as I finished off the remainder of the dinosaur chicken nuggets I made for Emmy and me earlier. I scooped each one directly from the pan and half-heartedly watched the news that only consisted of continued reports of widespread flooding and caution not to drive unless absolutely necessary.

As I poised to change the channel, my phone on the counter next to me vibrated against the gray granite. I bit back the smile that began when I saw Luke's name appear on the screen.

"Hi," I said, biting the head off a T.rex.

"Hi, Angel." Luke's voice was deep, and I swore I could feel it vibrate through me even over the phone. Not to mention every time he called me that damn name, I stopped breathing.

The little game we played between our windows was fun. The instant connection I felt between us was one I didn't think either of us was going to be able to shake. He knew exactly what to say to heighten every feeling and even my own touch seemed like too much for me when his low husky voice said such illicit things. He seemed to know my body so well already, watching the way I reacted to everything.

I wanted to do it all again, and I wanted more, but at the same time, I didn't know if I could handle more. When Luke was around, he consumed me, and that was terrifying. I needed to be sure that I was healed from my... abuse and that whatever was happening between us was going somewhere before I gave myself over completely.

I had to protect my heart and falling into bed with Luke too soon could prove disastrous.

"What's up?" I asked, my voice sounding unintentionally breathy around the chicken nugget still in my mouth.

"Just wanted to call and check on you. Looks like it's starting to get bad out again."

"Yeah, not looking so great. I'm currently eating chicken nuggets and trying not to watch the news."

He chuckled. "Sounds like a good night. The water is pretty high on the street, almost to the sidewalk up on the curb."

I cringed. "Shit. Doesn't look like it's going to stop anytime soon either."

"Nope. So, I was thinking maybe—"

He didn't get a chance to finish his sentence. To my right and just outside my back door was a large crashing noise before something scraped down the door. It sounded like metal sliding against the glass. The abrupt sound made me scream, and I almost toppled backward off the island.

Once I steadied myself and knew I wasn't falling to the hard tile floor, I checked that the door was locked. Even with the blood rushing behind my ears and my heart pounding what felt like a million beats a minute, my eyes first checked the lock. Then checked for broken panes of glass. Thankfully, whatever it had been hadn't shattered the glass.

"Hazel!" Luke yelled, breaking me from my panic. "What the hell just happened?"

"I don't know. There was a huge bang outside of my back door. Scared the fucking shit out of me."

"Don't move. I'm coming over," Luke barked.

"You don't have to. Let me turn the light on and see if I can see anything before you come running over in the pouring rain for nothing."

He was saying something about staying where I was and not going toward the door, but I wasn't necessarily listening. I had decent self-preservation instincts, and this didn't feel like someone trying to break in. Although, I wouldn't have put it past Michael to want to scare the shit out of me.

The thought made me pause for a second, my hand midair and reaching for the porch light, but I shook it off as quickly as it popped into my head.

I flicked the light on but still braced myself for what I might find. Directly in front of the door was the gutter that had been hanging above it only a second before. Water was still running down it toward the foundation of the house.

"Unlock your front door, I'm walking out of the house now."

"Yeah, yeah. Okay." I said, stealing one last glance at the downed gutter before hurrying to the front door.

Luke must have sprinted because he was climbing the last two steps up the porch when I made it to the door. I swung it open and was greeted by a toe-curling sight. Luke's dark hair was dripping wet and plastered to his forehead, as was his soaked white shirt. I could see the outline of his abs as well as his dark tattoos through the almost see-through material.

"What the hell happened?" he asked as he politely wiped his feet on the welcome rug. Not that it would actually do much, but it was a sweet gesture.

He walked past me, his jeans tucked awkwardly into the tops of his boots like he put them on in a rush and didn't have enough time to fix them properly.

"The umm... the gutter," I stuttered, taken aback by Luke's disheveled yet mouthwatering appearance. "The gutter at the back door fell."

Luke peered out the back before pulling the door open and quickly inspecting the damage. He stepped out onto the back patio and into the rain once again. The never-ending rain didn't seem to bother him much until he had to look up to inspect the damage near the roof. He covered his eyes with his hand and squinted against the harshness of the patio light and the torrential downpour.

He stooped down and inspected the gutter, shaking his head

softly before stepping back inside.

"When's the last time you cleaned out your gutters?" he asked with a raised eyebrow. There was something about the combination of the water dripping off him, along with his quick breaths, that made desire pool low in my stomach.

"Honestly?" I asked, and he gave me a nod that said *yes, honestly*. "I personally never have, and if I didn't, it's very likely Michael didn't either. Is that what happened?"

Luke shrugged and ran his hand through his hair. "Possibly, but I can't be completely sure. It's likely it just came loose."

"So, can we fix it?"

He thought for a moment, running his hand over his chin and cheek. "Do you have any two-by-fours or something like that?"

I furrowed my brow, not entirely sure where he was going with it. "Umm… yes. In the garage," I said as I hiked my thumb over my shoulder.

I led him into the garage, flicking on the light and grabbing a two-by-four from the corner where I had propped them out of the way just a few days before.

"You've done a lot of organizing."

"Yeah." I couldn't think of a better response; I didn't really want to discuss my imminent move and how my heart hurt a little knowing I wouldn't get to see Luke as frequently. Even if it was just a wave as we both walked into our separate houses, it was an interaction I looked forward to. The emotion made me feel stupid—we barely knew each other. "How many do we need?"

"Two should be fine. Let's go," he said, grabbing the one from my hands and taking another one before carefully navigating back through the house.

"Do you need help?" I asked after he walked back into the rain, stepping over the gutter with the two two-by-fours still in either hand.

When he didn't answer immediately, I took it upon myself to

just help whether he really needed me or not. I hiked up my joggers a little higher and braced myself for the pounding rain.

"What do you want me to do?" I hollered so he could hear me over the rain.

"I'm going to push the gutter up, and I want you to wedge one of the two-by-fours under it. Don't let go of it until I say so, though."

I nodded and grabbed a board. Like fucking Hulk, Luke gripped the gutter, water still rushing out of it, and heaved it over his head. Once it was flush with the part still mounted to the house, I wedged the piece of wood under it.

"Good girl," he said with a wink and my whole body flushed with excitement. "Now grab the other one and put it over there." He pointed just a few feet down, closer to where it was still attached. I repeated the process and was relieved that I could wedge the board into a seam in the cement of the patio.

"Is that going to hold?" I said as a bolt of lightning struck somewhere close and made me jump.

"It's the best idea I've got, so I hope so," he said, opening the door and waving me inside.

My clothes were sticking to every inch of my body like a second skin, and it felt like the cold was seeping down to the marrow of my bones. I hugged my arms around myself as Luke stepped inside—also shivering slightly—and closed the door behind him.

"Okay, we should be good—" he began to say but immediately stopped when he turned to look at me. He slowly closed his eyes, let his head fall back between his shoulders and took a deep breath. He let out a low chuckle and said, "Dear lord, Angel, you're trying to kill me, I swear."

"What are you talking about?" I asked, a flush creeping up my cheeks.

He leveled a heated gaze at me, and I watched his eyes flit down to my chest. "Your shirt is almost completely see-through," he said with another chuckle.

My eyes widened in horror. I looked down and immediately threw my arms over my chest. Sure enough, my white shirt was soaked through, and you could see the dark pink of my nipples through the thin material.

I groaned, my embarrassment growing the longer he watched me. "I'm just going to go…" I trailed off as I began to turn toward my bedroom.

"Wait," was all Luke said before he closed the distance between us. His clothes were also soaked through, and he had to be freezing, but I could still feel the heat rolling off him. "Don't run away. It's not like I haven't seen it before."

Another wave of embarrassment crashed over me, and my face was more red than it'd ever been. Even in my half-frozen state, I could feel the warmth on my cheeks.

I cleared my throat, trying not to look up at him, which was easier said than done as he smoothed his hands down my upper arms and inched closer into my space. I stared at the toes of his worn and wet boots instead.

"Yes, I'm aware, but I'm cold and wet. I think I should dry off and change."

"Hmm," he mused as he ran the fingers of his left hand back up my arm and over my shoulder. He wrapped his hand possessively around my neck and a shiver of want lit through me at the heat of his touch. He hooked the forefinger of his other hand under my chin and, using his thumb, urged my head up. I fought it for a moment, the desire was right there within reach, and I knew if I saw that same hungry look in his eyes again, I would be a goner.

I wanted to see, though. I wanted to see how much he wanted me, so I met his emerald-green gaze and sighed contentedly when they were blazing with a heat I'd never seen.

"Don't hide from me." His voice was a low whisper, also laced with the same desire that found a home in his eyes. When he lowered his mouth to mine, it was game fucking over.

I let my arms fall away from my chest so I could wrap them

around the back of his neck and string my fingers through his wet, messy hair. The kiss was urgent and filled with need. His tongue immediately found mine, and he ran his hands down my back and over my ass. He gripped the backs of my thighs and lifted me into his arms.

Reflexively, I wrapped my legs around his waist as we both deepened the kiss and hummed with pure lust. I had learned that Luke definitely enjoyed being in control, so it was no surprise when one of his large hands twisted into the back of my hair and moved me as he wanted me.

The urgency of our kiss made my head spin. I pulled back only for a moment, our foreheads still touching, and I looked into his eyes. On most days, Luke kept his emotions in check, but when he wanted me, it was obvious all over his face. I craved to see that face.

"Luke, I can't..." I said, my voice cracking as my core throbbed. I wanted it, I did, but I couldn't let myself go that far just yet. "I need more time..."

His fist tightened in my hair and a small moan escaped me as he licked at my open mouth. "We're on your time line, remember?"

I remembered but when he felt that good, it was hard to remember anything besides the need building inside of me.

He littered kisses up and down my neck, nipping at my collarbone and pulling at my earlobe. He kissed the soft spot behind my ear, and I ground against his stomach, trying to find any relief.

"I need to taste you," he growled into my ear. My eyes shot open in surprise. It was the last thing I thought he was going to say, but the mental images of his head between my thighs were sinful.

"Yes," I gasped. Relieved with the compromise. It was a good compromise, and I needed it more than I could comprehend.

TWENTY-NINE

Hazel

An unending desire coursed through me, and I nipped Luke's plump bottom lip between my teeth. The dark chuckle he purred against my lips was filled with naughty promises as he moved us around the kitchen. I figured he would take me to my bedroom, the couch, anywhere besides where he decided to set me down at the end of the kitchen table.

My legs and arms still wrapped around him, he laid me down on the hard wooden surface and whipped my wet T-shirt over my head. Yes, he'd seen my breasts before, from afar, but that was the first time he was there in person. He didn't give me a second to be self-conscious though, as he gripped both of them in his hands.

"So perfect," he mumbled before latching his mouth around one of my already hard nipples. My back bowed off the table as I tried to find more. More of everything. He swirled his tongue around the edges, licked, nipped, and even bit ever so carefully. I was a writhing mess by the time he switched to the other one and was clawing at his head and shoulders.

"Soon, I'm going to take my time. I'm going to lick and kiss every inch of your perfect little body," he said against my chest. His hands still kneaded my breasts, pinching my nipples between his fingers to the point that I thought I may come apart just from that. If his tongue was skilled enough to elicit that carnal of a reaction from me, excitement buzzed through me, imagining what else he could do.

He kissed his way down my stomach, pausing to kiss the birthmark on my left hip before he pulled my joggers down my legs. He did so slowly and methodically until my feet were freed, then he chunked them over his shoulder like he couldn't wait any longer.

He ran his hands down my sides, goose bumps erupting over every inch of my skin. When his hands tightened around my hips, he pulled me toward him and the edge of the table before pressing the inside of my thighs down and opening me up wider for him.

He let out a small groan and ran his thumb over my desperate cunt. I moaned and bucked against the soft touch. His dark hair hung in his face, and his eyes were appreciative as he looked down at me.

"Already so fucking wet for me," he said, circling his thumb around my aching clit with a little more pressure.

"We were just out in the rain," I said with a faint smile.

He growled and pinched my clit harder between his two fingers. The pain quickly morphed and twisted into a deepened pleasure.

"We both know this is all for me."

A moan and thrust of my hips were all the response I could muster. Behind my hooded eyes, I watched him tower over me, with one hand disappearing between my legs as he gazed at my face. He leaned down and placed a soft kiss on my lips as he continued playing with me.

"So beautiful," he said against my lips before he moved back down my body. He moved a chair over from the other side of the table and placed it in the perfect position directly in front of me.

"We're doing this right here?" I asked, the surprise evident in my voice. I thought we were just getting warmed up, and he'd move me.

He laughed. "Yes, Angel. Right here on your kitchen table. I am starving, so I don't think there's a better place."

He smiled down lustfully at my throbbing sex, and he wetted his lips. The pressure of his thumb disappeared from my clit and just when I groaned, pleading for something, he replaced it with his mouth.

I could have screamed.

He latched on to my clit, sucking it into his mouth before he licked me thoroughly from top to bottom over and over again. He closed his mouth over me and ate me like he was starving.

When I rolled against his face, my orgasm making itself known too soon, I tried to clench my thighs together, forcing him to slow down. But his hands were there, forcing my legs open again.

He slowed slightly, using light pressure to flick my clit with his tongue as he pushed one finger into me.

"Oh fuck," I gasped at the intrusion. My legs shook as he hooked his finger, finding the perfect spot immediately and latching back on to me. He fucked me with his finger as I clawed at the back of his head, grinding myself onto his face, chasing a release that was coming so soon.

I tried to do what I could to keep my orgasm from crescendoing, but he was playing me just right. I didn't want it to end, but when he slipped another finger into me, I realized I had no control.

He dipped down closer to my opening, where his fingers were pumping in and out of me with skilled precision. I couldn't even comprehend what he was doing. All I knew was that it felt more amazing than I remembered anything ever feeling.

When his tongue trailed back up to my clit, his fingers pushing deeper, and he grabbed my ass, pulling me closer to him, I came undone. My head fell back onto the table as a freight train of an orgasm plowed through me.

"Fuck, Luke, yes," I moaned, probably incoherently. I felt like my entire body was shaking and buzzing. Fireworks erupted behind my eyes, and I just let the feeling take me over.

When I felt it subside several seconds later, I released his hair from my grip. He didn't stop immediately but slowed his fingers inside of me, placing one last kiss between my legs.

"Are you satisfied?" I asked as a pleased smile crept across my face.

He chuckled, still slowly pumping a finger in and out of me. "I don't think I'm ever going to be satisfied. You taste sweeter than I could ever imagine. You're addicting."

I glanced down, and the sheen of my release covered his beard and lips that were upturned in a sly smile.

"How do you feel?" He placed a soft kiss on my inner thigh, still gripping my ass in his free hand.

"Amazing," I mumbled as my body began humming again. Much to my surprise, more desire was coursing through me as his finger picked up pace. It was like a drug that I could so easily become addicted to.

"I want to feel you tighten around my fingers again and hear you moan my name." He lightly licked me and pushed his fingers deeper.

"Again?" I asked, the surprise obvious in my voice. My body seemed ready, but I had never had two back-to-back orgasms before. I didn't know if I was actually capable.

Gauging my shocked expression and tone of my voice, he realized I wasn't expecting round two. "Baby girl," he muttered against me. "One is never enough."

Within minutes, between his skillful tongue and perfect fingers, he had another orgasm blazing through me just as strong as the first.

Knowing he liked it, I let his name fall from my lips as my vision blurred and my body was overcome.

It took me another minute to recover fully, and while I did, he kissed over my thighs, down my legs and over my stomach. As quickly as I could, I pushed up on my hands, eager to touch him and return the favor.

When I sat up, I gripped his face in my hands and kissed him thoroughly. I moaned when I tasted myself on him, but out of the corner of my eye, I caught his hand pushing against his erection that was bulging against his jeans. He was so turned on after pleasuring me, and I knew I needed to feel him in my mouth, probably as much as he said he needed to taste me.

Without another word, I released his face and slid off the table. He pushed his chair back, giving me room to shimmy off the table, and I watched his face closely as I slid to my knees in front of him.

"Angel, I'm not expecting you to reciprocate. I enjoyed that just as much as you did."

I smiled up at him, mustering as much confidence as I could and pressed my hand against his jeans. He groaned and my smile grew. "I can tell you did, and I know reciprocation isn't required. But what if I want to do this?"

His jaw dropped when I pressed down harder. He was big. So much bigger than I thought, and I was instantly nervous. There was no way I was going to fit him in my mouth completely, but I wanted to try.

"I guess if you want to…" His words trailed off when I unbuttoned his jeans and pulled them down his muscular thighs. I did the same to his black boxer briefs but not before I kissed his shaft through the material. His cock twitched even with my light kiss.

I pulled his briefs off and when his cock popped free, I sucked in a breath. He was thick and long, and my mouth watered to lick over the veins running up and down his shaft. The head was red and a bead of precum had already collected there. I continued pulling his jeans and underwear off until they were discarded near my clothes by the kitchen island. He settled deeper into the chair as I wrapped a hand around him.

My fingertips couldn't meet when I squeezed his shaft. I gripped him with both of my hands, squeezing gently and moving up and down. I had to admit that I was nervous, but with his eyes on me and drowning in desire because of what I was doing, I felt nothing but confidence.

"Fuck, this isn't going to take long. I already feel like I'm going to explode, and you've barely touched me."

I peered up at him as I twisted my hands around his cock in opposite directions. His eyes were hooded, and he was gripping the arms of the chair with such force I thought they may break. I didn't care though, I wanted to make him feel so good that he had to break shit if that's what it took.

"How do you like it?" I asked when his eyes met mine.

"Fuck, don't look at me like that?"

I frowned. "Like what?"

"Like you can't wait to suck my cock."

"But I can't wait." I leaned forward and licked the bead of precum from his head. He lurched in his seat with a strained *"fuck."*

"You didn't answer my question," I said with another teasing lick.

"What did you ask?"

"How do you like it?"

He gripped the back of my head. "Hard."

I squeezed my hands around him tighter, and he reacted just as I wanted him to—with a low sound of pleasure that rumbled through him and another drop of precum beaded at his head.

I couldn't resist anymore. I licked up one side of him, from base to tip and then the other until he was panting. I wanted to continue teasing him, but I knew he was right—he wouldn't last much longer, and I was tired of waiting. So, I took him into my mouth, as deep as I could. He thrust up into me, triggering my gag reflex, but I swallowed around it and around him.

"*Yesss*," he gathered my hair in his fist as I bobbed up and down around him. Each time I flicked the tip of his cock with my tongue, I could feel him resisting the urge to push up into me. I couldn't get all of him in my mouth at once, so I used a hand around his base, moving it in time with my mouth.

"God, you're such a good girl. You're so gorgeous when you suck my cock," Luke said through clenched teeth as his thumb ran around my lips which were stretched around his substantial length.

My eyes fluttered closed as his beautiful, dirty words urged me on. I could tell he was holding back, but I wanted to see him fall apart. He was watching me intently, taking in the entire sight of me on my knees in front of him, so I looked up, catching his gaze. I hoped I was actually capable of giving blow-job eyes because that's what I was aiming for.

Either way, I held his gaze as I squeezed the base of him tighter with one hand and gripped his balls with the other. His eyes began to close, but he forced them open again. I pushed him deeper into my mouth until he hit the very back of my throat. My eyes were watering, but I kept him as deep as I could, moving at a steady pace until I felt his balls draw up in my hand and the telltale stiffening of his cock at the base.

With only a few more thrusts up into my mouth, he was spilling between my lips, hitting the back of my throat in long, hot spurts. I swallowed every drop of him and didn't let up until I felt him slightly soften. Even then, I gave one last lick to his head before I sat back on my knees and released him.

"Holy shit," he groaned.

I stood on shaky legs, and he darted out his hands to steady me before I could tumble over. He kissed me again, thoroughly exploring my mouth with his tongue. I'm sure he could taste himself, but he didn't seem to care. His hands drifted higher on my hips until they were braced around my ribs.

Taking his lead, I leaned into his touch and placed my hands on his shoulders. Even after two orgasms, I didn't feel done with him.

"Shit, okay. We should stop," he said half-heartedly against my mouth. He kissed me once more softly and then pulled away. My eyes caught on his dick, which was hard against his stomach. An impressive turnaround time—good to know.

For a moment, with our eyes locked and an inexplicable energy buzzing between us, I second-guessed my decision not to go all the way. Was I kidding myself by thinking that my heart was going to be any less involved if his dick never wound up inside of me like that?

Whether my thinking was sound or not, it was kind of nice to just play and explore without the stress of sex hanging over us. And I knew I had made the decision for a reason. I had good, definitive reasons.

"I'll throw our clothes in the wash. What do you think about a hot shower?" I asked. I believed we could shower without me begging for him to be inside of me. Hopefully.

We showered without sex. It was difficult, and I, yet again, second-guessed myself. But Luke was skilled with his fingers, quickly drawing out another orgasm as I used my hands on him. My orgasm seemed to push him over the edge as he caged me in against the cold tile of the shower wall.

I chuckled as he pulled his lips away from my mouth. We were both still covered in soap, which was what we were supposed to be doing—cleaning each other—before we got caught up.

"We haven't even had sex yet, and you've already given me three times as many orgasms as I've ever had in one night." As much as I didn't want to compare Michael and Luke, I couldn't help it when it came to orgasms. With Michael, I was lucky to get out with one; most of the time, I'd hidden in my closet with my vibrator once he'd fallen asleep.

"I'm thinking of at least one more tonight," he winked and stepped under the water, pulling me with him to rinse us both off. "But you have the most beautiful face and make the most amazing sounds when you come. When you pretended to have an orgasm at that party, I seriously thought it was the best sound I'd ever heard. But it doesn't compare to the real thing. I could watch and listen to you all night."

I blushed but let him run his hands over me, rinsing away the soap.

"I think I'd be okay if we continued this all—" Night. I didn't finish my sentence as the bathroom was pitched into darkness.

"Well, that's pretty crappy timing," I mumbled, running my hands down my body and through my hair, hoping I hadn't missed anything.

"My phone is just on the counter. Let me jump out and turn on the flashlight before you try to get out," Luke said.

He pushed the door open, and I was about to tell him to be careful as I heard a wet slipping sound and a muffled *"shit"* before it sounded like something hit the counter. I reached to turn off the water and asked, "Are you okay?"

He groaned but had made it to his phone and flipped on the flashlight. I wrapped the large white towel around myself and thoroughly dried my feet on the rug in front of the glass shower door, not wanting to slip.

"What happened?" Luke was gripping the counter, dripping water all over the floor as I handed him his towel.

"It's wet, so I slipped."

I gave him a pointed look. He rolled his eyes and nodded that he understood it was stupid.

"Let me go switch your clothes. I would offer you some of Michael's, but I don't think they'd fit, to be honest."

He snorted and tucked the towel around his waist. In the dim light, with water dripping down his body and the towel perfectly poised around his waist, he was very reminiscent of the other night. "I wouldn't want to wear his clothes anyway."

"Well, if you're naked, then so am I." I smiled, taking his hand. I swear, I couldn't stop fucking smiling around him. My cheeks had begun to hurt, but it was a pain I was fond of, unlike other things I'd endured. I'd gladly take Luke's form of pain any day. "I have some candles in the living room, and I can turn on the fireplace."

Luke took it upon himself to light the fire, bathing the living room in a dim golden glow. I lit a candle on the coffee table and grabbed a bottle of my favorite red wine. Before I cuddled next to him on the couch, I grabbed the new comforter off my bed and walked back into the living room to find Luke completely naked, his towel puddled in a pile on the floor by his feet and lounging back on the couch.

"I don't mind the look of that," I said.

"Did I..." he began to say, beckoning me closer to him with a wave of his hand and a concerned expression. He eyed the inside of my thigh and swallowed. "I bruised you. Fuck, I didn't mean to bruise you. I didn't even know I was being that rough."

I shrugged. I hadn't noticed either, probably because I was a little concerned with other things going on. "Oh well. It doesn't hurt. I was a little preoccupied with what you were doing between my legs at the time."

The look on his face was angry and somber, though. "What's wrong? It's not a big deal."

"I told you I wouldn't hurt you." The conviction in his voice sent chills shivering through me. I tossed the comforter over both of us and snuggled into Luke's side. He was tense, and I ran my nails over his stomach, circling around the dark ink and through his dark hair.

"Luke, I would gladly accept these bruises, especially with what comes along with them. Don't make this something it's not. I'm... I'm happy for the first time in what feels like forever. If it doesn't bother me, it shouldn't bother you."

He nodded, handed each of us a glass of wine he'd poured and kissed my forehead. "Okay, Angel."

THIRTY

Luke

I rolled my neck back and forth along my shoulders, trying to relieve some of the tension. Hazel and I had fallen asleep on the couch, huddled together under the warmth of her comforter in an intense orgasm stupor. The fire crackling and the rain hitting the window was the perfect soundtrack. The power hadn't kicked back on until well into the early morning hours, breaking our blissful sleep by lighting up the house.

I had rushed around flipping off the lights and double-checking the locks on all the doors. I was eager to get back onto the couch with Hazel when I second-guessed myself that maybe us falling asleep together was an accident and she wouldn't want me to stay.

It came as a surprise when she pulled me back onto the couch with a tired yawn and cuddled back into me. She mumbled against my chest that she couldn't sleep in her bed with me. That it'd be weird and there were too many vivid memories she didn't want to think about while we slept together.

The woman already had me wrapped around her fucking finger, so whatever she wanted, I was game for. Although not fucking her was so much harder than I expected it to be. Even after the most mind-blowing, unexpected blow job and our time together in the shower, unexpended energy still coursed through me.

Waking up in the morning also proved to be harder than I thought it would be. We were tangled up in the comforter and Hazel's leg was slung over my waist and her tits were pressed into my side. With all the willpower I could muster, I slid out from under her and found my dry, yet wrinkled, clothes in the dryer. She was still asleep on the light-gray couch with the comforter only covering a leg and part of her chest when I was dressed. Her hair was fanned around her, and her features were soft and unworried.

I could tell that since she'd signed her lease on her new apartment and truly found a way out of her shitty relationship, she was less anxious. I wished the serene calm on her face when she slept was there all the time.

I brushed a few pieces of hair away from her face and kissed her forehead. I planned to sneak out and send her a text about coming over after work to help her pack, but I couldn't not touch her.

She stirred when my lips brushed her skin and a sleepy smile tugged at the corners of her swollen, pink lips. "Hi," she said in a drowsy voice.

"Good morning, Angel." I kissed her one last time and made to move away, only for her to grab my hand and tug me closer.

"Where are you going?"

"Work. I'll be back later to help you pack. Movers will be here tomorrow, right?"

She nodded and yawned as she stretched her arms over her head. The comforter fell and pooled around her waist, leaving her chest completely bare. I groaned internally and knew I had to leave soon, otherwise I'd have my head between her legs again.

"Okay, I'll be back this afternoon then." I held her face in one hand, ran my thumb over her smooth, slightly flushed cheek and kissed her.

She was still contemplating whether to get up or go back to sleep when I unlocked her front door and pulled it open. Her arms were lazily draped over the back of the couch and her head lay atop them.

I forced my feet to move forward and out into the fucking cold. Leaving her already felt like leaving something important behind.

The intense storms from the days before had sent through an impressive cold front, sending South Texas into the midthirties and everyone into a panic. At the clinic, we had received several calls from pet owners asking if it was too cold to leave their dogs outside.

It was a long day, but I was excited to see Hazel.

I jogged down the porch stairs after taking a shower and changing out of my scrubs. But rather than turn toward Hazel, I stopped at the bottom of the porch. In her driveway, Becky loaded Emmy into the back of her SUV.

It wouldn't have been enough to grab my attention, but nearly everything about Becky I'd grown used to in the years I'd lived next door to her was radically different. Becky often didn't leave the house—even to check the mail—unless she was completely made up.

"Hey, Becky," I said, trying to keep my tone casual as I began walking over to her.

She was wearing sweatpants and a large gray hoodie that swallowed her small frame. Her hair was disheveled and when she turned to greet me in return, her eyes were rimmed with red.

She gave me a tight smile and waved but didn't say anything as Emmy chanted her greeting from her booster seat.

Emmy was still talking about the doll she had in her hands,

but I turned my attention back to Becky. She closed the door on her talking daughter, and I heard Emmy's muffled *"heyyyy"* from inside the car.

Becky wasn't going to respond to my "hello," so I tried a different tactic. "Did you and Chris ever figure out anything about the break-in?"

I didn't miss the way her eyes slightly widened when I said her husband's name. The entire encounter eerily similar to one I'd had with Hazel not too long before; with that thought, my eyes automatically scanned her body for marks, bruises. She was completely covered, though. "Nope."

Please, not again. I thought for a moment and just decided to go for it. Repercussions be damned. "What's going on? Are you okay?"

She whipped her head around and glowered at me. She straightened from where she was about to open the driver's side door and crossed her arms over her chest. "What does that mean? Just because I don't look like I usually do doesn't mean something's wrong."

I tried to hide the shock on my face. I scrubbed a hand over my mouth, contemplating what to say next. I'd never seen Becky even a little defensive. Something was definitely going on.

"You... you look like you've been crying."

She threw her hands in the air in exasperation. "I'm a woman, I'm emotional. If that's all, I'm going to leave. Bye, Luke." And without another word, she hopped into her car and quickly backed out of the driveway.

Stunned, I didn't move until her car was long gone, and I looked awkward standing in the middle of her driveway.

"Umm... Luke?" A voice I knew and that lightened something in my heart said from somewhere behind me.

I turned to find Hazel hugging a large brown box in her hands right outside of her garage.

"Hey, Angel," I said, shaking off the strange interaction and crossing through the grass in our front yards. She set the box on top of another one labeled "living room" in black Sharpie and rearranged a few others that were stacked almost as tall as me.

"Were you talking to Becky?"

I nodded. "Yeah, she seemed weird. I think something's going on, but she wasn't going to give anything up."

She walked back into the house, and I followed her. "Do you want to grab those boxes? I'm just moving them to the garage to give us more room in here," she said as she attempted to lift one that was labeled "books" but quickly set it back down. I took the box instead, following her back out into the garage. "She brought Emmy over yesterday when it was pouring rain. She left her here for a few hours while she said she had to go handle a few things. She didn't look or seem like herself at all, but when I took Emmy home later last night, it was like nothing happened."

"Something's going on, and it really reminds me of…" I trailed off, not wanting to compare any situation, but it was hard not to.

"Reminds you of me?" she asked. She set the box on top of another one, and I smoothed a hand down her back.

"Yeah, a little."

She took a deep breath, turned around and wrapped her arms around my waist. The unprovoked display of affection felt like a few of her walls were slowly breaking down and she was letting me in. I was also thankful for her head against my chest that kept me from slipping into darker thoughts and her reading my expression that I fought to keep unreadable. Thoughts that made me question whether women who were abused or abusers just gravitated to me.

"Can you just keep an eye on her?"

"Of course, Angel," I said, smoothing down her hair and kissing the top of her head. "Come on, let's finish these boxes," I said, more than ready for a change of subject.

She pressed up on her toes and kissed me softly before she smiled and pulled me back into the house.

Even with her own darkness clouding some of her thoughts and my own right there with her's—just a lot older—it still all felt easier with her around.

We rearranged the packed boxes so it was easier for the movers to grab them and load them into the truck. And for a few hours, we easily worked side by side. I was more than happy to play Hazel's muscle to move around furniture, haul bigger boxes outside or anything in between.

Much to my surprise, their garage was still filled with a lot of stuff Hazel had used in college—old pots and pans, appliances, furniture.

"Why'd you keep everything? It's like you have two of everything." I asked as I climbed off the ladder, pulling down more empty plastic bins to use for a few of the kitchen items she was taking from inside the house.

First, she just shrugged but eventually said, "I don't know. When we moved in, so many people bought us new stuff, which replaced the stuff that's now out here. But when I went to throw it out, I couldn't. Something told me that I should keep it and maybe donate it later. Obviously, I never got around to it, and I'm glad I didn't." She dragged the bins back into the house and continued sifting through the few cabinets she hadn't gone through yet.

"What else do you need to do?" I asked, hovering by the kitchen table and reliving our previous night. Laying her out like a meal for me to devour was the best thing I could have asked for. The memories of her spread out on the table, writhing under my tongue, would stay with me forever.

"Umm... I'm not sure." I looked up at where she stood on the short step stool, hearing the obvious change in her tone just as one of her legs slipped out from under her. I sprang into action as quickly as I could, crossing the kitchen and darting my arms out to at least break her fall. I caught her in just enough time with one hand around her hip and the other gripped tightly around her arm.

She let out a small, panicked scream, and I lifted her to unsteady feet. "Damn," she breathed out. "That could have been bad."

"No shit. Are you okay?"

I looked her up and down, scanning for injuries, but I didn't see any.

"Yeah, thank you for catching me." Her breathing slowly went back to normal, and I eyed the red mark on her upper arm where I had caught her.

"That's going to bruise," I said, brushing my hand over the perfectly outlined red hand etched into her pale skin.

She shook her head and placed her hand on my cheek, drawing my attention to her face instead of her marked arm. "Different kinds of bruises, Luke. Thank you for catching me."

I nodded and tried not to think too much into it. Different types of bruises, and she was right. Fuckface's were to inflict pain, to abuse, and to degrade her. The bruises from me were to save her and bring her pleasure.

"What's that?" She was clutching a bottle tightly in her right hand. Her knuckles were white with the strain of holding it.

"It's—it's the...," she stuttered, "the bottle of champagne Michael bought us the night he proposed. He said we would drink it the morning of our wedding. I had completely forgotten I stored it above the fridge so no one would accidentally drink it."

For a long moment, her face was unreadable, and she stared flatly at the bottle. It looked expensive, with detailed, gold writing on the black label. I noticed her hand shaking ever so slightly before I saw the single tear slip down her cheek.

I swiped away the tear with my thumb. "Tell me what you're thinking, Angel."

She sniffed and peered up at me with pain-filled eyes. "It's stupid."

"I promise it's not."

She huffed out a breath and scrubbed a hand through her hair that was falling over her shoulder in effortless brown waves.

"When we got engaged, I was so happy, but I was so naive. The abuse had already started way before then, but I didn't see it. I was so blinded by love, but even that doesn't make sense. After everything that's happened, I don't think I ever really loved him, which is a scary fucking thing to think. How am I ever supposed to trust my feelings knowing they were way off the mark for so many damn years?" She took a shaky breath, gripped the neck of the bottle even harder and looked like she was contemplating smashing it over the granite countertops.

"He was manipulative. It was his manipulation, gaslighting and everything else that made you second-guess not only your emotions and feelings but all the other things." Her eyes were still locked on the damn champagne, and I wanted to smash it for her just to release some of her pain. If I thought it would have fixed it, I would've done it in a heartbeat.

"I think I was in love with the idea of him. A classic love that grew through each stage of life. It wasn't crazy or epic or anything like that. Other than the obvious, there wasn't a lot of drama and he seemed dependable. We had the same goals... I was just in love with the idea of what we could be. That's a hard pill to swallow and such a strange realization to come to after all this time. It makes me so sad that I wasted so much time."

I plucked the bottle from her hands and set it on the counter behind her. While she tried to argue with me, I scooped her up and planted her on the counter beside it.

"Look at me." It wasn't a request, and she complied, hearing the seriousness in my voice. I wrapped a hand around the back of her neck and let the other fall to her waist, positioning myself between her legs. Which was becoming my new favorite place to be.

I willed myself not to get lost in her hazel eyes that were

more green than usual and drowning in pain. "Healing from the pain he put you through—all of it—will take a lifetime. You will probably struggle with certain things for the rest of your life, and there's no telling what those things may be. But you're going to keep moving forward because that's all you can do. It's going to take a while, but you'll relearn how to live without him and his constant..." I struggled for the word. "Mistreatment."

She licked her lips, biting her bottom one between her teeth and nodded. Something like understanding flickered across her face and she leaned into my touch at her neck and against her cheek.

"You're right," she murmured. "Why does it sound like you have a lot of knowledge on this topic?" Her voice was quiet, and I could tell that she was trying not to pry but was curious, nonetheless.

I stiffened at the question. Forcing the memories that the question evoked to stay at the back of my head like I needed them to was becoming more and more difficult the more Hazel discussed her situation. My inability to deal with my own shit wasn't going to hinder me from helping her with hers, though. I would make sure of that, so I continued stroking her cheek with my thumb and kneaded her hip with my other hand.

I let the consternation and fear float away in their own time even as I felt Hazel's eyes on my face. I just watched her lips, slightly parted and letting out a steady breath every once in a while. I let the feeling of her in my hands, both of us safe, ground me as it all passed.

When I felt myself again, I slid my eyes to hers and lifted my mouth in the best smile I could muster.

"Conversation for another time, sweet girl." Then I kissed her like I was trying to kiss away her pain and my own. And she let me.

She moved her small hands over my shoulders and tugged at the back of my hair the way I loved for her to do. It made my dick throb in response, and I pulled her closer to the edge of the counter, where she was at the perfect height to see how quickly she got me going.

Her little moan in response to feeling me hard right between her legs made me deepen the kiss, eager to feel her tongue against my own. It wasn't much longer until we were both panting, and I forced myself to pull away.

I chuckled because, *God*, I felt like I was going to die if I didn't get inside of her soon.

"Luke, you know you can tell me anything, right? You listen to me, and I listen to you. That's how this would work…"

My chest tightened, and I nodded. I wanted to respond with something just as genuine, but I couldn't find the words with the hope swimming in her eyes holding me hostage.

When words failed me, it was easier to show how I felt through my actions. I leaned in for another kiss, bracing to show her my heart in the best way I knew how, when I was interrupted by the ringing of my phone.

I groaned, but Hazel just chuckled and placed a quick peck on my lips before pushing me back and hopping off the counter. She tapped my chest, "Go answer it. I'm just going to finish up in here."

"Okay, don't fall off of the damn step stool again." She rolled her eyes but muttered agreement that she'd be careful.

I stepped into the dining room and pulled my phone out of my pocket. It was a number with an Austin area code and knowing it could be one of the vet techs at work, I answered it without a second thought.

"This is Luke," I said.

"Hi, Bear. It's me." A voice I was all too familiar with purred down the phone. Thank God Hazel was preoccupied with packing the kitchen with her back turned to me because I couldn't hide my reaction. My breath caught in my throat, and I felt the world collapse in on me. I had to refrain from throwing my phone at the wall, but I was just barely holding it together, even with those four simple words.

THIRTY-ONE

Luke

"Valerie," I choked out her name and cringed at the way it tasted on my tongue.

"I knew you'd remember my voice. How are you? I've missed you."

I couldn't think or breathe or move. The muscles in my hand strained and begged me to loosen my grip on my phone, but I couldn't. The fucking panic of hearing her voice paralyzed me.

"Bear, talk to me. I want to hear your voice."

I growled at her use of my old nickname. "Don't fucking call me that." It was once a term of endearment that I longed to hear from her, but it had slowly morphed into a name that made my skin crawl.

Her chuckle was dark, and she sighed. "God, I used to love when you'd get all worked up. We had some great times, don't you think? I loved that voice you used."

I shut my eyes against the onslaught of disturbing memories. Rough sex was Valerie's favorite, and it didn't take me long into our relationship to realize she would start arguments and get me worked up for the sole purpose of knowing it would lead torturously long, never-ending arguments and eventually, hot, aggravated sex.

The first memory to cross my mind was one right before our final blowup. Maybe a week or two before I moved out, Valerie came home with what looked to be a hickey on her neck and the inside of her thigh. The rage I felt in that moment was unlike anything I'd felt since finding my parents dead and until finding Hazel beaten and bloody in her bathroom.

She pretended like she was attempting to hide it from me and making sorry excuses for where she'd been. I knew she was intentionally trying to get a rise out of me, and I let her. Looking back on it now, I realized I was so broken, I couldn't have held my anger for anything. So, we argued for hours before I fucked her harder than I ever had. By the time I was done with her, the hickey on her throat and her thigh were just two small marks among the many I had littered her body with.

She was so proud of herself and lived to wake the monster inside of me. She lay in the middle of our bed, my cum drying on her face and in her long, black hair. She quirked an evil smile in my direction when I came out of the bathroom, pulling my shorts on and ready to pack my shit.

The glint in her eyes stopped me dead in my tracks when she confessed that it was a girlfriend that marked her, and she only did it because she knew it would infuriate me.

She was so proud of herself for how well her plan had worked. I had played right into her hands, and I knew at that moment I was done with her mind games. If she wasn't putting herself in my destructive path, she had no problem doing it to other people. As long as she provoked me, she didn't care who got hurt along the way.

I left a week later only to find out she wasn't nearly close to being done.

"How did you get my number?" I hissed and moved down the hallway and into Hazel's office. Hazel knew about Valerie. As much as I didn't want her to have to deal with my shitty past, it was necessary to share at least a few details with her after my freak-out when searching for apartments. I didn't want to tell her everything though, it was in the past and that's where I wanted it to stay. Saying it out loud made it feel like it was bleeding into the present.

I cracked the door and ran a frustrated hand through my hair, yanking on it like the uncomfortable feeling would distract me from the torrent of pain in my chest and the rolling of my stomach.

"Oh, Bear. It doesn't matter how I got your number," she tsk-tsked. "I just want to talk. Don't you want to talk to me, too?"

I clenched my teeth, pressure radiating through my jaw. "I thought I made myself clear years ago when I left. We are divorced, and you don't get to just call me out of the fucking blue anymore after everything you've done." I tried to restrain myself, but the venomous words couldn't be contained. "You're psychotic. I'm glad to be rid of you, and it's no use trying to talk to me. I don't want to talk, and I never will. Leave me the fuck alone. You owe me that."

I caught my breath and when she didn't respond, I continued. "I'm blocking your fucking number. Don't try to contact me again."

I pulled the phone from my ear, my finger hovering above the "end" button when she cleared her throat like she would finally respond. But apparently, I was a masochist because I didn't end the call. Instead, I held it to my ear.

"I know there's someone else. Didn't have to go too far to find her, right, Bear?"

My temper flared, and my vision blurred. How the hell could she know about Hazel? When I didn't respond, she took my silence as her cue to keep going.

"She's beautiful, and I bet she's kind and generous and everything I'm not. But does she know about you, Bear? About how broken and sad you are." I seethed at her condescending tone but couldn't find the words to shut her the hell up. "I'm sure she doesn't know, and I'm sure she doesn't give you what I did. I challenged you in ways you know only I can. No one will ever compare to me. I made the sadness go away, didn't I?"

It was my worst nightmare—Valerie knowing about Hazel. I knew I could handle Valerie—I'd had years of practice—but I never wanted Hazel to know the violence and terror of my ex-wife. The way our relationship changed from something that pulled me from my darkness to a darkness I didn't know was possible was something I didn't want to relive. She was dangerous from the beginning, but I didn't see it until after we were married when I finally opened my eyes. And Hazel, by being associated with me, was in her direct path.

And comparing the two was absolutely ridiculous. Hazel was everything Valerie wasn't in all the best ways.

"Last time I'll say this, Valerie," I spat her name out like I'd spit the remnants of vomit in my mouth. "Leave me the fuck alone and leave her out of this."

"With that tone, I'd say she's pretty important to you, isn't she?"

"My tone is because I fucking hate you," I seethed. She had a way of getting under my skin like no one else.

She sighed deeply, and goose bumps erupted over my skin. I knew what that sigh meant. "Oh, Bear. You'll regret that. But I'll get you to listen to me and hear me out. I'll be back in your life soon enough. Tell your brother hello from me."

And she ended the call. There was no relief because Valerie didn't make threats lightly. She'd find a way to contact me again, so I'd need to be ready. I needed to protect Hazel, too. Every time Valerie threatened me before, she'd made good on her devious promise in spades. Knowing her only helped slightly, but I knew she'd hit me where it hurt. No one was safe from her wrath.

I couldn't begin to guess what she'd do.

First, I needed to know how she found my number, how she knew about Hazel, and why she mentioned Josh. Her mentioning Josh really stumped me—she always hated Josh and vice versa. That should have been the first sign that she was not who I thought she was—Josh liked everyone. So, with their rocky past, it seemed like he would be the last person she'd mention.

It wasn't a coincidence because nothing with Valerie was a coincidence.

Letting out an unsteady breath and scrubbing a hand over my jaw, trying to relieve some of the tension, I hit Josh's name with a shaky hand.

It only rang a few times before his chipper voice answered. "Hey, bro. What's up?"

I opened my mouth, but no words came out. What the fuck was I supposed to say? The call had completely destroyed the impenetrable walls I thought I'd built around the time Valerie and I'd spent together. The walls were fucking reinforced with the hardest material you could imagine, but just hearing her voice blew them right up. Obviously, I wasn't as past it as I had assumed I was.

"Luke?"

For the moment, with Josh waiting on the other end of the line, I did what I could to shove the worst of the memories back on the other side of the wall and rebuild it to whatever extent I could. It was a sad attempt and didn't help much, but it made me feel somewhat better. Luckily, I had decent experience compartmentalizing.

"Valerie," was all I was able to croak out.

"What about her?" Josh asked suspiciously.

"She called."

"The actual fuck? When? Just now?"

"Yeah, about a minute ago." I dropped my voice to a whisper when I thought I saw movement by the door. It was still cracked, but I could have sworn I saw a shadow or something out of the corner of my eye. Maybe I was just paranoid. Hearing a ghost made me feel like I was seeing them, too.

"What did she want?"

It wasn't a conversation I wanted to have over the phone, especially with the possibility that Hazel could come in at any moment when I was barely holding it together as it was. "Are you home?"

"Yeah, I was just getting ready for work, but I can let them know I'll be a little late. Where are you?"

"Hazel's."

He chuckled. "That's shitty timing to get that call. Wait—" he said and then cursed under his breath. The telling sound of a door slamming came after it, followed by more curses. "Shit, man, this is my fucking fault."

"What the fuck do you mean?" I was pacing the length of her office now, stepping around the white rug since I still had my boots on. Most of the room was packed away in boxes stacked in the corner save for her desk, desk chair, a standing lamp and the few pictures of her and fuckface hanging on the wall. It looked like they were pictures from over the many years they'd been together.

The most recent one was from when they got engaged—him on one knee in front of her holding out a box with that extra sparkly fucking ring. She was bent over, her hands covering her mouth in surprise. I'm sure she was probably crying, or was about to, and thought it was the second-best day of her life only to the wedding day.

Both of our previous relationships had ended in such an extraordinarily bad fashion. And my past was coming to haunt her. Over my dead body would I let anything happen to her. She'd survived Michael; I wouldn't let her have to survive Valerie, too.

I'm sure if I shattered a few of the photos, she wouldn't care, and God, did I fucking want to rip them off the wall and throw them across the room.

"She came into the bar on Halloween right after you left with Hazel. Tried to talk to me and wouldn't leave me the fuck alone for most of the night. I finally got security to escort her out, but not before she got in my face. The look on her face was fucking murderous, and she was talking about how much you needed her."

"Why the fuck didn't you tell me?" I don't know how Josh understood me, I was fucking seething and barely comprehended the words coming out of my own mouth.

"I know how you are about her, and you were doing well. I didn't want you backsliding just because she confronted me. It didn't seem like it was necessary to tell you."

"You said this happened on Halloween?"

"Yes…"

Fuck. It all clicked into place—how she got my number, knew about Hazel, knew where we lived and why she'd asked about Josh. My heart was hammering in my chest, and I couldn't catch my breath.

"I'm on my way home. Call Murphy's and let them know you'll be late." I didn't wait for him to respond before I ended the call. I gave myself two minutes to get a hold of my emotions before I saw Hazel again.

It took more than two minutes, but when I walked into the kitchen, Hazel didn't seem too concerned about my extended phone call. She was listening to a Justin Timberlake song on a low volume, swinging her hips and mouthing the words while she finished taping what looked like the final box of kitchen items.

She'd thrown her college alumni sweatshirt back on with her skintight black leggings.

I watched her for a moment. She was carefree and seemed happy, like for a minute the world wasn't weighing her down. Once she got past everything, I knew she'd just be sassy fucking sunshine all the damn time.

I'd do anything to protect that sassy sunshine; I wouldn't let Valerie ruin it. I would come up with a plan to keep her safe, and if it meant letting her go… I'd do it. It would quite literally kill me, but I'd do it. I'd suffer a million times over if it ensured her safety.

Knowing it was a possibility, I committed the scene in front of me—Hazel dancing in the kitchen—to memory. Something to call upon when life was shit. Which it would be without her.

She whirled with the chorus of the music, lip-syncing the words but stopped immediately, her eyes going wide when she caught me watching.

I cracked a smile, memorizing the embarrassment washing over her face and the blush on her cheeks and neck.

"How long have you been standing there?" she asked, turning the volume down even lower.

"Only for a minute or two." I crossed the living room and into the kitchen. "Did you finish in here?"

She nodded. "Yep. Now, I need to finish my bedroom and I'll be ready for tomorrow."

"Good, good." I didn't want to leave her. "I have to go. Josh needs me."

Her brow furrowed. "Is everything okay?"

"Yeah, just something with Zach. Everything's good, though." I internally cringed at using my nephew as an out, but I couldn't very well tell Hazel about my conversation with Valerie until I had a plan to keep her safe. If then even. Maybe it would be better if she never knew.

"Okay, I'll see you tomorrow then."

"Yeah."

She watched me curiously, but I tried to keep my face neutral.

"You sure everything's okay?" She crossed her arms over her chest, and I knew she saw through my facade.

I smoothed my hands down her arms and tugged her to me. "Yes," I said as I kissed her forehead. When I felt her lean into me, I relaxed a little, letting some of the tension dissipate. "I'll see you tomorrow." Even if it was just to help her move and say goodbye.

THIRTY-TWO

Luke

I found Josh pacing back and forth in front of the kitchen sink with his hands fisted in his hair.

He stopped when I came around the corner. With a pained, apologetic look on his face, he shook his head and opened his mouth to speak, but I held my hand up, stopping him.

"Your phone. Did you lose it the same night you saw Valerie? On Halloween, when I picked up Hazel?" He closed his eyes and ran his hands down his face but eventually nodded.

Nothing was ever a coincidence. Maybe Valerie had been trying to find me for a while, or she always knew where I was. If the latter was true, I'm sure it was Hazel that spurred her into action. The woman wouldn't let me have a day of peace if there was another woman in the picture, hence my lack of relationships since our divorce years before.

"I didn't put two and two together until just now. You have to believe me. I would have told you if I thought she had gotten ahold of my phone," Josh pleaded, bracing his hands on the island between us.

"I know. I believe you, but now we have this to deal with."

He hung his head, still shaking it in disbelief.

"What did she say? Word for word," he asked.

I gave him a play-by-play of my entire conversation while he grabbed us both beers. He downed his in one go when I told him about the part of the call where she mentioned Hazel and then immediately popped open another one.

"*Fuck*," he murmured halfway through the second bottle.

"Yeah, my thoughts exactly." Behind Josh and through the small window above the sink, I caught sight of Becky and Chris arm and arm walking down their front porch steps. In the dimness of their porch light, I could see that Becky was dressed in a formal red gown and Chris was wearing a suit. But what I was most surprised to see was a very toothy smile plastered on Becky's face.

"Talk me through what happened with Valerie," I said, deciding that my neighbors' fucked-up relationship would have to come after my own.

Josh cleared his throat and pulled out one of the barstools from around the corner of the island. "She approached me at the bar first and tried to say hi. Probably half an hour after y'all left. I told her to fuck right the hell off, and she disappeared, so I thought she had actually listened. Then I went to the bathroom and the bitch followed me. She got up in my face when I was trying to wash my hands. She was talking about how she knows we've had our differences, but I know deep down that y'all are meant to be together. I finally slipped past her and waved down the bouncer at the back door." He adjusted where he perched on the stool and looked uncomfortable with retelling the story. "After I got back to the bar from dealing with her, that's when I noticed my phone was gone. I thought I'd just misplaced it in the chaos of dealing with her. I'm not exactly sure how she swiped it, but it seems like the best explanation. I've deactivated the phone, and everything else that needs to be done, but I'm sure she probably got all the information she needed before I even realized it was missing."

I nodded my agreement.

"So, what the hell are you going to do? Are you going to change your number?"

"No," I said before I could really think about it. But I was tired of fucking running and doing exactly what Valerie wanted when she showed up once again. Changing my number, moving, it was all enough. I couldn't let her continue to rule my life.

"Fair enough, man," Josh said without needing an explanation. "But what about—"

"I don't know."

"How do you know what I was going to ask?"

I huffed out a humorless laugh. "Because it's the only goddamn thing I'm really concerned about right now. I can handle Valerie, but I don't want Hazel having to suffer from her psychotic bullshit just because she's with me."

I prodded my own finger in my chest just in case he didn't get it.

"With you, huh?"

I waved off his question and grabbed myself another beer—the last one, too, which meant I was switching to the hard shit after it. "You know what I mean. Valerie's always popped back up when another woman comes into my life, but anyone is fair game to her. And you know her, Josh. When she makes a threat, she makes good on it."

Before the divorce was final, when I was living in the apartment that she made a living hell, Josh was a victim of one of her torturous tactics. She called him pretending to be a nurse and told him Zach and Samantha were both in the hospital after a horrible car accident. That he should hurry to the hospital if he wanted to say goodbye to his son.

Josh was staying the night with me at the time and woke me up in a panic. We broke every traffic law imaginable trying to race to the hospital only to find that Samantha and Zach weren't there. But sitting in the emergency room waiting room was Valerie. I had to physically hold Josh back as rage-filled tears streamed down his face and he lunged at her again and again.

Then there was the incident with Blakely. While still living in that damned apartment, I hooked up with one of our friends. I was in the worst place I'd been since my parents died, and Blakely was willing to console me in more than one way.

We slept together three times total, and we both knew it wouldn't be anything more than that. Still, when Valerie found out, she went ballistic. She called Blakely, constantly threatening to kill her in the most gruesome ways possible.

When Blakely consistently promised it was over, Valerie turned it down a notch and only sent weekly texts reminding her. It was possible Valerie was a little easier on her since they'd once been friends. Valerie had been friends with all of us. Our entire group had been together since the beginning of college.

No one was safe with Valerie around.

"So, what are you going to do, break it off already?"

The thought of leaving Hazel before anything got started made anger sweep through me, heating my veins to a dangerous level. My hands shook when I imagined having to tell her that it wasn't working and slowly drifting away without a valid explanation. Because I couldn't possibly tell her, then leave her, likely putting her in even more danger. My entire body vibrated because I could see her broken face. I didn't want to break her, and I sure as fuck never wanted to cause her pain like her fuckface ex. The last thing I wanted to be was anything like him.

The rage was overwhelming, and it needed a fucking outlet, otherwise I felt like I was going to explode. I lurched forward and slammed my fist into the totally innocent refrigerator. Out of the corner of my eye, I saw Josh jump off his stool, but I waved him off, letting my head fall to the cool, stainless steel surface.

It was stupid, and all it did was make my fucking hand hurt and dent the fridge. I didn't feel any better, and I didn't know what the hell I was supposed to do.

"Wanna hear my thoughts?" Josh asked, carefully laying a

hand on my shoulder as he guided me back to a barstool. I flexed my hand—I'd feel that for a while—and rested my head on my arms.

I grunted.

"Based on your reaction just now, which I'm assuming was because you thought about ending it with Hazel, you shouldn't break it off." Shocked, I lifted my head and narrowed my eyes at him. "Don't look at me like that until you hear me out. What's going to happen? Val's probably going to come after you, me, and Hazel for sure, right? Probably everyone else as well, if necessary."

I nodded.

"Okay, so we can handle it. We've done this before, and when she fucks up this time, we're calling the cops and having her arrested. I'm over this shit." All I could do was grunt again. We tried that last time, and it didn't work. Even the restraining order only lasted a year and that was a bitch to get. "But whether you end it with Hazel or not, Valerie will go after her because, based on what you told me about your conversation, she knows you care about her. It's not important to Valerie that you're with Hazel; what's important to her is that you care about her. Maybe even love her."

My eyes widen at his word choice, but I don't argue. I can't argue.

"So, what do you think Hazel's best bet is, huh? You leaving her to face Valerie alone, *or* you staying with Hazel and doing whatever the fuck you can to protect her from the psycho bitch?"

The possibility of not having to leave Hazel did more to tamp down my anger than punching the fridge did, but I was still hesitant. Josh had a point—it was likely Valerie would continue to pursue Hazel even if we weren't together. But to bet on that being her plan meant that I could have possibly put Hazel in even more danger.

"But what if we're wrong? What if breaking it off with Hazel," I ground out the words like my entire body was telling me that it wasn't even an option, "will completely stop it all? Or what if I stay with her and Valerie just escalates?"

Josh just shrugged. "We can't be a hundred-percent sure, but look, I know Valerie, too. And I'm telling you, if you were thinking about this less emotionally, then you'd come to the same conclusion I am: she will continue going after Hazel whether or not you're fucking her. She knows ending a relationship doesn't always change the feelings. And she's all about the fucking feelings."

I glowered at him. His logic was sound, and if I pushed away my emotional attachment, I knew he was probably right. Valerie and I had ended our marriage years before, yet her feelings had never changed. During the few unfortunate times I'd seen her since the divorce was final, she'd said as much—that ending our marriage didn't change what she felt or how she imagined *our* future.

"I was trying to fucking help her. I didn't mean to get her mixed up in this shit." I shook my head and thought back to the small, broken woman that I carried out of her own home that night almost two weeks before. She'd already suffered more than enough and by trying to help, I unknowingly unleashed more hell into her life.

"No one is going to blame you, least of all Hazel. That woman is honestly too damn understanding. But if you want Valerie to stop controlling your life, I think this is a good step. We should contact the cop that helped with your restraining order, and then we stay extra vigilant."

"Fucking fine," I groaned, pulling out my phone and locating the number of the cop, Detective Bell, that I'd been put in contact with only a few years ago.

"And you should probably fill Hazel in."

"Like hell. She already has enough shit going on, the last thing I want to do is scare her when we don't know how Valerie is going to react."

He shrugged again and the gesture was starting to piss me

off. I wish I had Josh's blasé attitude toward a lot of things, but the situation we were in was not one of them. "Knowing's half the battle. She'd want to be prepared, so you should tell her."

With that lovely statement, I dialed Detective Bell's number and prepared to relay the entire story for the third fucking time.

THIRTY-THREE

Hazel

"Not everything's going. Most of it is in the garage, and the rest of it, I clearly labeled with green duct tape." The gruff older man nodded at me and jotted down a few notes on his clipboard.

"Okay, nothing we can't handle. And is this the correct address, ma'am?" He pointed at the apartment address on his paperwork, and I confirmed that, indeed, that was my new home.

He continued writing as two guys, probably not too much younger than me, wheeled in two dollies and a few blankets to wrap the furniture in. They both gave me long, lingering looks, and I internally groaned. It was going to be one of *those* days.

The only thing I missed about wearing my engagement ring was that it usually dissuaded men from trying anything. I made a mental note to pick up a cheap cubic zirconia ring from the store next time I was there.

"Not a problem. I brought the muscle with me since you're on the second floor," he joked, and I gave him a pity laugh. "We should have you all loaded up within the hour at most."

He nodded and turned to his guys, directing them on what to begin with and leading them out into the garage.

I hopped onto the kitchen counter, trying to stay out of the way as much as I could and trying to keep away from the freezing late-fall air pushing through the open front door.

I pulled my phone from the convenient pocket in my leggings and only saw three texts from my dad, sister, and my mom, all wishing me a happy moving day. They had all come around to the fact that I was staying in Austin, whether they liked it or not. Delilah was eternally supportive, but it took a few conversations with Mom to persuade both her and my dad that I would be perfectly fine.

I tapped out a response, letting them know that the day was off to a great start and I'd keep them updated. Delilah requested pictures, and I told her I'd send some as soon as I could.

My car was already mostly packed with a few items I didn't want them moving in the truck, along with a few odds and ends. So, my job was done, which meant that all I had to do for the next hour while the movers packed the truck was wait. Which also gave me a substantial amount of time to just sit with my thoughts.

I'd been so busy—both intentionally keeping myself busy and unintentionally—that I hadn't had much time to stop and really take in what was changing. With the movers slowly wheeling out my life, it all hit me.

I wasn't getting married; I wasn't in love; I wasn't living in my house anymore. My life had completely changed.

But I was mostly happy. I felt independent and free in a way I'd never known while I was under Michael's thumb. I was happy, but I was also terrified that I'd fuck it all up; I was independent, but I was alone. If I fucked it up, I didn't have a partner to fall back on.

However, I knew if I could survive Michael, I could survive reinventing my life or anything else the world decided to throw at me.

I had to admit that also having Luke around was a distraction I appreciated. Well, except for the day before.

I overheard part of a phone conversation that made me pause. I hadn't meant to eavesdrop, but I passed the door to my office that was slightly ajar when I was heading back to my bedroom for the other roll of packing tape. I wasn't planning on stopping, but when I heard the intensity of his hushed whisper and caught a glimpse of his tense posture in the crack of the door, my curiosity won out.

He was standing at the opposite side of the office, facing the window, and although the room wasn't large, it was still difficult to make out the entirety of the conversation. However, I did hear the words "she called" and a few "fucks" before he said my name, and with my heart pounding, I took that as my cue to move.

I hauled ass back into the kitchen and tried to continue what I was doing. Luckily, it was several more minutes before Luke appeared at the end of the hallway with an amused smile on his face.

The few minutes before he'd appeared had given me enough time to rationalize the conversation. My initial reaction was that he was talking about another woman that he was sleeping with or something even worse. But I talked myself down from the catastrophizing ledge—there were other women in Luke's life, including Josh's ex-girlfriend, Samantha, and his other close friends.

When Luke told me he had to go because of something with Josh and Zach, the idea that it was Samantha that had called made even more sense. But I could feel the change in his mood and noticed the tight set of his features. He also had a difficult time meeting my eyes and was abrupt when he left. He wasn't telling me the whole truth.

I hadn't slept at all, evidenced by the dark circles I had a hell of a time covering up that morning. Women never appreciated being lied to, and although I felt like I'd gotten closer to Luke in the few weeks we'd actually spent together, I still didn't *know* him. He was a closed fucking book for the most part, and with the way he left things, I was glad I had trusted my gut and kept his dick out of my vagina.

Pulling myself from my thoughts, I checked my phone again to see if I had any messages from Luke; he still said when he left the day before that he'd be here. It was still early—only a little past ten—but I was becoming more and more paranoid that he wasn't going to show up at all.

What better time to ghost me than when I was about to move?

I tried to not let myself think that I'd done something wrong because I knew I hadn't. But my mind had been trained by Michael to believe that everything that happened, including his bad moods, was my fault.

I hadn't done anything. I repeated it over and over again until I thought I might believe it.

I rolled my eyes at my stupidity. I was severely overthinking the situation, and I was irritated that I'd let myself become so emotionally invested in another person already.

Seriously, what the hell was wrong with me?

To take my mind off pretty much everything else, I pulled my laptop from its case on the counter next to me and opened my file. I was halfway through the first draft of my book, and I was mostly impressed with it so far. There were days when I wanted to delete the entire thing because it was garbage, but then there were other days when I smiled to myself and knew it could work.

I threw myself into it, easily picking up right where I left off and was only pulled out of my intense writing state when I heard the scuff of a pair of boots right in front of me.

When I peered up from my screen, I was greeted by one of the young movers. He was grinning from ear to ear, showing off his perfectly white teeth. Since the high was in the midforties, he was wearing thick pants and a sweatshirt, but I could still tell he was probably pretty built underneath his many layers.

He yanked off the beanie and scrubbed his hand through his disheveled, dirty-blond hair. "I'm so sorry to disturb you, ma'am, but I forgot my water this morning. Do you have any water bottles or maybe a glass I can use?"

My cheeks flushed because he'd approached me right in the middle of the main character's first actual sex scene and I'd hoped he hadn't noticed or taken it as me blushing at him.

I set my laptop aside and pushed off the counter. "Umm... I think I have water bottles in the laundry room. Let me see."

I returned with a few in my hands. "They aren't cold, if that's okay?" I held one out and he took it, letting his fingers linger over mine for a moment.

"Yes, ma'am, that's great. Thank you."

I cringed at him calling me "ma'am," but we were in the south and that's just how everyone spoke. With his characteristically Southern drawl, it was especially obvious he grew up in the South, and I wouldn't expect he'd call me anything less than "ma'am" whether I liked it or not. "I'll put the rest in the fridge in case y'all need anymore."

He downed the water bottle in a few slow gulps and tossed the empty container in the trash. He smiled again and even winked at me before he put his beanie back on and returned to work.

It took a little over an hour for the men to pack up the truck. I swept through the house one last time and confirmed they'd retrieved everything before they started closing the truck and grabbing their moving supplies from inside the house.

Hunter, the young mover from earlier, continued glancing in my direction each time he passed me, moving furniture from the bedrooms and my office. The older man, Bobby, was not amused with his lack of concentration and reprimanded him several times.

I couldn't lie, I had enjoyed the attention, and Hunter seemed innocent enough. He was telling me a joke about a woman they helped move who had a sex dungeon as he carried the final box that went in my car for me.

Walking down the porch stairs, he told me that the bottom had fallen out of one of the boxes while they were loading everything up and at least fifty dildos and other sex toys had fallen onto the driveway and began rolling down toward the street. They stood around and watched as the woman retrieved all of her dildos and retaped the box.

I was doubled over laughing at the insane story when I all but ran into a hard chest. Still giggling, I peered up into Luke's hard, green eyes. "Hey, Luke," I managed to say before I continued laughing. I swiped under my eyes, brushing away the tears. I had forgotten the last time I'd laughed so hard I cried.

When he didn't respond, I asked Hunter to put the box in my trunk. He eyed Luke suspiciously but only hesitated a moment before he continued walking to my car.

"Looks like things are going well here," Luke said, watching Hunter load the final box in my car and shut the trunk.

"I'll be right behind y'all," I said. Hunter glanced back at us one last time and hesitated as he hopped up into the truck next to the other two guys and backed out of the driveway.

I turned back to Luke and saw a glint of jealousy in his eyes which was only confirmed by his clenched jaw and the way he watched the moving truck slowly back out into the street. "Yeah, it went well. Didn't take them any time at all."

"Good. Do you have anything else that needs to go in your car? We can use my truck, too." I tried to keep my surprise off my face; I guess that meant he still planned to help me, whether he was later than I expected or not.

"No, everything's in my car. I just need to do one last walk-through and then lock up."

He waited in the entryway while I did my second walk-through of the day. Scanning every corner, opening every drawer, and taking one last peek at each room felt good.

I repacked my laptop in its case, grabbed my purse, and didn't shed a tear when I closed and locked the door for the last time.

"I'll meet you there," Luke said in a tight voice. His hands were shoved into the pockets of his jeans and all I wanted to do was confront him about his erratic behavior. But I caught myself before I could open my mouth. I knew it wasn't the right time to say anything.

So, I simply said "okay" over my shoulder as I headed toward my own car.

When we pulled up to my new apartment building, the movers were already backed into the parking lot and idling in front of the walkway up to the second floor.

I waved at the guys who were rolling up the door to the truck and jogged up the stairs to let them into my unit. When I opened the door, I was immediately met with the scent of clean carpet and new paint. I did a quick walk-through of the space—which didn't take long since it was a one-bedroom, one-bathroom apartment—making sure each room was completely clean before I ran back down the stairs to let the guys begin moving me in.

Luke hopped out of his truck which he parked next to my jeep and sauntered over to me. His hands were yet again tucked in his pockets, but he seemed a little more relaxed.

"Is your car unlocked? I'll start grabbing stuff out of the trunk," he said without meeting my eyes.

"Yeah, it's open." He headed back the way he came, and I scowled. What the heck was up his butt? But I didn't have a lot of time to continue contemplating his shitty attitude when Savannah strolled up to me.

"Our newest tenant. Welcome!" She threw her hands wide

and wrapped them around me in an awkward embrace. "I just wanted to come by and check in. How's it going so far?"

She was wearing skintight dark skinny jeans and a burgundy sweater with a deep enough V that it couldn't have provided any warmth. Her heels also made her several inches taller than me. Just like the first time I'd seen her, she looked like a Southern Barbie doll.

"We just got here, but the place looks great. Thanks for checking in," I said, trying to dismiss her without sounding too… dismissive.

"That's so great to hear. And look, you have your helper again." I swear I saw fucking hearts in her eyes when Luke stepped up next to me, a huge tub of my important papers in his arms.

My helper, huh? "Yes, Luke's helping me out," I said as Savannah twirled her hair in her fingers and licked her bottom lip. The girl was really laying it on.

Luke's only greeting to her was a tight smile and a nod. He looked down at me and said, "Won't take me too long to grab the stuff, so just relax, Angel." Then he leaned forward and kissed the top of my head before turning and jogging up the stairs with the box.

My heart thumped, and it was all I could do to not keep the smug grin of satisfaction off my face. He knew it bothered me last time—before much had even happened between us—that Savannah's attention was all on him. So, he made it a point to reaffirm that he wasn't interested in her.

It diminished some of the contempt I felt about his attitude. *Some* of it.

Savannah's face immediately dropped, but I was impressed with how quickly she recovered. She prattled on about the move-in checklist I needed to complete and return to the office by the following morning. She also instructed me that under no uncertain terms are tenants allowed overnight guests for more than three consecutive days.

I had to assure her three fucking times that it wouldn't be an issue.

I guess the third time was the charm, though, because she finally bounced her way back to the leasing office just on the other side of the parking lot.

"Always a pleasure, Savvy," I muttered under my breath as I grabbed a box out of my trunk.

Upstairs, Bobby and the other guy, whose name I never actually caught, were pushing boxes to the end of the kitchen while Hunter was unwrapping the one piece of living room furniture I actually had—a large gray chair that could fit two people comfortably.

He wrapped the plastic in a ball and winked at me when I passed through the living room and into my bedroom. Whether the grin on my face was intentional or not, whether it meant anything or not, Luke scowled when he noticed who I had smiled at as he walked out of the bedroom.

Hunter walked out of the front door, and Luke threw a death glare at his back. I stopped directly in front of him, the box still in my hands, and pushed up onto my toes until his focus was back on me.

"What was that for?"

He shrugged, and I lost it. Using the box in front of me, I shoved it into his hands. I pushed him back into the bedroom and into my small walk-in closet. I swung the door closed behind me.

"Okay, enough, dude. What is going on?"

He gaped at me for a moment and his jaw clenched. He set the box I'd aggressively shoved into his hands on the floor. And then I realized my mistake.

The space around us was too small and suddenly, the air was thicker. An all too familiar ache in my chest made it hard to breathe. And panic, like an old friend, bubbled inside of me.

The look on Luke's face was virtually unreadable, and when he lifted his hand, I knew what was coming. Like an omen of what the rest of my life would be, I flinched and prepared for the pain.

But it didn't come. Instead, I opened my eyes to see him scrub his hands down his face. He looked tired, exhausted really, and I felt a little sorry for losing it.

"I'm sorry," he said, the regret clear in his voice.

For a moment, I was embarrassed. But it wasn't my fault—my innate reaction wasn't my fault. Michael would've hit me for my outburst and made me regret saying anything against him. But I was standing in front of Luke. Luke was apologetic about his behavior, and his green eyes held all the sincerity I needed to see.

I was grateful he hadn't seen me flinch—I didn't want to explain myself or my unconscious reaction.

"Is everything okay with Josh and Zach?"

His brow tightened, and he looked confused for long enough that my earlier suspicions were confirmed—it was a lie. "You said last night when you left in a hurry that something happened with Josh and Zach. I'm guessing based on your face" —I pointed to the obvious expression—"that that's not why you left. So can you please tell me what the hell has you in such a shit mood?"

He sighed and reached for me, but I swerved out of the way. I needed to hear what was happening before I let him touch me because every time he touched me—as evidenced by the small kiss he gave me in front of Savannah—I turned into a foolish teenage girl and all sense went out the window. This was no time for butterflies.

He flinched when I moved out of the way of his hand but seemed like he understood.

"I promise I have an explanation for my shitty attitude. I'll tell you everything after the movers leave. But it's not necessarily a conversation I want to have an audience for."

My stomach dropped and my heart plummeted right along with it. My first instinct was that it was all over—that he was done with me before we even got started. I bit my bottom lip to keep it from quivering and willed the tears threatening to pool in my eyes not to fall.

His eyes were glued to my face, and he saw the hurt there. Damn it, why couldn't I keep my facial expressions controlled like he did?

"Whatever you're thinking right now, it's not that." His hand hesitantly reached for my face, and foolishly, I let him run his thumb down my cheek, which freed a tear from where I was holding it hostage. "Tell me what you're thinking."

"It doesn't matter," I muttered, his thumb holding my chin.

"It does matter."

"Why?" I countered.

He sighed and cupped both sides of my face in his hands. "So I can tell you that you're wrong." He waited for a moment, but I couldn't muster the words. They sounded weak in my head and obviously self-conscious, and I didn't want to sound like that. "Tell me," he said once more in a lower, more threatening, demanding tone.

My words were barely audible, but he was so close to me, I knew he'd hear. "I'm thinking that you're about to tell me that this was all fun, but that's all it was. It was fun, and now you're done."

A sly grin pulled at one side of his mouth, forming that intoxicating lopsided smile I couldn't get enough of. "Not even close, sweet girl." And then his mouth was on mine and reflexively, my arms slid from where they were crossed in front of my chest to wrap around his torso and pull him closer to me.

Swiftly and automatically, a hungry desire coursed through me, and I didn't really care what the fuck was going on with him as long as he still wanted me. And the way he tangled his tongue with mine, forcing our kiss deeper and deeper. I knew he did.

A loud bang from somewhere else inside the apartment finally pulled us free from one another. Both of us gasping, I smiled up at him as we caught our breath.

"Glad we cleared that up," he mumbled and reached for the door after he readjusted his thick erection.

"Wait," I said, stopping him as he twisted the knob. "What the hell are all the dirty looks at Hunter for?"

He gave me a nonchalant shrug. "He's giving you too much attention and staring at your ass every five seconds."

I rolled my eyes and pushed him lightly in the chest. "Oh no, sir. You do not get to be all possessive when you've had a shit attitude all morning. And it doesn't matter anyway. They can look as long as they don't touch or say anything to me."

"Did one of them say something to you? Or touch you?" he growled.

I rolled my eyes at his possessiveness. "No, Luke. That's what I'm saying: if they want to stare at my ass, I don't care."

He didn't seem satisfied, so I continued. "You're the only one I'm letting between my legs, so you have no reason to go all caveman on me."

That statement got me another sly smirk and darkness in his eyes. Both of those, along with the possessiveness, seriously had me turned on, although I wouldn't tell him that.

"You're mine," he said, wrapping an arm around my waist and pulling me flush against him. A thrill lit through me, and I think I moaned.

"If it makes you feel better to say that, then fine," I said in what was supposed to be a mocking tone, but with the arousal pulsing between my legs, it didn't come out that way at all.

His hands traveled down my back until he gripped my ass, squeezing tightly. "Did you have to wear your tightest pair of leggings, though? No wonder they're fucking staring."

"You're staring, too. Don't lie." I gasped when his tongue dragged a line up to my ear and his palms squeezed even tighter.

"I am," he murmured against my neck.

"Hey, Hazel? You in here?" A voice inside my bedroom called out. I noted the playfulness in Luke's eyes just before he tightened his grip around me with one hand while the other swung open the door. Sure enough, Hunter was walking past the closet and out of the bedroom when he turned at the door opening beside him.

Understanding and maybe a hint of jealousy crossed his face as he took in the sight before him: me breathing hard, standing flush against Luke with a healthy blush on my cheeks as his hand still palmed my ass.

I inwardly groaned but knew it would be foolish to try to pull away from Luke; he'd keep me hostage against his side until Hunter got the message. *Mine.*

"Umm… We…" Hunter stuttered, and I felt bad. He was a good kid, and I didn't want to hurt his feelings. "We're done out here. The boss just needs you to sign some papers."

On that note, Luke did loosen his grip, and I was able to step out of the closet. "That was fast," I remarked as I followed Hunter into the kitchen and threw a scowl over my shoulder at Luke, who wore a shit-eating grin.

THIRTY-FOUR

Hazel

As I signed the paperwork confirming all my belongings made it into the apartment and nothing was damaged, Luke stood behind me, his hand rubbing the back of my neck and then down my spine. The heat of his body pressed into me.

By the time the men left, my entire body was alive. But I remembered that he had things to tell me and talked myself down from jumping him.

Luke shut the door and turned to stare at me with a shake of his head. "That was interesting."

"Interesting?" I asked, grabbing my phone off the counter and pulling up the food delivery app. My stomach was growling, and after being stressed and busy, it was the first time food had crossed my mind.

"Apparently Hunter didn't get the message. Although I feel like I made myself pretty clear." He leaned back onto the counter, crossing his arms over his chest. He'd long since chucked off his jacket and how he stood showed off the muscles in his forearms and the detailed ink there.

"What are you talking about? He didn't try anything else." I pause scrolling through my app for a moment to mimic his posture. Crossing my arms over my chest, I, too, leaned my back against the counter directly across from him.

The kitchen was upgraded with white quartz counters I was sure to ruin sooner rather than later, along with stainless steel appliances and wood cabinets. But it was still a tight alley layout and even on "opposite" sides of the kitchen, we were fairly close together.

Luke smirked when I raised an eyebrow as an invitation to elaborate and answer my question.

"Look at the fridge. Right there on the side." He pointed behind me, and I slowly swung my head to the left. On the side of the fridge was the magnet with the management numbers the office had given me and the paper with the move-in checklist I had to complete. Then, farther to the back was another, smaller piece of paper. I squinted, leaning over the counter to see what it said.

My eyes widened in surprise, and I ripped it off the fridge, flinging the magnet holding it across the kitchen.

Luke chuckled and peered over my shoulder at a scrap of paper. Scrawled in messy handwriting was Hunter's name and his phone number.

"When the hell did he leave this?" I was actually surprised. I also thought Luke had made it more than obvious that I had my hands full, at least with him.

Luke shrugged and plucked the paper from between my fingers. For a second, he inspected it and then promptly ripped it in half and then in half again before he threw it in the trash can under the sink.

I gaped at him.

"You don't need it," he said in response to the look on my face.

I bit the inside of my cheek, trying not to smile or show him how much that little gesture affected me. I recrossed my arms over my chest and said, "How do you know? Maybe I'll tape it back together later. He was nice and funny and attractive…" I watched his face closely, seeing a flash of jealousy just before it was replaced by a look of amusement.

He licked his bottom lip and my heart thundered in my chest as he took a step to close the distance between us. I figured he'd come up with some smart remark or lay claim to me once again, but he didn't. He cupped my face in both of his hands and leaned in to kiss me.

Not even half a second after our lips met, an involuntary moan slipped from my throat. Luke smiled against my mouth, and I couldn't help but smile back. He knew the response he elicited from me without even trying and that was his point, I was guessing. The way I felt around him—with or without his hands or lips on me—was a way I had never felt before, a way I wasn't sure was actually possible until only a few weeks ago.

With one simple kiss, and without any words, he claimed me once again. *Mine.*

But the intensity of my feelings exacerbated my anxiety. My life was changing drastically every day, and I had to admit that my heart was still healing from Michael. Sometimes my thoughts were too intrusive, and I couldn't contain the images that appeared at random. It seemed even worse when I felt like I had less control over my life as a whole.

Thankfully, Luke, with his calming and unshakable presence, was a godsend during the rockiest transitional time. But it was all happening at warp speed while I felt like I was falling and flailing.

My thoughts were all over the place, and Luke noticed the immediate change. He leaned his forehead against mine and ran his hands down my arms. When his hands reached my own, he forced me to unfurl my fingers from the fists at my sides.

"You're too in your head, Angel. Talk to me," he whispered, coaxing me out of my thoughts.

"It's a lot."

"What is?" He kissed my forehead.

"Everything."

He raised my hands and looped them around his neck. My fingers tangled in the back of his hair, my nails running over his neck, and he shivered. The small movement made me smile, which he didn't miss.

"I love it when you do that," he said.

"I love doing it." He kissed me softly then. His lips barely grazed my own but still made me weak at the knees.

"Tell me about everything." I sighed, just wanting him to continue kissing me.

"You already know," I said, hoping he'd take it as his cue to put his mouth back on mine.

He nodded and brushed my hair out of my eyes as he leaned back. "I'm ready to listen whenever you want to talk."

His sincerity filled me with warmth, and I wanted to drown in it. Let it comfort me until there was only the warmth of him surrounding me. But there were other things going on.

So, I pushed the intrusive image of Michael's fist flying at my face out of my mind as well as the panic of the unknown and tried to enjoy the moment for what it was.

"Speaking of talking, you said you had something to tell me."

"Umm... I do." He took a deep breath and squeezed the back of his neck with one of his hands. "Food first, though. Might go over easier on a full stomach and I could hear yours growling from across the room."

My throat tightened, but I nodded. I'd faced everything that had been thrown my way thus far, and I'd face what was still to come, too.

The empty containers of Greek food were scattered on the floor of the living room. My stomach was fuller than I ever remembered it being and before I could control it, a fleeting thought had me worried that I shouldn't have eaten so much. But I remembered quickly that Michael was no longer in my life to critique what I put in my mouth.

Luke and I were sitting next to each other on the floor and leaned against the large chair. He was absentmindedly playing with my fingers, and I was waiting for him to start talking. He seemed lost in his own thoughts, just as I had been earlier.

Just when I thought he wasn't actually going to say anything, he sighed and pulled me onto his lap. My legs fell on either side of his, and he placed his hands on my hips.

"I think this might be easier to talk about with you close."

My hands fell softly onto his chest, and I made myself comfortable on his lap. He didn't speak for several minutes, only squeezing my hips every once in a while and looking at nothing in particular. His silence was freaking me out even more.

"You're starting to worry me," I said quietly.

"I'm sorry. I..." He cleared his throat, and it was easy enough to see how difficult it was for him. I was dying to know what was happening but seeing him struggle made me want to comfort him.

"I told you I was married before."

My brow furrowed, wondering where he was going with that, but I nodded. I didn't know much about the woman—Valerie—but still knew that she was bad news.

"We started dating right after I finished vet school. She'd been part of our friend group for a while, and I knew she'd always had a crush on me. But I never did anything about it until after I'd finished school. Those details aren't important, though." He waved his hand around like it wasn't, but I had a feeling every detail of their relationship was insanely important. "Almost as soon as we started dating, she became very possessive and attached to me, but I didn't realize it at the time. I was going through a tough time, and she was there."

He readjusted me on his lap. "Josh never liked her, even when she was just our friend, but he really didn't like her when we started dating. No one liked how she treated me, but I didn't listen. It was eight months to the day after we started dating that we got married. We were both twenty-five and thought we were in love."

He chuckled, but it was a hollow sound. "We lasted a full year, but I knew it wasn't going to work the first month in. I realized she would do things just to rile me up and make my temper flare. She was just nasty and hateful a lot of the time, but then she'd switch like someone had flipped something. There were other things, too, but let's just say it was not a healthy relationship. After that first month, the other eleven months we were together, I spent trying to convince myself that it wasn't that bad."

For the first time since he had begun talking, he raised his eyes to meet mine. The green of them was potent, but behind them was sadness like I'd never seen. I contemplated what I could do to take away even a small amount of that sadness, but I wasn't sure there was anything.

"She pretended to have cheated on me, even came home with hickeys and marks on her body as *'proof.'* She did it because she liked it when I got pissed, and if she couldn't get to me, she'd turn me against other people. She liked it, and..." He blew out a breath, and I almost told him to stop. That I didn't need to know if it was that hard to say. "She liked it because then we'd argue and I'd take it out on her... body. She got off on making me angry, actually angry. She told me afterward that she lied about cheating. I left within the week, stayed with a friend and then moved into that apartment as soon as I could.

"She was not happy when I filed for divorce. The day I filed the papers, she sent me hundreds of messages, called me over a hundred times, trying to get me to come back. She did some fucked-up shit to almost everyone in my life, including all our mutual friends, because they took my side according to her. But when she realized I was going to divorce her no matter what, she broke into my apartment. She was screaming incoherently and trashed the entire place."

Luke was shaking underneath me. His face was red, and he was deep in horrific memories. I cupped his face in both of my hands, brushing my thumbs over his black facial hair and urging him to look at me. "Luke, look at me," I said softly. He did immediately and I could see his pupils dilate and his eyes refocus.

He covered my hand with one of his still pressed to his cheek. "If I told you all the shit that she did, we'd be here all night. But she…" His voice broke over the words. But he cleared his throat and continued, "She almost hurt Sadie, tried to stab me. She was out of her mind."

I gasped, and the pain in my chest felt like my heart had broken into two or maybe several sharp pieces.

"I finally got her to leave and was able to get a protective order a few days later. That kept her away for a while."

He took a deep breath, and I tried to contain the tears pooling at the corners of my eyes. When one ran down my face, he wiped it away immediately. "Please don't cry, Angel. I'm okay, I promise."

But that didn't help. My heart still ached for him, and my gut churned at the thought of her hurting him. Or the thought of her hurting Sadie.

"Long story short, the divorce was finalized, and for a while, she was MIA. I thought she'd actually just decided to leave me the fuck alone until I started sleeping with one of our mutual friends. When Valerie found out I was sleeping with Blakely, she came after us both. It was casual and only happened a couple of times. But it was several months before Valerie finally believed that Blakely and I were never sleeping together again and weren't interested in each other like that."

He paused, rolling his neck along his shoulders and peering up at the ceiling. "That was more than two years ago and was the last time I heard from her until yesterday."

She called. My jaw dropped, but I quickly schooled my features.

"She stole Josh's phone Halloween night—the same night you were also at Murphy's. She found my number. When she called while I was at your house yesterday, it really freaked me out. Just hearing her fucking voice makes my skin crawl."

He shivered and closed his eyes. I gave him a moment to continue talking, but when he didn't say anything, I asked, "Why'd she call?" Seemed like the chick must have had a reason to contact him again after all that time.

I had an idea why she had, but I was sincerely hoping I was wrong.

His eyes darkened. "Mostly because of you."

My breath caught in my throat. In that moment, I didn't know what I was feeling. I was heartbroken and angry for Luke, but I was also worried and panicked and overwhelmed for us both.

"Angel, please listen," Luke pleaded. He gripped both sides of my face, forcing me to look at him and straightened. "I never meant to put you in the middle of this. The last thing I ever want to do is fucking hurt you. I know life's given you a shit hand recently, and I never meant to add to it just by being near you."

"I know," I said.

He nodded but didn't relax or release his grip on me. "Since that phone call yesterday, I've been going back and forth with what to do. You're in her sights now, and it's only a matter of time before she begins terrorizing you."

Much to my surprise, I wasn't as scared as I imagined I would be when faced with the impending wrath of Luke's psychotic ex. Maybe it was because I had survived Michael, so in my mind, I could survive anything. I thought he'd be the worst I'd have to face.

"You said she eventually left Blakely alone, right? So, don't you think she'd do the same thing to me? If she thinks we're just casually hooking up?" I was careful with my word choice because all signs led to us not being a casual hookup. But I didn't want to lay it all out there right that second.

He shook his head adamantly. His green eyes bore into mine. "She knows I care about you. She knows how important you are to me, and I don't think this is going to be anything like the last time."

Well, fuck.

"What do we do?"

One corner of his mouth quirked up in a small smile, and my brow furrowed in confusion. Why the ever-loving hell was he smiling in a time like this?

"You said we." He said, explaining his smile. "I've been going back and forth with what to do, and there're only two options I can think of. Your safety is my number one priority, and with that being said, the first option is that we both move on."

Before he could expand on the first option, I was already shaking my head, which he still had cupped in his hands, making it harder for me to move.

"Let me explain before you start arguing. If we go our separate ways, it's more likely that she'll give up on going after you, seeing as you'd no longer be in my life."

"But that's not foolproof, right?"

"No, it's not. But it's the only option that has the greatest possibility of keeping you safe. We at least do it until I can figure out how to get her out of my life forever."

"What's the second option?"

He dropped his hands from my face to grip my hands between us. "We keep living our lives and don't let Valerie's threats stop us from this." He motioned between us. "If we do, then I'll do everything in my power to protect you, and we should be more vigilant about watching our backs. I've already spoken to the detective that helped me with my restraining order, and I'm going to keep him updated on anything that happens. But it's possible she'll do whatever she can to make both of our lives a living hell."

I opened my mouth to respond, but before I could say

anything, he clamped his hand over my mouth. "Before you say anything, I want you to think about what you're going to say. And seriously think about your response."

When I didn't do anything, he tilted his head to the side and raised his eyebrows, silently asking me to acknowledge his request. Begrudgingly I nodded, and he slowly removed his hand.

I contemplated ignoring his request and just blurting out the first thing that popped into my head, but he was right. I should take more than a second to think it over, so I quickly ran through the pros and cons of all two options.

Based on everything Luke told me, the possibility that Valerie would just let me walk away seemed unlikely. Between her previous treatment of him and his friends, along with the fact that she stole Josh's phone, meant this chick was actually obsessed.

And after hearing Luke's story and the abuse he also endured at the hand of a partner, I felt even more pulled to him. No wonder he understood me in ways I didn't think possible. He was cautious when I needed him to be and pushed me when necessary. He read my facial expressions and posture like he was actually in my head, probably because he had gone through some of the same things.

The first option may have sounded like the best option for my self-preservation. But I kept going back to the same two thoughts: I had survived Michael, and I wanted Luke in whatever way I could have him.

"I'll take the red pill," I said confidently.

"Did you... did you just quote *The Matrix*?" he spluttered.

I laughed, extremely glad he got the reference. "Yes."

He shook his head. "So, I'm assuming the red pill is option two."

I nodded as he shifted and gripped the back of my neck with one hand and forced me closer to him by wrapping the other around my waist. He buried his head in my neck and took a deep breath as I said, "I'm not ready for our story to end."

He chuckled against me, and I felt the warmth of his breath against my neck. I could feel his relief in his deep sigh and the way his entire body relaxed into me. My fingers automatically ran through his thick, black hair and he shivered before he kissed my neck.

"I'm so selfish, but that's what I wanted you to say," he groaned. "I will protect you, Hazel."

"I know you will." I knew he would try, but I hoped, for both of our sakes, that he wouldn't have to. That we were done with the curveballs and the unexpected.

THIRTY-FIVE

Hazel

When I woke up early the following morning to find Luke and I had fallen asleep on the chair in my living room, I contemplated asking him to move with me to my bed. But I realized that would require digging through a box to find sheets and putting them on. So instead, I snuggled back into his chest, and we both slept soundly for another few hours until the shrill ringing of his phone woke us both with a start.

Josh actually had an issue this time; his car wouldn't start, and he was supposed to pick up Zach earlier that morning. So, Luke rushed out with the promise to be back later and help me unpack. And with the reminder that I should be careful.

I was counting down the minutes until I saw him again like a freaking crazy person.

Having taken the day off work, I had the day to myself and time to organize my new space. I also wanted to do anything to keep my mind occupied and hopefully far away from the topic of Valerie.

I wasn't second-guessing my decision that Luke and I should continue on with our lives and not let her ruin something that I felt could be good. But the idea that she was unpredictable and obsessive had me on edge in a way I hadn't been since Michael left. So, I tackled the stupid move-in checklist first since Savannah had already emailed me by ten a.m. reminding me it was due.

After inspecting my entire apartment, the only issue I found was with the lock on my balcony door. It didn't latch properly even when I tried to force it down. I noted the issue on the form before grabbing my keys and heading out of my apartment.

Luckily, the front door lock was working as it should with the magnetic key the complex had provided.

It was still early in the morning and the cold November air whipped around me even with the hood of my jacket pulled snug around my head. It was because of the thick hood that I didn't realize my new neighbor was also leaving until I heard a faint yet chipper "Hi!"

Startled, my keys fell from my hand, along with the move-in checklist, when I whipped my head around to see who was speaking.

"Oh shit. I'm sorry. I didn't mean to startle you," she apologized and scooped both my keys and the paper off the floor. "I'm just excited to have a new neighbor."

She handed my belongings back to me, and I thanked her as my heart rate settled back down to normal.

"I'm Lexi," she said, sticking out her hand and straightening her shoulders. She was probably around my age, maybe a little older, with vibrant orange hair. It was a stark contrast to her pale skin.

I shook her hand. "I'm Hazel. It's nice to meet you."

When our hands met, she tensed a little at my freezing cold touch, confidently squeezing my hand.

"How was your first night here?" she asked with a large, seemingly genuine smile plastered to her face.

"It was good."

"Do you live alone, or do you have a roommate?" For a

second, I thought about how odd it would be to have a roommate in a one-bedroom apartment, but I guessed it wouldn't be completely unheard of.

"Nope, just me."

"Me too. Well, I was just off to work, but we should hang out sometime."

I hesitated for a moment. The only things I knew about the woman was that she lived next to me, and her name was Lexi. But I needed more friends; if I was going to make a serious go of living in the city, I had to make more friends that didn't consist of my work friend, Stephanie, who I was rarely able to see, and Luke. Lexi reminded me of a friend from my childhood anyway. She was warm and exuded happiness with an unfaltering smile.

So, I pushed away my insecurities and my hesitance and agreed. "Yeah, that sounds great."

"Perfect," she said, bouncing on her toes as she pulled her phone out of her back pocket. "Here. Give me your number and we can find a time that works for both of us."

I typed my name and number in her phone before handing it back to her.

"Okay, I'll text you and we can find a time to meet up."

"Absolutely," I said, trying to match her level of glee but knowing I was likely far from it.

She waved before she hurried down the stairs with her large bag slung over one shoulder and her laptop gripped in her hands.

I continued to the office just across the parking lot and turned in the move-in checklist. Savannah was less than enthusiastic about putting in the service request for my patio door; however, when I mentioned that I'm sure Luke wouldn't mind coming over and fixing it for me if the maintenance guy was as busy as Savannah made him out to be, she immediately input the request and let me know he would be there the same afternoon.

The chick had it bad for him, and I mean, I couldn't blame her—I also had it bad. But, come on. Enough was enough.

Back in my apartment, staring at the boxes stacked against most of the walls, I was feeling slightly overwhelmed. Restarting by myself and reorganizing my life was part of it, and I was accustomed to being alone since Michael was gone so frequently anyway. As I stared at those plentiful cardboard boxes that held my life, I realized that what was most overwhelming was that, for the first time in my life, I wasn't dreading what was coming next.

The weight of my new life was heavy, but I didn't feel it necessary to constantly look over my shoulder to make sure Michael wasn't lurking and ready to start an argument. I didn't feel the need to check my phone several times an hour to make sure I didn't miss a call or a text from him. And I wasn't staring at the clock, calculating how much longer I had to be in peace before he came back home.

Hindsight is a bitch. Looking back, I could identify that I should have never felt the need to do any of those things; I was scared to live my life in my own house. But in the moment, I rationalized all of it.

So, the cardboard boxes, and the new life, although daunting, were absolutely liberating in the best way. And in true form, I began to cry, happy and relieved tears. And each day, I seemed to mend and heal more of myself.

I was *so* tired of crying all the time but emotions were high.

The tears slowly subsided, and I was eager to get everything organized. I was in the middle of trying to decide which shelf my glasses should go on when my phone buzzed on the counter. Seeing Delilah's name roll across the screen made me cringe—I had completely forgotten to give her an update yesterday, and I knew she'd be upset.

"Hi, D," I said.

"Don't 'Hi, D,' me. You were supposed to call me last night and you didn't respond this morning either. I've been worried."

I rolled my eyes but didn't say anything as she continued giving me her usual spiel about how she was just concerned about me being on my own again and that I couldn't blame her for being a worried big sister.

"I don't blame you, D. I'm sorry I didn't call or text."

She huffed. "I accept your apology. Now, how'd it go?"

"It went well. It didn't take them long at all, which isn't a surprise since I don't have that much stuff anymore. But I'm excited. This—this feels good."

"Is the place nice?"

"Yeah, it's a normal apartment. It's nothing fancy, but it will work until I decide on my next move. It's been updated and cleaned, so it hits all of the major points."

"I'm really proud of you, Hazel," Delilah said, and I could hear the smile in her voice. My chest tightened hearing her say it. "You've done something that's unimaginably difficult and done it with as much care and grace in your heart as ever. I understand that you want to keep this under wraps, and you don't want to go to the authorities. Although we're in complete disagreement on that, I want you to know that I will continue to support you no matter what. You're my hero, babe."

By the time she's done, I'm on the verge of crying again. God, even the happy tears are exhausting.

"That means a lot, D. I just want to move on. Like I told you the other day, an investigation means more of my energy will have to be spent on him and that's really the last thing I want. I might change my mind, we'll see what happens, but I need to make sure I'm completely away from him first."

Delilah had been a big proponent of getting the cops involved immediately, but I just couldn't do it. Just not yet. Luke had also mentioned it once or twice, but when I told him I needed to get out first, he stopped pressing the subject. I was sure that now that his ex was in the picture, we would possibly have bigger issues on our plate.

"One thing at a time—I get it. But, umm…"

I could hear the hesitance in her tone, and knowing my sister, she didn't hesitate to state what was on her mind—it had to be *something* then.

"What's wrong?"

"Michael's back in Austin. According to Mom, his mom told her he flew out super early this morning and probably landed only an hour or two ago. I wanted to make sure that you knew. That you weren't surprised, just in case."

I groaned and scrubbed a hand through my hair that seriously needed to be washed. I knew what that meant.

"So, it's only a matter of time before I get an *'I wanna talk'* text, I'm assuming?" I phrased it as a question, but I knew it was going to happen whether she confirmed it or not.

"That's part of it, yeah. A lot has happened the past few days, Hazel, and with you moving and everything, no one wanted to bother you, but..."

My heart beat wildly in my chest, and I felt my stomach turn at her unspoken words.

"D, tell me. You're scaring me."

She sighed. "Mom confronted Michael's mom. Told Joanie everything about Michael—his abuse and just everything. She felt so bad since you didn't want her to say anything, but she got fed up with the rumors that Joanie was contributing to with her own baseless bullshit. So, Mom kind of snapped. She only told Joanie, and it was when they were screaming at each other in the middle of the Flanigan's kitchen that Michael came in. Joanie immediately asked Michael if it was true, and according to Mom, he didn't deny it. Joanie believed her then. That was a few days ago, but yesterday she told Mom that he promised to go to therapy and get help for his obvious issues. Joanie also told Mom that Michael was going to make amends with you."

I was pacing the kitchen as she continued. I knew my mom couldn't keep quiet for very long, especially when she told me at least every other day that there were new rumors in their neighborhood and within their friend group. God, suburban women could freaking gossip.

"He wants to make amends with me?"

Over the phone, I could hear her shushing her children and talking quietly to who I assumed was Tony.

"Yes," she said breathlessly. "Of course, you do not have to see him or do anything for that asshole. I just wanted you to know. Mom went back and forth about telling you, but she kept fucking crying. So, I thought it would be better coming from me."

She was right. Hearing my mother bawling her eyes out was never going to help the situation, and I probably would have just been pissed. But I knew she had only told Joanie out of trying to protect me and trying to stick up for me. It was the motherly thing to do.

"Thanks for telling me, D," I mumbled. Just the thought of seeing Michael again was poking holes in my carefully crafted and comfortable bubble. I knew it had been too easy to separate myself from what had begun to feel like a previous life, even if it was only a few weeks that had passed.

"Just be prepared because Joanie made it sound like she was going to require him to make amends with you, just like she was going to make him go to therapy. I don't know what she threatened him with, probably with that damn trust fund, but knowing that, he's probably going to be pretty serious about meeting up with you. He always was a demanding little shit."

I paused my pacing, regretting that my boots were thudding against the hardwood floor and likely disturbing my neighbors below if they were home. Another matter of apartment life I had to get used to. The floors and walls were thin.

"Yeah, I understand."

"So, are you going to meet with him?" she asked, and I had no idea what the hell to say. Did I need the closure that meeting with him may provide?

"I don't know. It'll have to be a decision I make when, or if, he reaches out."

"Yeah, that makes sense. Well, if you do meet him, I think

you should meet at a public place and take someone with you. It's only smart."

"You're right. I'll consider that."

She cleared her throat. "Do you have someone that can go with you?"

The way she asked the question was like she already knew the answer. My first thought was that Luke would be more than happy to go with me and sit beside me while I let Michael try to explain away his actions, which he invariably would try to do. But Luke's presence would grate on Michael in a way that was sure to cause an incident. Part of me would be excited to see Michael pissed off, but that would be putting Luke in a situation he never asked for.

"Yeah, I have someone, but if we meet in a public place, that wouldn't be necessary."

"Who?" Delilah asked without missing a beat. And I didn't say anything. "Hazel, who would you bring with you?" The expectation was clear in her tone.

"Damn, D. I have friends, okay? I have a friend that can come with me if absolutely necessary."

She laughed. "What's his name?"

I groaned and wanted to throw a fit like a child. I didn't want to go into that with her, at least not at that moment, with the possibility of having to confront Michael hanging over my head. But I couldn't keep anything from my sister—my best friend.

"Luke," I sighed.

"I knew it!" she squealed, and I could hear her clapping. "Tell me."

I knew my sister was trying to be supportive and was genuinely interested in the new person in my life, but I didn't want to share him with anyone just yet. Especially with Valerie now back in his life, or our lives.

"Luke's just a friend, D. Please don't make this a whole thing."

"Are you dating?"

"I don't know… no. We're friends."

She scoffed. "You're lying. Seriously, tell me. I need to know what's going on and you're too far away for me to just stop by." Thank goodness for small miracles.

"D, I've just got a lot going on right now, and I don't want to go into it. For now, Luke is just a friend and he's been helping me a lot with moving and everything."

"I'm sure he has been helping," she said facetiously.

"Delilah, I'm serious."

"Okay, okay," she finally conceded. "But I want to hear all about him soon. Like really soon." And then screaming erupted from somewhere in her house as a door slammed, eliciting even more screams.

"Shit. I'll call you back later, Hazel. Miles and Amber have decided to fight about every damn thing lately. Let me know if Michael reaches out and what you decide to do."

I opened my mouth to respond, but a screeching interrupted me, and the phone disconnected. Often, that's how our conversations ended. Delilah only had enough time to talk when she wasn't at the office, and when she was at home, she liked to relieve Tony of his stay-at-home dad duties. And as great of a mother as my sister was, she was not so great at dealing with her children while also doing anything else. So, our phone calls ended with some sort of catastrophe, and I'd always get a text explanation after the fact.

At least that was one text I was looking forward to.

THIRTY-SIX

Luke

It had been a long day. I chugged a cup of coffee on the way back to Hazel's apartment from a day of shuttling Josh around and then stopping by the clinic for a few hours of work. I was deliriously tired even after a couple of espressos and then the cup of coffee as I pulled up to Hazel's apartment.

I took the stairs two at a time, heading to her second-floor apartment, and more eager than I thought I could be to see another person.

When I made it to the second floor, I was staring down at my phone, reading a text from Josh saying that he was going to get someone from Murphy's to take him home. Reading the text and not watching in front of me, it was no surprise that I ran directly into someone as I approached Hazel's door.

"Oh shit. I'm so sorry." I almost knocked the person down as I stumbled for my footing and the empty coffee cup flew out of my hand. My phone also fell directly in front of Hazel's door, and I stooped down to grab it as I said, "I should probably pay attention to where I'm going."

I tried to laugh it off, but the person didn't say anything.

When I stood up straight, with my phone clutched in one hand, all I saw was a flash of red hair before the woman hurried into the apartment next to Hazel's without a word to me.

The entire exchange was odd, but I retrieved the empty coffee cup from across the hall and didn't have to knock as Hazel's door swung open.

"I heard thudding and then raised voices. What happened?" she said with a confused look.

"Hi to you too, Angel," I said, pressing a kiss to her forehead before I stepped around her. She closed and locked the door, and I took a minute to look at her. Her dark-brown hair was hanging in loose waves over her shoulders, she was wearing a long-sleeved dark-red top that dipped into a deep V, and her legs were hugged in dark jeans that cupped her ass mouthwateringly well.

She was unimaginably gorgeous in more than one way.

When she turned back, she looked at me expectantly with raised eyebrows. "Whatcha lookin' at?"

I smiled. "You," I said, not even trying to hide my obvious gawking. But watching the appreciative smile as it crossed her face, I couldn't help but think about Valerie. God, she was the last person I wanted to think about when I looked at Hazel's face, but it happened. She had already begun tainting everything and nothing much had even happened. I didn't want her to taint Hazel even more, but I was too selfish to let her go. She was brave and hopeful for staying.

"I actually don't mind it when you stare," she said, casually strolling over to me and kissing my cheek. I tilted my head and leaned into her calming presence. It was hard to be anything but utterly and completely calm when I buried my nose in her freshly washed hair.

"Good, because I plan on staring a lot," I mumbled into her hair, wrapping my arms around her and pulling her to my chest.

"How was your day?" she asked after a minute, still clinging to me.

I pulled back to look at her as I spoke. "It was good. I toted Josh around and then went into the clinic for a few hours to get some work done." I kissed her softly on the lips, no longer being able to hold back and she laughed against my mouth. The normalcy of the act brought up an ache in my chest I hadn't felt in years at least.

"You smell and taste like coffee." She kissed me again yet lingered a few seconds longer. "I love coffee."

"I know you do." We stood there, arms wrapped around each other, our lips connecting and grazing and hovering over each other's.

"I have to tell you something." Hazel stepped away, and she immediately began chewing her thumbnail. It was a sign of her apprehension I'd caught on to as the weeks had passed.

"What's wrong?" I asked as I urged her to let go of her thumb. My first thought was Valerie, but I had hoped if something had happened, Hazel would have called me earlier. Either way, I thought the absolute worst.

"Michael's back," she said. And I took a breath.

"Okay, well, you knew he'd be back, and—"

"And he wants to meet."

I frowned. "Are you going to meet with him?"

She shrugged, and I scrubbed a hand over my face while backing farther into the apartment. The small little entryway didn't seem like the place for that conversation, but, yet again, neither did the kitchen or the living room because I didn't want to have the damn conversation. I had gone over there with the intention of taking her out on a casual date, just dinner and maybe hot chocolate afterward. I wanted to do something that seemed normal even when the rest of our lives weren't necessarily normal at all.

My jaw clenched even though I tried to stop it, but I was able to smooth my hands on the cold quartz counter instead of clenching them at my sides.

"I'm not sure what I'm going to do yet, but his mom found out about everything. She's making him go to mandatory therapy and part of his required shit is making amends with me. Or at least attempting to because I don't believe he can actually make amends."

"Therapy is great and everything, but I'm not sure what it's going to do for him. And do you think meeting him is going to benefit you? Because who gives a fuck what he needs to do. If you don't want to do it, or if you don't think it'll help you, then he can rot. You never have to speak to him again."

I so badly wanted to demand that she not go and that she never see him again. That we never speak to him or about him for the rest of our lives. But I knew that was unrealistic, no matter if the idea of her even being in the same room with him made me want to flip the fuck out. That also made me a controlling asshole much like the man she'd left.

"I think it might be good. Moving out without even saying another word to him just felt wrong and odd. I think it'd be good for me to get some closure and then move on the right way."

"I don't think you should." So much for not being controlling.

She gave me a look that told me she was going to go no matter what my opinion on the subject was.

Not the answer I wanted, but I nodded as I shifted on my feet. I stared down at my hands still flat against the counter to keep them from noticeably shaking.

"We're going to meet at Roast right around the corner in like twenty minutes," she said, stepping up next to me and running a hand down my arm.

"Good that you're meeting in a public place."

"Yeah, it was a condition if he wanted to see me."

I huffed out a long breath, feeling a little more in control of my emotions and turned to face her. "I'm going with you."

In another reaction I wasn't expecting, she smiled and bit her bottom lip between her teeth. "I figured as much. But I think it would be best if you stayed somewhere where he can't see you. You can still come in and listen and whatever else. But if Michael sees you..." She shook her head and her eyes fell closed.

As hard as it was for me to let her walk in there and meet the bastard, I knew it was a thousand times harder for her to confront her abuser. I needed to keep that in mind. It wasn't about me.

"That's fine. I can do that, but if he touches you, I'm getting involved. No questions asked."

"I know," she said quietly.

I pushed her hair back over her shoulders and cupped my hands around her neck, using my thumbs to push her chin up so she'd look at me instead of at our feet. "Talk to me, Hazel. What are you thinking?"

She wetted her lips as her eyes darted around my face. "I'm running through every damn scenario of how this could play out. None of them include him apologizing or being regretful of his actions, but I just hope he lets me leave without a fight. I hope you don't have to get involved. And I hope that he doesn't cause a damn scene because he loves to cause a scene."

"He won't get a chance," I promised, and I meant it more than I think I'd meant anything in my life up until that point.

"Okay, we should probably go then and drive separately. He said he was already there, but I told him it would be a little while until I could make it."

I agreed and hovered by the door as Hazel flitted around the apartment, turning off the lights and grabbing her things. She was running off nervous energy as she bounced from one room to the next, and I was saying a silent prayer to all the coffee I'd consumed that it'd actually keep me awake.

. . .

Pulling up to the coffee shop at a little past seven that night, there weren't many people inside. The front of the business was made entirely of large glass windows, so it wasn't hard to spot Michael, who was dressed casually for once—not in his usual designer suit—seated at a table by the far door.

Hazel hopped out of her car only a second before I shut my truck off. She made eye contact with me and nodded before she approached the door. With the metal door handle in her hand, she stopped. She stared at her hand for a moment, wrapping the other jacket-clad arm around her body before she shook off the doubts that were likely simmering in her mind and flung the glass door wide.

I followed suit on the opposite side of the coffee shop. Luckily, Michael's back was to me, and I easily slipped in without him noticing.

When he saw Hazel in front of his table, I was still approaching, so I couldn't hear what he said, but I saw the forced smile cross her face. Her eyes were tight, and she nervously worried her lip as he stood and gave her an awkward hug.

Every muscle in my body tensed as I approached the table behind them. I had the urge to rip him off her, and I knew I needed to get my shit in check and fast—their entire conversation was going to make me want to rip him apart. That was just a fact. But watching him touch her was even worse.

A gangly-looking teenage guy was seated at the table behind them. Once he noticed I was stalking directly toward him, he stiffened in his seat, eyes wide.

I fished my wallet out of my back pocket, grabbed a twenty and tossed it on the table in front of him. He watched the money fall to the table and then looked back at me. Without saying a word, I pointed to the cash and then motioned with my thumb for him to get the fuck away.

He shrugged but grabbed the money, took his coffee, and found a new table just a few feet away.

I sat down at the opposite side of the table from the seat the boy had just vacated, so I could not only hear but also see what was happening.

By the time I sat down, Michael was already speaking a mile a minute. Seemed like he had consumed nearly as much caffeine as I had.

Hazel's eyes stayed planted on the paper cup in front of her —how sweet, he'd ordered her coffee—as he spoke. Chewing her thumbnail in intense worry.

"These two weeks apart have been the worst two weeks of my life. And the fact that I couldn't talk to you made it so much worse. I wish you hadn't blocked me, I have so much to tell you. I've made some serious improvements, and I'm going to work on being the man you need me to be." He shook his head, looking down at his coffee and Hazel took the opportunity to peer over his shoulder at me. I gave her a tight, hopefully reassuring smile which she returned. "I am so, so, desperately sorry for what I did to you. I should have never hurt you. But you have to know that I'm not that man anymore. I'm going to be better, and I went by the house. I know you already moved out and that broke my heart, baby. Seeing all your stuff gone broke me. But I want to make another go of this. I want to be better for you. We both have stuff to work on, and maybe living apart and working on it would be for the best. It would give us some space while we figured us out. What do you think?"

Hazel didn't speak and didn't lift her eyes from her cup. She was nervously pulling at the label, and I could see under the table that her leg was bouncing. She was so uncomfortable, and there was nothing I could do about it without causing a scene. I wished we'd come up with a signal that told me she wanted out.

Michael reached his hand out to touch her, but she flinched away.

"Hazel, baby. Please don't do this. We had a good thing going for so many years. I know the last year has been rough, but—"

"Rough, Michael? Rough? You beat the shit out of me," she seethed.

There it was. I didn't know what her reaction would be—if she would be submissive and nonconfrontational, or maybe indifferent and just let him talk to himself. But anger wasn't the first thing I'd expected. Good for her, though, she deserved to get angry.

Apparently, it wasn't what Michael expected either because his shoulders tensed as he leaned back.

"Hazel, please don't—"

"Don't what? Don't call you out on the shit you did?" She heaved a heavy breath, glanced in my direction and then, with newfound confidence, stared back at Michael. "It wasn't just physical abuse, you know. When you hit me or pushed me, it hurt so bad, but you were also emotionally abusive and manipulative. Not to mention you cheated on me. This last year hasn't just been rough, and it wasn't just the last year. It all started a long time ago, and yeah, maybe you didn't start hitting me until a year ago. But everything else started long before that."

She was out of breath, and her cup was shaking between her palms.

Michael shook his head and leaned forward. He was speaking softer, and I strained to hear what he said.

"I take responsibility for my part in the end of our relationship. I should have done better... Let's not throw out words like abuse though, because that really changes the tone and escalates the situation... did not manipulate you at all... take accountability for your own part in this."

He had leaned forward and reflexively, so had I. The expression passing over Hazel's face morphed from shock to confusion to anger. I wanted to get her out of there. He was no longer apologetic, and it wasn't going to end well.

"... you were also fucking our neighbor..." he said, and Hazel actually laughed.

"Are you serious right now? After everything you've done,

including cheating on me with several women, you think if I had slept with Luke—which I haven't—that would make what you did okay?"

"That's not what I'm saying." His voice was louder, and the tension was clear in his tone.

"Then what are you saying? Because bringing that up isn't helping anything. That is a weak argument—any argument that includes something I apparently did wrong is a weak argument because it isn't true. The only thing I did wrong was stick around for as long as I did."

I wanted to give her a standing ovation, but Michael had other ideas. He reached forward and snatched her hand, pulling her toward him as much as the table would allow before she even had a chance to react.

On instinct, I stood from my chair, ready to pry his hand off her. But Hazel quickly widened her eyes and shook her head in an almost imperceptible motion, silently telling me not to. My jaw clenched and the need to get his hands off her hummed through me like electricity.

I didn't sit back down, though. We were done with this conversation as soon as Hazel looked at me again.

"Listen to me, Hazel. I was supposed to be your husband, and you were supposed to be my wife. You were supposed to listen to me, but you didn't know what the fuck was good for you. It's not my fault that I had to resort to lesser methods to get shit through your head. It's also not my fault that I couldn't get what I needed from you sexually, so I had to find it elsewhere. Maybe we are better off apart if you can't see what I was trying to do for us."

Hazel stared at him for a long moment after he'd finished speaking, and I tried to silently will her to look at me. But she just stared at him.

"Do you have anything else to say?"

Michael scoffed and pushed Hazel's hand away before he stood and rounded the table. He leaned over her in a dominant stance and spat the words close to her face. "So, this is how you're going to end it, huh? How many fucking years did we put into this dead-end relationship, and you're just going to walk away like that? If you know what's good for you, you'll tell your mom and your stupid fucking sister that we made amends and split amicably. Don't go feeding them some bullshit lies about what an asshole I am. Do at least that for me."

And with that, he hustled out the door, and hopefully, out of her fucking life.

Once he was out of sight, I crossed the few feet to Hazel. She was sitting stock-still in her wooden chair with her hands still cupping the coffee she hadn't even taken a sip from. Hesitantly, I took Michael's seat across from her and even sitting in a chair his ass had been in made me uncomfortable.

"You heard all of that?" she asked, finally lifting her head from the spot she was staring at on the table to look at me. Her hazel eyes were drowning in sadness, but there weren't any tears.

"I heard enough." I wanted to touch her. My fingers longed to pry her hands from the coffee cup and wrap them in my own, but I knew it could be a bad idea.

"Then I don't want to talk about it right now, okay?"

I nodded. "Let's go home."

Without another word, she grabbed her purse from where it hung on the back of the chair and walked toward the door. Like it was poison, she tossed the full coffee in the trash as soon as she could.

I walked her to her car and paused with my hand on the door handle. "Are you okay to drive? We could leave your car here and get it tomorrow."

"No, I'll be okay. You're coming over, right?"

I smiled. "Of course, I wouldn't—"

The words were whipped from me. Something flashed in front of me and pain radiated from my cheek. I stumbled backward with a grunt and just barely got my footing before an enraged Michael leaped toward me.

"I fucking knew it, you motherfucker!" he yelled as he tried to hit me again. But I knew it was coming this time and dipped out of the way. He wasn't fighting smart, and his fists were propelled by his anger. I knew he would be easy enough to subdue.

When his punch missed by a mile and I ducked around him, he stumbled forward, almost eating shit on the curb. As he righted himself, I peered behind me to see Hazel frozen in shock, her mouth hanging open as she stood near the rear of her car.

Michael lunged for me again, fist swinging toward my face, but I popped him quickly in the nose. Blood started pouring down his face and drenching the front of his shirt. He let out a wet yelp, and his hands instinctively flew to his face.

"Not a good idea, dude. Go the fuck home," I said, making sure I stayed between Hazel and the crazy idiot in front of me.

"You're fucking my fiancé!" he half groaned and half yelled, it was pathetic.

"She's not your fiancé anymore, so get the fuck out of here and stay away from her. Come around her again, and I won't be so forgiving a second time. I've nearly killed men twice your fucking size."

Blood continued flowing out of his nose, but he snarled at me nonetheless.

"Michael, just go," Hazel said in a small voice behind me. His eyes flashed to her like he'd forgotten she was there. I pivoted into his line of sight and shook my head.

He seemed to think about it for a moment—maybe contemplating if he could take me or if he could get a shot in on Hazel—but it wasn't too long before he turned back to his car parked only a few spaces down.

"I'm going to charge you with assault!" he bellowed before getting in his car and peeling out.

Once he was gone that time, I turned to Hazel.

"Fuck, Luke. I'm so sorry. Are you okay?" She stepped up to me and gently prodded my right cheek where Michael had landed a lucky shot.

I cringed because it was tender, and she huffed a breath. "Let's go home, so I can look at that."

"I promise I'm fine, Angel. It's just—"

She leveled me with a look that said I shouldn't be arguing, so I stopped and helped her in her car.

When I got in my truck, I quickly glanced at myself in the rearview mirror and saw the spot was red and there was a small cut where one of his rings had glanced off my cheek. It didn't need stitches or anything, but I guess it did look like it would hurt.

I was too used to that type of pain after the years and years of fighting, but I'd let Hazel look it over if it made her feel better. Fuck, I'd take a million punches for that woman.

THIRTY-SEVEN

Hazel

"Sit," I commanded Luke, pointing to a chair at the dining table as I hurried into the bathroom to grab my first aid kit. The same first aid kit I bought because I had to patch up my own Michael-inflicted wounds.

When I entered the small dining area, Luke had done as I asked. He was sitting in the chair—which seemed small when he was in it—with his legs spread and a nonchalant look on his face. It was like it didn't even hurt, but I heard it when Michael punched him.

I set the first aid kit on the table and fished out an antiseptic wipe.

"You don't have to—"

"Don't argue. Just sit back and let me make sure you're okay."

He sighed and leaned back in the chair even farther.

Ripping open the small package containing the wipe shouldn't have been hard, but my hands were shaking furiously. Between listening to Michael degrade me and casually speak about the things he did and then witnessing him attack Luke for just being there, I was shaken up.

I never meant to get Luke pulled into my shit, and I'd done just that and more. He'd gotten hurt because of me, and so I needed to fix him.

I had to force myself not to replay Michael's heinous words as I stepped between Luke's legs and softly dabbed the scratch on his right cheek.

Whether I ever believed a thing Michael said or not, his words and his own brand of venom always impacted me and, at one point, nearly debilitated me. The way he spewed vitriol with no remorse absolutely destroyed every part of me. It made me come undone, which was always the point, and then when I was left broken and bleeding, he'd change his tune to make me feel safe once again.

It was a tormented life. But it was one I wasn't stuck in any longer.

Although his tongue had just as much bite as it once did, his words weren't as potent and lacked the impact. It was an eye-opening feeling to know that he lacked the power he once had over me. It still hurt that he completely disregarded my experience and his role in it, but it was progress to know that I was no longer a prisoner to the way he made me feel.

I still felt like I needed a shower after speaking to him though. Seeing him reminded me of too much and the memories were vivid. I felt his words smack me across the face, his yelling reverberating off the kitchen cabinets, his hands creeping over me and his palm slapping me across one cheek and then the other.

His words might not have impacted me the way they used to, but just seeing him was like putting my memories on instant replay.

Luke's firm grip around my wrist pulled me from my thoughts. I tensed against his touch but remembered it was him, not Michael touching me, and relaxed.

"You've been dabbing at my face for a while now. I think it's clean."

I tried to smile, but I knew he'd see right through it. Luke always saw right through me. I set the wipe on the table and surveyed the damage to his face and then on his hand.

"I've had worse injuries, Angel. Years of fighting made for some pretty gnarly cuts and bruises. Few broken bones and several concussions, so this is nothing."

Although his confession didn't do much to ease my worry about him, it did keep my mind from running back to the same things.

"Are you ever going to explain why you settled on fighting? It was before Valerie, right? So, it couldn't have been her that led you to it." I was hoping to keep my thoughts from my own past and discussing his seemed like a good way to do that.

His hand had slipped from my wrist and gripped my fingers as his thumb lazily caressed the back of my hand in slow circles.

His expression was unreadable, except I saw a flash of something across his eyes. Something that made his pupils dilate and his eyelids tighten. But then he chuckled. "If you tell me all of your secrets, I'll tell you mine."

I rolled my eyes at his avoidance of the topic. There were only two topics in which he did that now: fighting and his parents. Maybe I was trying to find something where there was actually nothing, but they seemed to be connected.

I wanted to press him for information but was overtaken by my exhaustion from the night. It couldn't have been past nine p.m., but it felt like it'd been hours since we'd left to go to that damn coffee shop which I would not be stepping foot back into.

With an exhausted sigh, I let him get away with skating around the topic once again. "I don't think I have any secrets left."

"Then tell me what's on your mind right now." He squeezed my hand, urging me to talk to him. And I wanted to talk to him, but I didn't know what to say.

"I'm sorry you were pulled into the middle of this. I'm sorry that you got hurt because of me."

Luke's hands reached out, cupping the back of my thighs, and pulled me closer to him. My thighs rested on the inside of his own as his hands held me to him in a possessive touch that sent shivers up and down every inch of me.

"I would take that same punch a million times over if it kept him away from you." He was serious, too, I could see in his eyes that he'd do that and likely even more if it meant I wouldn't have to confront Michael again. "Honestly, I wish he'd been less of a fumbling mess so I could have actually beat the shit out of him."

I scoffed. "Well, I'm pretty sure you broke his nose, so if that's any consolation…"

"What else are you thinking about?" He scrubbed away the tension between my eyebrows with his thumb. Luke was so much taller than me, and I'd gotten used to having to stare up at him when we were talking, so it was strange to see him looking up at me from where he sat in his chair.

My fingers itched to trace the planes of his face. I wanted to run my fingers through his thick, black facial hair and over the scar on his opposite cheek. I wanted to stroke his slightly creased forehead and run my finger across his hairline before I dipped my hands into his hair. I wanted to do all those things over and over again while his bright-green eyes watched me until they eventually closed with the feeling of my hands on him.

I wanted to memorize the man before me, who would happily spill blood for me. I wanted to memorize him inside and out.

"His words hurt, but not like they used to. I don't feel so powerless against him anymore and that's a good feeling."

"That's so good, Angel," he whispered, not breaking our eye contact and not moving his hands from the backs of my thighs. Not being able to hold back anymore, my fingers brushed his uninjured cheek, grazed his jaw, and fell down his neck.

His eyes fluttered closed for a moment, and I bit my lip to keep from smiling. It was good to know that my touch affected him as much as his touch affected me.

"But…" I continued. "Seeing him and sitting across from him brought back all of the memories again."

He nodded but didn't speak as I continued trailing my fingers wherever they wanted to go, with no rhyme or reason, along the planes of his face.

"I thought I'd moved past a lot of it, but I'm not sure if I have or if I ever will. I know it'll get better, though. That over time, it won't feel as fresh and raw as it does right now and knowing that makes me feel better. It also makes me want to replace those stained, awful memories with new, good memories."

He wetted his lips, and I traced around them. I wanted to kiss him.

"You've already helped me create new memories. That stupid Halloween party was one of them. And then eating burgers after I rescued Sadie. And my birthday when you made me dinner and bought me a cake. Our little tryst through our bedroom windows. The night of the storm was also such a good memory after you fixed the gutter and then laid me out on my kitchen table and made me come again and again." At my mention of our night together, his hands flexed on the back of my thighs. I took it as a sign to continue. "And I think we're going to create so many new memories. But there's one specific memory I want to create tonight."

And I replaced my fingers along his lips with my own.

I meant to take it slow, but the moment I pressed my mouth to his, I felt an urgency to know what he felt like inside me. I tilted my head and deepened the kiss as I threaded my hands through his hair and let his tongue duel with my own. He gripped the back of my thighs tighter and pulled me onto his lap.

I straddled his thighs and even through the thick material of our jeans, I could easily feel his hard length as I fell onto his lap.

The pressure hit my clit perfectly, and I moaned into Luke's mouth in response.

At one moment, his hands were on my hips then they were running up my sides to cup my breasts through my shirt. His hands clasped my face and tugged my hair. He pulled my hair and his mouth left mine but quickly found its place again on my neck as he trailed open-mouthed kisses down to my collarbone. He ran his tongue back up my neck in a move that made me nearly combust.

I felt like I was flying. That I was no longer inside of my body but was above it, watching myself feel all the new, incredible sensations.

His hands lit a fire inside of me and knowing he wanted me as much as I wanted him was enough foreplay in and of itself.

"We have to make it to the bed this time," I gasped as he kissed from my chin along my jaw to my ear. The kitchen table wouldn't do this time around.

"Mmm… yes," he said into my ear, immediately standing and carrying me into the bedroom. In the few seconds it took to cross the living room and walk into the bedroom, I returned the favor, trailing wet kisses up his neck.

I bounced off the bed as he laid me down. In one swift move, he ripped my shirt off over my head and pulled down a cup of my bra, exposing one of my breasts and pulling my nipple into his mouth. He sucked it gently at first, and I instantly writhed against him. His strong hips settled between my own, pinning me to the bed, and he sucked my nipple harder. When his teeth bit into my sensitive skin, I let out an erotic gasp and pressed myself farther up into his mouth.

I needed more of everything. In that moment, I needed it like I needed fucking oxygen.

My hands worked his shirt up his body, and he begrudgingly let go of my breast so I could pull it over his head. I ran my nails down his taut stomach, tattoos, and the dark hair trailing down the center of his body that led to something I needed to feel inside of me sooner rather than later.

I immediately began to work on the button of his jeans as he reached around my back with one hand and popped the clasp of my bra. I slid myself free and savored the warmth of our naked bodies pressed together and his firm chest against my own.

"*Fuck.*" He groaned when I slid my hand beneath the waistband of his boxer briefs and wrapped my fingers around his long, hard length. His skin was so soft but so powerful and pulsing in my palm. I wanted to feel it all.

I pumped him a few times as he ravished my mouth, biting my bottom lip and sucking it into his mouth.

"I need you inside of me," I pleaded as I tried to force his jeans down his legs with one hand while still holding his cock with the other. "Fuck me."

"Music to my fucking ears, beautiful girl." He stood at the end of the bed to pull off his jeans, but I immediately missed his warmth. It felt good to have him on top of me, his weight pushing me down into the mattress.

He kicked his jeans toward my desk near the window, and I gawked at him. Lucas Shepherd was all muscle and man; his chest was broad and beautifully covered in intricate tattoos that circled his arms and ended at his wrists. I wanted to trace the dips between each of his abdominal muscles with my tongue, and when he stood in the dim light of my bedroom, he looked like my dark angel.

He made quick work of my own pants, and I scooted farther back to the pillows propped at the top of the bed.

Frozen at the end of the bed, it seemed he was doing the same to me. His eyes were devouring my naked body, and to ensure he received the full effect, I let my legs fall apart. I was so wet, and the cooler air around the room hit between my legs, making me shiver. As his eyes trailed over me—over my feet, up my legs, between my legs, my stomach, pausing on my breasts and my face—they blazed a trail of need. He watched me like he wanted to claim me in all the ways I wanted to be claimed.

My entire body thrummed with need and desire coursed through me as he kneeled on the bed. The anticipation of what was about to happen had my hands shaking and my breathing uneven. I assumed he'd crawl over me completely, but he stopped with his head between my legs, dark hair falling into his face as he leaned down and licked me from bottom to top. His tongue swirled around my pulsing clit, sucking it into his mouth before pushing two fingers inside of me.

I moaned and clenched hard around his fingers. He twisted them and hit the perfect spot as he continued to devour me.

"Please, Luke," I begged only a few seconds later. When I felt the orgasm beginning at the base of my spine, I knew I wanted my first orgasm of the night to be around his cock.

Like I knew he would, Luke knew exactly what I was asking. He licked his fingers, and I grabbed his face to kiss myself off him as he positioned himself over me.

"Wait, condom?" he asked.

I sighed. We'd gotten that fucking far, how cruel the universe was to now withhold it.

"I'm clean, I just got tested. Are you?"

He nodded. "Yes, but—"

"I'm on the pill," I confirmed, knowing what the next question would be, and I was done waiting.

Apparently, Luke was as well because as soon as the words left my mouth, I felt the wide head of his cock beginning to breach my entrance. My hands stayed on either side of his face, his green eyes locked on mine as he slowly pushed into me, inch by inch.

He was big, like *big*, and it did hurt a little, but that ache was so good because I knew what would come after. I wanted him to stretch me and claim me. He worked slowly, and although I appreciated the attention, I wanted him completely inside of me immediately.

"Luke," I begged, but his name barely left my mouth before he pushed home. Fully seated inside of me, he blew out a low "*fuck*" as I moaned and arched my back, savoring the feeling of him inside of me for the first time.

His eyes closed as he let out a deep breath, but when they opened, they were back on me. I shifted my hands to his arms that were braced around my head as he began to pump in and out of me at a steady pace.

"You feel so fucking good, Angel," he groaned before capturing my lips. He devoured my mouth as he picked up the pace. Eventually, I began to meet him stroke for stroke, lifting my hips in such a way that he was hitting deeper than I ever imagined.

A muffled "yes, yes, please" was all I could manage as he shifted. He sat up and took hold of my hips in his huge hands. It was such a stark contrast, my pale, unmarked skin compared to his tanned and tattooed arms.

"You're such a good girl," he said, running one hand up and down the middle of my stomach, my chest and then gripping one of my breasts. "You take my cock so well."

I think I whimpered when he pinched my nipple between his calloused fingers. His face was twisted in arousal, and my eyes wanted to close of their own accord, but I wouldn't let it happen. I wanted to see everything. Every drop of sweat, every expression, every time his mouth parted, and dirty words spilled from his plump lips.

When his fingers trailed down my body again and met my clit, I knew I was lost. My release was imminent, and Luke knew. His fingers expertly swirled over me as he continued the long, hard strokes.

Sweat was beading on his brow, and I could feel the beginning of it collecting on my back. But neither of us cared as we lost ourselves in each other.

"That's it, sweet girl, clench around my cock. Just like that. I want to feel you as you come. *God*, you're so perfect." His words and his fingers and his perfect strokes inside of me were the intense combination I needed as the orgasm washed over me.

I couldn't stand it anymore, my eyes closed, and my back arched as a moan ripped through me. I gripped one of Luke's hands that was tightening around my hip as I rode wave after wave of intense pleasure.

"*Fuck, Luke,*" I said during the aftershocks that didn't seem to abate for several long minutes.

When I opened my eyes again, Luke leaned down over me with a sly smile on his face. His eyes were dark with arousal. He braced his hands on either side of my head and kissed my neck and my chest.

"I could watch you fall apart over and over again. The most perfect thing I've ever seen."

There was something about the man's dirty mouth that really pushed me over the edge. I felt my pussy gush with warm heat around him, and he groaned in response.

"I need to see it again." And without warning, he banded an arm around my hips and flipped onto his back without pulling out of me. I braced my hands on his chest as I lowered myself back onto him completely. In this position, it felt like so much more. He felt longer and thicker and just more.

As I settled onto my knees around his thick thighs and started to bounce up and down on him, my mind went to the last person I wanted to think about during a time like that. But I hadn't been on top in a while, and I could already feel it in my legs.

It was the look on Luke's face, though, and the way he pushed up into me each time I moved that kept me going. I wanted to make him feel as good as he made me feel.

I leaned forward slightly, keeping my hands on his stomach and over an intricate tattoo of a snake, so I could pick up the pace. I isolated my hips and slammed up and down on him, grinding when I was fully seated on him each time.

"*Shit, yes,*" he sighed and took hold of my hips again. His touch was bruising and urged me on. Before him, I didn't know I was capable of back-to-back orgasms, but the tingling low in my stomach combined with the squeezing of my pussy around his cock was a sign I apparently was capable of it.

At the perfect moment, and right when the orgasm was making itself known, his fingers shifted, and he found my clit once again. I detonated around him after only a few seconds of his skillful touch.

Whether it was the position or his mumbled, "Good girl. Yes, just like that," that did me in, I didn't know. But the orgasm that whipped through me stole my breath and I bore down on him as I rode through it.

I clenched hard around him as my mouth parted on a half moan, half scream. The best part was that as I was at the peak, I had the sense to open my eyes and witness Luke's face twist as his own release found him. He yelled into the room that was filled with our combined noises of pleasure and ecstasy.

He kept his eyes on me as he pumped his hot cum inside of me. I could feel it hitting my walls that were still clenching in time. His cock pulsed in a way that I thought was going to spur another orgasm.

We maintained eye contact until we both came down and our breathing was slightly slower. With him still inside of me and slowly softening, he pulled me down toward him and made love to my mouth just as he had done to my body.

He tormented my mouth with his skillful tongue, his hands running down my sides sending goose bumps over each part of me, until I was buzzing to go again.

I eventually slipped off him and plopped myself rather ungracefully on the white sheets next to him. The world was a daze as I lay there, our faces barely an inch apart, our lips sometimes brushing and our hands roaming the other's body.

His hands had their own purpose, I was sure, but my hands traced each plane and divot and scar, hoping to solidify the memory. Push it to the front, even, and the others so far down the line that it was never their turn.

The only light in the room was a small lamp in the corner near my desk and the lone window. It was enough to bathe the room in dim, warm light but not enough for us to clearly see each other. It was cozy and warm, and I felt safe, well and truly safe, in that room.

"If I could sit here and touch you and kiss you forever, then I would. Leave the rest of the shit behind that door, and it just be the two of us."

I smiled and pressed my lips to his in response. In a post-orgasm haze, words seemed more difficult than usual, but I knew he understood what my actions were trying to say when he climbed on top of me once again.

The pulse between my legs had been growing steadily as we touched and when he barely swiped his hands over my core in a teasing stroke, a small gasp escaped my kiss-swollen lips.

"That's so good. I knew you'd be ready for me again, my beautiful, beautiful girl," he said in a low voice as he pressed a kiss between my breasts. Like he was following a path he'd set for himself, or the path he, not a minute earlier, was drawing with the tips of his fingers, he trailed his tongue over my collarbone to the shallow dips on either side of the bone. He meandered lower to my breasts, teasingly circling each nipple with just the tip of his tongue until they were both mercilessly hard and pebbled. He continued down my body, not forgetting my arms, placing kisses on the inside of my forearms and my palms. His fingers followed the path his mouth set. Sometimes they quickly moved against me, while other times he massaged and traced specific spots, like the birthmark on my hip or the few scars on my legs.

He worshipped my body and didn't leave one place untouched. Without hesitating, I flipped over on my stomach when he asked me to. His groan made me smile as his touch feathered down my back before he gripped my ass with both hands.

"Do you know what I'm doing, Angel?"

"It feels like you're worshiping me," I mewled. The words sounded kind of ridiculous coming out of my mouth, but Luke laughed and continued his worship at my neck just behind my ear.

Feeling his heaviness over me was so relaxing. I knew it was a sensation I'd later crave, like a weighted blanket.

"Yes, but do you know why?"

The moment he asked the question, his teeth sank into my earlobe, and all sense went out the window. My thoughts fluttered away, and all I could think about was the similar intense flutter between my legs.

When I didn't respond, he continued, "I'm not going to leave an inch of your body untouched. When you look in the mirror or see yourself at all, even if it's just looking at your hands while writing your book, I want you to remember me. I want you to remember this moment and all of the moments that will come after, because there will be so many moments after this. You're mine, Angel. And I take care of what's mine." He peppered kisses, licks, and bites between his words, and I was a writhing mess underneath him. Trembling with want, I pushed my ass up against him where I could feel him hard and ready.

He chuckled but shifted until he moved down my legs. He didn't even leave my feet or my toes untouched. And when he was finally done, he moved back over me, nudged my legs apart slightly, and began to press into me.

"Yes, Luke," I muttered against the pillow. I twisted my head to see him and melted at the beautiful desire twisting his features.

Once he was fully seated, he leaned down, moving all my hair to one side, and kissing my neck. His strokes were slow and languid and hitting all the right spots. Between the weight of him on top of me and how much he'd prepared me, I was already too close to the edge.

So close, in fact, that when he continued speaking and stoking the fire in me with the whipping of his magical tongue, I was lost to all of it.

"I'm going to touch every part of you. I'm going to imprint you with the memory of my tongue, my teeth, my hands, my cock, so that you have no choice but to replace all of the bad shit with me."

THIRTY-EIGHT

Luke

It was the morning sun peeking through the blinds in Hazel's room that woke me. Without its intrusion, I would have likely slept well into the morning.

I couldn't remember the last time I'd woken up and immediately been content and excited. The feeling was foreign and had been since I was old enough to remember. There had been moments where I felt like my life had been moving in the direction where I'd feel that hope again: when I graduated college and when I started seeing Valerie. Even when I treated my first patients as a vet. None of those moments compared, though, to the hope blooming in my chest when I woke up with Hazel's body twisted around mine.

It all felt different for some reason. A reason I hadn't yet pinpointed, but with one of her legs draped over my waist, her arm curved over my chest and her head nestled into my shoulder, I knew it was different.

Of all the women I'd been with—both before and after Valerie—none of them felt like Hazel did. For lack of a better explanation, I settled that it could have been that our demons looked eerily similar. Whether I'd ever admit it out loud or not, Valerie had been her own version of the monster Michael had been. The effects of which I'd continued to feel long after "enough" time had passed.

But I hoped that our connection was less about our similar pasts and troubling situations—although those couldn't be completely disregarded—because if that were the case, it could have defined our entire relationship. If our mutual pain was all that pulled us together, there had to be something else that made it stick. In my mind, our relationship would never succeed if all we contributed was the effects of our pasts.

It also didn't escape me that I hadn't yet confessed all my past to her; she was still in the dark about my parents and the beginning of everything. I had begun to say it a million times and a million different ways the past several weeks, but I couldn't make myself do it. With Michael trying to stay in Hazel's life and Valerie suddenly popping up again like a fucking virus I couldn't kick, it wasn't that I was worried about adding anything to our newfound relationship. I just wanted for a while longer to not have someone look at me like I was once a broken teenager who got a shit hand earlier in life.

More past demons meant more our relationship would be based on.

But watching the steady rise and fall of Hazel's bare back with the sheets twisted around her waist, I knew it was more between us than our pasts, whether spoken or not.

To me, she felt like the fucking sunshine pouring through the window.

With that realization and the constricting feeling in my heart, I kissed the top of her head before I reached over to the bedside table for my phone. Josh had texted that Sadie was out of food, so I made a mental note to stop by the store before heading home whenever that was.

When I slid my phone back onto the bedside table, Hazel stirred, turning away from me and pressing her back against my side. She was still naked, and only her arm covered her chest as her hair tumbled over her shoulder. I folded my body around hers, pulled her closer to me and buried my face in her clean hair.

The floral from her shampoo was still potent from the night before. I'd made her come so many times I lost count (I'd make her count next time so that wouldn't happen again). And when she was completely sated and only partially coherent at the end of the bed, I carried her into the shower and washed every part of her with the floral soap I craved to smell.

She let me wash her and then dry her when we stepped out of the shower until she dropped to her knees on the mat. With the water still dripping off of my body, it only took a few minutes until I was spilling down her throat.

Back in the bedroom, it was only moments after we curled up under her clean white sheets that I heard the even sound of her breath and knew she was asleep.

I fell asleep with my head in her damp hair, inhaling her floral-scented shampoo, and it was made even better waking up to it and knowing we could do it all over again.

"It's too early. Go back to sleep," Hazel whispered before patting my arm that was banded around her midsection. Trying to settle deeper into the bed, she pushed her ass back directly into my morning wood. She was warm, and I was sensitive and the combination of the two was enough to make me groan.

Before I could gain total control of my body or my thoughts, she did it again. The head of my dick perfectly pressed against that mostly unexplored hole. I spent a little time kissing and licking the area just as I said I would—no inch of her was left untouched or uncherished.

Her eagerly pressing up against me made me question whether I should explore the area more, especially when she chuckled softly against my arm. It was almost quiet enough that I didn't hear it, but I felt the telltale vibration of it against my bare arm.

"Don't start something unless you plan to finish it," I whispered into her ear after brushing her hair away from her neck. I kissed the tender place behind her ear, and as I learned she would, she sighed and tilted her head to expose even more of her skin to me. It was one of her favorite places.

"I don't know what you're talking about. I'm trying to get comfortable, so I can go back to sleep."

I sank my teeth into the outside of her ear and chuckled darkly. She gasped and continued to wiggle against me in direct contradiction to her words. I decided to call her bluff by running my free hand down her chest. I pinched a nipple before pushing lower and lower until I circled her clit with the pad of my middle finger.

My touch was light and teasing and I kept it that way even when she moved her hips and tried to intensify the pressure. I swirled my finger around and around, letting the pressure increase slightly with each movement. When she was all but panting beside me, I dipped my finger lower, finding her wet and ready.

I pushed one finger inside her perfect cunt, and every time I did, I was even more taken aback by how warm she was. She immediately gripped my finger, trying to pull it deeper, but I hooked it toward her front wall. That soft spot was easy to find, just a few inches in, and she let me know I'd found it by whispering my name in a lyrical moan. Like a plea falling from her lips.

"Do you want me to stop?"

"Don't you fucking dare," she snapped.

I withdrew my finger and before she had time to argue, I pressed it to her lips. "Suck. Taste yourself."

And she did. She licked her lips and wrapped them around my finger, pushing it to the back of her mouth and sucking hard. Flicking her tongue around my finger like she loves to do with the head of me, was going to drive me mad.

I withdrew my finger and replaced it between her thighs. "Are you sore?"

"A little, but it's a good kind of sore. Like my body is reminding me of last night without me having to try."

I smiled against her hair. Mission accomplished.

"Too sore to—"

"No," she said without a minute of hesitation. And I wasn't one to question her or deny her what she wanted.

I hooked her top leg over mine and with one thrust, I pushed inside of her, her warmth enveloping me immediately.

"*Shit*, Angel." I sighed against her neck and kissed her. If I wasn't cautious, I thought I'd come the minute she pulled me in. Because that's what she did. She clenched around me and pulled me deeper, and when I didn't begin moving the first moment I entered her, she began backing up into me. She ground her hips against me the best she could, even though the position didn't allow her much range of motion.

Once I had calmed myself enough and given myself a pep talk to at least hold out until her orgasm, I withdrew to the tip and plunged back deeper. That earned me a throaty moan that slipped from her too-sweet lips. So, I did it again and again and again.

The hand she wasn't on top of, I used to grip her hip. I kept each stroke lazy and dragged in and out of her while I whispered in her ear how beautiful she was.

"You feel so good wrapped around me. You're beautiful in the sunlight, curled against me, making the sweetest fucking sounds I've ever heard." Every few words were punctuated with a deep stroke inside of her, but as I pulled out, I kissed and licked and nibbled at the side of her neck.

I savored every part of our lazy lovemaking because that's what it was. It wasn't fucking as much as it had been the night before with an untethered desire that crashed over us both and ensured we marked each other's bodies. I was sure when I got up, I'd see scratches up and down my back and chest from her nails and teeth marks in several places.

I'd already spotted bruises on her hips and a few bite marks and hickeys on her own skin. They just further proved she was mine.

Our unhurried pace that morning was more about savoring each other and soaking up the glow of the morning after.

It was only mere minutes before I felt the beginning clenches of her impending orgasm. Her breath quickened in sync with the new tension inside of her and she mumbled quiet pleas, "Right there, Luke. Yes, don't stop."

"Come all over my cock, sweet girl. Show me how much you love it."

Over her shoulder, I watched her face contort in overwhelming pleasure as she peppered the air with pleading moans and did just what I asked. I felt the warmth of her pleasure drenching me, and the tightening of her walls spurred on my own release.

The orgasm that was sitting low in my stomach since I slid my fingers between her legs was done waiting and hurtled forward. I pushed deep and spilled inside of her as her own release drew out longer. I wanted to continue watching her, but I was overcome by every sensation building and spilling over.

Long after we were both spent and I had slowly slipped out of her, we were still curled together. The sun was clearly higher in the sky now as the room was glowing in the rays escaping between the blinds.

"I wish we could stay here all day."

"Why can't we?" It seemed simple enough to me: I'd call into work for the day and ask Josh to watch Sadie if it meant we could spend time together and have even more mind-blowing sex.

"I actually have work to do today."

I let out a disappointed groan and Hazel laughed. *God*, I loved her laugh. My heart clenched again at the feeling her laugh elicited. I didn't think I'd ever get used to how she made me feel, especially how she made me feel when she was happy.

"Do we have to get up right this second?"

She chuckled before pulling my hand to her mouth and kissing the back of it. As her lips found my bruised knuckles from punching her ex-fiancé in the face the night before, she took the opportunity to roll out of the bed and scurry into the bathroom.

I shook my head and took off after her. One more round before we started our days couldn't hurt.

The second round on the tiny bathroom counter then turned into a long shower, and by the time I was dressed and as prepared to leave as I could be, it was well past ten.

We lingered at the door for several minutes, sharing slow kisses and careful touches before I finally pulled away to let her get to work.

"Oh, before I go, we do a Friendsgiving every year, and it's at our house this year. It's this coming weekend actually."

She nodded as she gave me a skeptical look.

"I want you to come," I clarified.

Her face dropped. She opened her mouth but immediately snapped it shut before repeating the action. "Really? I don't know if... I just think that..." Her voice trailed off, and her thumb slid between her lips as she chewed it in worry.

"Angel, why are you worried about it? My friends are going to love you." *Almost as much as I do.* The thought made me backpedal for a moment, but only a moment, because I was done hiding from shit like that. Hazel had only ever given me reason to trust her and want to move forward, and that's what we were going to do.

I was falling for her, no matter if it was too fast or not. I couldn't change it. I had no power over it. It was a force greater than us both.

"It's all the friends you always have over, right?"

I nodded until I realized her concern. "The past is in the past, Hazel. We'll start over fresh, and none of them will hold anything that happened before over you."

She gave me an incredulous look but withdrew her thumb from her lips as I gave her a reassuring squeeze.

"Okay."

"Okay," I repeated and kissed her quickly.

"Should I bring anything?"

"Just your sparkling personality."

She rolled her eyes but laughed. "That's a given. It's actually a two-for-one deal: you get the personality and all of this." She flourished her hands up and down her sides and winked.

"Thank God for that."

THIRTY-NINE

Hazel

I was going to shit my pants. Or maybe puke, but I was hoping it wouldn't be both.

I had paced my apartment for an hour while I waited for the cobbler I'd baked to finish in the oven. Once I quadruple-checked that it was thoroughly cooked but not overcooked, I focused my attention on my outfit that I hadn't even had the brainpower to think about before that moment.

The week had sped by. Work was picking up day by day, which left me less time to write. I found myself working and taking frequent breaks to jot down notes of dialogue and key issues in the story I hadn't yet addressed.

My closet was just a smaller version of what my entire apartment, my entire life looked like. Shit was scattered everywhere and there wasn't a rhyme or reason to any of it.

To simplify the process, I pulled out my favorite pair of black jeans and black boots—it was a classic combo that always worked. But I went back and forth with which top would best fit the occasion. I went through almost everything in my closet before I settled on a black, simple yet slightly girly top. The cinched hem skimmed the top of my high-waisted black jeans and the buttons up the front hit the perfect spot where my cleavage was there, but it was tasteful.

By the time I left my apartment with an apple cobbler in one hand and a decently priced bottle of wine in the other, my hair was curled and my makeup was done. I felt confident and pretty—especially with my light makeup and bold red lip—which did a lot for the nerves churning in my stomach.

It wasn't until I was about to turn down Luke's street—my old street—that the possibility of shitting myself appeared. I was stopped at the stop sign at the end of the street for so long, I turned on my hazards and pretended that something was wrong with my car.

I expected to be nervous about meeting Luke's friends. Well, remeeting them after being a colossal bitch on several occasions. And I realized only a few days before that they had all likely been witness to my mortifying performance imitating an orgasm at the last party. But most of the nerves were from being so close to my old home again.

I'd just left, and I was relatively settled at my new place. I was happy there, and I knew I did what I did for the rightest reasons anyone was ever faced with. But that didn't keep my anxiety from building, knowing that I would be so close to the damn house without living there for the first time. Then there was the possibility that Michael was there. He could be sitting there on the porch and watch me walk up and confront me and I wasn't going to be okay if he did.

Just as the real panic was setting in, tapping on my passenger side window pulled me from my thoughts and sent my heart into my throat. I whipped my head to the side to find Luke leaning down and waving at me through the window.

Fuck. I sighed but rolled the window down.

"Josh just pulled up and saw you sitting out here," he said as I began preparing my less ridiculous excuses until he continued, "He's not here, Hazel."

Oh.

"You'll see. Just pull up behind my truck, I saved that spot for you." He reached into the window and unlocked the door before he hopped in.

I hadn't seen Luke as much as I would have preferred since earlier in the week. Neither of our schedules was conducive to seeing much of each other. Josh's car was still out of commission, so Luke was chauffeuring him around or letting him use his truck. And Luke was putting in extra hours at the emergency vet hospital.

He told me his schedule that week hadn't been usual, though, and it just so happened to fall on a week when all we wanted to do was stay in bed constantly.

So, when he hopped in my passenger seat and his intoxicatingly manly scent filled the small space, my brain was having trouble focusing on anything besides *him*.

Luckily, I was able to drive the ten seconds down to Luke's house and pull in behind his truck without an issue.

"I was wondering why it smelled like cinnamon apples in here," Luke said, scooping up the bottle of wine and apple cobbler from the back seat. I slung my purse across my body and smiled as he took a whiff of the dessert even through the tinfoil.

But my smile quickly vanished when I attempted to just swing my eyes across my old house without seeing much. That plan backfired when my eyes narrowed in on the "For Sale" sign planted in the grass near the curb.

The range of emotions I felt in the moment confused me. I was surprised he'd put it up for sale so fast, but I was also sad that a house I was once so excited about was no longer a possibility and ended up being the place where some of my worst memories took place.

"Sign went up yesterday as soon as the movers showed up."

That information was even more shocking. "He's gone?"

Luke nodded, leaning against the side of the car next to me. "Josh watched the guys load up the entire rest of the house in no time at all apparently. I'm sure it'll go fast, but it's completely empty right now."

"Good—good for him." My voice was quiet and didn't match the words coming out of my mouth. I didn't really have the capacity at that moment to comprehend what I felt about the situation, so instead, I decided to save it for later. "Ready?"

"Only if you are," Luke said, peering down at me and carefully scrutinizing my face.

"I'm okay," I told him before reaching for the cobbler. When I held the large glass dish in my hands, he cupped my chin with his now free hand and pressed a soft kiss to my lips. He lingered for a moment, but it evened out my mood and reset me the best it could.

"Everyone's excited to meet you again," he said as we headed up the driveway and around to the walkway.

I grunted, unsure if he was just comforting my growing nerves or if he was actually serious.

"I'm serious, Hazel. No one cares about any of the shit that happened before now."

"Is it because you told them about Michael?" I asked, suddenly realizing that they could all be fine with meeting me again—even after I'd been such a big bitch—because they pitied my situation. I was the abused woman next door that Luke took in and all but rescued.

He stopped in the middle of the stairs leading to the front porch and turned to me. "I told them that you called off your engagement, but nothing more than that. I wouldn't tell them that without your say-so. Your story is not mine to tell."

Luke had never given me any reason to distrust him, but I found myself hunting his face for any sign of deceit. There wasn't any. And I knew I was being ridiculous. But the thought of anyone pitying me made me want to run in the other direction.

"Okay. Thank you."

And with no other words, we walked the rest of the way up the stairs and entered the house.

The inside of the house was warm, and the scent of delicious food immediately wafted into the entryway from the kitchen at the back of the house. Following the smell was the jovial sound of raised voices and laughter also coming from the living room area. It was inviting to walk into, but it did only a little to relieve my anxiety about walking into a room of Luke and Josh's friends.

"Hazel!" Josh appeared at the end of the entryway and entrance to the living room as he bellowed my name. He threw his arms wide and made his way to me. His arms wrapped around me, the dish of cobbler awkward between us, but he didn't seem to care. "We're so glad you're here. Oh, what is this?"

He pulled the dish from my hands and lifted the foil to see the contents. "Shit, this looks so good!"

"It's apple cobbler. I hope it tastes as good as it looks," I said.

"I'm sure it will," he smiled at me, his genuine Josh smile that lit up his entire face and the room around him. "Hey, guys! Hazel brought cobbler!" Josh yelled to the people gathered as he headed to the kitchen with the dish.

Luke slid his fingers between my own and squeezed them in silent reassurance before he led us both into the living room. "Everyone, I'm sure y'all remember Hazel," he said when we walked into the room.

The fireplace was roaring and heating the space and music filtered from the TV speakers as five faces scattered throughout the room said their polite hellos and watched me.

"Hi," I said with a small wave. My fingers tensed around Luke's, but he drew soothing circles on the back of my hand before lifting it and kissing my knuckles. He gave me a crooked smile when he dropped our hands back between us, and I gawked at him. We obviously weren't wasting any time letting everyone know exactly where we stood. Not that I minded, but I also didn't know what Luke had actually told them.

Had he told them we were friends or more than that?

Before I had even a second to overthink it, a tall blond guy with a smile as wide as Josh's stepped up beside me. In his hands was a glass that was filled to the brim with what I was assuming was a hot toddy, given the heavenly cinnamon scent and the yellowish coloring.

"I'm James," the man—James, apparently—said as he stuck out his hand. I released my tight grip on my purse so I could properly introduce myself.

"It's nice to meet you," I said politely.

"And I'm Reed," a deep voice bellowed from the opposite direction. I turned just in time to see a man with boyish brown hair stride over to us and elbow Luke out of the way.

He stopped just in front of me, and I shook his offered hand.

"It's nice to meet you," I said again, but with a laugh this time. The joy radiated off him and was highly contagious. Reed also looked like he hadn't missed a day at the gym. Ever.

"Oh, we've met. I still think about that last party when you—" Luke cut him off by punching Reed in the arm and leveling him with a look.

I was utterly mortified, and I could feel the blush blanket my face and neck.

"What?" Reed barked at Luke, not even flinching at Luke's murderous gaze. "It was the most memorable part of that night!"

A hand clamped over Reed's mouth before he could say anything else. It was a perfectly manicured hand with deep-green nail polish, and I was forever grateful for it inserting itself into the situation.

The owner of the hand was a woman about my height with long, blonde hair pulled to the top of her head in an effortless bun. Her dark-rimmed glasses drew attention to her sapphire-blue eyes.

Were all of Luke's friends attractive? Did he only surround himself with attractive people?

"Seriously, Reed. She just got here. Let's try not to make her uncomfortable just yet." Her tone was serious, but she ended with a beautiful smile. Reed rolled his eyes.

"I'm Amanda and ignore him. He gets off on being the clown of our group sometimes." She went past the handshake and instead wrapped her arms around me in a friendly hug. "It's so good to see you again," she said into my ear and my skin pricked with awareness at the sincerity in her voice. I knew I was going to like her.

She pulled away and gave me another friendly smile before she motioned behind her.

"And the quiet one on the couch is Devon," she gave him a wink and he huffed and shook his head as he stood.

"Nice to see you again, Hazel," he said. I was immediately jealous of his dark-red hair that seemed so effortlessly tousled. He gave me a shy smile, but he also had kind eyes.

"What do you want to drink?" Amanda queried from next to me with a little bounce in her step. "I made hot toddies since it's fucking freezing outside."

"That sounds amazing," I smiled.

"Okay, I'll be right back," she said, holding up a finger.

Luke replaced Amanda in front of me and leaned down until his head was next to mine. He brushed my hair over my shoulder and with his hot breath on my neck came plentiful goose bumps all over my skin. He kissed my neck softly before he asked, "What do you think?"

He already knew exactly what got me going, like soft kisses on my neck and the way he held me possessively. He knew it and he used it to his advantage because I had to force my knees from buckling and my breath from catching when his husky voice asked such a simple question.

"They're all really nice, and your house looks so cozy," I managed to say somehow. "It also smells like heaven."

He chuckled against my neck and added, "You smell like heaven." Then he licked me, and I pulled away.

"Dude, all of your friends are here," I chastised him, trying to also compose and remind myself that I wanted and needed to make a better impression than last time. "I know how much they mean to you," I pleaded. "So, it's really important to me that they like me. I don't want to fuck it up *again*."

Luke's expression was one of amusement as he looked down at me, still rubbing up and down the back of my arms, and I narrowed my eyes at him.

"Honestly, there's not much you could do to fuck it up," Amanda spoke up from behind me. I winced and shut my eyes for a second, embarrassed that she overheard my pleas to Luke.

I turned toward her, ready to explain, but she held up a hand and offered me the hot toddy with the other. "Don't worry about it. Seriously. Before you got here, we were all discussing how much less of a grump he's been since you came into the picture."

"Seriously, Amanda?" Luke questioned but in a playful tone.

"Yes, Luke. You were a grade *A* grump most of the damn time."

I couldn't help the smile that pulled at the corners of my mouth as I took a sip of my hot toddy. If I cured the grump, I'd be okay with that. Or if he wanted to be my grump, that was also fine.

Luke and Amanda moved on from the grump topic and began discussing how to go about dinner. I was content just listening to their rambling and occasionally sipping my hot toddy, especially when Reed jumped in with his own two cents.

"Hey, Luke." A woman appeared at my side, and I immediately recognized her from the last party I'd been to. Her jet-black hair was as pin straight as it had been the month prior, and she donned a shade of red lipstick similar to mine. Between the hair and the lips and her high bone structure, she was strikingly beautiful.

"I was wondering where you were. Hazel, this is Blakely."

Oh, great. A woman that's seen my man's cock.

I cringed at myself internally because technically, he wasn't my man—or at least not officially—but the thought elicited the same reaction no matter what our relationship status was.

I tried not to second-guess anything, but I immediately began questioning whether she was better in bed than me or had less baggage or knew what the next few years of her life were going to look like.

"Hi," I said, sticking out my hand, which she took with a less than interested look in my direction.

She dropped my hand in the same second and turned back to Luke. "Could I talk to you?"

"Blake, I don't—" Amanda began just to be immediately cut off by Blakely's raised palm in her direction. Amanda rolled her eyes and mumbled, "Fucking hell. You don't know when to quit, do you?"

Luke's eyes darted between the two women in obvious discomfort. He crossed his arms over his chest and shrugged. "What's up?"

"I want to talk in private," Blakely said with a pointed look in my direction. I raised my eyebrows, surprised by her brazenness, but looked to Luke. If I wanted to make a good impression, the way to do it wasn't to make enemies of his exes.

He huffed and hung his head. "You have five minutes," he said. Blakely turned on her heels and exited the living room, heading down the hall and into what I knew was Luke's bedroom. We'd probably both spent the night there…

Just as the thought crossed my mind, Luke stepped forward and smoothed out the furrow between my brows. "Whatever you're thinking right now, stop."

I laughed. "That's awfully presumptive of you. How do you know I wasn't thinking something that you definitely wanted me to think?"

"I can see it written all over your face, Angel. I can read you like one of your books. I'll be back in a few minutes," he said and pressed a lingering kiss to my lips. I swayed slightly when he let me go, both drunk on my extra-strong hot toddy and Lucas Shepherd.

Half an hour later and we were all sitting in the living room crying with laughter at another story of the shit Josh and Reed got up to in college. They were dumb and dumber in most of their college and post-graduate years. Apparently, they'd both figured their shit out at thirty, but their crazy antics proved the perfect party stories.

What made the stories even more hilarious was the fact that they interrupted each other every minute or two, adding additional details that they couldn't exactly agree on.

"No, he was wearing a gorilla mask and was carrying the stuffed tiger, not the other way around."

"Actually, I jumped off the bridge and that random chick found me on the shore and then we fucked. Craziest sex of my life."

Most of them were drunken nights they only vaguely remembered, but others were wildly colorful stories about the times when all their friends—most of whom were sitting in the room around us—had long since gone home.

We were all comfortably lounging on the sectional, listening to Reed seated on the edge of the fireplace and Josh, who I realized couldn't sit down for any length of time. Amanda took up the spot to my right, giving me additional details and insight into the entire group.

On my other side, Devon added his own versions with lightning-fast wit, and farther down the couch, James enjoyed chiming in when he overheard part of our subconversation.

Even as an outsider in their long-since-established group, I didn't feel that way at all. They had all met in college, and they'd been friends ever since. People had apparently come and gone—

names I didn't recognize appeared in several of the stories—but the core group of seven had stayed.

I was curious how Valerie had fit into the group. Had they liked her? Had she fit in seamlessly before everything went to shit? No one had brought up her name, and I couldn't tell whether it was intentional or not. But I had a feeling it was a long-held standard to not mention her name, given the way Luke spoke about her and what was happening then.

It was in the middle of a story Amanda was telling about Reed and Josh trying to pursue the same woman when there were raised voices from Luke's bedroom. Amanda stopped midsentence and they all peered at each other, careful not to look at me.

With the liquor of my third hot toddy coursing through me and feeling comfortable, I spoke up. "Anyone know what they're talking about?"

They all glanced at each other again before James said, "Blake and Luke have always butted heads. They look at things in very different ways, so that means they argue a lot. It's been like that for as long as we've all been friends."

"Not to mention, Blake can be a tad opinionated and argumentative," Reed quipped, taking a long pull from his cider.

Josh scrubbed a hand through his hair as Amanda patted my leg. "I'm sure it's fine. Want to help me get everything out for dinner?"

Ready to find a different topic and move farther away from the bedroom, I agreed.

For the twenty minutes it took me, Amanda, and Devon to lay out all the parts of the meal—most of which had been warming in the oven or staying cool in the fridge—Luke and Blakely still hadn't surfaced. We had been engaged in light conversation about what we all did for a living and other somewhat mundane details of our lives.

Amanda was a middle school teacher, which didn't surprise me in the least when she used her "teacher" voice on everyone, including me, more than once. Devon was a genius; he was working for a start-up company that was working on a new form of artificial intelligence technology. He began to ramble on about the details of his daily work until Amanda gave him a "teacher" look and he chuckled.

"Sorry, I get a little carried away and forget that not everyone understands, nor wants to hear, the nerdy shit."

I laughed. "You're passionate about what you do, that's not a bad thing. Besides, I get that way with books and writing."

That spawned the conversation of what I did for a living, and whether it was the liquor or what, I wasn't sure, but I told them that I was writing a book. They asked all of the usual questions, but I kept the details surface level. Just telling them was a big step for me, and I was thankful they didn't push too much.

They both expressed their eagerness to read it, and I didn't have to pretend to be excited. Slowly, the idea of others reading my work was becoming less terrifying.

When everything was set and Amanda was poised to break up the arguing still happening in the bedroom, I interrupted her and said I'd go. She contemplated it for a moment but stepped aside.

Josh gave me a sympathetic smile as I walked past where he sat on the fireplace. Uneasiness filled my stomach as I approached the door, my heels clicking on the hardwood, and I heard angry whispered voices.

The door was slightly ajar, and through the small crack I could see Luke leaning against the windowsill with his arms crossed defensively across his chest. He was shaking his head and his expression portrayed his frustration.

They'd been arguing for nearly an hour, and dinner was ready. So, I pushed the door open just in time to hear Blakely say, "She's not going to survive it, Luke. You've put her in the worst possible situation because you're being selfish. Flaunting your relationship or whatever the fuck this is, is just going to bring Valerie's wrath down on her harder."

Having heard enough, I cleared my throat. I stood my ground as both of their heads whipped to me, standing in the open doorway, and I said in an even voice, "Dinner's ready."

Blakely opened her mouth like she was going to argue, but I said again, "Dinner's ready." She glanced over at Luke, who was watching me carefully with deep-green eyes. When he didn't acknowledge her, she brushed past me and headed back down the hall.

When she was well and truly gone, I closed the door behind me and faced Luke. "You were arguing about Valerie?"

He nodded but didn't add anything to my assessment.

"She doesn't think you're handling it correctly?"

He shook his head and scrubbed a palm over his beard. "She thinks I should stay all but in hiding while the police try to handle it, which I've done before and it didn't help jack shit. She was around when it all happened, and I stayed cooped up for weeks hoping they'd handle it. Nothing ever came of it because Valerie has always played on the cusp of legality. She straddles the line of stalking and never leaves fucking evidence, and it just won't help. I'm tired of hiding and playing by her rules."

I crossed the distance between us in a few purposeful strides. "I agree, Luke. I understand."

"But she's right about me being selfish," he said, drilling me with a guilty look.

I was shaking my head before he could finish the thought or even think about adding to it. "No. You gave me a choice, you left it up to me whether I wanted to be involved or not, and like you said, Valerie will come after me even if we aren't together. She did it to Blakely, right?"

He gave a slight nod. I knew that was probably part of why she was so defensive—she had been on the receiving end of Valerie's terror and didn't want that for another woman or for her friend. I could appreciate that, but I wasn't her.

"So not being together makes no sense when either way, I'm a target."

"There's just more to it that I didn't know. We'll... we'll have to talk about it after dinner."

He brushed my hair over my shoulder and cupped the back of my neck, pulling me forward until our foreheads met. I braced my hands against his chest and beneath the hard muscle, I could feel his heart frantically pounding against my palm.

I stepped forward between his legs and pressed my chest against his, needing to feel more of him against me. It was unusual and somewhat strange that I was so calm about the situation, but something about my lack of freaking out made me believe I was making the correct decision. Even with whatever we might have needed to discuss.

Luke pulled back and watched my face. His eyes glued to my lips as I licked them in invitation.

"I like the red," he said, his voice dripping in barely restrained desire.

"Thank you." I flashed him a smile.

"How much of it is going to come off if I kiss you right now?"

I threw my head back and laughed. Of course, that's what he was worried about. "It's pretty budge-proof. I don't think it's going anywhere."

There was a playful gleam dancing in his eyes as I straightened myself and he grasped his hand that wasn't tangled in the back of my hair around my waist.

"What a shame. I think I'd like to see it smeared around my cock later."

The desire I saw in his eyes found its way between my legs and then he slammed his mouth to mine. For a minute, we kissed like we were starving for each other. I clawed at his arms, his chest, his neck, but he took charge of the kiss, tilting my head so he could dive his tongue deeper into my mouth. He claimed me in all of the ways I didn't know you could be claimed by a kiss.

Although neither of us wanted to stop, the all-consuming

want still pulsing between us, we parted at the same time, leaning our foreheads together and catching our breath.

Luke smoothed his hands down my face like he was making sure I was real.

Before we could get caught up again, I peered at his mouth. "Doesn't look like anything came off. But we can test it around your cock later."

He groaned at my promise but followed as I led us back to his waiting friends.

FORTY

Hazel

With a little rearranging, we were able to manage fitting two additional chairs around Luke's dining table even after he insisted that I could just sit on his lap while we ate.

"Y'all are already gross with the PDA, we don't need you having a hard-on the entire dinner," James quipped from the dining room while the rest of us stood in the kitchen loading up our plates.

Josh and Reed agreed with James's assessment as they both piled mountains of mashed potatoes and corn casserole on their plates. Everything smelled and looked amazing. Each of them had brought a different dish, although apparently, Luke and Devon were usually the ones that cooked most of their big meals.

They had all the usual suspects: potatoes, green beans, dinner rolls, turkey, *and* ham. It was when my plate was relatively full that I began second-guessing my choices. There were several carbs on my plate, and I knew the ham had a sugary glaze on the top.

Standing in front of the dinner rolls that were smothered in butter, I glanced at everyone around me. Each of them was piling their own plates with everything offered. Amanda was even eagerly adding additional potatoes to Blakely's plate as she said something about her grandmother's secret recipe making them even better.

No one was looking in my direction or paying attention to what was on my plate. It was the first holiday in a while that I didn't restrict what I was eating, and my stomach rumbled. Could I eat all of this?

My new normal was more difficult to get used to than I imagined it would be. It was things like the food I chose to put on my plate that seemed to bother me the most. I figured that it would be a seamless transition to more healthy habits and with little input from anyone else, but that wasn't the case. Michael's opinion was ingrained in me, and his voice was still hanging out in my head whenever I ate what he'd believed was too much or too unhealthy.

It was Josh leaning around me to grab two rolls that pulled me from my thoughts. He smiled down at me, and I decided to not let my ex-fiancé ruin another delicious meal for me. I smiled back and, in a move I wasn't expecting, Josh kissed the top of my head. It was an innocent kiss, but the gesture warmed my heart.

"We're glad you're here," he said before smiling once more and heading into the dining room.

With my plate full of food, I followed Josh into the now crowded room and squeezed into the last open seat between Amanda and Luke.

"Are we going to say what we're thankful for?" Amanda spoke up over the several conversations happening around the table. Everyone groaned simultaneously as they began shoveling food into their mouths.

"We go through this every year," Reed mumbled around a mouthful of potatoes he not so gracefully scooped up a moment earlier.

"I know, but I just think it's a nice sentiment," Amanda

explained. "Life is crazy sometimes, and it's good to remind ourselves that we should continue to be thankful even when shit is tough."

Luke's hand found its way to my thigh underneath the table as he ate like it was second nature to touch me when we were close. I loved that he couldn't stop touching me. I reflexively leaned into his touch and slid my legs apart so mine brushed his own. His fingers trailed a path up the inside of my leg until his hand found its place at my midthigh.

The residual heat from our kiss earlier pulsed between my legs as his thumb stroked in lazy circles. Even through the thick fabric of my jeans, I could feel his touch to my skin, and through my muscle and into my bone. Like each time he touched me, he embedded in me another piece of himself.

"Well, I think it's a fucking great idea," Luke said. "And I damn well know what I'm thankful for this year." His eyes darted to me, and I felt the blush creep up my face. If there wasn't enough sincerity already in his voice, his eyes held it in spades.

I gave him a smile that hopefully conveyed how much I agreed, but to ensure he received the message, I dropped my hand under the table and squeezed his.

I wasn't a woman that felt she needed a man to make her happy or complete her. But *damn*, was it nice. I had spent too much time with someone who quite obviously didn't appreciate me and didn't care, so it felt easier now to identify when the opposite was true. Like you'd only eaten the absolute worst food on the planet for years on end and eventually concluded that the horrible food would be all you'd eat ever again. The food was awful and somewhere inside, you knew that, but that thought grew smaller and smaller as you became more comfortable with the disgusting food. Then, out of nowhere, you slowly tasted some of the best food ever made. It was baked, and glazed, and grilled, and fried, and it seemed indulgent and out of reach. But it wasn't. And then, once you tasted the food, you knew you'd never go back.

It would be easier then to identify the good food just based on smell, sight or even touch.

Luke seemed like the finest food I could find, and God, did I hope I was right.

From across the table, someone cleared their throat, and my eyes found Blakely's boring into me. If a look could have set me on fire, hers would have done it. Luke's hand flexed on my thigh, and he stared at Blakely with annoyance.

Reed took the opportunity to elbow her, but she didn't flinch as I tried to ignore her and continue eating. With one small sound, Blakely silenced the entire room. The only noises were the scraping of utensils on the plates and chewing, which grated my nerves.

"Josh, how's Zach? Is he with Samantha this year?" Devon asked, cutting through the tension with a single question. Thankfully, the question spurred follow-up questions after Josh explained that Samantha had taken Zach out of the country without his say-so, and thus, a new conversation commenced.

It was easy to tell that no one liked Samantha either, and it seemed like both Luke and his brother had had pretty bad luck when it came to the women front.

"What about the brunette from a few weeks ago? You said things were going well with her, right? What the hell was her name?" James asked before slumping back into his seat and taking a large pull from his beer.

Josh scoffed and mimicked James's posture. "Her name was Georgia, and everything was going well until I found out she was engaged. And then she tells me that the only reason she started dating me was because she was questioning her relationship. Apparently, I made her question her engagement so much that she broke it off and wanted to start something with me."

Reed laughed and nudged Josh. "Damn, dude, I swear you have the worst luck sometimes."

Josh threw him a look and knocked back the rest of the beer. "Once a cheater, always a fucking cheater. I didn't want any part of that bad juju."

I couldn't help but laugh, and Luke slung his arm over my chair, tracing circles on my opposite shoulder.

"Well, there're plenty of women out there, right?" Reed said but with little conviction like he didn't actually believe it.

Josh's eyes whipped to our side of the table and landed on Amanda, who was totally unaware and eating her mashed potatoes. She scooped them into her mouth and licked the fork like it was ice cream, her eyes fluttering closed. As Josh watched her for half a second, I saw something flit over his expression that I couldn't exactly place.

"I don't think so, and one woman has absolutely ruined the rest for me," Josh said, not tearing his gaze away from Amanda, who, when she registered the comment, lifted her eyes to his. The tension was back, but it was different this time. That time it felt a lot like sexual tension, but who was I to know?

Their eye contact only held for a moment before Amanda cleared her throat and took another, less indulgent bite of potatoes. As I glanced around the room, I realized I was not the only one who had witnessed the interaction.

"So, how are you liking your new apartment?" Amanda asked from beside me, changing the subject easily.

"Yeah, you're living at the Ella Apartments, right?" Devon asked, and I nodded, trying to finish the bite of green beans I'd just taken. "I lived there for a few months before I moved closer into town. Pretty nice place, but that fucking leasing office woman. What was her name?"

I bit my lip and tried to hold back my laughter. "Blonde with huge boobs? Looks every bit the part of a Southern Barbie?"

"Yes!" Devon exclaimed.

"Yeah, Savannah. She's still there and loves Luke," I said with a wink in his direction. He shook his head and finished off the food on his plate.

"Pretty sure any guy that walks in there who looks half-decent is a target for her," James quipped and then added to Luke, "no offense, man."

"None taken," Luke said.

"But the apartment's nice and everything?" Amanda asked, bringing the topic back to *my* apartment, not the busty blonde working the leasing office.

"It is nice. It's good enough for now, which is all I wanted. I like my neighbors, and it seems like a good area. So, it checks all the boxes."

"That's really great. My ex and I *officially* broke up a couple months ago, so I'm also back in an apartment from a house. It's a weird transition." Her eyes were sad, but I could hear a little hope in her voice that made me think it wasn't such a bad thing that they broke up.

"It is. I got rid of so much stuff before I moved, but I still have way too much for a one-bedroom apartment. I'm unpacking and organizing and trying to go through everything I already went through for a second time."

Amanda smiled and nodded before picking up her wine. "I didn't think I was a hoarder, but…"

I laughed because the exact same thought had crossed my mind several times in the week since I'd moved in. "I'm going to rethink saving anything in the future. It's seriously all going to go in the garbage. My boss randomly requested a video call one day this past week while I was sorting through papers and whatever else on my desk. I had to prop my laptop on a box and then sit on another box to talk to him. It's a mess."

"Well, you're in better shape than I am. I've lived in my apartment for almost two months now and still haven't completely unpacked my kitchen. I pull pots and pans and plates out of boxes as I need them, and once I finally empty a box, I toss it. It's worked so far." She shrugged.

I knew we were going to be friends.

"Is that what you're thankful for?" James asked. "Finally

getting rid of that guy?

Amanda rolled her eyes but didn't argue.

"I know what I'm thankful for," he said. "Of course, all of you." Everyone awed as was appropriate, and James continued, "and a damn good job that gave me a fifteen percent raise this year."

We all raised our glasses and congratulated him. Luke whispered in my ear that James was the hardest worker of them all, that his career was, at that point, the most important thing in his life. He was some bigwig finance guy at an oil and gas company and still wasn't done trying to climb the corporate ladder.

James ruffled a hand through his shaggy, blond hair and wore a coy smile, but I could tell he was proud of himself as he should be.

"You deserve it, man. More than anyone," Devon said, raising his drink and taking a sip.

"Your turn," James said, pointing at Josh.

Josh sighed and seemed less than enthusiastic about coming up with something he was thankful for. It couldn't have been that hard, right?

After a long second, Josh looked around the table at his friends before stopping on Luke and then flicking his eyes to Amanda. He held her gaze as he stated plainly, "I'm thankful for second chances."

Another moment staring at each other, and they both looked away at the same time. I'd have to ask Luke about that later.

Reed was next to Josh and immediately piped up. "I'm thankful for good friends, good beer, and opening a kick-ass gym."

Amanda rolled her eyes but cracked a smile as she toasted Reed, who reached across the table and tapped her glass with his.

"Your turn, Blake," Reed informed Blakely as he slouched back in his seat. Luke's hand tensed on my shoulder, and out of the corner of my eye, I could see his jaw tic. I pushed away my empty plate and let my hand fall to Luke's thick jean-clad thigh beneath the table. If she hadn't been staring at us, Blakely would have missed the movement, but she didn't because her eyes were glued to us both.

"Pass," she said with annoyance, although her face was trying to convey indifference.

"But, Blake, everyone else—" Reed stammered.

She cut her eyes to him. "I don't care what everyone else is doing, Reed. *Pass.*"

Reed held his hands up in defense, his eyes were wide as he scooted closer to Josh and away from Blakely. Based on her attitude and what appeared to be absolute contempt for me, I couldn't believe it was only due to the Valerie situation. There was something more there, and I hoped it wasn't some unrequited feelings for Luke. Dealing with two scorned lovers was more than I had bargained for.

"On that note," Devon said. "I'm thankful that Mom's doing better and is currently at MD Anderson in a trial program. It's her best shot, so I'm thankful I could help her get there."

My heart broke at Devon's words and the sad smile that graced his freckled face. From personal experience, I knew MD Anderson was a cancer treatment center in Houston. My best friend's dad was diagnosed with stage IV colon cancer when we were in second grade; she and her entire family moved to Houston so he could seek treatment in one of the best facilities in the world.

We all raised our glasses to Devon's mom.

"Glad to hear she's doing better, dude. She's settled in her apartment okay?" Luke asked.

"Yeah. It's going to be a lot, me going back and forth to Houston to help her and my sister, but we'll handle it."

Luke nodded. "Well, we're all here to help with whatever you might need. Next time you go, let me know. I wanna tag along."

In a gesture I wasn't expecting, Blakely reached over and

gripped Devon's hand. I watched from the other side of the table as she squeezed it once. The look of disdain had vanished from her face, replaced by a warmth I didn't know she was capable of.

Devon returned the look and gave her a small, appreciative smile before he turned back to Luke.

"She'd really like that," Devon said, and then he cleared his throat. "Your turn."

Luke laughed and moved his hand from my shoulder to the back of my neck, sweeping the hair behind me. He brushed his thumb over the sensitive spot behind my ear and gazed at me with sparkling green eyes before he broke into a smile that lit up his entire face.

I hoped he'd always look at me like that, like I was everything.

"I think I already said what I was thankful for, but—"

"Actually, I know what I'm thankful for," Blakely spoke up. Every eye landed on her, the look of hatred firmly back in place. She didn't wait for our attention to continue, "I'm thankful for being independent and being able to think critically about a situation. Because at this point, I think I may be the only person at this table that can do so. And you know what—"

Amanda shot out of her seat suddenly as the rest of the group shook their heads and urged Blakely to "seriously shut the hell up," as Reed so eloquently put it. Luke's hand was shaking on the back of my neck and with my mouth still agape from Blakely's obvious speech directed mostly toward him or us, I looked over at him. It seemed like his jaw was permanently tense in her presence, and from my position next to him, I could still see the pulsing veins in his forehead and neck. The veins I'd only seen a few times in the past few weeks, and they only appeared when he was straining to control his anger.

"Blakely, I need to talk to you," Amanda said through clenched teeth. Her hands were balled in fists at her sides and the small, blonde woman looked like she was going to beat her friend's ass at that moment.

"Amanda—" Blakely attempted to say, but Amanda cut her off.

"Unless the next words out of your mouth are, 'Okay, Amanda, let's go outside and chat,' I don't want to hear it."

Blakely closed her mouth, grabbed her wineglass, and with one last glance in our direction, left the table. But the scathing look I expected to see wasn't there. Instead, I swore I saw fear, or maybe even pain, across her features.

Luke was vibrating with rage next to me while everyone else looked around at each other for a moment before James said something about clearing the table.

All four of the remaining men at the table stood and made quick work of clearing the plates, utensils, and empty glasses. Luke didn't move, though, so neither did I. As soon as Blakely left the table, Luke removed his hand from my neck, and I immediately missed the warmth and security of his touch. His hands were steepled under his chin and his eyes were somewhere far away from where we sat.

I was completely out of my element in how to help him. His leg was bouncing under the table and his shoulders were bunched together. I could feel waves of intense emotion and frustration rolling off him. With no other good ideas coming to mind, I twisted my fingers in the shorter hair at the base of his neck, scraping my nails lightly against his scalp.

His response was immediate. He dropped his head lower, his palms pressed against his face, and sighed into my touch. Shoulders instantly relaxing, the change was palpable. So, I continued to weave my hands in and out of his hair, scratching his scalp and along the sides of his neck, hoping to coax away the stress.

"It's been less than a week since I told you about Valerie, and I'm already second-guessing everything." He slumped farther forward. I waited for him to continue talking, but when he didn't say anything for a long moment, and the quiet clanking of dishes and his heavy breathing was all that filled the air, I had to break the silence.

"What's the full story? What else did Blakely have to say?"

He sighed and sat up to look at me. For a moment, it seemed like he wasn't going to tell me, but with a shake of his head, he said, "Blakely omitted some information about what happened with Valerie last time. She told me Valerie only called her and threatened her and backed off when Blake said we were done... but that's apparently not what happened. Earlier, she told me the actual story, and now, Angel, I'm fucking terrified for you. I'm furious that Blake would leave out anything, especially the information she did, and especially when it comes to Valerie."

He was fuming and my hand in his hair was no longer working to calm him—I didn't know if anything would. Not to mention, this revelation had my panic spiking. My chest constricted and I dropped my hands to my lap, trying and failing to control my breathing and the vicious intrusive thoughts.

"What—what do you mean?" I stuttered. I wasn't so concerned when I thought Blakely was just jealous that Luke was giving another woman attention or when I believed that she was concerned enough for me. Knowing there was more to the story may have changed everything.

I could handle incessant phone calls and veiled threats because I was working off the assumption that Valerie never actually made good on any of them. But judging by the look on Luke's face, he was genuinely worried for me.

His only response was to place his hand on one side of my face and run his thumb over the corner of my mouth before he kissed me softly and with such emotion that I almost broke. Never had a kiss conveyed so much in such a brief time; it was only a second or two—not long enough to build any additional tension—and he pulled back.

"I'd rather have this conversation alone. Can you stay tonight?"

I nodded, and he gave a half-hearted smile.

FORTY-ONE

Hazel

Sadly, the aftermath of Blakely's outburst lasted the rest of the night. Even after several not-so-subtle hints from all her friends, Blakely stayed until the bitter end, throwing annoyed glances at me and Luke. Her attitude put a stain on what would have been a really fun night.

We were able to play a few games and sat outside drinking and laughing around a small fire and the heater before it became too cold.

Blakely and Amanda were the first to leave, and Amanda and I exchanged numbers. She promised to text me soon and said that she was excited to have a new friend. I didn't miss the look Blakely sent my direction when her supposed best friend made the comment, but I had a comfortable buzz going from a few glasses of wine and hot toddies, so I didn't care as much.

I hugged Amanda tightly as Blakely walked out the front door.

James and Devon weren't too far behind them. Throughout the night, Devon began to open up more and more and his dry sense of humor made me laugh so much my stomach hurt. They were both so much fun and easygoing. James's commentary on Reed's shenanigans could have possibly been my favorite part.

The entire group was amazing, and I knew why Luke liked them all so much. They fed off each other and there was never a dull moment.

When I walked back into the living room, I found Luke covering a passed-out Reed with a blanket. He was starfished on the couch, one leg and arm hanging off the edge.

"He can stay there for tonight," he said and then hiked his thumb over his shoulder with a raised eyebrow.

I knew he was asking if I was ready to pass out, and God was I ever. But we still had a conversation to have. I managed to push the thought out almost entirely for the rest of the evening, but then my eyes would land on Blakely, and I couldn't help but wonder what Valerie had put her through.

Luke shut off all the lights and Sadie followed us down the hallway. I'd long since lost my heels somewhere in the living room, so I quietly padded to his bedroom and flung myself on the made-up bed the moment I saw it.

Exhaustion wanted to overcome me and pull me under into a deep sleep, but I fought it hard and sat back up on the bed. The moment I turned around, Luke appeared from the bathroom door in low-slung gray joggers and no shirt.

With his tattoos and broad muscled chest on full display, I couldn't help but gawk at him. Instantly, I felt a pull to run my nails up and down the dark hair speckled over his chest and stomach and through the happy trail until I would push below his waistband. Just looking at him made my panties wet and after lingering touches and heated glances all night—even with Blakely's drama—I was aching.

As I gawked, Luke tossed one of his old T-shirts into my lap.

With a saccharine smile, he said, "I didn't know if you brought anything for tonight but figured you wouldn't mind sleeping in one of my shirts."

Eager to take my bra off after an entire evening wearing one with underwire, I hopped off the bed and whipped my shirt over my head. I placed it on the bed, which was quickly followed by my bra. It was pure bliss. Once completely undressed—aside from my soaked panties—I tugged the shirt on and placed my clothes on the blue chair in the corner of his room. The same one he lounged in when we had our tryst through the windows. I smiled at the memory but tried not to think too hard about the house just on the other side of his bedroom window.

Big arms wrapped around me from behind and large hands flattened against my stomach and just below my breasts.

"I love seeing you wearing my clothes," Luke said in a husky voice as his proud erection ground into my lower back, grazing the top of my ass.

"I can tell," I mused as I rose on my toes just enough to ground my ass back into him. He grunted in response and his hands automatically found my breasts which were aching from the damned bra. He massaged them, his thumbs pressing from the outside and moving inward until he tugged both of my nipples. An illicit moan ripped through my throat and I pushed back again.

"I honestly thought you'd want me to sleep naked," I whispered because I couldn't get my voice any louder.

He chuckled and kissed my shoulder, running his tongue along my skin until he found my neck and kissed me there, too.

"I'm sure you will, but we should talk if you're up for it. And I can't talk to you if you're naked—I'll be too distracted to have any type of constructive conversation."

I laughed but then gasped as his hands gripped my hips and spun me around. My hands landed on his chest, and I was immediately distracted by everything about him.

"Then you need a shirt, too," I said and he rolled his eyes with a chuckle. He disappeared into his closet and returned a second later wearing a tight black T-shirt that was only a little better than him being shirtless.

He positioned himself against the headboard, and I found a

place beside him. As he always did when I was close, his hand found me and fell onto my knee. Sadie was already snoring at the bottom of the bed, and the entire situation felt eerily comfortable—being in bed with the man I'd only just begun seeing with his dog curled up like my being there was a common occurrence.

"*Fuck*, I don't know where to start," Luke said and dragged a hand through his hair. It was perfectly messed up from him dragging his hands through it all night long.

"Just start. And don't sugarcoat it—I've been on edge all night, and I just want to know what the hell I can expect from her."

"I don't know if there is a way to sugarcoat it," Luke muttered and sighed. "So, like I said before, I was under the impression that Valerie incessantly called Blakely, texted her, too, but eventually gave up. Her threats were disturbing, but I didn't think she'd ever acted on them. Blakely told me one day she just suddenly stopped, and we both figured she'd gotten bored. That's the story Blakely told me, but that's not actually what happened."

His hand tensed on my knee, and my gut twisted at what I assumed he'd tell me next—what really happened. And I knew he wanted to give me the entire story, but I was eager to know. I needed him to hurry, so I could figure out how it impacted my—our—situation.

"Turns out, Valerie made good on some of her threats." The second the words left his mouth, I swore my heart stopped beating and time stood still. With his head down, staring at his free hand in his lap, he continued, "Valerie broke into her house and held her at gunpoint for hours. Apparently, she didn't do much besides scaring the absolute shit out of her. Valerie cut off her hair and knocked her around a little bit. Blakely tried to reason with her and told her we'd broken it off, but Valerie was past reasoning. She's long been past reasoning, but Valerie told her that if she ever told me or the cops, she'd come after us both again. Blakely was terrified and believed Valerie would do it, so she did as she asked and didn't tell anyone."

As Luke spoke, it felt like someone steadily turned the heat warmer and warmer in his bedroom. "But she told you now." I croaked out.

"Yeah, because she knows that Valerie's back. Blakely's terrified that she's going to escalate even more this time, but since she called me, she's been silent. Which is honestly worse than when she's active—when she's quiet, I can't predict her next move. Blakely manages Murphy's, the bar where Josh also works, and they've thrown her out a couple of times, but that's child's play for Valerie."

My brain was working overtime to keep up with all the moving parts while fighting the several other emotions and thoughts that were at war within me.

"Blakely thinks we should stop seeing each other," he said, dropping his voice low. "She wanted me to march into the fucking living room and tell you to leave. Make a big scene, so you wouldn't have any desire to come back."

The only thing keeping my emotions in check was the knowledge that he hadn't done what Blakely asked. It would have been humiliating to be dismissed so abruptly, but it would have also broken my fucking heart. At that moment, I realized I was too far gone for the man in front of me. No matter how it ended, it would be an utter and all-consuming heartbreak.

"But you didn't." My words were quiet, and I wished I could muster up some sort of confidence, but it wasn't possible.

"No, I couldn't and wouldn't do that to you. I've seen you hurt, and I swore I would never be the person to do that to you. That's the reason I told you about Valerie in the first place. My first thought was to just break it off, go cold turkey, but I knew it would hurt you. I knew you'd internalize it and assume it was your fault."

He was right, that's exactly how I would have reacted. And

although things between us had escalated even in the past week, a week ago, I still would have been upset if he'd disappeared.

"So, my next best option was to tell you. I wasn't going to completely leave the decision up to you, but you deserved to know what was happening and have input on what would happen next. I'm not going to control you or make decisions for you. So, when you said you'd want to see where this goes, the selfish part of me agreed. That decision was also based on incredibly different information, and Hazel, I refuse to put you in harm's way."

I opened my mouth to speak, but he held up a hand. "Wait, just let me finish and then you can say anything you need to."

Reluctantly, I nodded and shifted to sit on my legs. "I've already talked to the dumbass detective that doesn't seem to give a fuck about it anymore. I texted him right after Blakely told me. He said he'd reach out to her, but she's got to talk to him and then *maybe* they can do something. But until Valerie's behind bars or fucking dead, you're in danger."

He took a deep breath, but I could tell he wasn't finished. I also didn't know if I could form words, so I waited for him to continue and all the while, I tried to come up with any sort of solution.

"My fear is that she's planning something big for one of us. That she's gone silent because she's biding her time, and at this point, I wish I could end things with you. I wish I could walk away."

His words hit me like a fucking train and my entire body tensed. His hand was still on my knee, and he must have felt my reaction because, finally, his blazing green eyes met my own.

"If it meant it would keep you safe, then I'd do it in a heartbeat, beautiful girl. I would hate every fucking second of it, and I would be utterly miserable, but it would be nothing if it meant she wouldn't go near you. I can handle her threatening me. But I can't handle her doing the same to you."

His hand shifted from my knee, and he tangled our fingers.

Staring at our intertwined hands, he said, "But I think we're past that. I think no matter what, you're going to be in danger. But I'm leaving it up to you. If you want to end things, I will understand. I would continue to do what I could to protect you, though, even if you didn't want to be with me. Even if..."

I couldn't lie to myself and say I didn't contemplate the decision for at least a moment. My self-preservation instincts told me that flight would likely be the best option in the situation in front of me. But my heart and the rest of my body were telling me something different.

What he was saying made sense—I was already a target whether I was with Luke or not. What didn't make sense was distancing myself from the one person who swore to do anything to keep me safe and made me feel safe.

"I'm not going anywhere," I said, and my voice sounded more confident than it had in my head when I'd only thought the words a second earlier.

I didn't know what I expected Luke's reaction to be, but the solemn head nod he gave me was not it. I knew it was his internal turmoil that provided his less than enthusiastic reaction. He didn't like that either of us had to choose, given the options presented or lack thereof.

"If that's the case, then we need to do more to make sure you're safe."

It made sense, but I was wary of his suggestions.

"My first instinct is to have you move in here with me and Josh. Most often, at least one of us is home which means you'd have someone with you twenty-four seven."

The idea, in theory, made sense, but I had just gained a small bit of my independence back. It was independence that I craved and thoroughly enjoyed and really did not want to give up.

"Do I have another option?"

Luke chuckled like he expected me to ask just that question.

"If you don't move in here, then I'm going to all but move in with you. I'll be there every night and we'll add extra security. Those are the two options if you still want to be with me."

Butterflies set flight in my stomach at his final words, *"be with me."* They sounded good coming out of his mouth and in his deep voice.

"That's a lot of work for you and what about Sadie?"

"I'll bring her with me. She loves the car and you." I was sure my apartment would have an issue with overnight pet guests that weren't on my lease, but that was a problem we could solve once we got there.

"Let me first say that it's not so much that I don't want to move in with you—"

Luke shook his head before I could finish my statement. "You don't have to explain. I get it, and that's why I came up with a second option."

With the decision made and the most realistic plan agreed upon, I tried to focus on what I could control. Valerie was clearly out of my control and her actions were her own—there was nothing I could do at that moment to stop her.

I could, however, control my reaction to the situation and how I handled it. Those stupid fucking podcasts I listened to about healing and blah blah blah taught me that, and I wanted to put it to good use. If there was ever a time to try, it was then.

Lost in thought, I stared at our intertwined fingers and the stark differences. Luke's hands were large, his fingers were thick and were obviously worn, as were his palms which were littered with calluses. The backs of his hands were dusted with black hair and his knuckles were covered in scars and marks. The scars were old and had long since healed and turned a cloudy white.

Either way, it hurt me to know he was once hurt. That he inflicted pain because he was in pain. I didn't know more than it had to do with his parents. I wanted to know, and the question crossed my mind every time I stared at the healed parts of his hands. But it wasn't the time.

"I thought you would freak out," Luke said, pulling my attention from his hands.

"Oh, I'm sorry my reaction didn't meet your expectations. Should I become hysterical? Maybe start throwing things?" My tone was sarcastic, but my eyes searched the room for something that would be good to throw. "That lamp would shatter nicely and so would the pictures there." I pointed, but Luke's grip on my chin pulled me back to look at him.

The humor in his eyes had replaced the sadness I'd seen there only moments ago.

"I like my shit, so maybe don't break it."

I shrugged. "If you say so."

"I'm being serious, though. You're taking this all too well."

I sighed and covered his hand that still cupped my face with my own.

"I'm trying this new thing where I only worry about the things I can control. And right now, I can't control Valerie or what she will do, so I'm not going to spend more brainpower on it than I have to. I'm worried and, honestly, slightly terrified, but I'm safe *right now*. I'm safe with you, so that's what I'm going to focus on."

A small smile tugged at the corner of Luke's lips which made me smile, too. His hand slid to the back of my neck as his other found its place on my waist. He tugged me onto his lap, and I fell onto him like it was the place I was always meant to be. I loved that position; we were face to face and there was no way to hide from the other.

His lips ghosted over mine. "That's very admirable, Angel."

Realization struck as he tossed my hair over my shoulder and nuzzled my neck. "Accepting my circumstances and the situation I'm in has never been an issue for me." It was a thought I hadn't meant to say out loud, but the sensation of Luke enjoying me was overpowering the rest of my senses.

He froze as my words and their meaning rang out around us.

"Hazel, I—" Luke began, the sadness had reentered his eyes and I was going to do whatever I could to immediately remove it.

I clamped my hand over his mouth before he could say anymore. "No, Luke. That's not what I meant. This is not your fault. It's not your fault you have an insane ex-wife that can't stand the prospect of you being with another woman. It's not your fault that Blakely lied to you. And it's not your fault that I got caught up in it. Please stop apologizing to me, and stop looking at me with sad, pity-filled eyes. My situation with Michael and our situation are worlds apart. It was all his fault, but I accepted the hand I'd been dealt because I thought that's what I was supposed to do. With you, it's different. Everything's different in an unexpectedly good way. I'm accepting this situation because the alternative's not having you and that seems like a seriously shitty alternative."

I paused, catching my breath and watching him watch me. There was a curious look there, and I could feel his mouth flex underneath my hand as he mumbled something into my palm.

I didn't pull my hand away immediately, instead, I warned, "If the next words out of your mouth aren't about how badly you want to fuck me, then I don't want to hear them, and you might as well not say anything at all."

Slowly, I dropped my hand from his mouth and before it could fall to rest on his chest, Luke spun me around and pinned me to the mattress with his body on top of mine.

"I think we should test out this red lipstick," he growled before slamming his mouth over mine. He didn't have to say it twice; I had been thinking about getting every inch of him in my mouth all night.

FORTY-TWO

Hazel

Our kiss was carnal and frenzied. As our tongues tangled, I pushed my hand down between us and immediately found him hard and ready. It was easy enough to slip my hand inside his loose gray sweatpants, and just below his waistband, I found his tip large and already leaking. My hand wrapped around him, and I reveled in his size and the weight of him in my palm as my fingertips almost touched, but not quite. He was heavy and as I pumped him, he lurched into my hand with a low, growl-like groan.

The sound alone had me craving more.

I pumped him a few more times, eliciting more erotic noises before I pushed him off the edge of the bed. He stumbled back a few paces, but I stepped off the bed and reached for him. By the waistband of his sweatpants, I pulled him to me. I jerked the soft material down his legs as I found myself on my knees at his feet.

His head fell back, resting on his shoulders after one look of me kneeling before him.

I stared at his cock directly in front of my face and took a breath to renew my courage. God, it was fucking intimidating.

Thick, pulsing veins ran up and down his shaft, and the size of his tip was daunting as I wrapped my hands around him. With both of my hands, I was able to cover most of his shaft, but the tip of his cock was still exposed.

I stuck my tongue out and licked the bead of precum before it dripped.

"Fuck, yes. I love your tongue. I love your mouth," Luke mused, finally looking down at me. His thumb traced the outline of my lips around his shaft as I pushed him deeper. "You're so pretty when you're on your knees for me."

His filthy words spurred me on, and I fluttered my tongue underneath his head. His hand wrapped around my hair, and he thrust deeper into my mouth. With my hands twisting and pumping up and down him, I bobbed my head down and back up, slowly easing him deeper and toward the back of my throat.

Every once in a while, I looked up at him and watched as he was taken prisoner by the pleasure I was giving him. The muscles in his toned stomach flexed each time I swallowed around him or sucked just a little harder.

He continued mumbling dirty words and praises. "You're such a good girl sucking my cock like that. Yes, that's so good."

When he called me a good girl, my eyelids fluttered closed on their own accord, and I basked in his praises. I knew I was doing a good job because my jaw burned, and saliva was running down my chin and dropping onto his T-shirt I was still wearing.

With a loud pop, I pulled my mouth off him and ripped the shirt over my head. I was back on him in a second, and I could feel the vibration of his pleasurable growl through his dick.

"God, the things I want to fucking do to you," he said, winding his fingers back in my hair. He tugged it at the root and the bite of pain quickly gave way to pleasure. My responsive moan was desperate.

"I want it all," I confirmed. Luke didn't have to be told twice and slid his cock deeper. He prodded the back of my throat just barely before he drew out once more.

"I don't want to hurt you."

I chuckled around him and said, "You won't hurt me. I can handle it and if I can't, I'll tell you. Now, give me your worst."

He chuckled darkly and slammed his cock into the back of my throat. That time he held himself there as I gagged around him. My eyes watered at the intrusion, but I couldn't care as I focused on giving him more pleasure. With one hand still wrapped around his base, I used the other to grip his balls and squeeze just hard enough.

He groaned and continued fucking my face. I knew my mascara was running down my face, and it seemed like my gagging was spurring him on. I was overcome by the depravity of the act.

Abruptly, he backed away, breathing heavy and leaving me in the middle of the floor, still on my knees. I was a mess, but once he composed himself, he gripped me under my arms and lifted me to the bed, where he laid me out.

"Lipstick wasn't invincible. It looks so good smeared all over my cock." I propped myself on my elbows to look toward the edge of the bed where, sure enough, I could see the base of his cock was covered in my lipstick.

I smiled but then realized it was also likely all over my face. I sat up and wiped at the corners of my mouth like it was going to do anything at all to help my disheveled appearance.

"No, don't fix it," Luke said, gripping my chin between his thumb and his forefinger. "It looks even better smeared around your mouth with your makeup running down your face. You looked like a fucking siren crying while my cock was in your throat."

He stared into my eyes as he spoke, pulling my flimsy, wet panties down my legs, and I fell apart in a mess of desire and lust. He pushed me back into the bed, positioned himself between my legs and lined himself up with my entrance. I was panting for it and watching him above me, so lost in his own desire, with his only mission being to send us both over the edge, making me spread my legs wider. Unlike the first time, he didn't wait or tease me with shallow thrusts; he pushed all the way home with the first thrust, most definitely hitting my cervix.

I all but yelled as he kept himself buried deep inside of me. The two other men in the house were absolutely awake then. There was no way they were sleeping through my yell or my subsequent loud moans. My inner walls clenched around him, and I slowly relaxed to let his full length comfortably in.

After a few moments, he began to pump in and out of me at an unrelenting pace. Giving him head wasn't only for his benefit; it also had me wet and ready for it—for all of him grinding into me. Watching him come undone for me was the best foreplay.

He dipped his head down and flattened his tongue against one of my nipples. I gripped each of my breasts and pushed them toward him, eager for his mouth to ravish me. My nipples were like a direct line to my clit, which was already pulsing as he ground against me.

I met him thrust for thrust, pushing up to him, hoping to get even closer. My orgasm was climbing and twisting at the base of my spine.

Luke let go of my nipple with a pop and focused on steadying his thrusts and stoking that raging fire within me. One of his hands gripped my hip while the other swept around my neck, pulling my mouth to his.

His wicked tongue swept into my mouth as I clawed at his back. The man put every emotion into the way his lips danced with mine. He fused our mouths together with expert precision, and I melted into him, feeling his need whip through me and tangle with my own.

His hips slowed slightly as he rolled in and out of me, hitting a spot so deep before pulling out. He hit every spot so perfectly that I cried out for more. I was lost to his touch and his movements blanketed me.

The hand at the back of my neck tightened just before the one at my hip did, too. A few more thrusts and I knew I would fall apart. Luke also seemed to sense it as he continued the same pace but pushed even deeper.

"Open your eyes, beautiful. I want to watch you come. Look at me," Luke demanded, and I wasn't going to deny him.

The second I forced my eyes open, even through the sublime sensations running all over my skin and deep into the marrow of my bones, my breath hitched. Luke's eyes were deep green and intent on my face. His mouth was parted on a moan, and I could see the pleasure etched into his features, but there was more there than just that.

Behind the outward expression of his pleasure, it was like I could see his soul and his heart through the minute details of his face and the way his eyes bore into my own.

Like he had earlier that night, he looked at me like I was everything. And the look in his eyes made me explode and implode and combust.

The entire time the orgasm ripped through my body, I kept my eyes trained on Luke. He pushed himself deep and ground into me, letting me wring out as much pleasure as possible.

When the pulsing subsided what seemed like minutes later, Luke resumed his thrusting only to pull out abruptly and spin me to my stomach. I felt languid and orgasm drunk, but Luke lifted me to all fours, and I managed to keep myself up.

He nudged my legs wider with his hands, pushing the inside of each thigh before he positioned himself between them. With my legs wide, I let my chest and face press down into the mattress and thrust my ass higher for him. He audibly groaned and palmed my ass roughly.

"God, your ass," Luke said, smoothing the spot he had just grabbed with delicate fingers. "Your ass was made for this position. Keep your ass in the air for me, Angel. Can you do that?"

"Yes," I moaned as he ran a finger over my swollen lips and twirled it over my sensitive clit. Suddenly, his finger was replaced by his tongue licking me thoroughly as his hands spread me apart. His moans vibrated against my entrance and the feeling was uncanny. The same wicked tongue that ravished my mouth went to town on my pussy, thrusting in and out as he did with his cock.

"You taste so good," he said with one more lick before I felt the bed move beneath me and watched him kneel behind me once again. "Are you going to stay like this for me?"

"Yes," I repeated in a breathy gasp.

The engulfed head of his cock prodded my entrance and as he pushed inside of me, he groaned, "Good girl."

The position we were in was a mind-blowing sensation. He was so deep that, for a moment, it felt like he would split me in two. But as always, the slight pain gave way to intense pleasure. Each thrust was measured with greedy hands splayed on my hips, digging into my sides, and I could feel my ass bounce and recoil each time he slammed into me.

Another orgasm was already making itself known as I pushed back into him, earning a string of curses. He pushed my cheeks apart, and I pushed up to my hands to watch him. His eyes were cast down, and he was intently eyeing where we were joined with his lips parted and a look of barely restrained desire.

He glanced up to see me panting and studying him from over my shoulder. His dark laugh was one I knew only came with even more positively amazing sensations. "We fit together so well, baby girl. I could watch my cock slip in and out of your pussy forever. You're so wet for me and look at you pushing back onto me."

He growled low as I picked up the pace and the vibration pulsed through him and his big cock and straight into me. Everything was overwhelming, and I felt like I was no longer in my body.

He had electrified each of my nerves and I wanted to do the same to him.

I fell back to the bed, still pushing back into him and trying to keep time with his thrusts, I snaked my hand under my body and found his balls hanging behind me. The instant my hand wrapped around their silkiness, he yelled some indecipherable expletive and launched himself deeper. I didn't stop, though, even when he remained still and buried deep inside of me. I squeezed his balls just as I had done earlier and clenched my inner walls around him.

"That's it, play with my balls and squeeze around my cock. *Fuck*, you're going to make me come," he groaned. I could sense he was holding back and probably fighting off his own release, but I needed his release like I needed my own. I wanted to feel him pulse inside of me or watch the ropes of cum decorate my back or my front.

"Come inside of me, come on my ass, or my tits, I don't care. Please, Luke," I moaned the rest of his name as he began bucking wildly.

There was a change to him as something primal was unleashed. It was less about giving me pleasure and more about taking his own from my body. It was erotic, and knowing he wanted me, that only I could give that to him and make him hungry, was enough to push me over the edge.

He hiked one of his knees up next to me as he pushed my head into the comforter and gripped my hip with punishing savagery. Even with my body contorted how it was, there was no way I was letting go of his balls when it meant he completely unleashed on me.

His touch was possessive but appreciative, and his thrusts were selfish as he took and took from me.

With a groan followed by hurried breaths, Luke gave in to it all, letting the pleasure wash over him. His cum was warm and feeling the pulsing of his cock as he shot into me propelled me headfirst into another orgasm. One that was no less earth shattering as we shared it together.

Luke removed his hand from the back of my neck and smoothed a loving hand down my spine. When he withdrew a moment later, my body gave out and I slumped to the bed in pure exhaustion.

The bed moved under his weight, and I let myself sink deeper into the comforter as I listened to him shuffle into the bathroom. Even in the few seconds he was gone, I was well on my way to succumbing to sleep. The two orgasms had pushed me over the edge, and I didn't know how much longer I could stand to keep my eyes open. That was until Luke placed a warm cloth between my legs, cleaning me as well as he could.

"I think I could get used to this," he said while making another pass before gently flipping me over. I raised my eyebrows in question, silently asking him to clarify. "Watching my cum spilling out of you while you lay fully satisfied on my bed."

Sex hung everywhere in the room and his words made me want to go again and again and again, but the rest of my body was not on the same page as the aching, pulsing area between my legs.

But it wasn't just the sex between us, and that was the part that scared me. His words didn't just make me want to jump his bones, they made me want him in every part of my life every single day. They made my chest ache and made me want to spend more time in and out of his bed with him.

Even though we had despised each other for the past few years, I was amazed at the switch that flipped the night he found me in my bathroom. He didn't pity me—although, at one point, I thought he might. He was worried and truly concerned, and I wholeheartedly believed that he would have killed Michael had he been given the opportunity.

I didn't condone murder but knowing a man would willingly kill for you was honestly a turn-on.

The way he approached my situation was an eye-opener; he wasn't the person I had assumed he was and that shifted our relationship. But I was still going to be cautious. I knew Luke was a good person and a good man, even with his somewhat secretive and tumultuous past.

He wasn't defined by his past and neither was I.

But the last person I gave my heart to didn't deserve it at all —he beat it to a fucking pulp, which made me second-guess giving it away completely again. I didn't think I could handle a second heartbreak so close to the first.

Luke leaned down and softly kissed me before escaping back to the bathroom. I watched the muscles in his back and his perfectly circular ass as he walked through the doorway and flipped on the light. When I heard the shower turn on, I knew it was exactly what I needed, too, before curling up in bed.

Rolling out of bed, my legs shook slightly with my weight, and I smiled to myself. The man knew what he was doing in the bedroom.

Once I regained my balance, I trudged into the bathroom, squinting against the bright light. I stepped into the room as steam began permeating the air but stopped in my tracks when I caught sight of Luke. His head was downturned as the spray cascaded over his black hair, which was falling into his face.

He seemed so impossibly vulnerable in that moment that a small gasp almost escaped my throat. I felt a pull in my chest that urged me toward him, and I wasn't one to ignore my pull to him.

I knew he heard the glass shower door open, but he didn't move his position. I took the opportunity to wrap my arms around him from behind, pressing my front into him. He groaned softly in response and finally lifted his head.

"I was hoping you'd join me," he said, spinning to face me and then rotating us again so I was directly under the spray.

He gave my hair a slight tug, and I leaned my head back, letting the water drench my hair. Luke's hands tugged through the tangled strands, carefully combing them out.

"I'm eager to know: what did you think of everyone? I'm sure you have an opinion."

I laughed and shrugged. "I usually do have an opinion, you're right about that."

"So..." he prompted, and I tightened my arms around him as he squeezed a likely way too small amount of shampoo in his hands.

"They were all really nice. They all seem like genuinely good people. I just think it's cool that y'all have been friends for so long and have managed to stay friends even through everything life has thrown at you."

He nodded and squirted more shampoo in his hands as I knew he would. I groaned as he massaged my scalp, working the shampoo into my hair and pulling it through the strands. "They are amazing. We've all been through a lot, but we've supported each other through everything. Not having any blood relatives left, they're the closest thing to a family that Josh and I have. That's why when things like Blakely's outburst happen, we figure it out. Most of the time, when we have arguments, it's because we give too many fucks about something else."

Finished with the shampoo, he tipped my head back again and methodically rinsed it out.

The curious part of myself perked up again, wondering more about his parents. But I couldn't muster the strength to initiate the conversation. I was too relaxed and exhausted to think about tough conversations.

"I can see that. Maybe one day Blakely and I will be friends," I mused, but really I had no idea.

Luke chuckled and moved on to the conditioner. "Maybe, but I wouldn't get your hopes up."

"Trust me, I'm not, but I don't want to cause issues between all of you."

He shook his head. "You won't. Blakely is just the most difficult among us about certain things—especially about Valerie. She'll come around, I promise."

I just rolled my eyes but hoped he was right.

"It seemed like you and Amanda got along, though."

"Yeah, I really like her. We exchanged numbers and she's supposed to text me sometime this week so we can hang out."

Rinsing out the conditioner, I was overcome by the feeling of his large, rough hands tenderly stroking my hair and carefully removing all the product. It was taking all of my willpower to pay attention to what he was saying, but his hands were hypnotic and dominated my attention.

"What?" I asked, just catching the end of his sentence. When I opened my eyes, Luke was shaking his head and smoothed his hands down the sides of my neck and over my shoulders.

"I said that if you really want to learn about Amanda, you should go get margaritas. She's very chatty when she drinks tequila. But I know she'll love you."

I threw my head back and laughed. I also enjoyed margaritas, but was it the best idea for a first friend date? "I'm hoping we'll get along. This is embarrassing to admit, but I don't have a lot of friends after—" Emotion lodged in my throat unexpectedly, but I pushed it away, trying not to acknowledge it. "Michael really tried to keep me isolated, so I don't have friends. Stephanie, my work friend, is the only friend I've had here, and she's moving. So, I'm excited to hang out with Amanda. My new neighbor, Lexi, seems nice, too."

Without a word, Luke gripped under my ass and lifted me with ease, pinning me between the slightly chilled shower wall and his warm, hard chest. His eyes were intently glued to mine and he squeezed my thighs.

"Hazel, they would be stupid to not want to be friends with you. Don't stress about it. They will love you."

"How do you know? It's absolutely possible they won't."

It was a legitimate question. But the way Luke watched me, I questioned the validity of it. His lips were set in a stiff line and his jaw ticced slightly. A few drops of water slid down his face as I watched his eyes study my face in detail. His eyes were brimming with something I couldn't decipher as he said, "I just know they will. Trust me."

As the words fell from his lips, I thought I began to recognize the look in his eyes. Not as something I had truly seen before, I realized, but something I'd attempted to write about in my book. I'd attempted to explain it, but I couldn't find the words yet. The look was inexplicable and so was the feeling in my chest.

FORTY-THREE

Hazel

I slumped into the booth at the corner of the bright Mexican restaurant, sliding my full shopping bags down to the corner and against the wall. Even the day before Thanksgiving, the restaurant was lively and full of children since they had the week off.

That was also how Amanda was able to spend the afternoon shopping with me. Luke was taking me on our official first date. So, I bought a dress with Amanda's help.

"Oh, shit. You've got to be kidding me," she groaned but smiled brightly and waved at someone behind me. "One of my shit kids is here, and he's spotted me. Now, I have to say hi. Oh, God, his mother is awful. Order me a frozen margarita with salt while I'm gone. A *big* one." She cupped her hands in front of her, demonstrating the bowl-sized margarita she wanted.

I chuckled a little but told her I would.

Just a few tables behind us, I could hear who I thought was the kid's mother eagerly exclaim how excited she was to see Amanda or Ms. Allan, as the children called her. Amanda returned the sentiment in a voice that perfectly disguised her annoyance at being seen in public.

When the waiter, a young, skinny teenager who seemed less than thrilled to be working the day before a holiday, approached our table, I ordered two huge-ass margaritas and queso. He did not return my smile and merely grunted when he walked away.

I heard Amanda speaking to her student and laughed in amazement. How she was able to deal with hormone-driven twelve-, thirteen- and fourteen-year-olds would always be a mystery to me. But I'd learned throughout the day she really did enjoy her job and had an unparalleled passion for teaching.

She was currently one of two middle school science teachers at one of the elite private schools in the area. Her stories about the students and parents alike had me laughing most of our day shopping together.

By the time Amanda returned, the condensation from our margarita glasses was dripping onto the table and I'd eaten my fair share of queso. Before she even muttered a word in my direction, Amanda sucked down half of her margarita and then scrunched her eyes shut.

"Fucking brain freeze," she mumbled, rubbing her fingers across her head.

I stared at her across the table with my eyebrows raised. "That bad?"

She sighed and grabbed a chip, scooping up a plentiful amount of the cheese. "She's one of the PTA moms, so she began ranting that the children should have also received the Monday after Thanksgiving off because too many families travel and should get an additional travel day. I just gave her some bullshit about understanding and blah blah blah." She took a bite and continued talking around the chip in her mouth. "So, yes, that bad, but also the same old shit."

I laughed, and we perused the menus. We sucked down our margaritas quickly and decided to order another because why the hell not?

Being with Amanda was easy. The conversation rolled smoothly, and we were similar yet different enough to keep things interesting. It was a good first friend date as I had called it and then Luke had continued to call it when I told him I'd be going with Amanda to find something to wear for our date.

He'd been at my house every evening since the night he told me he would be. It was all oddly comfortable and normal. He got to my apartment around six thirty after stopping at his house to pick up clothes and Sadie. We ate dinner and afterward, he watched TV while I wrote. He not so subtly attempted to sneak peeks over my shoulder, but I still hadn't let him see any part of it.

Then, after at least a round or two of sex, we went to bed, the three of us cuddled up on my queen-size mattress. I'd thought it would have been big enough, but between a full-sized dog and an extra-large man, I was sorely mistaken.

Luke got up and left for work long before I did, but before he left, he always kissed my forehead and told me he'd see me that night. He took Sadie with him and dropped her back at his house with Josh, although I told him she could stay. Apparently, Josh missed her too much when she was gone all day.

We easily fell into a cohabiting routine, and as far as I could tell, we'd only grown closer even if it only had been a few days; at least we hadn't wanted to kill each other. And I couldn't help but admit that having him there every night eased some of the worries I'd begun to have about Valerie. She was unpredictable and the last thing I wanted was to be on the wrong end of her rage if I could help it.

Once the second margarita arrived, and since I was already feeling the first one, I had the courage to finally ask the question that had been on my mind since the Friendsgiving party.

"What happened with you and Josh?"

Midsip, Amanda's eyes went wide, really showing off the brilliant, deep blue. She took an extra second to take an even longer sip, then, with a sigh, crossed her arms in front of her on the table.

"You noticed that, huh?"

She didn't seem upset that I'd asked the question but did seem slightly uncomfortable talking about it.

"I noticed that Josh couldn't keep his eyes off of you and seemed to be directing his thankfulness for second chances toward you."

She groaned and threw her head back into the shiny red cushion of the booth. She took a deep breath and said, "Subtlety is not that man's best trait."

I chuckled but waited for her to continue; I had already pushed enough but was eager to hear more, so I kept my eyes expectant and my mouth shut.

"I'm not sure what everyone else knows at this point, meaning I don't know what Josh and Reed have told Blake, Devon and James, so just don't say anything even to Luke, please."

I made a cross over my heart with my finger as I chewed the rest of my chip. "I swear."

"So, at the end of July, all of us were hanging out at Reed's parents' house. They have this amazing house on the other side of Austin, right off the lake, with a beautiful pool. We go there pretty often and that weekend, all seven of us were there. We hung out by the pool and by the lake and drank pretty much all day. We had so much fun, and before we knew it, everyone else was passed out in their rooms besides me and Josh. We had been on the back porch talking for hours but hadn't even realized we'd been out there for that long. We were cozy on their couch, just talking about anything and for the most part, it felt like it always has between us, completely platonic and friendly. But then something flipped, and I can't even pinpoint it, but I know we both felt it. I was especially raw from everything going on with my ex. But then one thing led to another, and we kissed," she paused for a second, flipping all her hair over one shoulder and playing with it between her fingers.

"We kissed and it was such a *good* kiss. Then I was on his lap, and at that point, whether we wanted to or not, neither of us was going to stop. So, we went upstairs to the bedroom I was supposed to be sleeping in, only when I opened the door, the room wasn't fucking empty. Reed was sitting at the end of the bed with his head in his hands. We were caught red-handed, and I had no idea what to do. I asked him what he was doing there, and after a few minutes of pulling the answer from him, he said he came to find me."

My eyes had to have been the size of golf balls, and I was mindlessly sipping my margarita, slowly heightening my buzz as she continued.

"I'm not going to bore you with the details of the conversation, and to be honest, I don't remember them all that well because I was slightly drunk. But… we had a threesome."

Margarita could have come out of my nose with the way I gasped when she added the final confession. "What?" I asked between coughs and gasps.

She nodded slowly; an unamused smile perched on her lips. "Yup, all three of us together, and it was *fucking amazing*."

My jaw was slack, and I honestly had no words. For once in my life, I was fucking speechless. "Wait, so what happened afterward?"

"Afterward, we didn't really talk about it. It hasn't really come up since then, and I'm hoping it won't. Friendsgiving was the first time either of them has said anything about it, really."

"You mean Reed hasn't said anything? Josh seemed to insinuate pretty heavily that he wants something, right? That's what he meant by a second chance."

She rolled her eyes and paused the story as the waiter dropped off our steaming plates of food and grunted after we thanked him.

"I'm guessing so. Reed has stayed quiet, but there's been a

change there. I haven't wanted to ask, though, because if anything happens, it'll fuck up our entire dynamic and everyone will be pissed. I thought it was an unspoken rule between the three of us—we weren't going to talk about that one time at the lake."

I shrugged and blew on a bite of the creamy cheese enchiladas that my mouth was watering for.

"If you weren't worried about how it would impact your group, what would you want to do?"

Amanda stopped chewing midbite and gave me a quizzical look. She set her fork back down and the furrow in her brow deepened further.

"I seriously haven't even thought about it because there's no point. It doesn't matter what I would want; it would ruin everything."

"I really don't think it would ruin everything. Everyone seemed pretty accepting and you all genuinely care about each other. If you wanted to be with either of them, then I'm sure they'd accept it and support you."

Her shoulders slumped and she put her head in her hands, leaning over her plate. "I don't know, Hazel. If they both pursued me, I don't know if I'd be able to choose. And choosing one over the other could mean breaking one of their hearts."

My enchilada had finally cooled off enough that I could take a bite, and I moaned when the gravy and cheese hit my tongue.

"I think it would be worth it if you feel like one of them could be your person."

"Yeah, one of them…" she murmured around another bite of food before looking off to the side. Even though I didn't know Amanda all that well, I did know the look in her eye well enough. There was something she wasn't telling me, and it seemed like it had everything to do with choosing between the two men.

Changing the subject abruptly, Amanda turned back to me

and asked, "So you're staying here for Thanksgiving this year? Not going home?"

Home, that was a loaded word. I hadn't lived in my parents' house for nearly ten years, so that felt less like home and more like their house. And then, moving to Austin, I figured the house Michael bought for us would be our home, but it never felt that way. The closest I'd gotten in the last ten years to feeling like I was at home was my college dorm and then my new one-bedroom apartment.

"No, I'm staying here. Since I just moved in, I didn't want to travel right now, and I don't want to even think about running into Michael."

Amanda nodded in understanding. I'd given her the Cliffs-Notes version of the story between Michael and me and how Luke and I had transitioned from neighbor enemies to whatever the hell we were. In the middle of a dressing room, with clothes strewn everywhere, she quietly listened to everything I had to say. She'd been open and genuinely concerned for me and how I was doing after the fact. And there was something about Amanda that made me want to be open and share my story with her.

"That makes sense. So, you'll be with Josh and Luke then?"

"Yeah, it'll just be the three of us. It's the first Thanksgiving in almost ten years that I'm not going up to Nashville, but I just can't manage it. Even thinking about going up there and seeing all the places where Michael and I have so many memories, along with the possibility of seeing *him*, it's too much. My family was going to come down, but that changed."

"You know, with everything Luke's been through, it doesn't surprise me that he was drawn to you. Don't get me wrong, you're an absolute catch, and I'm not sure there is a person better suited for him than you. But I think people who are similar are drawn to one another, especially when your experience almost mirrors someone else's."

"You mean with everything he went through with Valerie," I

said, remembering that I'd had the same thought not too long after he told me about her.

"Absolutely, yes. Once we really got to know her, none of us liked Valerie all that much. She ended up being controlling, manipulative, and selfish, along with a million other nasty words. Even Blakely, who was honestly the closest to her, took Luke's side seeing who Valerie *truly* was. What he went through was horrible and I wouldn't wish it on my worst enemy, but there is also everything with his parents. That can really fuck a kid up, you know?"

For a split second, I paused before continuing to take a sip of my drink. She'd mentioned the infernal question I'd had spinning around in my head—the reason why Luke sought out fighting and told me he was a messed-up kid. The one topic he refused to broach.

The need to know vibrated inside of me, and I was sure that if I played it right, Amanda would tell me. But that also seemed like I was going behind Luke's back. I knew he should be the one to tell me and he probably had a reason for not doing so, but I heard the words, "Right, his parents," come out of my mouth before I knew what I was doing.

My voice was confident, and Amanda didn't suspect the actual question my words held.

"Everything with Valerie was just the icing on top of the cake, really. Growing up in a house like he and Josh did with a constantly pissed-off father who beat their mother had to wear on them both. Luke really protected Josh from a lot of it, though, even after he found his parents in their bedroom."

All the background noise in the restaurant went silent as I replayed each of Amanda's words over again in my head. He found his parents? I'm assuming she means that he found them dead, but how did they die?

Even with the tequila blazing through my system, my acting skills seemed to be on par because Amanda didn't notice the quickening of my breath nor the tensing in every part of my body.

"Yeah, right."

Amanda nodded with her mouth full. "Luke told me before that he thinks about it every day, which is no surprise when you find your parents dead. In college, we had all fallen asleep in the living room after a night out. Luke and I had called dibs on the sectional, and I woke up in the middle of the night to him kicking the shit out of my shoulder. He was having a nightmare and ended up telling me the next day that he still has them every once in a while. It broke my heart. Does he still have nightmares?"

"I'm not sure. I haven't noticed them if he does," I said honestly. My brain was working overtime trying to comprehend the new information and hearing that his parents died in their house—and that he was the one to find them—did wonders to sober me up completely.

"That's good. And God, do I ever hope that this is the end for Valerie. She's been a fucking leech in his life for too damn long."

My head was spinning, but I managed to say, "Yeah, me too."

"I'm glad he has you, though. And for what it's worth, I don't agree with Blakely even if she is my best friend. Valerie won't stop even if you break up, so you might as well live your lives."

I nodded again because I was well and truly incapable of forming a single syllable of a single word. Luke's mom had been a victim of abuse and then he had as well. It was amazing that he trusted anyone at all. It also well explained his need to fight and release the likely onslaught of emotions it brought on, especially as a teenager with no other outlet. The grief was probably debilitating.

My heart broke for him over and over, and I felt the tears pricking the back of my eyes as I thought of a heartbroken teenage Luke.

"Thanks. Anyway, what are your plans for tomorrow?" I asked, trying to change the subject with as much grace as I could muster.

Amanda easily transitioned into an account of her and her family's plans for the following day. Luke was right, though, I not only got to know Amanda over margs, I felt like I got to know him, too.

FORTY-FOUR

Luke

The small, folded piece of white paper that was in the mailbox of the vet clinic was unfolded and lay on my desk when I felt the urge to fucking pummel something.

It was the third time in the past few days that I'd received a letter from Valerie at the clinic. Besides the contents of each letter, the only way of identifying they were each from Valerie was her nickname for me, written precisely in a basic typeface on the front of each.

"Bear."

The first one was a standard letter claiming that she missed me and was still in love with me. She said she was more than happy waiting as long as I needed to go back to her. Then she went into detail about our first date. She described every feeling she had that night and how the tension of our years-long friendship made that first date all the better. She went into graphic detail about the things we did together in the alley behind the place.

The second letter was less sexually graphic but was her recap of the day I asked her to marry me. Like she was writing the next great American novel, she described in perfect detail the night I took her to hear one of my favorite bands play live and asked her to be my wife during my favorite song. They were playing a surprise show in a run-down converted warehouse outside of the city. The song described an imperfect love with the best intentions, and it was a song I played over and over and over again, annoying everyone around me except for her.

I never listened to that fucking song again.

The third was a letter reminiscing on another old memory—we'd gone to Murphy's, and after too many shots of whiskey, I almost fought a guy just for bumping into Valerie in the middle of the dance floor. It took both Devon and Reed pulling me away from the encounter and shoving me out the back door to calm me down.

Rhonda, the owner, threatened to never let me enter the bar again if I didn't calm down. It was the second time that month that I almost got into a fight, and she wasn't having it any longer.

It was embarrassing to know that I couldn't control my anger even over the simplest accident. But that's not the way Valerie remembered it. She remembered it as I was her knight in shining armor fucking saving her from the rest of the men in the world. That's also the way I saw it back then, which is how we ended up escaping to the upper levels of the bar, which were only used for storage and fucking against cases of beer and liquor.

The third letter was a detailed recap of that night and how she'd felt when I got kicked out and when we snuck back in.

I read about a quarter of it before I realized where she was going with the extra emotional and distorted details. There was something more in the words of the third letter that there hadn't been in the others. My stomach lurched when I read the words "beautifully explosive rage." It was a night that I too often thought of when I second-guessed if I'd turn into my own father. Apparently, it had also been memorable for her but in radically different ways.

I skimmed the rest of the letter, but she also included a message to let me know that my happiness meant more than anything to her. That my happiness was the key to her own and that's all she cared about. I gagged, threw up a little in my mouth and then promptly texted Detective Bell.

I was beginning to lose hope in him and the police in general. In the weeks since the phone call with Valerie, nothing had changed. Even after Blakely's confession, she had yet to speak to any of the officers that contacted her, and when I confronted her, she said it was for our own safety.

I called her twice a day and she explained each time that she'd told me so that I knew what to expect when Valerie went after Hazel. She still believed talking to the police would mean Valerie would find her or pursue me harder.

Without Blakely's statement, the police claimed there wasn't enough evidence to support a new restraining order—like it would do any good anyway—and they were unable to arrest her for letters and a phone call.

According to Detective Bell, they'd even so much as gone to Valerie's house—our old house—and spoken with her in person. She, of course, told them exactly what they wanted to hear, including that the phone call was not supposed to be threatening and that she merely missed me. The woman wasn't capable of such intense emotion.

Like she had so often done before, she was walking the line of legal and illegal, annoying, and obsessive stalking. But I wouldn't let her cross the line when it came to Hazel.

I'd stayed with her every night and would continue until the threat no longer existed. I'd keep her safe no matter what it took because I was falling for her. Well, I had fallen for her already; *falling* made it seem like it was happening, but I'd already smacked into the fucking ground. I was done falling and thinking of Valerie getting anywhere near Hazel was the worst-case scenario.

We had found a rhythm just in the few days we'd partially

lived together and moved around each other seamlessly. We ate dinner together; I annoyed the shit out of her when she tried to write, and she was never excited to tell me goodbye when I left in the morning. It was just that it wasn't my home she was in, and every day I felt more of a pull to make her even more mine.

But Hazel had been hesitant from the start and understandably so. So, I decided to keep my feelings to myself for a while longer and let things naturally develop, although my heart was more than ready to speed it all up. It wasn't about me—that's what I needed to remember.

I was silently telling myself that when I knocked on Hazel's apartment door and she swung it open with her sunshine smile pasted to her face. My eyes didn't linger on her face for long, though. Her eye makeup was slightly darker than usual, and she was wearing a kissable pink lipstick that wouldn't be as stark of a difference around my cock as the red.

But quickly, my eyes shifted down the rest of her body, and my jaw dropped open. It took everything in me not to fist-pump the air and push her back into the apartment. Fuck the dinner, I wanted her right then and there.

Her curves were wrapped in a crushed red velvet dress with a deep neckline and a short hem that only met her midthigh. The fabric covered her arms and shimmered in the fluorescent hallway lights and my fingers twitched to touch her everywhere and feel the material for myself.

I swiped a hand over my mouth, stunned silent by the magnificent woman in front of me. Along with the dress, she had thrown her hair back into a messy updo and paired it with tall black heels.

Was I drooling?

"You have a key, or did you forget it?" When I didn't respond for several seconds, my eyes still taking in her entire ensemble, she laughed a bright, cheerful laugh and shook her head. "Put your eyes back in your head and come inside, I need to grab my coat."

My feet moved of their own accord, but I made it inside.

"I wanted to knock and pick you up like you're supposed to for a first date," I croaked out as I watched her ass sway. She disappeared into her closet and said something I couldn't make out.

"What?" I asked, still standing in the doorway and trying to resituate the situation in my slacks so it wasn't pressing against the zipper and threatening to split my pants in two.

"Aren't you supposed to bring flowers, too?" she asked with a playful smile as she threw her jacket over her shoulders.

I sighed. "I did buy flowers, but one of the dogs at work ripped them apart. It was a mess, and it was either pick up more flowers or be late. So, I thought you'd forgive me for the lack of flowers as long as I was on time."

She quirked a brow and grabbed her bag from the kitchen counter. She flipped off the light and walked to me with a mischievous glint in her eye. Her playful mood wasn't helping my erection, but I didn't give a shit.

With one final step, she stopped only an inch from me and, through dark lashes, peered up. In heels, she was to my chin, so she didn't have to look up as much as normal, but it had the same effect.

"You clean up nice, too," she said in a low voice. I didn't have many suits because they were mostly unnecessary as a veterinarian, but I did have a few. The one I chose for our date was black, and I paired it with a crisp white shirt. Classic.

"You look absolutely incredible. The most beautiful woman I've ever seen." I slid a hand out of my pocket and trailed it down the center of her body, starting at her throat and trailing down to her ample cleavage, over her taut stomach and finally brushing the hem of her dress and over the smooth skin of her thigh. She gasped at my touch and my own body thrummed in excitement at her responsiveness. "How am I supposed to get through an entire dinner with you sitting across from me looking like that?"

Her eyes had drifted closed as I appreciated her and the soft, luxurious fabric. When she slowly lifted her eyes open once more, I saw my own need mirrored there. Her normal hazel eyes were almost the color of whiskey and did I ever want to drown in the amber liquid.

"Same way I have to sit across from you and not think about the large erection I know you'll be sporting all night." As she spoke, she gripped my cock through my slacks and squeezed. She was playing dirty, and I was all about it.

"Don't start something you don't plan to finish, Angel."

Her face lit up at the pet name, and it was difficult not to smile when she did. But I kept my expression serious like my comment had been.

"I'll finish it, and that's a promise. But I won't easily forget the lack of flowers." She stepped around me and grabbed her keys from the table near the door. She opened it and didn't even flinch when the cold wind whipped around her, pulling a few strands of her hair loose. Her eyes found mine again as she said, "But I think you should make up for it in orgasms."

A low rumble of pleasure started in my chest as we hurried out the door. I used my key to lock it behind us as she hugged her coat around her tighter against the wind.

I slung my arm around her and pressed her into my side as we headed down the steps and to the truck. "Do you want one for every flower I was going to bring you? I think twelve would more than make up for it, but we could push it to thirteen just to be safe." I whispered into her ear, and a shiver—one I didn't think was due to the cold—whipped through her.

She didn't have a sassy comeback for that, and I smiled smugly to myself as I opened her door and walked around to my side.

When I turned on the truck, I made sure both of our seat warmers were on and backed out of the spot. Like it was second nature, my palm found the warm, exposed skin of her thigh just next to the hem of the dress. With tentative fingers, I slowly inched them higher. Her breath caught in her throat as she allowed me further access.

I was almost to the apex and the very place I needed to feel more than anything when her hand shot out and grabbed my wrist, stopping my exploration. It had only been a few minutes since we'd left her apartment, but we'd driven those few minutes in almost complete silence except for the classic rock station and her hurried breaths that served as background music.

"This is so unsafe," she said. I could multitask no problem, but she set my hand back on the gearshift and tapped it once, which sparked an idea.

"I need to know how wet you are."

She groaned and gripped the back of her neck with her black-painted nails. "I'm wet. Trust me."

Amused, I pushed her further. Her playful attitude had rubbed off on me, and I really wanted to fucking play. "Prove it."

I glanced away from the highway just for a moment to see her giving me a tempting side-eye. "And how would you like for me to do that?"

"Touch yourself and show me the evidence."

Her jaw dropped, and she stared at me like she was waiting for me to say I was kidding. When I motioned her on with my hand that had been perched on her thigh, she spluttered, "You're serious?"

"I don't joke about pleasuring my woman. Now, show me how wet you are."

Hesitantly, she shifted on the seat—and only after eyeing me for a few more seconds—did she lean her head back and push her hips lower on the seat.

Her hand, with the shiny black nails, disappeared under her dress and I was jealous of her own fingertips. "Good girl," I praised, and her hips bucked against her hand as she moaned at what was likely only a light touch against her wet heat.

Thankfully, we were stopped at a red light after I'd exited the freeway, so I was able to watch Hazel's hand reappear. Her wetness coating the tips of her fingers glinted in the streetlights as she held her hand up between us.

Without another thought, I gripped her hand and sucked her arousal off her fingers. When her sweet creaminess hit my tongue, my mouth began watering and I sucked harder.

Her fingers popped out of my mouth, and I moved her hand back to her thighs as the light turned green. I caught a glimpse of her face before I looked back to the road. Her eyes were wide, and her jaw was slack. The needy look on her face broke my self-control.

I gripped her thigh again and pulled it toward me with a slightly rough tug. "Keep going. We'll be there in a few minutes, but until I park this car, I want you to touch yourself. Touch yourself, but don't come."

There was no hesitation in her movements. Her thighs fell farther apart, hiking her dress up higher on her thighs, but not high enough where I could see the color of her panties or if they were soaking wet, too.

With another brush of her fingers, Hazel closed her eyes and stuttered a breath under her own touch.

"Tell me what you're doing," I demanded.

My grip on her thigh tightened and she moved with the force of my hand. Stopped at another light roughly two minutes from the restaurant, I pulled her dress higher. Her black lace thong was pushed to the side and her fingers were working overtime, slipping between her folds.

"Use one finger and rub your clit with your thumb." Hazel moaned as she slipped her middle finger inside of herself, and I groaned, thinking about how tight I knew she was and where I knew she should hook her finger and press against to push herself closer to an orgasm.

I was so mesmerized by the movement of her hips against her fingers and the small gasps escaping her glossy lips that I didn't realize the light had turned green until the person behind me honked.

Hazel's eyes popped open, and her hand and hips stopped. "Keep going," I demanded, not wanting her to have a second of a break.

She continued with my urging, pushing her hips back onto her finger and rubbing furiously with her thumb. I could smell her arousal throughout the car as she became more and more wet.

I was so turned on that when I absentmindedly brushed the heel of my palm against my erection, I groaned and thrust my hips toward it. Rather than pushing it down, I stimulated it even more. My own desire was coursing through me at such a pace that my left leg shook, and my hand trembled against the wheel.

"How close are you?"

"So close. I want to come."

"Not yet," I said as I sped the car up over the speed limit on the small side street near the restaurant. I couldn't get to the damn restaurant quick enough. "What are you doing? What do you feel?"

"I—" She cleared her throat. "I am..." she moaned.

"Tell me, Angel. Use your words."

"I'm fingering myself with two fingers and rubbing my clit against my hand. I can feel myself getting wetter, and if you keep talking like that, I'm going to come before you want me to."

"Does my voice turn you on, beautiful girl? Do you like the dirty things I say and the way it makes your body feel?"

"Yes," she sighed, and I could tell she was getting close as her cheeks flushed and her movements became urgent and erratic.

"Do not come. You are only allowed to come when my fingers are buried deep inside of you."

"But, Luke," she pleaded as I almost screeched the tires swerving into the parking lot. I found a spot near the back but not far enough away that someone would be suspicious.

I already had my seat belt unbuckled before I threw the car in park. As the truck settled, I was popping Hazel's seat buckle and giving her directions.

"Turn around so your back is on the door and spread your legs so I can make you come."

She opened her eyes and looked around. "Luke, someone could see—"

I pulled at her thigh, and she began to move. "I will pay attention and make sure no one sees us, Angel. This is for my eyes only because you're mine."

She was easy to persuade as her head hit the window with a soft thud and her legs parted. Her black coat fell open and removed some of the shadows from around her. The black of her panties was so pretty and delicate, but I ripped them off, not wanting anything in the way of her pleasure.

With her panties gone, I could see her wetness dripping down her folds and closer to her ass. Her clit was swollen and eager for more, and I wouldn't let her suffer for long. I couldn't keep my hands off of her anyway.

I plunged two fingers into her, and she gasped at the intrusion. But the gasp quickly turned to a deep, throaty moan and her hips bucked against my fingers.

"Yes, use my fingers. Fuck my fingers just like that."

Her hand latched around my wrist, but this time, instead of forcing me off, she tried to push my hands even deeper as her heat enveloped me. I let her control most of it, but I pressed the tips of my fingers against her inner walls and used my other hand to draw small, tight circles over her clit.

As soon as I touched her needy bud, she detonated on my fingers. The warmth rushed over them as she squeezed more pleasure and writhed, not keeping quiet as beautiful noises slipped from her mouth.

Her head lolled against the glass, and I blinked back the desire fogging my vision. If I didn't get myself under control, I was going to come in my pants by just one look at her fully sated, relaxed expression.

She laughed casually and cleared her throat. "This is already the best date I've ever been on, and we haven't even gotten out of the car yet."

"I agree," I mumbled as I withdrew my fingers and held them up in front of me. It was so much more than before as my fingers stuck together, but my mouth watered just the same.

Hazel was straightening in her seat, her whiskey-colored eyes watching me intently as I licked my lips and then sucked her pleasure off my fingers. Just as I had only minutes prior, I savored the tangy creaminess of it and knew we had to get out of the car immediately.

"Get out of the car, Hazel." The words weren't meant to be demanding, but they were.

Hazel didn't question me, though, grabbing her bag and slipping out of the truck. I rounded the truck quickly and pressed her against the passenger door with a hand to the base of her throat before I slammed my lips on hers. My tongue immediately breached her lips, and she sighed into me.

"Can you taste yourself on my tongue? So fucking sweet."

She was past words and held me close by the lapels of my suit jacket. Breaking the kiss was miserable, but we had a reservation. She also already knew that I could fuck her like I owned her, but I wanted to show her I was well rounded, not just a one-trick pony.

"You're extra bossy tonight," she smiled up at me before kissing just my bottom lip.

"If we had stayed in that truck for two more seconds, I was going to make you get in the back seat so you could ride me to kingdom come. And if we stay out here another second, I'm going to take you up against the truck. I have twelve more orgasms to give you." Her eyes flared, but I returned a look that promised so much later.

I'd tell her all I wanted to do to her later over dinner.

FORTY-FIVE

Luke

The hostess sat us in a circular booth at the back of the restaurant, which may or may not have been because I requested one. Our time in the truck wasn't enough, and I needed easy access to her all night.

I was addicted to everything about her.

The waiter, Ronnie, an older man with a handlebar mustache, had already taken our drink orders and left us to "peruse the menu and enjoy the ambience" while he was gone. Those were his words, not mine, but Hazel and I were both doing just that.

The place I'd decided on was recommended by Reed and I'd have to thank him later if the food turned out to be as good as everything else. It was a renovated fire station inside the city limits that they'd turned into one of the best Italian restaurants in the area, at least according to the internet.

The exposed brick on each of the walls was charming and the old fire station paraphernalia kept the history of the place alive. Outside it still looked like the old fire station, but inside it had been transformed into a romantic dinner spot with numerous candles and fancy green velvet booths.

I wasn't accustomed to places like that, where the waiters scraped the pristine white tablecloths with the fancy crumb scraper tool and asked you if you wanted still or sparkling water. But we both looked the part—and might I add, we looked damn good together—and when I focused on Hazel, most of the rest of the world disappeared.

The soft candlelight reflected off Hazel's dress as she bit her lower lip scouring the menu. It appeared by the deep furrow in her brow that she was having the same trouble I was—I could barely pronounce half of the words and had to decipher the eloquently written descriptions of the dishes to have any possible clue what they were.

But whether she was worried or confused or angry or frustrated, she looked breathtaking.

"What do you think about trying the bruschetta and the mushroom strudel to start with?" She pulled her eyes away from the menu to find her answer, but I was too taken aback by the light dancing in her eyes.

"Sounds great, whatever you want."

She rolled her hazel eyes and closed the menu in front of her, peering around at the other patrons enjoying the food, drinks and the "ambience."

I brushed my fingers against the back of her exposed neck and placed my hand there just beneath the small curls that didn't fit into her bun. She seemed to relax into my touch and watched the opposite corner of the restaurant where a woman with long gray hair was playing a baby grand piano. Each note and stroke of the keys was soft, but the whisper of music perfectly matched the rest of the restaurant.

"Here we are," Ronnie said, setting the drinks in front of us both. "A cabernet for the lady and a Macallan neat for the gentlemen. Have you had enough time to decide on your appetizers for this evening?"

I ordered the appetizers with a nod of approval from Hazel.

Ronnie scurried away as quickly as a man who was probably

pushing seventy could as I palmed my glass in my free hand. With my other, I gently squeezed the back of Hazel's neck to grab her attention, enjoying the way her skin felt beneath mine.

She picked up her glass and turned to me slightly and just enough that I could see the curve of her breasts beneath the velvet of the dress and along the deep V of the neckline.

"This place is amazing," she whispered, her eyes darting around the restaurant once again.

"I'm glad you like it, but why are you whispering?" I asked, whispering just as she had.

A laugh bubbled up from her throat, but she clamped a hand over her mouth to stifle it. "I don't know. It just feels like a place where you whisper. Like speaking too loudly would disrupt the *ambience.*" She mimicked Ronnie's earlier words which made me laugh, but I didn't try to stifle it.

Out of the corner of my eye, I noticed a few heads turn in our direction, but we both ignored them. We were in our own little bubble in our circular booth, and it was going to stay that way.

I held up my glass to hers, thinking back to our first night together and remembering her words. "To new memories."

Her smile returned and she watched me with unyielded happiness in her eyes before she sipped the wine. She groaned in approval and took another decent-sized sip. "Even the wine is good. If the food sucks, I'm going to be sorely disappointed."

"You can blame it on Reed. He's the one that recommended this place." She nodded and relaxed farther back into the booth. She crossed one leg over the other, which hiked her dress farther up her thigh.

I placed my hand on her exposed thigh and began rubbing small circles over her smooth skin with my thumb. Small goose bumps erupted over her flesh, and I smiled to myself, taking another sip of my drink before placing it back on the white tablecloth and in front of the large candles in the center of the table.

"Did you hear from Becky today?" I asked, trying to distract myself from anything but the dirty thoughts running through my head. It was the first topic I could think of that wasn't as intense as telling her about the third letter from Valerie.

Partially living together didn't leave much room for keeping secrets. When I came home the days before after having just received the first two letters, Hazel knew the moment I walked through the door that something was off. She'd guessed it was Valerie, and although I hadn't wanted to burden her with the truth, I couldn't keep anything from her. The compassion in her eyes and the sweetness of her words were always my undoing.

But it went both ways—I couldn't hide anything, and neither could she. After we'd discussed the second Valerie letter only a short time ago, I could tell there was more going on with her.

Apparently, Becky had texted her and asked if she could watch Emmy during the day. Even in the middle of a workday, Hazel couldn't tell her no. She'd been Emmy's safe place from her parents' bickering for so long, she couldn't strip that away from her then.

We also both suspected that something more was going on between Becky and Chris, and if being there for Becky meant taking care of Emmy, she would do it.

Emmy had stayed at Hazel's apartment from ten in the morning until well after five that evening, and when Becky both dropped and picked up Emmy, she had little to say besides profusely thanking Hazel.

"Yeah, she may bring Emmy by sometime this weekend, but she didn't say much more than that. It's just so interesting to me that Emmy wouldn't tell me much either. She's usually so talkative and has no problem telling me about when they fight, but she had nothing to say on the subject the other day. Even Lexi tried to get her to talk, but nothing."

Lexi, Hazel's neighbor, had apparently come over to help Hazel with Emmy while she had a meeting with her boss. Hazel had talked up Lexi's help, and even Emmy requested that Lexi play with them the next time she came over.

When I'd first heard Hazel mention Lexi as more than a

neighbor and a potential friend, my hackles went up. In the middle of the day, I called the leasing office and prayed Savannah would answer the phone.

When she did, I turned on the charm and laid it on thick. I only felt a little guilty because ultimately, it was to protect Hazel and I didn't actually mean anything I insinuated.

After promising to come by the office next time I was around, she verified that Lexi Johnson, or Alexandra, was Hazel's next-door neighbor and had moved in a few weeks prior. Even though my charm helped a lot, I knew that without a reason or a warrant, I wouldn't be able to get much more information.

I'd even gone as far as to investigate Hazel's coworker, Stephanie. All the women in her life eventually checked out and my paranoia eased.

"Did Becky say why she needs you to watch her again? What was the last reason?"

Hazel sipped her wine, and I watched her slim throat bob as she swallowed. "She said she was doing last-minute Thanksgiving preparations. She didn't give me a reason for this weekend, but I'll ask her when she drops Emmy off. I don't want to be too pushy, but something's going on. Has she been acting strange from what you can tell, or what about Chris?"

I shook my head as Ronnie set two large plates with colorful food in front of us.

"Have you had a chance to review the dinner menu, or would you like a few more minutes?"

"We haven't even looked yet. A few more minutes would be great," I said.

"Of course," he said with a bow of his head.

I placed a small appetizer plate in front of each of us and scooted both the larger plates toward Hazel, motioning for her to go first.

"Since staying with you, I haven't been home much lately. I'll ask Josh, though, and see if he's noticed any changes."

Hazel scooped a bruschetta onto her plate but worried her

lower lip between her teeth. I knew it was bothering her that she couldn't do more to help Becky, but we'd both agreed that helping when she asked for it was the best method to get her to open up.

"We're doing what we can," I said, pulling her lower lip free of her teeth with my thumb. "Try not to worry too much."

She sighed and fell back into the booth. "I know, it's just that..." She shook her head, another small piece of hair freeing itself from her bun. "I don't want any woman to find themselves in the position I was in and not have anyone to turn to. They should all have a Luke, even if the person is grumpy and pushy sometimes. If I can be Becky's Luke, then I want to be. I want to advocate for her safety and her needs like you did for me."

I love you.

The words were on the tip of my tongue as her sentiment washed over me. My heart constricted in my chest, and the rest of the restaurant noise filtered away.

I wanted to tell her about all the emotion building in my chest and how I'd never felt it before, but expressing it was going to be difficult. But I knew she'd understand.

But I promised myself I wouldn't push her and that meant not blurting out those three little words just because I felt like it. I wanted her to feel secure and want it just as much. Each step, she had been hesitant about giving more of herself, but we made it that far and I didn't want to ruin it.

So, instead of saying anything, I kissed her. I put the words into the kiss and the way our lips moved against one another's had to be enough in the moment.

"You're too good at that," she murmured against my mouth before pulling away and scooping up the bruschetta.

I also loaded my plate with the appetizers and dove in as my stomach yelled at me. "It's not my fault. You've turned me into this monster."

She laughed around the food in her mouth. "Okay, well, let's change the subject then so we don't get in trouble for doing anything in public that we shouldn't be doing. How was your day?"

I paused with my third bite of strudel hovering near my mouth. Hazel caught the change and dropped her fork. "What happened?"

"This is the last thing I wanted to talk about tonight. I don't want our first date to be all about the bullshit going on in our lives. This," I said, waving my hands at the beautiful place around us. "Should be an escape from that."

"Although that sounds amazing, I think that's wishful thinking, Luke." She laced her small fingers through my own and squeezed. "Our lives don't just stop because we're in a pretty restaurant with *really* good food. And besides, this date is already perfect because it's us."

Reluctantly, I agreed and raised her hand to my lips to kiss her knuckles. It would all be over one day.

"So, what happened? Another letter from Valerie?"

"Yeah, same as the past two times. It was typed on the computer, printed, and stuck in the clinic's mailbox. I already texted Detective Bell and he picked it up before I left this evening."

"What did this one say?"

I scrubbed a hand over my face and downed the rest of my very expensive whiskey. I savored the burn as I remembered the contents of the letter. I hadn't recounted every detail of each letter to Hazel; I had only told her the very basic plot points. "It was about a fight I got into at Murphy's a few years ago. Then it said that my happiness was the most important thing to her and that's it. I just don't know what she's playing at anymore."

"Oh, crap, here comes Ronnie. I have no clue what I want," Hazel mumbled as our waiter approached.

We both quickly ordered our meals and another round of drinks as well.

"It's all mind games. She's trying to keep your mind on her

and thinking about what her next move might be. She wants you on your toes and cautious. At least that's what I think."

She had a point; Valerie never took too kindly to me giving anyone else attention, whether it was friends, colleagues, or the waitstaff at a fucking restaurant. She wanted to monopolize my every thought and feeling.

Ronnie dropped off our new drinks and Hazel gave him a soft, polite smile as I brooded over my ex-wife. Her tenderness toward the man eased something in me, though, as I watched her gracefully interact with him like we weren't just talking about what we were.

When the waiter left to check on his other tables, she said, "Has Blakely spoken to the police? Wouldn't her statement have some weight in all of this?"

I shook my head and instead of reaching for the glass of whiskey, I pulled Hazel closer to me so her thigh was pressed against my own. She grounded me and I needed her closer.

"No, she won't talk to them. I've told her every day since we found out that she needs to return their calls, but she's still terrified. She told me today that her only reason for telling me was to scare me into breaking things off with you and to try and protect you. She never planned on actually telling the police."

"Amanda said pretty much the same thing. For the record, she completely disagrees with how Blakely is handling everything because she practically holds the cards to putting Valerie behind bars but refuses to. She's also tried reasoning with her on multiple occasions, but nothing seems to be getting through. I wonder if she's actually been in contact with Valerie recently. Maybe she's contacted Blakely again this time around, which has renewed her fear."

"I'll ask her tomorrow when I do my daily phone call to get her to talk to the cops."

In the craziness of the rest of my day, I had completely forgotten that she was spending the day with Amanda shopping for tonight.

"You bought this dress today?" I asked with a smile.

"Yeah, it took a few hours to find, but it was worth it." She ran her hands down the sleeves of the dress that just brushed her wrists and pulled down the hem slightly. I pushed it back up and she swatted my hand away.

"How was it, though? Did y'all have fun?"

Hazel chuckled and pushed away her appetizer plate. "We had so much fun. She's a fucking riot, and I already love her."

There was a small twinge of jealousy in my chest hearing her so casually throw around the word that was tormenting me inside, but I shook it off.

"What'd you do?" I asked just in time for our food to arrive. With a large smile, Ronnie left us to eat.

Both of us were overcome with the delicious smells wafting off our bowls of pasta and didn't wait even a minute before diving in. Around a groan, Hazel said, "We went shopping for a few hours and literally did not stop talking the entire time. I ended up telling her about Michael, and it felt good to get to tell someone about it in the past tense. I didn't have to explain that it was currently happening but that it was done, over with, and had already happened. Then we ate lunch at a Mexican restaurant downtown and drank the place out of margaritas."

I cut my eyes over to her as she smiled and slurped a few noodles into her mouth. "You took my advice seriously, then? Let me guess, now you know her whole life story?"

She giggled and shrugged. "First of all, the margaritas were her idea, and second of all, yes."

"I told you, tequila makes her talk."

"I think tequila does that to a lot of people and it wasn't like I didn't participate. But we didn't just talk about her, she talked about all of you."

I narrowed my eyes at her, concerned about what Amanda might have spilled and its impact on how Hazel viewed me and my friends. I knew Hazel wasn't judgmental, but our group wasn't always rainbows and sunshine.

"She tell you all our deep dark secrets?"

"No, but she did ask me if your dick is as big as she thinks it is," Hazel quipped.

Whiskey almost came out of my nose, and I coughed several times before I was able to compose myself. Wiping the tears from my eyes, I asked, "Why the hell does she want to know?"

Hazel was laughing at my reaction and trying not to choke on her pasta when I was able to look back at her. "It's not *that* weird of a question, honestly. Apparently, yours is the only one she hasn't seen, and Blakely didn't spill, so she thought I might. She said it must be big or really small if you've kept it so tightly under wraps for that many years."

I gawked at her, amazed at the turn in the conversation and the contradiction between the fancy restaurant and our conversation about my penis size.

"Did you tell her that I'm hung like a fucking horse?"

"Not exactly." Her tone was nonchalant, which I knew meant I was not going to appreciate what she actually told Amanda.

"What the hell does that mean, Hazel?"

"I told her that it was memorable."

"That could go both ways. She could assume that I have a small dick now."

She made an unconvinced expression and leveled me with a serious look. "Why does it matter what anyone besides me thinks about it? I'm the one that reaps the benefits of your horse cock."

I had no words because she was right. It was only her opinion that mattered.

When I didn't respond, she smiled and seemed pleased with herself, picking at her remaining pasta.

The music lifted louder around us, and the voices in the restaurant grew louder with it. Finishing our meals, we sat in companionable silence as we watched the people around us enjoying their dinner. There were a few older couples that appeared to be on date nights and a family just a few tables away that was celebrating a birthday. But what caught my eye was Ronnie, leaning against the baby grand piano, chatting with the woman playing.

He threw his head back, laughing, and so did she. And I assumed he was just casually flirting until he leaned in and kissed her.

"Do you see them?" Hazel asked, elbowing me in the side and moving closer to me for a better angle.

With one hand holding her half-empty wineglass, the other dropped to my thigh and wrapped around it. I could feel her nails slightly dig into my skin through my pants, and the one small touch may have appeared insignificant to anyone else— that we were just a normal couple having dinner together the day before Thanksgiving. But that wasn't the case.

The touch meant she wanted to be near me and wanted to feel the heat of my skin against her own. With each voluntary touch, she claimed me as much as I claimed her.

Those little words were once again on the tip of my tongue as I wrapped an arm around her shoulder and buried my nose into her hair. It was freshly washed and soft against my rough skin. I breathed her in and let her surround me just as the music did, holding me to this moment and the calmness I felt with my woman in my arms.

Hazel tilted her face up toward me and her eyes met mine. There was a spark of joy there and it lit my entire world on fire to see it in her eyes. If necessary, I'd light the entire world on fire to make sure it stayed there, captured in her hazel eyes forever.

Her nose brushed mine and then her lips ghosted over my own.

"Are you finished with your—oops." Ronnie had the most perfect timing. I smothered a groan when he blushed. "I'm so sorry to interrupt, but are you finished with your plates?"

"Yes, thank you so much. It was delicious," Hazel said. Ronnie grabbed them both and began to walk away. But before he could get too far, he turned around and reapproached the table with a curious look.

"Are you celebrating something tonight? An anniversary perhaps?"

"Actually, this is our first official date," I answered honestly, although too much had happened before we could even get to the first date.

Ronnie's eyes widened like he was shocked to hear it. "By the way you interact, I could have sworn you'd been together for years. Well, either way, I like to give advice to young couples whether they want to hear it or not. It makes an old man like me feel important when I have an audience once in a while."

"We'd love to hear your advice. Go for it." Hazel prompted, leaning forward against the table and placing her chin on her fist. Her other hand didn't leave my thigh, and I covered it with my own, matching her curiosity as the older man set our bowls back on the table.

"Well, there's three things really. The beautiful woman playing the piano has been with me for fifty years and hasn't killed me yet, so I'd say it's worked. But if you want a love that lasts, first you must be honest. Nothing good ever came from lying about anything, and if the person really loves you, there isn't much that they won't understand. Second, love them every day like it's the last day you'll do so because you don't know when that last day might be. And last, but certainly not least, make new memories all the time. Never stop creating new memories together. There may come a time, and sometimes it's sooner than you would have hoped, when all you have left are those treasured memories."

With a final nod, Ronnie slid the dessert menu onto our table and shuffled off.

His words hung around us, and I knew we were both internalizing his advice. It was easy enough advice to follow, and I didn't doubt for a second that it was something we could manage for years. Because I needed years with her—I needed forever at least, but even that didn't seem like long enough.

Hazel was still seated in the same position, staring into the rest of the restaurant. I smoothed my rough, calloused hand down her smooth arm, eager to have her attention back, but when she turned to me, I wasn't prepared for tears welling in her eyes nor the one that broke free and slipped down her cheek.

"Whoa, Angel. Why the tears?"

She sniffled and wiped them away before I could. Turning to face me, she pulled her knee up and tucked it against my thigh. She used her napkin to dab under her eyes and took a deep breath, exhaling completely, before she looked at me again.

In a shaky voice that instantly put me on edge, she said, "There was something else that came up at lunch with Amanda that I need to talk to you about."

I scrubbed a hand through my hair and attempted to mentally prepare myself for anything from my past that might have arisen in their conversation. There wasn't much that Hazel didn't know, and what little she didn't know wasn't because I intentionally kept anything from her but was because it hadn't come up in conversation.

Most was unimportant information or stupid shit. She knew about Valerie and the only other...

It dawned on me exactly what she could have learned about my past that would put tears in her eyes. I let my head slump forward as I steadied myself for the conversation.

"She told you about my parents," I said matter-of-factly.

Not hearing a response, I looked up as Hazel gave me a sad nod. Decades of emotion flooded back to me, seeing the way she looked at me. I'd done so much to not be that scared little teenager anymore; I wasn't him, and I never would be again.

Trying to think clearly, I remembered that the woman in front of me only cared about me and it was likely not pity in her eyes but genuine concern and heartache.

"What'd she tell you?"

She took a steadying breath. "She didn't mean to, so please don't be upset with her. She assumed that I knew, and when I didn't tell her otherwise, she just kept talking. I should have stopped her," she pleaded, her words becoming increasingly desperate. "I should have told her that it was something you would talk to me about when you were ready, but my curiosity won over. And by the time she started, I realized she had already said too much. I'm so, so sorry. I feel like I broke your trust or something, and I—"

"Angel," I pleaded, her tears were freely flowing, and she was speaking so fast her words were blurring together. I reached forward with the intention of cupping her cheek in my hand and hopefully calming her rapid breathing. But it had the opposite effect.

As my hand moved toward her face, she gasped and flinched away, cowering back into the booth. I froze instantly and began rethinking my entire plan.

She thought I would be mad at her, that I would be upset that she found out about my parents through someone who wasn't me and someone who had probably had way more tequila than they ever should have. She thought I'd be mad, and after years of abuse and not knowing how I would react to being upset with her, her body's reaction was to hide and cower. Because the last man that was angry with her beat her.

Touching her wasn't going to help the situation, and by the time I lowered my hand, Hazel was also realizing what her reaction had been.

I kept my voice calm and whispered, "Hazel, I'm not angry and I'm not even upset. Honestly, Amanda probably did me a favor by telling you because I had been holding off for weeks now. It's a story I'm not fond of telling, but I know it's a necessary part of my past. But please hear me when I say that if I was upset or angry or pissed off at you, I would never hit you or want to inflict pain on you. Recovering from what that piece of shit put you through is going to be an uphill battle, so I will be careful with my actions, and I will tell you as many times as you need to hear that I will never hurt you."

Her tears had slowed, and her eyes stayed steady on my face, so I knew she heard me.

"Now, may I touch you?"

"Yes, please," she said and so slowly that it was actually painful, I cupped both sides of her face in my hands. I brushed away a few stray tears with my thumbs.

"I'm not upset, and I'm not going to hurt you. So, please stop crying. It breaks my fucking heart when you cry."

Out of nowhere, she laughed, and although I was taken aback by the sound, I didn't question it and just smiled down at her.

"That's not what you said the other night when I was choking on your cock and crying off my makeup."

My laugh could be heard throughout the restaurant, and I didn't care who I disturbed. "Damn right, beautiful girl. I loved those tears, but I'm not a fan of them when you're sad."

I kissed her forehead, letting my lips linger for a moment before dropping my hands and reaching for the dessert menu.

"We don't need to talk about it, but I just wanted you to know," she said, taking the menu when I handed it to her. "It felt like I was keeping something from you, and after what Ronnie just said about honesty..."

"When I was sixteen, I came home from a friend's house to find that both of my parents were dead. My dad lay next to their bed, slumped onto the ground with two gunshot wounds through the chest. Once I kicked down the bathroom door," I began, cutting right to the chase. "I found my mom leaning against the bathtub, sitting in a pool of her own blood. There was so much blood I could taste it when I walked into that bathroom. I thought it had been a break-in and told the cops that when I called 9-1-1. But when they showed up, they found the gun had fallen between my mother's body and the bathtub. It had fingerprints from both my mom and my dad, and as they continued investigating, they found obvious signs of abuse. My dad—" The automatic story I had told what seemed like too often in the nearly fifteen years since my parents' death cut off just as the part where I usually described, in a few words, the abuse my father put my mother through. The words were stuck in my throat, and for a moment, I didn't know if I could force them out. "My dad had been hitting my mom off and on for my entire life and probably before that. She had several broken bones that hadn't healed properly and had bruises from that night. She also kept journals that described a few of the worst arguments. The police believed that my mom fought back after he shot her, fought him for the gun and shot him before she died."

She died. My beautiful, caring, enthusiastic and book-loving mom was killed by my father.

"My father drank a lot and some of the worst fights were on the nights when he'd binged the entire day. But my mom shielded Josh and me from it our entire lives. She tried, but I also knew that something was happening. I knew something was going on, but when I was a kid, I didn't understand and when I was a teenager, I didn't *want* to understand."

After years of therapy and soul-searching, I knew that it wasn't my fault. That I was the child, and it wasn't my job to protect my parents. The guilt and rage I felt that led me to fight —a lot of illegal fighting—I was eventually able to control, and until I met Hazel, I thought it had almost gone away completely after Valerie and I divorced.

I didn't catch on to all the signs that my dad was hitting my mom, but I knew when they'd at least had a bad argument and would steer Josh clear of them the best I could. He eventually caught on, but not until right before they died.

Lost in memories of that time, I was overcome by them until I felt the faint brush of hands on my face. I blinked a few times and watched Hazel's sympathetic face form a soft smile as her hands moved over my face. "Now, you're the one crying," she said.

Was I? My hands brushed over my cheeks and sure enough, they were wet. I hadn't even noticed that the tears had begun to fall. I sniffled and brushed away the tears as her hands dropped to my thigh.

"Now you know, and that's enough sad shit for one night."

She opened her mouth to say something but quickly snapped it shut, nodded, and picked up the dessert menu. "Cheesecake for me and don't even think about asking to share."

"I wouldn't dare," I laughed.

"Have we decided on dessert?" Ronnie asked, appearing out of thin air.

We ordered and settled back into the booth to finish our drinks. No more sad shit for the night, but the shit wasn't nearly over.

FORTY-SIX

Luke

"We're ready for the check, thank you," I told Ronnie, who took away our dessert plates.

Once he turned his back on us, I was touching Hazel. It'd been a long night of trying to keep my hands to myself but having to watch her glow in that damn red dress, I was itching to get my hands on her and that dress off her.

"I'm excited to see what this dress looks like on your bedroom floor," I whispered into her ear, eliciting a pretty little shiver through her body.

She bit her bottom lip to stifle a smile, and I knew she was thinking the same things I was. My fingers trailed a path up her thigh and under the table where no one could see, and I pushed her dress slightly higher, watching her lips part just barely as I brushed along the inside of her thighs. Her eyes dilated and her breath hitched.

I was planning another orgasm or two for her on our drive home when she cleared her throat and sat up straighter. With a faint blush on her cheeks, she was radiant.

"I'm going to the bathroom before we go," she said, and I

couldn't tell if it was code for *follow me in the bathroom so we can fuck against the wall* or if she just needed to use the restroom.

I chose the former and decided to follow her, hopefully after Ronnie promptly brought our check back.

She scooted around the curve of the table and when she stood to walk down the hallway to the bathroom, I was able to watch her ass sway. That damn dress was going to be the death of me.

I was imagining the many ways I could keep the dress on her, at least for the first couple of times, when Ronnie approached the table sans the bill.

"Mr. Luke, someone has actually paid for your meal. She said she's a friend of yours and saw you dining together. I forgot her name, but she's a beautiful young woman with black—oh, there she is now. Hello," Ronnie said, swiveling his head to look at the woman strutting to the table.

It wasn't until she was seated that my brain began to comprehend what was happening. She was wearing a blue velvet dress, something eerily similar to Hazel's, and her straight black hair hung around her face like a shield. But her face was a face I'd only seen in my nightmares over the past three years. A face I would have been fine going my entire life without seeing again.

"Thank you so much, Ronnie. You've been such a delight all evening. I've made sure to leave you a sizable tip on both of our checks."

Out of the corner of my eye, I watched Ronnie nod and leave after thanking her profusely. But I didn't take my eyes off her. At first, I assumed she was an apparition, but Ronnie saw her as well, so that couldn't be true.

Then the room began to close in around me as she swiveled her gaze back to me and a small smile curled her lips. She crossed her legs and folded her hands into her lap like she was getting comfortable.

She hadn't changed much in the years since I'd seen her. She still had that air of poisonous cockiness surrounding her and could easily switch from one mask to another. The smile she gave me was nothing like the somewhat genuine smile she gave our waiter.

Beads of sweat formed on my brow, and I realized I hadn't taken a breath since she slid into the seat Hazel had occupied only minutes earlier.

Hazel. She'd be back soon and the last thing I wanted was for her to see the devil incarnate sitting in front of me.

"What are you doing here?" I seethed. My composure was lost just like it had always been around her; she made me angrier than almost any person could.

She smiled and tilted her head. "It's been so long, Bear. Is that really any way to greet your wife?"

"You're not my wife. We've been divorced for three fucking years, Valerie. So, I'll ask again: what the fuck are you doing here? What do you want from me?"

"The same thing I've always wanted: I want to make you happy. I'm the only one that can make you happy, Bear."

I was no longer holding my breath, but each breath felt like my lungs were burning. My whole body itched to get away from her.

"I am happy, but you just can't stand it because it's not with you."

She tsk-tsked and waved her hand like it didn't matter. "She won't make you happy like I can, Bear. I know you better than anyone." I shook my head and she leaned closer. "Of course, I do. We were together for so long and went through so much. I know you have a darkness inside of you that must be fed. I also know exactly when you've had enough and need a softer touch. It's a balance– one I've perfected."

She reached for me like she was going to demonstrate, but I ripped my hand away before she could. The thought of her touching me made bile twist in my stomach.

She brushed off my rejection and returned to her casual posture. Where the hell was Hazel?

"What is it going to take to make you go away for good, huh?"

"*You.*"

"That's not how this works, I want you out of my life, not in it."

She shrugged. "It's either you give me a second chance, or I never go away. Your sweet new girl was right about one thing: I want to be on your mind. I want you to dream about me, fantasize about me in the shower, and recognize me in everything that you do. It's always been me, and the quicker you realize that, the quicker things can go back to normal. *Our* normal."

My right eye began twitching as the anger pulsing through me threatened to release. It was something that often happened when I was with Valerie—she pushed my buttons like no one else and knew exactly what to say to fire me up.

My stupid eye twitching along with the vein I could feel throbbing in my forehead were the only signs that I was close to losing it. And Valerie didn't miss either of them. I was twice her size, easy, and could choke her out with one hand, yet she smiled like I was her favorite fucking toy finally being returned to her.

"There he is. There's my Bear. I was starting to think you'd gone soft on me and that you'd reverted to that scared little teenager who didn't do shit to help his poor mommy. But I can see the explosion waiting in your eyes. Do you protect the new one like you protected me from all those guys pawing over me? That always really got you going, defending me—your woman. I still think about how you'd claim me in every part of our lives and whisper to me *'mine'* like saying it made it even more true."

There was a thread left of my self-control, holding back the monster she would surely unleash if she kept talking, and she was fucking dancing on it. But I couldn't. I wouldn't hit her, and I wouldn't cause a scene. I was more in control of myself than I ever had been before. And I owed it to Hazel not to let those stupid demons out. My rage didn't have to control me, and I wouldn't let it.

If I kept staring at her stupid smirking face, I was going to explode, so whether it was a smart decision or not, I closed my eyes briefly and counted to ten. A technique I hadn't sincerely needed for years but was helpful, nonetheless. I counted to ten and focused on my breathing. Then I did it again.

Once I felt more in control of myself, I opened my eyes again to find Valerie watching me through narrowed black eyes. My eye was no longer twitching and the throbbing from the vein in my head had dulled.

"I'm going to say this one more time, and let's hope it gets through your thick fucking skull: I will *never* want you *ever* again. I've witnessed the blackness of your soul and the way you incinerate everything good you touch. That is not something I, or anyone else, will ever want in their life. You look back on our time together with fondness, but it is legitimately the thing of nightmares. You are twisted, deluded and a fucking sociopath. I promise you will get what's coming for you if it's the last thing I do. Now, I'm done with the fucking games. Stay away from me, and stay away from anyone else I care about, or so help me God, you will see the goddamn monster. But this time, I'll make sure you don't enjoy a single fucking second of it."

My nails were digging into my palms when I finished speaking, and slowly, I lowered the finger I had been jabbing in her direction.

For a moment, I thought she understood what I was saying and gathered the weight of my words. Her eyes were no longer narrowed but wide and surprised. Her lips were parted, and she was taking in quick breaths. But her expression morphed when I sat back.

The smirk returned and there was a new challenge in her brown, almost black eyes. She licked her bottom lip before she clicked her tongue.

"Wrong move, Bear," she said, sliding out of the booth and straightening her dress, brushing invisible lint off of her sleeves. "You know how I feel about lying, and you're lying to yourself right now. And I'll prove it to you. Picking her over me is the worst decision you could make for either of you. But don't worry… the games, as you like to call them, are almost over. It'll *all* be over soon enough."

And with that cryptic response, she turned on her heels and strutted out the front door. When the click of her heels faded and the door closed behind her, I finally took a breath and was out of the booth in the next second.

Valerie was sitting in our booth for several minutes, and the fact that Hazel hadn't returned from the bathroom during that time made a whole new type of fear pulse through me.

I turned down the dimly lit hallway with the "Restrooms" sign hanging above it and broke into a sprint. The fucking boots I was wearing weren't conducive for running and I skidded to an ungraceful stop in front of the door labeled "Women." Propped against the doorknob was a dining chair that I had seen plenty of throughout the restaurant.

Memories of walking into Hazel's bathroom, into my mother's bathroom, were instant as I ripped the chair away, throwing it to the side. In another breath, I pushed through the door and almost stumbled over a disheveled Hazel.

She was seated on the floor near the door in the fetal position. She lurched, ready to flee, but when she saw it was me barreling through the door, relief washed over her features.

She scrambled to her feet and flung her arms around me before I could even ask her if she was okay. She was shaking and I snaked my arms around her, holding her close and reveling in the warmth of her body. For a minute, we stood in the women's restroom, clinging to each other like we hadn't seen each other in years.

Reluctantly, I pulled back and stepped away to get a better look at her. Other than the fact that her hair was spilling out of its updo, she seemed fine. Her eyes were dry as well, so she hadn't been crying.

"Are you okay? What happened?"

"I'm fine, just shaken up a little." I smoothed my hands down her arms and closely inspected her from head to toe to make sure she was telling the truth. "I was walking into the bathroom when I saw a flash. Someone shoved me so hard that I lost my balance and fell into the side of the sink," she pointed to the granite countertop just beside us. "It knocked the air out of me, and by the time I was able to stand back up, the door was locked from the outside. I left my phone and purse at the table, but I figured you'd come looking for me eventually. It took you a while, though. How long do you think it takes me to go to the bathroom?"

I wished I could laugh, but nothing seemed funny at that moment. Even when I did everything in my power to protect her, Hazel was still in danger. Valerie found a way to her, and it could have ended so much worse.

"Valerie paid for our dinner, then made a special trip to our table. I'm sure she's the one who locked you in here."

Hazel was stone faced aside from a flash of understanding in her eyes. "She wanted to talk to you alone."

I nodded and pulled her into me, needing to feel her with me and against me. I was still feeling the effects of the fear I felt for those several minutes of not knowing where she was or if she was okay. "This could have been so much worse, Angel. She could have fucking hurt you, and I was just sitting at our table."

"Don't do that," Hazel said, jerking her head back to look at me. Her small hand landed on my cheek. "Don't blame yourself for your psychotic ex-wife. It's not your fucking fault, and I will keep telling you that until you actually believe it."

"How can you be so calm right now? Neither of us had any idea—"

She cut me off by pressing her lips to mine in a bruising sort of kiss that made me forget everything else. Even in heels, I felt her push onto her toes to meet my mouth and force her tongue between my lips. Her urgent lips against mine felt like coming home.

She pulled back after a minute, panting against my mouth, and gave my lower lip one final lick. In her eyes, I saw her resolve, and I tried to let it steady me.

"You've done everything you can, but she's a loose cannon. Trying to figure out what she's going to do next isn't going to work. We can be more careful, but we can't stop living our lives because of her and you can't follow me to the bathroom all the time either."

"We should have been more careful since the beginning," I muttered. Looking around, I figured it was about time to get the hell out of the restroom.

"Let's go home."

I took the long way back to Hazel's apartment and carefully watched every car behind us.

When we left the restaurant, I didn't notice any odd cars in the parking lot or anyone lurking, preparing to follow us. But I wasn't going to give anyone a chance and my paranoia was on full blast.

I was beginning to believe what Hazel said about us just needing to be more careful, but that changed when she grunted in pain getting into the truck. She waved me off when I tried to help and said she'd be fine, but I was sure there'd be a bruise along her stomach by morning.

Hazel asked me to tell her exactly what Valerie said, and I did, word for word. After hearing it all, she agreed with me that Valerie was nearing the end of whatever she had planned. Her next move would be something big. Once we both came to that realization, we were silent for the rest of the drive.

Hazel was moving in with me. Whether she wanted to or not, I wasn't letting her need for independence win out over her safety. She'd stay with me until Valerie was dealt with or, if I played my cards right, hopefully forever.

As we approached her apartment, I decided I'd tell her my

decision about her living situation the following day. I would be staying with her that night and we'd immediately go to my house for Thanksgiving the next morning. I didn't want to start an argument when so much had already happened.

We lumbered up the stairs, still silent, and I hoped I'd feel less paranoid once we made it behind the closed, locked door. I'd even parked in front of another building so anyone that might see my truck wouldn't know which building we were in exactly.

I followed behind Hazel as we approached the second floor but almost ran her over when she paused at the top of the steps. With a grunt, my chest collided with her back, but I wrapped an arm around her to steady her before she could fall forward. I steadied us both, using the railing for support.

"Mom?" Hazel exclaimed after we'd gained our balance. "What are you doing here?"

She removed herself from my grip and crossed the space between the stairs and her front door in a second. The woman was as short as Hazel without heels on and had long salt-and-pepper hair. Her smile was huge, and the resemblance was obvious.

"Now, is that any way to greet your mother?" She flung her arms around her daughter and smoothed her hands down her back. "I'm sorry to surprise you, but surprise! I couldn't be without my girl on Thanksgiving." She eyed Hazel up and down with her eyebrows raised. "Well, aren't you something else. I tried to call you, but you didn't answer."

"I'm so happy you're here," Hazel said, and I could hear the emotion in her voice as I approached them. "And my phone died at the restaurant. I hope you weren't standing here for long."

"Oh, no. Your lovely neighbor right there"—she pointed to the door immediately to the right of Hazel's—"let me in for a few minutes and gave me a glass of wine. I actually just came out when I saw you walking up the steps."

"It's so good to see you, Mom," Hazel said with a smile that matched her mom's. If Hazel looked like her mother in the next thirty years, those were some damn good genes.

"Now, who is this?" Hazel's mom said, pivoting to look at me with raised brows. I was standing close, but not too close, with my hands in my pockets, trying to wait my turn and not freeze my ass off. While also hoping we could hurry along the greetings and head inside.

"Mom, this is Luke. Luke, this is my mom, Laurie."

Just as my own mom taught me, I greeted her with a smile and stuck out my hand. "It's very nice to meet you, Mrs. Cooper."

Her eyes never left mine and she didn't make a move to take my hand. Her gaze was observant and contemplative, and I eventually glanced over at Hazel in question as I lowered my hand. Hazel returned my look with a look of her own and a shrug.

"So, you're the young man that has bulldozed his way into my daughter's life just after she's broken off her engagement. Oh, and beat up my ex-future son-in-law."

"Mom—" Hazel chastised, but Laurie waved her off.

"I'm glad we've met. Hazel, let's go inside, I'm chilly and I'd really like to spend some time with my daughter. There seems to be quite a lot you have failed to mention to me."

Hazel closed her eyes for a moment and took a deep breath. It was hard to not watch her chest rise and fall, but I could feel her mom's eyes still boring into my head, so I watched her face instead.

"Yes, let's go inside."

Hazel unlocked the door, and I went to grab her mom's bag that was propped against the wall.

"Oh, I've got that," Laurie said just as I reached for it. Not one to argue with the mother of the woman I love, I pulled back and let them both walk inside in front of me.

Before I could even close the door, Laurie said, "Will we see you tomorrow for Thanksgiving, Lucas?"

I opened my mouth to respond, but Hazel beat me to it. "Actually, Mom. I was going to go over to Luke's tomorrow and have Thanksgiving with him and his brother."

"Well, I was hoping we could have dinner here, honey. In your new apartment." Her voice was sweet, and I knew Hazel probably wouldn't be able to tell her mom no.

"We can talk about it," Hazel said. "Luke, let me walk you out. Mom, make yourself at home."

It was obvious Laurie wanted some alone time with her daughter, but I was still hesitant about leaving her alone with Valerie on the loose.

We walked back out into the cold just in time for the wind to whip around us and chill me through my suit jacket and all. When I turned back around, Hazel closed the door and began apologizing.

"I'm so, so sorry. I had absolutely no idea she was coming down here, otherwise, I would have told you."

I could see the panic in her face, and just like at the restaurant, I knew she was worried I'd be mad. So carefully, I wiggled my hand into her open jacket and wrapped it around her waist, resting it just above the curve of her ass.

"Don't be sorry, it's not your fault," I said, repeating the words she'd told me earlier. "I had the best time tonight before Valerie showed up, I hope you know that."

She pressed into me, and I could feel her chest through my shirt. She licked her bottom lip, and I wanted to taste what she tasted when she did that. "I did, too. It was a memorable first date."

"And there will be many more memorable dates, Angel. I can promise you that." I brushed my lips against hers before gently kissing them. "The only thing I'm upset about is that I didn't get to give you the other twelve orgasms you're owed."

She giggled against my lips and crushed her mouth to mine with a moan that I felt in my toes. "I can't wait to cash that in."

Lowering herself back onto her feet, she sighed against me,

pressing her face to my chest. "I'll let you know about tomorrow, okay?"

"No worries, Angel. I can be here if you want me here."

Through dark lashes, she peered up at me, and I saw my whole world. "I always want you here."

FORTY-SEVEN

Hazel

THE FIRST THING I DID WHEN I WALKED BACK INTO MY APARTMENT was let my mom know she couldn't just show up without forewarning. This comment started an argument I wasn't prepared for from her.

My mom had always been rather submissive and wasn't quick to argue, but since my broken engagement, she was ready to go toe to toe with me over most everything.

It started out with her telling me that I should have gone to Nashville and that she would have made sure Michael was far away from the family gathering. This was a moot point because I knew, for a fact, she wouldn't be able to manage that—we always had Thanksgiving with Michael's family, and even if he wasn't in attendance, I didn't want to be around them either.

This turned into her getting upset because she was wholly less involved with my life for the past few months. When I explained to her that that's what happens when your children grow up, I thought she was going to have a heart attack, so I backed off slightly.

I conceded to telling her more about my life in the future,

although I did not agree to the daily phone calls she really wanted.

Once we had agreed that we should communicate more, she then broached the topic of my love life. I knew it was coming, but it didn't make talking about it any easier.

I hadn't told my mom or my sister much about Luke. Delilah knew who he was and sort of knew who he was to me, but I swore her to secrecy.

At first, I didn't tell them because we were just friends, and there was nothing groundbreaking about a new friend, even if that friend also made you come harder than any person ever had and kissed you like he was made to do it. But then, when it became obvious that something more was happening, I didn't tell them because I wanted to keep it to myself. I knew they would both judge me or at least be very concerned about my jumping into something new after a breakup.

But what no one realized, and what I explained to my mom, was that after weeks of reflecting on my and Michael's relationship, I came to the realization that I had been done much earlier than it seemed. Mentally, I had checked out of our relationship months, if not a year, before the literal bloody ending.

I couldn't identify the exact moment it happened, but after he graduated law school, he wasn't around often enough for us to even have a relationship. Then when he was around, he was constantly belittling and controlling and angry and abusive. None of those things added up to a relationship, and although I wore the ring and did his laundry and plastered a stupid fucking smile on my face, it was all over.

So, whatever the hell was going on with Luke, wasn't the quick jump from one man to another as it appeared. What happened with Luke did start quickly and picked up at warp speed, but he wasn't a rebound as my mom so nicely referred to him.

"So, he's your boyfriend then?"

I sighed, falling back deeper into the couch in all-consuming exhaustion. She wanted to know every single detail of every single thing she missed. "We haven't had the conversation yet, but he's as good as."

"Well, don't assume that until you have the conversation, honey. You know men will mess around until you lock them down."

I scrubbed my hands over my face for the umpteenth time and peeked at my bed through the open door of my bedroom. I had promptly changed out of the red velvet dress and into sweats and a T-shirt after showing Luke out. My bed was calling my name and I longed to curl up in it.

I also found it difficult to explain to my mom everything that had happened while still reeling from learning Valerie had practically attacked me to get Luke by himself. My ribs would most definitely be bruised the following day, but I was more concerned about Luke. The entire ride home, he was silent, even when I tried to make conversation, it was like he wasn't even there.

He also didn't touch me, which may be insignificant to most people, but for a man who couldn't stop touching me no matter where we were or who was around, it was a stark difference.

I needed to see him again to make sure he was actually okay. He seemed better when we said goodbye, but I wasn't ready to part for the night.

"Where'd you go, Hazel?" my mom said, scooting toward my side of the couch and waving her hand in my face.

I shook off the myriad of thoughts and focused on her. "Nowhere, just tired. It's been the longest day."

"Well, just answer me this, and I'll leave you alone: does he treat you well? And treating you well doesn't just mean that he does the basic things a man is supposed to do, like not hit you." Her voice cracked over the words, and I was sure I knew what she was thinking about when it did. "But does he treat you well?"

I reached out and gripped her hand in mine. Even at almost

sixty, she was beautiful. She'd aged gracefully. The lines around her eyes and her mouth were just proof that she'd had a happy life, and she still had the same spark for it as she did when I was a kid.

"Yeah, Mom. He treats me better than I could have ever imagined a man could treat a woman. He makes me feel like I'm his everything."

Her green eyes roamed my face for a moment as a smile pulled at the corners of her lips. It was the first smile I'd seen from her all night, and I couldn't help but smile back.

"You love him," she stated, and my face dropped.

Since Luke had been staying with me, the word had rattled around in my head a few times, and I'd felt myself more inclined to randomly blurt it out at the most unusual times. Earlier that week, we were sitting on my new couch after dinner. I was writing—as I could be found doing most of the time—and Luke was eating a bowl of cereal as dessert. He had muted the wilderness TV show he was watching because I mentioned I was writing an extra intense scene having to do with my main characters and the villain. He didn't want to distract me and didn't want me to go into the other room, so he muted the TV and turned on the subtitles.

I was curled up next to him, but with my laptop facing away, since he liked to peek, when I suddenly also really wanted some cereal. Without thinking too hard about it, I looked over my laptop at him and Sadie and said, "Bite, please." Immediately after I said it, I opened my mouth, waiting for the bite of cereal I had so nicely requested.

Luke glanced over at me, scooped a bite with the perfect cereal to milk ratio and fed it to me over my laptop. Once I took the bite, he returned to eating and reading the subtitles.

The entire interaction was so familiar and comfortable that my heart squeezed in my chest like it might explode with what could be love. It was the first time I thought about it, and I quickly went back to writing and didn't ask for another bite.

The second time I thought about it was later that night when he was buried between my legs, coaxing the fourth orgasm out of me with just his tongue and fingers.

"It's a little early for that word," I finally managed to say, but nothing got past her.

"Oh, honey, if you don't know by now, love does *not* have a time line. But on that note, let me get out of your hair. I already booked a hotel, so I wouldn't be too much of an imposition."

"Mom, no, please—"

She waved me off before I could tell her to stay. "Don't argue with me. I'll see you bright and early tomorrow morning. I've already got all the groceries in my suite, so I'll bring them for Thanksgiving dinner here. I'll see you and Luke tomorrow."

I walked her to her car, where she gave me a long hug, and with another promise to be here close to dawn, she was gone.

The moment I returned to my apartment and closed and locked the door behind me, I had my phone out to text Luke.

Me: Mom got a hotel for the night. If you're not already asleep, do you want to come back?

It was well past eleven and it was completely possible that he was already asleep in his own bed with Sadie curled up in the crook of his legs. I didn't have to sleep with him, I could very well spend a night on my own without a problem, but I wanted him there with me.

Only a second had passed when my phone buzzed.

Luke: I'm on my way up.

When he knocked on my door less than a minute later, Sadie trotted through first, but Luke was steady on her heels. There wasn't even a hello between him opening the door and scooping me into his arms. He kicked the door closed behind him and locked both locks. Like we didn't know if we'd see each other again, our lips crashed together. Our hands were everywhere all at once, and I couldn't get close enough to him.

With my legs wrapped around his hips, he walked us into the bedroom like I weighed nothing while Sadie found her spot on the couch. He pressed me up against my closed bedroom door as we tore at each other's clothes, and I bucked against him. His erection hit me perfectly, and I knew I was already close. The need within me burned bright like white-hot flames.

We'd undressed each other in seconds, and after having set me down to rip my sweats off, Luke scooped me back up and plunged in deep.

My release had me screaming. And those three little words were taking up so much space in my head that I felt them clawing at the back of my tongue, also taunting me for release.

FORTY-EIGHT

Hazel

THE MORNING WAS A DISASTER. MOM WAS FREAKING OUT OVER cooking in my tiny-ass apartment kitchen while I tried to refrain from drinking until at least eleven. I gave up at around nine and poured us both mimosas. She scoffed at it at first, but when she almost caught the dish towel on fire, she downed the entire thing in one go.

Luke had left around six, and I missed him the moment he was gone. But just past ten, he returned freshly showered and with two pies.

I kissed him thoroughly in the doorway before we turned the corner into the kitchen, where my mom was peeling potatoes.

She instructed Luke to set the pies wherever he could find a place and to not worry about helping—not that there was much room to help anyway.

I grabbed a cider from the fridge, and he didn't even hesitate before popping it open.

"Is Josh not coming?" I asked, plopping down next to him on the couch while Mom banged around in the kitchen.

"No, he went over to Amanda's parents' house and took Sadie with him."

I raised my eyebrows, remembering Amanda's confession at lunch the day before and if Josh's change of plans had anything to do with it. Luckily, Luke was too busy trying to find the football game he wanted, so he didn't catch my expression.

"Oh, that's fun. So, it'll be the two of them plus her parents and younger brother?"

Luke found the channel and leaned back into the couch before adding, "And Reed. I think he's going over there as well. His parents are out of the country."

And the plot thickened.

"Hazel!" my mom bellowed from the kitchen like she would have if we were in their six-thousand-square-foot house and not my six-hundred-square-foot apartment. "You are not exempt from helping."

As far as Cooper Thanksgiving feasts were concerned, the one my mom made in my kitchen was more on the tame side. We still had all the usual sides along with turkey *and* ham, but it was only a little more food than what you would likely cook for at least six people.

We would have leftovers for days, but I wasn't surprised. Mom went all out for every holiday, including decorations and photos. Every holiday was an event in our house, and I wouldn't have it any other way.

It was almost noon and I had moved on to the cider Luke was also drinking when my doorbell rang.

Through the living room and over the bar in the kitchen, Luke and I made eye contact, both giving each other concerned looks. He stood and announced that he would get it.

The door opened a second later, and all I heard as I dusted my hands off on a towel was, "You've got to be fucking kidding me," in a voice I knew all too damn well.

I rushed around the bar and saw my sister gawking at Luke with her jaw dropped.

"Delilah," I said, trying to break her attention from him.

"Hazel!" she squealed and barreled past Luke to wrap me in a hug. There's nothing quite like a hug from your sister.

"What are you doing here? Jeez, does anyone call anymore?" I asked while still squeezing the shit out of her.

"Thought it would be more fun to see the look on your face. Mom knew I was coming," she said as she pulled back and glanced over her shoulder as Luke shut the door.

"In all of our conversations, you couldn't have warned me at least once that he is that fucking hot?" Her voice was well above a whisper, and Luke chuckled behind her. I narrowed my eyes at both of them but couldn't stay mad at her for long.

God, I missed her.

"Come in, it's almost ready. It's like you planned to get here right when all of the work is done."

Mom laughed and kissed Delilah on the cheek when we walked into the kitchen. "She'll be on dish duty with Luke."

Delilah and I discussed her flight and how she was able to get away from Tony and the kids for even a day while Mom hurried around the kitchen and directed Luke in the proper way to set the table.

"Tony is over at Mom and Dad's house with the kids. I talked to them on the way over here, and they seem to be having a blast. Mom made them an entire dinner before she left, so they just popped everything in the oven."

I took another sip of my cider and handed one to Delilah. "That's impressive."

She nodded. "Yes, but what's more impressive is your fucking man."

Her eyes were wide, but she whispered that time as she hiked her thumb over her shoulder. Luke noticed, though, like he had a sixth sense that told him we were talking about him.

"Yeah, I know," I said casually. I wasn't going to pretend like he wasn't something to look at because most of the time, that's all it took for me to be in the mood.

"Oh, I know that look." Delilah waggled her eyebrows suggestively, which made me giggle, especially after the mimosas and several ciders in my system.

"D, stop."

"Okay, but tell me, it's serious, isn't it?"

I peeked over at Luke again as he grabbed something out of the top cabinet for my mom, who was directing him all over the place. Even on the step stool I had in the kitchen, she wasn't tall enough to reach the top of the upper cabinets, and I watched Luke go to assist her without hesitation. So far, he was fitting in well, and I smiled at the smile on my mom's face when he handed her the dish and helped her off the stool.

"Yeah, it is." I couldn't lie to my sister because she'd see right through it, so I opted for the truth.

"God, and I'm sure the sex is amazing." I whipped my head around to her in surprise.

She gave me a *"what?"* expression, and I shook my head at her. "Are you sure that's your first one?" I pointed to her cider, and she rolled her eyes at me.

"Sometimes you can just tell if a man is good in bed. It's not my fault I'm intuitive about these things. I'm sure he likes dirty talk, too."

I choked on my cider at the accuracy of her statement.

"I'm taking that as a yes. Good for you, sis. I still need to talk to him and gather more intel, but as of right now, I like him. He's a serious upgrade at the very least."

"It's ready!" My mom beckoned us to the table which was pristinely set thanks to Luke with Mom's guidance. The food covered every inch of counter space I did and did not have, and we had to take turns individually loading our plates because there wasn't enough room for more than one person in the tiny kitchen.

"Hazel, can I open this champagne?" my sister asked from the kitchen.

"No!" I all but yelled at her. I recognized the label and the note I had written on it even from across the room. It was the bottle Michael had gifted me after our engagement to be opened on our wedding day.

I didn't have a definitive reason why she couldn't open it, but I wanted to dispose of it in my own way, I guessed.

"Sorry, there should be some in the fridge," I said before I took my seat, not missing the curious look Luke directed toward me.

We each took our seats, and after Mom said grace, we all dug in. It was delicious, as always, and no one spoke for a long while as we shoveled food into our mouths. The football game still on the TV was the only background noise.

It felt good to have them here.

Although we were missing a few people, and the apartment was a little too warm from the oven and stove, and the space was also a little tiny for even four grown people, it was nice.

Much to my surprise, the conversation started out pleasant enough, even after the champagne incident. Everyone kept the topics light for the most part. Luke asked about Delilah's marketing business and about Mom's hobbies. He seemed interested when Delilah began prattling on about Amber and Miles and even asked questions when she scrolled through her entire camera roll.

Then Mom started in. "Luke, what do you do for a living?"

"I'm a small animal veterinarian specializing mostly in dogs and cats."

"Very nice. And you enjoy it?"

"Yes, very much so."

"I'm sure that makes you a good living as well."

"Mom," I warned through gritted teeth, but Luke gripped my thigh under the table, telling me it was okay.

"Yes, I'm very fortunate that I have a job I enjoy with a decent salary."

Mom hummed in approval and took another bite of green beans. "And you live alone?"

I groaned internally and prepared for twenty questions. "No, I own a home next door to Hazel's old house, and my brother lives with me."

"So, was that for any particular reason, or…?" She let her question trail off as she glanced up at Luke from her plate.

"He was between places and needed a place to live, so I let him stay with me. It's worked out pretty well so far."

My legs were crossed on the wooden chair, and Luke's hand on the inside of my thigh was slightly distracting. With one hand, I continued to pick at my mashed potatoes while the nails of my other hand trailed up and down his forearm. His eyes cut over to me as a small smirk lifted one corner of his mouth.

I hadn't seen that lopsided smile in a while, and it was the sexiest damn thing I'd ever seen. It promised lots of dirty things when we were alone later.

"How old are you?"

"I'm thirty-one."

"And when was your last long-term relationship?"

Luke's hand tensed on my thigh, and I circled my hand around his wrist. "Mom," I said again, but Luke squeezed my leg harder.

"I was married for about a year, and we divorced three years ago," he said matter-of-factly, not giving away a single sign that he was uncomfortable with the topic. But I could tell by the way his arm tensed against me that he didn't want to discuss it.

"And what was the reason for the divorce?"

"Irreconcilable differences."

Mom eyed him, and I watched her contemplate questioning him further as the expression on her face morphed.

"I'm sure that's what the paperwork said, but was that really the reason?"

"Yes, it was. We were young when we got married and as we grew, we realized we wanted different things out of life."

Mom was still hesitant, but thankfully, she let the topic drop, and Luke obviously relaxed next to me.

Delilah looked across the table at me over the rim of her wineglass with her eyebrows raised. I widened my eyes at her and then quickly flicked them in Mom's direction, trying to silently convey that she should help or step in next time. She rolled her eyes.

"I would like to discuss Michael, though," Mom announced.

"Okay, seriously?" My fork clattered to my mostly empty plate, and I contemplated just leaving the table. "Are you trying to make this *the* most awkward Thanksgiving dinner ever? Why do we need to talk about him?"

"I just want to know what happened at that damn coffee shop or whatever it was. Michael's version of the story doesn't add up, and you only told me there was an altercation. But Michael's nose is broken, so I'd like to know."

I looked over at my sister again for help, but she was also looking at me like she wanted to hear the entire story. Even though he wasn't there, he was still torturing me from thirteen hours away.

With a long sigh, I pushed my plate away and put my head in my hands. I immediately felt Luke's hand on my lower back, and the feeling of him grounded me. I was out of that house. I had made it out, and I wasn't going back, and I would never be hurt like that again.

His hand cautiously trailed up my spine until it settled on the back of my neck.

No one said anything else and when I looked up, my mom and sister were watching me expectantly while Luke continued to eat with his other hand. There was something about the way he acknowledged how uncomfortable I was with his hand on my neck while he continued eating that made it seem less climactic. I needed that.

"I'm not going to rehash our entire conversation at the coffee shop, so if that's what you're looking for, you're not going to get it." I looked up from my hands to find them both still staring. I took that as confirmation to continue. "Michael and I met at a coffee shop around the corner. He felt no remorse for what he did and was the utter definition of a piece of shit. Luke stayed in the background because I didn't feel comfortable being alone with Michael, even in a public place. Michael didn't see Luke until we were about to leave. He attacked him out of nowhere and Luke subdued him by punching him in the face, and it worked. That's it, that's what happened."

Mom nodded thoughtfully, and Delilah seemed amused.

"Good for you, Luke. He deserved a million times worse," Delilah mused, and I couldn't help but laugh.

"Well, it wasn't the last punch he took," Mom added and continued eating like she hadn't said anything at all. Delilah and I looked at each other and then looked back at her.

"What the hell are you talking about?" Delilah finally asked.

"Your father kind of went off on him, ended up punching him in the face as well. Didn't do as much damage as Luke did, but your dad hit him."

Both Delilah and I wore twin expressions of shock. My dad was the last person on earth I would imagine could hit someone. He was laid back and eternally calm, which was rather unsettling as a child when we got in trouble.

Luke chuckled beside me, running his thumb up and down the side of my neck. "I like your dad already."

"He's also a fan of yours," Mom added, which made me smile. I didn't doubt Dad and Luke would get along swimmingly; they had a lot in common, not including me.

Delilah immediately went on a tangent about Mom not telling her things even though they live in the same city.

She continued as we all got up and set our dirty dishes in the sink. Once everyone stepped out of the kitchen, I opened the dishwasher, which earned me a dirty look from Luke.

"Go sit down. I can handle the dishes." And with a kiss on my forehead and a tap on my ass, he sent me off.

Delilah, Mom, and I all fell onto the couch with our drinks in hand and fell back into our usual rhythm. There was clanging and water running in the kitchen for a while, but when I glanced up—expecting to see Luke with soap up to his elbows—he was actually staring down at his phone. He had a definitive tic in his jaw, and even from across the living room, I could see the vein in his forehead pulsing.

I crossed the room and stood next to him at the sink. I peeked over his shoulder and noticed the ten missed calls from the same phone number as well as a text message that had just come through.

While I looked over his shoulder, he opened the text.

Unknown: Can't wait to see you soon, Bear.

The woman didn't waste any time with the sinister, obscure threats.

"Is that the first text she's sent you?" I whispered.

His phone was gripped tight, his knuckles white with the force, and his only response was a quick nod. The frustration and anger were sweeping off him in waves. I wanted to do something to lessen the impact of it all, but the only thing that came to mind was to run my nails down his back. He shivered under my touch and relaxed slightly.

"How about a game?" Mom asked no one in particular.

"Clue!" Delilah volunteered, and Mom and I groaned in unison.

"I don't have Clue, D. It's either Scrabble or Dominoes."

"Seriously? You have to keep Clue around so when I'm here, we can play."

I turned to Luke who was watching all of us with an amused smirk as he leaned over the sink.

"When we were kids, Delilah got so angry while playing

Clue that she raged and threw the entire board at my head. That's what the scar just above my lip is from," I said, pointing to the faint scar above my upper lip.

"That's a lie!" Delilah hollered from behind the bathroom door.

"No, it's not!"

"But it's also happened a few times since. So, now, we do not play Clue."

Luke's smirk turned into a smile that lit his green eyes as well. With his arms banded around my waist, he leaned forward and pressed his lips to mine briefly. My heart pounded in my chest, and my body craved more even with just a small kiss.

"I like Clue, too," he muttered against my mouth.

Distraction was complete, but not for long as his phone buzzed on the counter one more time.

FORTY-NINE

Hazel

THANKSGIVING WAS A SUCCESS. AFTER SEVERAL ROUNDS OF dominoes and a very heated game of Monopoly, which I found in one of the many boxes I'd yet to unpack, we had two additional empty bottles of wine. Mom, Luke, and I were crying tears of laughter as we watched Delilah storm out of the room in a rage that she'd been beaten.

Their flight was early the next day, and I was truly sad to see them go. Having them there made the little space feel more like home. All it needed was some laughter and Monopoly, I guessed.

On their way out, they both told me that they approved of Luke. Mom told me that Luke seemed like a "sweet soul" while Delilah said he was "yummy."

I left them with a promise to go to Nashville for Christmas. It was a lot less likely I'd run into Michael or his family since they usually spent the holiday with their extended family out of state, and that gave me enough peace of mind to plan ahead of time.

Mom and Delilah also requested that I bring Luke, and as much as I wanted to tell them he'd be there, that seemed like only something you bring a boyfriend to or someone you've committed to, and we technically weren't either yet.

I let them go with the promise that we'd see how the next month went.

After they left, I'd spent the day cleaning and finally unpacking the rest of my boxes. With Luke at work and my paranoia at an all-time high, I didn't want to leave my apartment for anything unnecessary.

Luke had received several text messages from Valerie, but none of them amounted to much other than promises to see him soon or random shared memories that appeared to not mean anything to him.

After our run-in with her only two days prior, I could tell a change in him. He'd done his best with my mom and sister, and neither of them could tell since they hadn't met him before. But I could. He didn't relax for a second, and even in the apartment, his head was on a swivel. The few times one of us left the apartment—to get something out of the car or tour the complex on Mom's request—he made it a point to go with us and watch intently.

Each time his phone vibrated, he visibly tensed and at one point, his eye began twitching, which was something I hadn't seen before but figured was due to stress.

I desperately wanted to do something to relieve the tension, but there wasn't much I could do. He refused to block the number she was contacting him from because that would be the end of gathering evidence.

It was evidence we ended up personally taking with us to the precinct handling Valerie's case.

Luke picked me up during his lunch break and drove us both there. It was a silent ride, and I longed for anything to talk about to break the tension in the air. He was brooding like it was an Olympic sport, and it was driving me nuts.

We were taking all the steps either of us could think of to deal with the Valerie situation the right way. He contacted the police every time there was a new development, and he provided them as much information as he could. The rest of it was clearly out of our control, and he was going to let the stress of it eat him alive.

And I knew the turning point of it all had been when I got hurt. There was a blue bruise running the width of my ribs where I'd slammed into the granite counter of the bathroom sinks. When Luke had taken my shirt off, he'd paid extra close attention to the forming bruise. He ran his fingers over it and kissed along it softly. It would have been sweet had I not known that he was busy blaming himself while he did it. It didn't matter how many times I told him that I was okay. It wasn't okay to him, and I felt helpless against his fear and self-pity.

"So, these are all the messages you've received?" Detective Bell asked from across his disheveled desk.

Luke nodded at the man who was finishing off his coffee as he sighed and leaned back in his shitty old office chair.

Detective Bell wasn't necessarily what I expected. He was tall and looked only a few years older than us, but with quite a lot of gray hair around his temples. I'm sure the job was stressful and caused the gray hair in spades.

And I wasn't overly impressed with his laid-back attitude toward everything we'd told him.

We'd both explained what had happened at the restaurant in detail. We also showed him the missed calls and texts on Luke's phone. Whether he meant to or not, he seemed unimpressed.

Luke's self-control was thinning, and I was watching it happen right in front of my eyes. Detective Bell was discussing the issue with the text messages as Luke shook his head and clenched his fists in his lap.

"So, what do you plan to do?" I piped up, interrupting Detective Bell's meaningless explanation of the issue with text messages.

"Excuse me?" he asked like he wasn't prepared for me to speak.

"Are you going to ask the restaurant for their cameras? Or maybe talk to our waiter from that evening? There had to be witnesses that watched Luke and Valerie's interaction, so you could also talk to them."

Detective Bell nodded along like he had been thinking of all those things in the first place, but I doubted him.

"Yes, of course, ma'am. We will do all of those things and more. I'm also going to go over to Valerie's house and speak with her once I have a chance to review the footage from the restaurant and speak to..." He leaned forward and picked up his flimsy notepad from the desk. "Ronnie, your waiter. I have it all covered."

I eyed him and tried to give him my best *"you better"* look. His face dropped slightly so he must have gotten my message loud and clear.

"Great, we look forward to hearing what you've uncovered by tomorrow morning." With newfound confidence, I stood from my metal chair on the opposite side of his desk and stuck out my hand.

Detective Bell was five steps behind me and scrambled to stand and take my hand. When he did, his palm was clammy, and I quickly pulled my hand away after the required second had passed.

Luke followed my lead. He stood, shook the detective's hand and then grabbed mine to lead us out of the station.

"Oh, before you go," Detective Bell called out before we were a few steps away. "I was able to get a hold of your friend Blakely, and she has agreed to come in for an interview on Monday."

As the words left Bell's mouth, Luke visibly relaxed. We both thanked him for his time and headed out of the station.

We'd spent a few hours in the boring, cement building, so by the time we walked back outside, the midday sun had warmed the still slightly chilly November air.

Luke opened the passenger side door and waited for me to hop in before closing it behind me. He rounded the front of the truck and rolled his head back and forth, dissipating some of the tension I knew was probably accumulating there.

As he climbed in and took a seat on the black leather, it gave me an opportunity to appreciate him in his dark-blue scrubs. I'd seen him in them a lot since he'd often go straight from work to pick up Sadie, and he'd only change once he returned to my apartment. I never tired of it, though—the way the material hugged his arms and his legs and showed off the sculpted muscles of his chest. If he turned a certain way, I could even see a line or two of his defined stomach.

"I have to run back to the clinic and finish up a few things before I'm really done for the day. Do you want to come with me?" he asked, completely ignorant to the fact that I was drooling over him.

"Sure," I said, interested in getting to actually see what he did every day instead of just hearing about it secondhand. "I guess it'll be bring your girl—"

I clamped my mouth shut before the entire word could escape. Mentally, I berated myself for my slip of the tongue, while on the outside, I pressed my lips into a firm line and stared out the windshield.

We hadn't had *the* conversation or anything close to it, so slipping up and almost calling myself his girlfriend without any prior discussion was not my best move. Granted, we were partially living together and had hit all the other milestones of a relationship. And to an outsider, it would appear that we were just that: in a relationship. We were also planning to move me into his house the following day. But still…

It was important to me to have the conversation and to set up expectations, otherwise, we were both just assuming the other knew what was going on. We didn't have time for assumptions.

We stopped at a red light, and I could feel Luke's eyes burning a hole into the side of my face. But I stayed strong and continued looking forward even though every nerve in my body was crawling to see the expression on his face. I needed to know what he was thinking like I needed to breathe.

He could have reacted a few ways and I was getting anxious the longer the silence continued and the longer he stared.

Finally, after what seemed like years, Luke asked, "Who am I bringing to work?"

My whole body deflated, and I chanced a glance in his direction. The light turned green as I peeked over at him, so thankfully, he had to break his stare down, but I caught what I thought was a smirk before I faced forward again.

"You're taking me," I said in a tone that didn't exactly exude the confidence I hoped it would.

"And who are you?"

"I'm Hazel, Luke. Don't be dense, you know who I am."

He snorted and reached over the center console to grasp my thigh, which I had propped up. My whole body shivered with just one single touch and under the warmth of his large hand.

"Okay, let me rephrase. Hazel, who are you to me?"

"Well, I'm still Hazel," I said, but I caught the unimpressed expression he threw my way out of the corner of my eye. "This isn't fair, aren't you supposed to ask me?"

"What am I supposed to ask you?" he threw back, taking a right turn onto the street where the clinic was located.

I groaned and threw my hands up in the air. "Are we really going to play this game right now?"

"You're so cute when you're flustered," he said. He was so amused about my current state, but I wasn't.

I finally looked over at him with a hard set to my expression. "What have I told you about calling grown women cute, Lucas?"

"Oh, we're using my full name now?"

"Yes, it's come to that."

His amused lopsided smile didn't move as he flipped on his right turn signal and pulled into the parking lot at the back of the building. He put the truck in park and immediately turned it off. As he jumped out, I hesitantly unbuckled my belt and grabbed my purse from the floorboard.

Luke had my door open as I lifted the bag over my head and around my shoulder. He practically pulled me from the truck with a hand around my wrist. The urgent look in his eye was something I hadn't seen in quite some time; it replaced the worry and concern that had been there for days.

In one swift motion, he pulled me to the side, shut the passenger door, and pressed me into the cold exterior of the truck. One hand cupped the side of my throat, twisting into the back of my hair, while the other gripped my hip. My breath caught in my throat as his lips slammed down onto mine. I wasn't prepared for it, but I quickly gave in to the feeling of him pressed against me and all the emotions that brought with it.

I liked him like that—like he couldn't wait and was starving for me.

His lips were urgent against mine, but he pulled back before it could go too far, which was probably for the best since we were outside of his place of work.

His forehead rested on my own as his thumb traced my lips.

"You're mine, Angel. Whatever you want to call it, it's that. You've been mine ever since you barged into that stupid fucking party and had us all dumbfounded by you. I wasn't ever going to let you go. So, we can call it whatever you want. If the girlfriend/boyfriend titles are what you want, then you can have them and all of the other expectations that go with them. Because I'm all in."

I think I forgot how to breathe as the weight of his words washed over me and hung around us. I felt them on my heart and my soul, and I saw the truth of them in his eyes as he watched me. He was so good, even in times like that one, at keeping his face neutral and waiting for a reaction while his eyes told the story.

"I know with everything going on, it's maybe not the best

circumstances to begin a relationship, but I'm hoping the worst of it is behind us. If we can make it through this, then..." He trailed off, lost in thought and a million miles away. He was watching my face, but I could tell he was thinking of something else.

I presumed he was thinking of the small amount of time from that party at his house to us standing beside his truck and what a whirlwind it had been. But I wouldn't change it for anything, and when a soft smile pulled at the corner of his lips, I knew he felt the same.

"You're my sunshine, Angel. A bright light when everything feels dark."

With emotion thick in my throat, I pressed to my toes and kissed him with all the emotion his words made me feel. I hoped my kiss conveyed what my words would miss because what I was feeling was bigger than words.

"I don't know if I can top that. But I don't mind being yours, as you so eloquently stated. And I'll be your light the best I can."

His smile was bright, and he took my face in both of his hands to kiss me once again, but his lips didn't get a chance to meet mine. The back door to the building swung open behind him, and a blonde I remember oh so well stepped into the parking lot.

"Oh, I'm sorry," she said, stopping dead in her tracks. "I didn't mean to umm..." Her eyes dragged up and down Luke's back, obviously ogling the ass I had been checking out before, as he spun around to face her.

Luke chuckled, placed his hand on the back of my neck and led us to the door Crystal had just exited.

"Crystal, you remember my girlfriend Hazel, right?" Luke said, reintroducing me as his girlfriend like it was something he did all the time.

"Yes, of course. Nice to see you again." She half smiled. "I was just heading out for the day. I'll see you tomorrow, Luke."

And with that, she was gone quicker than we could manage another word.

I rolled my eyes and shook my head. "Do you ever get tired of women checking you out and so obviously throwing themselves at you?" I asked as he opened the metal door and motioned for me to enter.

"Yes," he said simply with a slight tilt to his lips.

"Liar."

FIFTY

Hazel

Luke stole a rolly chair for me from one of the other desks around the back room before he set up at a computer in the far corner.

It was only a minute or two before he had files and papers spread out before him and was immersed in whatever he was doing. He'd asked me if I wanted to use one of the computers to continue writing, but in the same breath, he'd also said it wouldn't be too long.

So, instead, I spun around in my chair, high off Luke's declaration.

"You're making me dizzy just watching you spin around in that thing," Luke said, barely glancing up from the computer. His hands were flying over the keys as he flipped through papers.

"Then stop watching me," I said, sticking my foot out and hitting the edge of a desk to stop the spinning. I was making myself dizzy, too.

"You look happy." He leaned back in his chair and turned to

me. His eyes blazed a trail over my body as the room stopped spinning.

"I am happy," I responded confidently.

His eyes lingered on me for another moment, and I was happy we were alone otherwise, anyone else would be able to see that he was so obviously undressing me. I didn't want to share that look in his deep-green eyes with anyone.

"Now, stop distracting me, so I can hurry up and finish this."

I pulled out the book I had in my purse—a romantic thriller I couldn't get enough of—and flipped to the page with my floral bookmark. The clicking of the keys as Luke typed along with the brush of paper against paper was decent background noise, but I hadn't read more than ten pages when my phone buzzed in my back pocket.

Ever since Luke began receiving incessant text messages from Valerie, any time one of our phones buzzed or rang, I tensed instinctively.

I set my book down on the desk and dragged my phone out of my back pocket. It was a text from a number I didn't recognize.

Hi, Hazel, this is Blakely. I was hoping we could have lunch tomorrow. I feel so bad about the way we left things, and I just wanted a chance to talk.

"Can I see your phone, please?" I asked Luke. Without looking up, he pulled it from his jacket pocket and handed it to me.

"What's your passcode?"

"Ten twenty-two."

I punched it in and began to type the number from my phone into his contacts when it dawned on me what his passcode could possibly be.

"Do those numbers mean something?"

"Yup," he quipped, still not looking up at me.

"What do they mean?"

He sighed and spun his chair. "It's the date of the party you crashed, Angel. Do you have any other questions?"

"Nope," I said, looking back down at the two phones in my hands and trying to focus on typing in the simple four-digit number. But it was an effort to keep my fingers from shaking.

Every day he continued to surprise me; it wasn't that long ago that we were at each other's throats as next-door neighbors. It was like a switch flipped and suddenly, the date everything changed for us was his passcode.

Once I typed the number in Luke's phone, it pulled up Blakely's contact, and I slumped in my chair with relief.

I slid Luke's phone back across the desk and hovered my thumbs over my own phone screen as I contemplated how to respond. Having lunch with Blakely didn't mean that I condoned the way she had been acting and it could provide additional insight into why she had a sudden change of heart and decided to speak to the police.

It was also obvious that Luke's group of friends meant more to him than just a normal group of friends usually did. He was broken up about Blakely lying to him and not feeling safe enough to approach him sooner, and I thought it would go a long way if I showed that I cared as well.

"Blakely just texted me. She wants to have lunch tomorrow."

That caught Luke's attention. "Are you sure it's her?"

"Yes, that's what I was doing, looking up her number on your phone."

He stuck his hand out, palm up, silently requesting my phone. I set it in his hand, and he read over the simple text.

"Do you want to go?" he asked and handed it back to me.

"I think it might be a good idea. She may want to clear the air before she goes to talk to the police on Monday, and it would be nice to start over. I know she's your friend, so I should probably figure out how to be friends with her and vice versa," I said with a shrug. Honestly, if Luke told me it wasn't a good idea, I'd probably still go to try to make amends. Maybe I was too forgiving, but it was more difficult to go through life holding grudges against everyone. It required more emotional currency than I had to spend.

"If you want to go, I'm not going to stop you. But I have surgery tomorrow during lunch. It's already been rescheduled once, so it has to happen tomorrow. And I don't know how I feel about you going anywhere alone, though. Especially right now..."

I waved a hand, dismissing his concerns. "Luke, I'm just going to lunch with her. I'll be fine for an hour-long lunch, I promise."

He wasn't convinced and based on the look on his face, I knew it was going to take a lot more than that to persuade him otherwise.

"What if I shared my location with you?" I said, tapping on my phone screen and pulling up our text messages so I could set it to share my location for an indefinite amount of time.

"I guess that would help."

I understood his concern, I really did, but I also knew I couldn't live my life with a bodyguard constantly by my side.

"There," I said. "Now you can see exactly where I am. Just don't be creepy about watching it, okay?"

"I am incapable of being creepy," he said, turning back to his work. I guess my solution was good enough because he didn't utter another word in argument.

While Luke finished up his work, I mulled over a response to Blakely. I went back and forth with how to approach it but ended up deciding that simplicity was likely the best option.

Hi, Blakely! It's good to hear from you. I would love to go to lunch tomorrow. Just let me know the time and place.

I hit send just as Luke was combining his papers and putting files away in a few trays above the desk. One of the women that worked up front walked into the back room to discuss next week's schedule with Luke, and he again introduced me as his girlfriend.

I didn't think I'd ever tire of hearing him call me that.

"Okay, let's go. We have very urgent things to attend to."

Luke ushered me out the back door and hurried us to his truck. He didn't forget to open my door, but he quickly shut it and jogged to his side. The moment the truck was on, he peeled out of the lot like we were in a fucking getaway car.

"What the hell is the rush? What urgent things do you need to attend to?" I asked, holding on to anything in the truck cabin that would keep me from swinging back and forth even with my seat belt firmly buckled.

"I need to fuck my girlfriend. That's the urgent thing I must attend to," he said as he made a sharp right out of the parking lot.

I threw my head back, laughing at his dramatics. "Is it really that urgent?"

"Yes!" he exclaimed, huffing out a frustrated breath when we were stopped by a red light. I guess it wasn't urgent enough to mean running red lights. "This is a historic moment; sex as a couple for the first time is a special occasion."

I raised my eyebrows in interest and decided to play along. "You're absolutely right. You know, it's been a while since I've done this, though. Can you explain to me how this differs from sex as a not couple?"

When the light turned green, he gunned it up to the speed limit and then let off the gas slightly. "Well, it varies from couple to couple, but I know you'll enjoy the things I have planned for you."

I wanted specifics, but I decided it wasn't a bad thing to be surprised every once in a while.

. . .

The normal fifteen-minute drive took half that time, and I swore Luke was going to leap from the car before he'd put it in park.

The guy really wanted to get laid.

I already had my door open and was hopping out when he made it to my side. Without a word, he gripped my hand and tugged me to the stairs, which he began trying to take two at a time.

"Okay, I have short legs, dude. I cannot go up the stairs like that. You go ahead"—I waved him forward—"and unlock the door."

He bounded the rest of the way up the stairs and was through my apartment door before I had even made it to the top of the second set.

His enthusiasm was cute, though. I contemplated telling him that he was cute and seeing how he felt about the word when Lexi stepped out of her apartment.

"Oh, hey. Long time no see," I said. "How are you?"

She'd dyed her hair nearly black, and it honestly fit her better than the orange. She also looked like she was heading to the store with several reusable grocery bags in her hands.

"Hey, Hazel. I'm good. How was your Thanksgiving?"

"It was actually really great. My mom and my—" My apartment door opened abruptly and cut off my words. I didn't have a chance to finish my conversation as Luke's hand darted out and caught me by the wrist.

"Hey!"

Luke peered out into the hall and was wearing a no-nonsense face which excited me. "Sorry, Lexi, Hazel needs to fuck her boyfriend right now. She'll talk later," he said as he shut and locked the door behind us.

"Okay, that was rude. And you don't have to advertise our sex life to all of my neighbors."

Luke shrugged and scooped me into his arms. Reflexively my legs tightened around his waist, and I could tell how hard he already was. "Angel, they're going to know when they hear you screaming my name."

"Oh, and you're so sure that I'm going to scream?"

"I'm undefeated so far." His voice was low and dripping with lust. I assumed he'd carry me into the bedroom, but he stopped at the couch. We'd had sex on almost every square inch of my apartment besides the couch, so I guessed he wanted to rectify that issue.

He sat down with me on his lap, and rather than come at me like a dog in heat, Luke pushed my jacket off my shoulders as I dropped my purse to the floor behind me and pried my shoes off.

Left only in my jeans and a T-shirt, Luke tangled his hands in my hair and pulled me to him. The eagerness I felt in his kiss outside of his truck was there again yet intensified. He immediately urged my lips apart with his tongue, and I moaned at the first caress of it against my own. His hands stayed tangled in my hair as we became a mess of lips and teeth and tongues. But I let my hands roam over his neck, shoulders, arms, and chest; I wanted to feel him everywhere.

We broke apart only for a second so he could pull my shirt over my head, and I pulled his off before we were back together again. My breasts pushed against his hard chest, and I could feel my nipples harden beneath the fabric of my bra. I took his lower lip between my teeth and bit down slightly. He growled in response and pushed his hips up into mine.

We had too many clothes on, both of us still dressed from the waist down, and I needed him as close to me as he could be.

"I want to feel my girlfriend's mouth around my cock," he said before pushing me off his lap and loosening the tie of his scrubs around his waist. Without hesitation, I dropped to my knees in front of him, but he shook his head.

"Take off your pants and come up here." He patted the couch next to him, sliding his pants down his toned legs. "I need to touch you, too."

Eagerly, I slipped out of my jeans, leaving them in a puddle on the floor beneath me. I climbed up next to him on all fours with my head bowed over his thick length.

With the hair tie on my wrist, I pulled my hair back into a low ponytail, then gripped Luke's shaft with one hand. His skin was so soft, and I could feel him pulsing beneath my palm. As I stroked him up and down with a twist in my wrist, his hands smoothed down my spine and palmed my ass.

His hand trailed lower until the calloused tip of a finger circled the tight hole he hadn't yet explored. "Has anyone ever fucked you here before?"

"No," I said before licking the drop of precum at the tip of his engorged head. His dick twitched and a satisfied smile crossed my face.

"Have you used a toy back here?"

"No," I said again, then I licked slowly up the side of him and twirled my tongue around his tip. I sucked the head in my mouth just for a moment, then released it with a pop.

"Fuck, Angel. We'll have to work you up to it, but I'm going to fuck you here soon."

I didn't say anything because I was too lost in what I was doing and what I hoped to accomplish. I only hummed in approval as I swallowed him as deep as I could and until he triggered my gag reflex at the back of my throat.

He moaned, and I continued working my mouth up and down him at what I was hoping was a satisfyingly slow pace. Each time I tried to push him deeper. I held him far back in my throat for a second or two before pulling back up.

All the while, Luke teased my throbbing clit with small, hurried circles. In such a short time, he'd become an expert when it came to my pleasure and my body. He knew exactly how to work me so I would fall apart at just the right time. With every twist of his fingers, I could feel myself growing more wet and the craving for release growing closer.

One of his fingers finally dipped inside of me, and I pushed back into it, wanting him deeper. His finger pushed in and out of me while his thumb continued circling my clit, and I was nearly overcome with the sensation of it so I momentarily stopped what I was doing.

When I paused with my mouth only over the tip of him and my hand around his slick shaft, his movements also stopped.

"You stop, I stop," he said, and I immediately continued at a quicker pace because I needed more.

He kept going but withdrew his finger from my pussy only a few seconds later. I was about to protest when I felt his finger pushing at a different entrance.

"Don't tense up," he said, prodding at my tight hole while his other hand smoothed down my ass and then moved around my front to continue stimulating my clit. "Just keep sucking my cock like a good girl. *God*, that feels so good," he groaned, and the sound of his hunger was evident in his voice, which spurred me on. I pushed my hesitation to the side because I wanted everything Luke could give me.

Slowly, he pushed his finger into me. He talked me through each step and explained what my body was doing as he moved. It didn't hurt as much as it felt uncomfortable for a few minutes, but once I got used to the intrusion, the pleasure overwhelmed any thoughts of pain or unease.

My hips jerked back into his finger, pushing it deeper, and I moaned around his cock. The heat I felt growing low in my stomach suddenly propelled through me with a fierce intensity.

"Don't stop," I pleaded. His clever fingers thumbed my clit and pushed into me at such an expert pace that I couldn't do anything but succumb to the torrent of pleasure that washed over me.

I ground back into him, sighed his name, and then yelled it as my sex clenched, and I could feel his finger deep inside of my ass.

The new sensations and type of orgasm had me slumping over his lap and licking up and down the sides of his cock in hopes of recovering for a few moments. But Luke had a different idea. With a growl, he lifted me up and twisted me to the other side of him. My back landed on the forgiving couch cushion, and he poised himself on top of me. He ripped a pillow from the other side of the couch and positioned it underneath my lower back, lifting my hips for easier access. His forearms were braced on either side of my head and his eyes scanned my face as he pushed into me in one long thrust.

I gasped and immediately clenched around him, and although my eyes wanted to fall closed, I forced them open to watch his expression contort in undeniable pleasure. I clasped his face in my hands and melted into him, kissing him deep and long. His thrusts were punishing and the pillow beneath my hips only forced him deeper into me. Each time he pulled back, the tip of his cock grazed that perfect spot within me, and I tried to meet him in the middle, thrust for thrust.

I craved his groans and gasps and mumbled dirty words.

He was deep, so deep, but I wanted more of all of it. I didn't think I could ever get enough. I slung one leg over the back of the couch, opening myself up wider and allowing him to drive deeper. With an open invitation, Luke leaned back, gripping my hip in one hand as the other palmed my breast, pinching my nipple.

"You're so beautiful, Hazel. And so fucking addicting," he breathed. I could feel my arousal coating us both, slipping over my thighs and allowing him easy access.

"You feel so good, Luke," I gasped. Scraping my nails down his stomach and the tattoos on his chest, I left small red marks in their wake. His eyes rolled back as the pain propelled his pleasure forward; I knew how he liked it. His thrusts became frenzied, and I knew he was close as his eyes closed and his grip tightened around both of my hips.

In a second, Luke fell backward into the couch cushions as he planted his feet on the ground. He was still partially inside of me, but I got the satisfaction of sliding back down onto him completely. His fingers dug into my hips as he guided me back down; we both groaned simultaneously at the connection.

My need for him burned under my skin, and I watched between us as his thick length disappeared inside of me. Once I was fully seated, I glanced up to watch his expression.

The desire and need and unfathomable pleasure were all still there, flickering in his deep-green eyes. But there was more that time. It was something that took my breath away, and I knew he saw it reflected in my own eyes.

We were drowning and pulling each other deeper and whether I could breathe or not, I didn't care.

It felt like a culmination and the creation of something I couldn't describe. I knew I was frozen in the feeling, and it felt like Luke was too, as he stilled beneath me. But no matter what was newly buzzing between us, the fiery desire urged me to move.

My fingers threaded through his soft, nearly black hair, and I scraped my nails against his scalp. His eyelids fluttered but didn't close. With his hair gripped in my fingers, I began bouncing, falling on top of him and pushing him so deep I felt him in my stomach. Then I rose to the tip only to do it all again.

Our foreheads fell together as his huge hands continued to guide me up and down his cock. Our noses brushed and our lips ghosted over each other's. Each kiss was slow, like we were trying to savor the other and maintain the deepening connection. My pace quickened as Luke's hands eagerly gripped my ass and squeezed. My head lolled back, and my long hair fell down my spine. Luke gripped my hair and pulled my head back even farther as he took the opportunity to lick up my neck from my collarbone, where he teased and nipped up to my ear.

With calloused fingers, he glided his hands up my back and

pressed me closer to him. Our chests collided, my soft breasts against his toned muscles as he whispered, "You're mine. All mine. These legs are mine; this ass is mine. Your stomach, arms, and tits are all mine. And with the way your pussy responds to me, and your mouth sucks my cock, those are definitely mine as well."

His hands touched each part of me that he referred to with an intoxicatingly possessive caress, and I could feel his words bury themselves into my soul.

I'm his.

"Then you're also mine," I sighed, letting him claim me and doing the same to him. The only sound in the apartment was our heavy breathing and the wet noises of our fucking.

"*Yes,*" he groaned and unleashed himself on me. My hips were firmly in his hands, and I craved their bruising force as he held me up and pistoned into me from below. I wanted to push back down onto him, but there was no way I could move. So, I held on to his shoulders, then behind his neck. The beauty of his masculine features twisted in the pleasure I was giving him with his watchful eyes filled with raw emotion, didn't just push me toward my release but incinerated me in its wicked light.

"Oh, fuck, Hazel," Luke cried as I screamed my release, and he lost himself in me. My inner walls clenched around him with such force that I pushed him over the edge along with me. My vision went white and blurred as we each rode out our release, and I felt the warmth pulsing from his cock inside of me.

Several seconds later and we were both still trying to catch our breath. My head rested on his shoulder as I regained my strength. As Luke's hands passed over my back, I shivered into him. He pressed a kiss to the side of my head, and his lips gently lingered over my damp skin.

We were both a mess of sweaty, tangled limbs, and I'd never felt more sated.

I chanced a look into his face after he brushed away a few

pieces of hair that had fallen from my ponytail and were plastered to my forehead.

No words were spoken between the two of us—none were needed—but I hoped he read the words in my eyes that I couldn't yet let myself say. The same words I would bet my life were also running through his own mind.

FIFTY-ONE

Hazel

I input the address Blakely sent me into my phone GPS and set it to connect to the screen in my car. It was only a twenty-minute drive into town from my apartment, but it was also pouring, so I left a few minutes earlier than necessary.

"What's the name of the restaurant again?" Luke asked over the phone. He was at the clinic, and I heard what sounded like the door to the back parking lot slam closed.

"I just texted you the address, but you have my location. Luke, I'll be fine."

He sighed and there was the faint sound of dogs barking in the distance.

"I know, Angel. I have surgery in thirty minutes, but I'll have one of the techs watch my phone. If you need me, call me. She'll make sure to answer. And again, I'd prefer if one of the guys, or even Amanda, went with you. If I call any of them right now, they can meet you there."

I rolled my eyes at my overly protective man, but it felt good. He was *my* man.

"I promise I don't need a chaperone. I'll text you when I get there, and I'll text you before I leave just for good measure and if it'll make you feel better."

"Good, yes. Do that," he said in a low, serious tone that sounded similar to the voice he used when he was being bossy in bed.

"The room is prepped whenever you're ready," a voice said over the phone.

"Okay, I'm on my way," he said to the person and then there was the slamming of the metal door again. "Okay, I've gotta go, but let me know how it goes."

"I will. Good luck with whatever surgery you're performing."

He chuckled, and it was a sound I couldn't get enough of.

"Thanks, Angel. I'll talk to you later."

"Yes, you will. Bye, Luke." I exhaled a long breath, hearing the hesitation in my own voice. There was a decently long pause and had I not heard him breathing on the other side of the phone, I would have thought he'd hung up on me, or the line had been disconnected.

It felt like my sternum wanted to cave into my chest, and the possibility hanging in that pause twisted my gut. The possibility of words neither of us had spoken, but I knew that I at least felt, were obvious within that pause.

"Bye, Hazel," Luke finally said. Five seconds passed before I hung up the phone and reversed out of my parking spot.

The rain dinging off the car, along with the low hum of the music, kept me company on the short drive. My thoughts were in a million different places, and it was nice to get lost in them as the buildings and numerous other cars on the road flew past.

My thoughts first drifted to Michael, but I knew thinking about him would only lead to panicking about something that was well and truly in the past. So, instead, I acknowledged each feeling—terror, guilt, hope, anger, and so many others—and let each of them pass like a wave breaking over the shore. A technique one of those podcasts recommended.

My thoughts about Valerie were more chaotic, and the feelings were scrambled up in what I felt for Luke. But I knew everything with her would end one way or another. My mind immediately went to the worst-case scenario, but I didn't survive an abusive ex-fiancé to be taken down by my boyfriend's abusive ex-wife.

And Luke didn't endure everything with his parents and Valerie to have to worry about her any longer.

When I pulled up to the quaint restaurant, I had decided that I would tell Luke that I loved him that night. Whether it seemed too early didn't matter much anymore, and I felt positive the feeling was mutual. Life was too short to pretend like it wasn't what I felt.

The exterior of the restaurant was a red brick that looked like it had been restored within the past several years. I double-checked the street number on the gold plaque next to the door with the address in Blakely's text before I got out of the car and slung my purse across my body.

The rain had let up enough that I didn't need an umbrella, I just quickly scurried under the awning in front of the door. The black metal doors were heavy, but after a tug, they opened, and the warmth enveloped me.

"Hi, just one today?" a tall blonde woman asked from behind the hostess booth.

"I'm actually meeting a friend, but I'm not sure if she's here yet." I peered around the wall dividing the entrance from the rest of the dining room and searched for Blakely's distinctive dark hair and defined bone structure.

"Did she make a reservation?" the hostess asked as she began tapping at the screen in front of her.

"I'm not sure. It may be under Blakely?"

"Oh, yes. She hasn't arrived yet, but I can take you to your table now."

"That would be great, thanks," I said, returning her smile and following her between the tables.

It was an older building that had been renovated with industrial and contemporary touches in the fixtures and furniture. It fit well within the gentrified area of the city.

"Here you are," she said with a bright smile, motioning to the round wooden table tucked in the back of the restaurant.

"Thanks," I said, returning her smile and taking one of the matching wood chairs.

She handed me one menu while she sat the other in front of the spot across from me and pointed to the drink specials on the small table tent. With another bright smile, she let me know that our waiter would be there momentarily. For longer than necessary, she stood there smiling at me expectantly. When I realized she wasn't walking away, my eyes darted around, wondering if I'd missed something. Or maybe the answer to why she was still standing there would be found at one of the other tables near us. I gave her a hesitant smile, and she finally skipped off like she could think of nothing more rewarding than seating the older couple that had just walked in.

The entire time her smile never faltered, and I felt like I wasn't in on the joke.

Before I opened the menu, I found my phone in my purse and texted Luke to let him know that I had made it to the restaurant. He'd be in surgery for likely more than an hour, so I wasn't expecting a response. I placed my phone screen down on the table next to me and picked up the menu.

It was several pages long, and I wasn't even halfway through when the waiter stopped by to take my drink order. He gave me water when I told him I'd wait for Blakely and added his recommendations for his favorite dishes.

Further into the menu and several minutes later, I was growing more nervous that Blakely hadn't shown up. I peeked at my phone and didn't see any missed texts or calls. Although it's hard to detect a person's real feelings and intentions over text, she seemed genuinely interested in talking and starting over. I was beginning to think the worst had happened, and she was stuck in a ditch somewhere and had even begun typing out a concerned text when the chair across the table was pulled out.

I looked up from my phone, smiling that Blakely had finally arrived, only for the corners of my mouth to drop immediately upon seeing her.

Her black hair was slightly curled, and she was wearing a dress I had contemplated purchasing only a few days prior after seeing it online. If it hadn't been for her red-rimmed eyes that were wide with what I could only describe as pure, outright fear, I wouldn't have known anything was wrong.

"Blakely," I whispered, reaching for her hand that lay on the table and trembling so hard that it moved the wood underneath it.

She jerked her hand back and her eyes widened even more.

My heart thudded in my chest, sensing her fear.

She took in a quick breath and said in a breathy voice, "I'm so sorry. Don't scream."

It was the last thing I heard before there was a sharp stabbing pain in my neck, a cold heat radiating from the point, and then utter and complete blackness.

FIFTY-TWO

Luke

The house was quiet, and it was later than I expected to be home. Sadie greeted me at the door like I'd been gone for years instead of a few hours. I stooped down in the entryway and buried my nose in her coat as I scratched behind her ears.

The plan was to shower, change, and head over to Hazel's apartment to be there when she returned from her lunch with Blakely. She'd been there for almost two hours, and I was continuously checking her location to make sure she hadn't left even after she texted me and said it was going well less than an hour ago.

Nervous didn't even begin to describe how I felt about their impromptu lunch reunion. Blakely had many redeeming qualities and was a good friend, but she was also stubborn and hard to get along with on a good day. I didn't doubt that Hazel could stand up for herself, though, if the need arose.

It only took a few seconds for the water in the shower to begin steaming and just the thought of stepping under the spray made my muscles relax. I stripped off the sweaty scrubs and immediately let the hot water wash away the stress and uncertainty for at least a few minutes.

Since Hazel had catapulted herself into my life, my favorite way to relax had become replaying the multitude of ways and places we'd fucked. I also frequently found myself imagining the ways I wanted to have her and hadn't yet had the opportunity to try. But we had forever; I knew we would try everything, experience all the new things we could, both inside and outside of the bedroom. A lifetime of making new memories.

I was halfway through one of my favorite imaginary scenarios, which included Hazel naked in the bed of my truck, when my phone began ringing from the bathroom counter right outside the shower. I pulled the towel from where I tossed it over the shower door and casually dried off before I stepped out of the shower and immediately grabbed my phone.

It was only a missed call from Josh, and I was slightly disappointed it wasn't Hazel letting me know she was on her way back. I put my phone back on the counter and grabbed jeans and a T-shirt—a navy-blue one that Hazel said she liked—from the dresser in my room. As I draped the wet towel back over the shower door, Josh's name scrolled across my locked phone screen once again.

Begrudgingly, I answered.

"Hello?"

"Where are you?" he asked in a hurry.

"At our house. What's up?" At his clipped, exasperated tone, I instantly stiffened.

"You need to check Hazel's social media. Now."

My heart thundered in my chest at the mention of Hazel. "What the hell are you talking about? I deleted all that shit years ago after the Valerie and Blakely shit went down. Why?"

"Fuck!" he bellowed, and I yanked the phone from my ear. "I'm pulling in the driveway now."

Without another word, he ended the call at the same time I heard the squealing of tires outside.

I met him at the garage door, which he whipped through like a bat out of hell. His face was red with rage as he thrust his phone toward me.

I didn't know what I was expecting—possibly a picture of her and Blakely from lunch or something of the two of us since she'd been keen on snapping photos frequently. But neither of those was the picture that filled the screen.

It was a close-up shot of two faces that were pressed together in familiarity. At the bottom of the photo, you could see partially full wineglasses in their hands like they were toasting, and both were smiling. As usual, Hazel was beautiful, with a slight flush to her cheeks which made me guess it wasn't her first glass. There was nothing wrong with her half of the picture, and there wouldn't have been anything wrong with the picture at all except the person she was standing next to.

Her black hair was pin straight, framing her heart-shaped face. And although her mouth was smiling, Valerie's dead eyes still lacked any warmth.

"Is this some kind of joke, Josh? Because if you're trying to be funny right now, you've missed the mark by several miles."

Josh was still fuming and ripped the phone out of my hand. "No, Luke. You've gotta be fucking kidding me. You really think I'd do something like this? It's not a joke; this is a *real* post on Hazel's *real* account. Look," Josh said as he pointed to the text at the top that had her account handle @hazel.cooper just above the photo.

"It's her account. She hasn't posted in a while, but this photo of her and Valerie was just posted to Hazel's account. Now, look at the caption."

He pointed to the text below the photo like I didn't know what I was looking at. I grabbed the phone back from him and read the few words slowly: "To new neighbors and new friendships." At the end of the caption, there was a wineglass and a red heart emoji. I continued scanning the post, noting that a few dozen people had liked it in the past thirty minutes since it had been posted.

There was too much information to intake and analyze. My mind was racing to a million different conclusions, each of them leading to Hazel being in danger.

My own phone said hers was still located at the restaurant she was supposedly at with Blakely. I dialed her number and tried to tamp down the panic that was threatening to rip through me. I paced the entryway, thrusting Josh's phone back into his unsuspecting hands, as Hazel's phone rang and rang and rang. When her voice mail picked up, I waited and left a simple message asking her to call me back. Then I texted her and locked my phone.

"She's not answering," I told Josh.

"Yeah, I figured as much when you left the voice mail," he quipped.

"Josh, don't fucking joke around right now. I'm in over my head and don't know what the fuck to do. I swear, if anything happens—" My voice cut off because I couldn't actually say the words that were going through my head. Nothing could happen to Hazel; I wouldn't let anything happen to Hazel which meant we needed to move quickly.

"Oh fuck." I was still pacing when Josh showed me his phone once again. "Look at the profile that's tagged in the picture." Josh clicked on it and the entire profile was only pictures of Valerie. In a few of them, her hair was dyed a faded-orange color, but it wasn't difficult to identify that it was still her. Then in the more recent ones, her hair was back to what was very close to her original color. A couple of the photos were just of her, but there were a few taken within the past couple of weeks with both her and Hazel.

The entire room collapsed in on me, and I braced my hand on Josh's shoulder to keep myself standing.

The name at the top of the profile was "Lexi." No last name, just Lexi, but the description read:

ATX
Cat Mom
Go *GREEN*
My motto: expect the unexpected

The last one stopped me. This was all for me. That final line sealed the deal that I was meant to find that profile at some point.

I'd heard the name, that stupid name before, but I couldn't think of where I heard it from. It was Valerie, not Lexi, and the photos proved it unless someone was using her photos. My head was spinning, and I felt like I was in a thick fog until it all clicked together.

Rage like I'd never known pulsed through me in increasing waves. The fog around me lifted, but it was anger, red and intense, that blurred my vision. I looked for the nearest object. My hand landed on a decorative vase that Blakely, of all people, had gifted me last Christmas. It shattered into a million pretty little pieces when I threw it at the wall. It was a good sound, but it didn't do anything to make me feel better.

"Whoa there, dude. I understand this is bad, but I feel like I'm missing something. Why is Valerie pretending to be someone named Lexi?"

I scrubbed my hands down my face and pulled at my hair. "Lexi," I said through clenched teeth, "is Hazel's new neighbor."

Josh's brow furrowed and his eyes narrowed to slits as he peered down at his phone once more. In another few seconds, his confused expression morphed into one of understanding. "You've never met Lexi, I'm assuming?"

I shook my head because in that moment, I was beyond words. And I was already past the realization—I was on to planning and figuring out what the fuck was going on.

"While you contemplate that, I'm going to go get my fucking shoes, and we're going to the restaurant where her fucking phone says she is."

"Do you really think she's still there? I don't think—" I stopped my retreat from the entryway and cut off Josh's words by whirling on him.

"Do not finish that sentence. Do you have a better idea?"

Gauging my reaction, Josh only shook his head and waved me off.

In a matter of seconds, I was leaning against the doorframe of my closet, pulling on my boots. It wasn't even a thought to grab my gun and holster and position it at my back, partially below my belt. I grabbed another loaded magazine and shoved it into my front pocket.

I didn't know what I was walking into, but I knew Valerie had been planning this. We were so many steps behind her that I couldn't even begin to fathom where she was going with it. We thought she had been biding her time or taking a back seat and settling on mind games, but she had been plotting.

How she figured out where Hazel was moving and had leased the unit immediately next to hers under a fake name was beyond me. But I had sorely underestimated her and doing so meant Hazel was in danger.

I positioned the gun that I hadn't carried in a while at my back and tried to keep the anger at bay. I hadn't carried a gun since just before I left Valerie.

Getting angry and letting it take over was not going to help find Hazel, even if it was doing a damn good job of overwhelming the rest of my emotions and rationale. I would keep a lid on it if it meant we had a better chance of finding her. I did not have the luxury of panic.

I shut off the light to the bathroom and pulled my phone back out to try Hazel again. It continued ringing like it had before, but I lifted it from my ear when something outside of my bedroom window caught my eye.

We hadn't left the house yet, and I was already pulling my gun from where I'd just placed it. Slowly, I pushed aside the partially open curtain and lifted one of the blinds. I squinted through the small opening and tried to identify what I'd seen. I scanned the ground between the houses, looking carefully from left to right, but didn't see anything out of the ordinary there.

I parted the dark curtains and lifted the blinds all the way to the top of the window with one quick pull of the cord. With the curtains parted and the blinds open, it was obvious what had caught my attention. The space between the houses was empty, just as I thought it would be, but written on what used to be Hazel's bedroom window, in large, red letters, were the words: Game's Almost Over.

My gun was at the ready, poised in front of me, but as I read the text, I lowered it, realizing the threat wasn't in front of me. I'd heard those words recently, directly from Valerie's mouth and in the same breath as when she claimed picking Hazel over her would be the worst decision and that I was lying to myself. As if there was a decision to be made or she knew my thoughts, she said that it would all be over soon enough.

I heard Josh enter the room behind me and when he noticed the words on Hazel's old window, he mumbled a few curses. "That's not blood, is it?" he asked, worry evident in his voice.

I shook my head. It was paint, that much I could tell by the opacity and the way the bottom of each letter only ran slightly. Her intention was obvious, though. She wanted to make me second-guess if it was blood. But I tried to take what little comfort I could in the fact that it wasn't and that she'd used the word "almost." It would have been simpler to just write Game Over.

"I cleaned up the broken vase, and I tried to call Blakely. No answer, though. So, let's go," Josh said, snapping a picture of the window and turning on his heels. "Do you want me to drive, or —?" he asked, throwing open the front door.

I locked the door, and we jogged down the porch stairs to where I'd left my truck parked in the driveway. "No, I'll drive, you call the restaurant and see if they're still there or whatever else you can find out."

I needed some type of control and driving seemed to be the only thing I could control in that moment.

When I input the address into the truck's GPS, it said the place was twenty minutes away, but we didn't have time to waste. I would make it in at least half the time.

FIFTY-THREE

Luke

Josh put the call with the restaurant on speakerphone, but they didn't have much to say. The man we spoke to didn't have a clue who we were talking about and claimed he was uncomfortable providing people he didn't know with that kind of information anyway. My hands began to hurt from the tight grip I was keeping on the steering wheel, and my jaw was sore from clenching it.

Finally, after Josh had gone back and forth with the guy for several minutes, I reached over and ended the call. Then I proceeded to break every speed limit, run every red light, and pass on the shoulder to get to the restaurant in nearly ten minutes. I only slowed long enough to make sure we were at the correct place. I found a spot near the front door and leaped from the truck.

I spotted Hazel's car also in a spot by the door, and I couldn't decide if it was a good or a bad sign that it was still there. I peered through the windows as Josh headed inside, but there wasn't a fucking thing out of place.

When I opened the large black door and stepped into the

warm restaurant, it was like stepping back in time. The memories assaulted me from every direction. Although it had changed since, I would never be able to forget the restaurant where Valerie and I had our first date and my life changed forever. It was a time I would do anything not to ever think about again. But the restaurant was a time capsule holding and spawning so many of those memories.

There wasn't anyone up front at the hostess stand, although there were a few people at the tables I could see over the short, half wall on the opposite side of it. Raised voices from the back of the restaurant meant I didn't have to go searching for my brother. I brushed past a man asking me to wait to be seated as I headed toward the sound of Josh's voice.

"Yes, I saw her and her, but not this one," said a tall, blonde woman who was probably only in college. You could tell she was unsettled by Josh's attitude. When I approached, the blonde's eyes went wide. I would usually try to temper my approach—soften my eyes, relax my jaw, seem shorter and less scary—but I didn't have the capability at that moment.

"What's up?" I directed the question at my brother, but an older man behind him began talking.

"You cannot just barge into my restaurant and demand—"

I pushed Josh to the side and twisted the man's shirt into my fist. Just like the blonde, his eyes went wide with terror. "Someone has just kidnapped the fucking love of my life from your restaurant. I will do as I damn well please if it means getting her back. And so help me God if you stand in my way..." I let the man go along with the threat, and he slumped back into the wall, breathless and shaken up. Turning back to Josh, I asked again. "What's going on?"

Josh's eyebrows were raised, but he didn't say anything about my behavior.

"The hostess says she seated Hazel first at this table, then approximately fifteen minutes later, she seated Blakely. Apparently, Blake looked upset but made some excuse about a bad breakup and just needing her friend, a.k.a. Hazel."

"I knew she was lying," the hostess interrupted. "She was shaking like a leaf, like she was terrified. I pointed to the table where the first girl was sitting, and it wasn't a few minutes later that I asked the waiter if the other girl had stopped crying. That's when he told me the table had walked out."

There were tears in her eyes, and I knew she was telling the truth. "Tell him about the reservation," Josh prompted, and the woman nodded.

"It was a woman that called to make the reservation. She said she was going to surprise her two best friends, and all I needed to do was make a reservation under the name Blakely and seat them at that exact table so she could sneak up on them. Since, you know, you can't see the door from the table or vice versa."

"Did the caller give you her name?"

"Yes, her name was Lexi. Lexi Shepherd."

My blood boiled and my fury spiked at that name. She was setting everything up so I would play into the palm of her hand, and my lack of control was maddening. What was her endgame? She said she wanted me, but what would she do to Hazel in the meantime?

This was my fault, and I should have listened to my gut. The text message from Blakely and her random change of heart when it came to talking to the police didn't seem right from the start. I knew there was more to her invitation than a lunch date to make amends. It meant that Blakely was also a part of the plan. It wasn't possible that her being here was a mere coincidence.

"Find Blakely," I directed Josh. "Call Amanda or any of the guys, but she was involved, and we need to know what the fuck she knows *now*." He didn't hesitate to thank the hostess before heading off in the direction of the front door to track down our missing, back-stabbing friend.

While he tried to find her, I hunted for Hazel's phone. It said it was still in the restaurant, so I searched around the other tables, apologizing to each patron when I bumped into them or found myself in their personal space. Once I knew the dining room was clear, I started toward the back and had a thought.

I took an immediate right, knocking on the opaque glass of the women's restroom door, but not waiting for a response. Luckily, the space was empty, and in the trash can near the door, I found exactly what I assumed would be in there somewhere.

Tucked beneath several paper towels was Hazel's little black purse. I carefully pulled it from the can and set it on the counter. Right inside was her phone, placed in the same pocket where she usually kept it. The inside of her bag smelled like the perfume she kept in it, and a memory of nuzzling her neck right after she'd put it on made my heart constrict.

And then true fear set in. They had left the restaurant at least two hours before and the entire time, I thought she was having lunch. But her phone was shoved down to the bottom of the fucking trash can along with the rest of her belongings.

Valerie knew. She had to have known that the location was on and that I would find Hazel's stuff eventually.

Knowing that her phone may not provide any clues, I pressed the unlock button anyway. A string of profanities spilled from my lips as I saw the new photo placed just behind the time and the missed call notifications from me.

My chest constricted as I swiped away the notifications and saw the picture that had replaced the one she'd taken of herself and Sadie. It was a blood-chilling and unnerving sight, and I dropped it to the counter like it had stung me. Hazel, wearing the same jeans and sweater I'd seen her dress in earlier that day, was bound and lay on her side with her knees pressed to her chest. She was in the trunk of a car, given how tight the space was, with her arms and ankles bound using a rope. Her mouth, the soft, pink lips I'd kissed a million times and planned to kiss a million more, were covered in silver duct tape. Her eyes were open, but she was looking somewhere too far in the distance.

Time stood still as I dissected the photo. I was utterly petrified for Hazel. I'd promised that I would protect her, that I wouldn't let Valerie anywhere near her. And I'd wholly and completely failed in the worst possible way.

"Dude, I've been looking fucking everywhere for you, what are you—" Josh began to ask when he busted into the bathroom, but when he glanced over my shoulder, his words cut off.

"Fuck!" he roared, and it echoed off the walls. He paced to the door and back, fists clenching and unclenching as I stood there frozen. "Look, I had the manager guy pull the security tapes. They went through the back of the place in the alley."

"Have you gone back there?" I asked, replacing Hazel's phone in her purse and taking it with me as we hustled into the dark hallway. I slammed into the emergency exit door and stumbled into the alley. I didn't know what I expected, but I was disappointed that it wasn't immediately apparent where they went or what the fuck was going on.

"Wait, the camera's here," Josh pointed to it over his left shoulder and just above the restaurant's dumpster was a camera pointing to where we stood. "We're standing where the car was, but Valerie walked to the dumpster before she got in the car."

Josh retraced Valerie's steps, maneuvering around trash at the front of the dumpster until he kneeled to the side of it. While he looked around, I did the only thing I could think of and tried to call the number Valerie had been texting me from. It didn't even ring, just gave the normal message stating the number had been disconnected. That would have been too easy anyway.

When Josh popped back up, he was holding a manila envelope. He came back and handed the envelope to me.

"This appears to be for you." Sure enough, written on the front in Valerie's loopy, large handwriting was "Bear."

The envelope was heavy in my hands. If I could have done anything besides open it, I would have. Valerie had already proven how sick she was, but I knew it was only going to get worse.

My stomach twisted, and I had to choke back bile as I pulled a stack of photos from the envelope. The first one was enough to tell me what to expect from the rest. Hazel and I were standing on her front porch. She was halfway hidden by the partially open front door and her eyes were not on me but on her surroundings. My hand was reaching for her, and I knew the moment it was taken. When I had shown up, terrified Michael was going to hurt her again. The vulnerability in her sad eyes tore me apart.

Each photo was even more private than the previous. The last one was a photo from just outside of Hazel's bedroom at her apartment. It appeared to have been taken from just across the street and was level with her second-floor unit. All you could see of me were my legs and feet as Hazel straddled me on top of her bed. She was in the throes of pleasure, her hands twisted in her long, brown hair and her head thrown back. The contours of her back cast careful shadows across her ivory skin. It would have been a beautiful picture had it not been taken under those circumstances. And to only make matters worse, Valerie had drawn over Hazel's head a halo and, on her back, wings—angel's wings. Written in her signature handwriting on the bottom of the photo was, "Maybe your Angel deserves her wings."

I flung the pictures at the emergency exit door and yelled at the sky. Hazel was the only thing that mattered anymore. The rest of the world could go fuck itself because I was about to burn it all down to bring her home safe. Fuck it, she was my home.

The intention of Valerie's words was obvious—Hazel would have to die to get her wings. But I couldn't live in a world where Hazel didn't exist.

"Did you get a hold of Blakely?" I asked Josh, having completely forgotten about what he was doing before he busted down the bathroom door.

He stooped back down, retrieved the photos, and reviewed them as he shook his head and ignored my outburst. "Her phone's off, of course. I called Amanda, though, and she said

Blakely told her that she was driving to Arkansas to see her parents. Then I called Reed, and he said the same thing."

"Keep trying to call her. We need to know how the fuck she got involved and what Valerie told her."

"I will, man, but do you really think it's going to get us anywhere? The way the hostess made it seem, Blake was torn up. Don't you think it makes more sense that Valerie only used Blakely to maybe get Hazel here under false pretenses?"

"I don't know what makes fucking sense anymore!" I bellowed and whirled on Josh. He stood from his position near the ground, still unfazed. Other than Valerie, it was Josh who had put up with my anger and outbursts for years; he knew when to fight and when to let me be.

"We're going to find her," he said.

"How?" I asked, unconvinced he had any type of plan that would mean finding Hazel at that moment.

"I don't fucking know, but what you're doing right now isn't going to help."

I took a deep breath and tried to slow my rapidly beating heart. He was right and pacing back and forth down the alley, gripping Hazel's purse in my hand, and yelling at him was not going to get me to her quicker.

Rationalizing Valerie's motives and predicting her behavior was almost completely impossible. Valerie was not thinking like a normal person; a person does not kidnap their ex-husband's new girlfriend because they're jealous. But either way, whether she was rational or not, I knew Valerie well. After years of being together, I had begun to follow her reasoning as well as explain her behaviors and her thought processes. It was when that had begun to happen that I took a step back and reevaluated our relationship. Nonetheless, I could follow her train of thought.

I just had to do it again. Think like Valerie.

"The most important thing to Valerie is me. She said all she wants is me." Valerie may not have been a good person, but she didn't lie. She always told the truth, or at least her version of it.

So, we could take her words at face value. We had at least that to fall back on.

Josh nodded, pressing his phone to his ear, likely trying to get ahold of Blakely again.

"Right, so the point of taking Hazel...?" Josh said with a frustrated sigh.

"Getting my attention," I stated.

"And she clearly wanted you to see her in the video and find the photos—she was perfectly in the frame the entire time," he added.

The possibilities of what Valerie was doing to Hazel at the very moment we were standing there gnawed at me relentlessly. Valerie knew that Hazel mattered to me, and she was sure to make her suffer. My eye began twitching at the thought of Hazel tied up in the trunk of a car and transported to some unknown location where Valerie would likely do her worst. My mouth was dry, and I couldn't swallow past my fear.

"So, it's most likely Valerie took her somewhere you would know, right? Otherwise, she's going to bide her time and appear just when she wants to. She hasn't tried to contact you..."

I began filtering through the memories of anything Valerie had ever said to me. I went over and over it all. The wind picked up around us, and I held out my hand to Josh for the photos.

I gripped them tightly, shuffling them back into order and flipping through them. Her text messages didn't contain much, and neither did our conversation at the restaurant. But recently, in the letters she sent to the clinic, there were three dates she mentioned, and they were fresh in my mind after reading her own version of each. Our first date was from the first letter, the date I proposed was the second, and the third was the night I almost killed that random guy for accidentally bumping into her.

She'd specifically mentioned those three for a reason—everything Valerie had done up until that point had been for a reason. And something told me in my gut that the answer had to do with that night at Murphy's. If she wanted me to find her, I knew that's where she'd go.

"Have you called work to tell them you won't be there?" I asked Josh, who was staring intently at his phone.

"Reed is going over to Hazel's apartment just in case, and no. The bar's closed until Monday for the Thanksgiving holiday and Rhonda is taking the opportunity to do some renovations."

"She's at Murphy's. Hopefully, they're both there."

"Whoa, whoa. I mean, fine, we can go by there, but you totally just came up with that out of left field. Care to explain your thinking?" Josh asked as I shoved the photos back into the manila envelope and jogged down the alleyway and back around the building.

"I'll explain on the way," I said, hearing Josh's footfalls close behind me.

When we were both in the truck and I was flying down the highway, explaining my thoughts to Josh, I started to pray for the first time since my parents died. It felt like the right thing to do, and I knew I needed all the help I could find to get there on time or find Hazel at all.

FIFTY-FOUR

Hazel

All there was, was pain. Pain in my neck like small, hot needles pressing into my skin. Pain around my wrists and ankles burning like fire. Pain in my nose radiating up into my skull. Pain in my mouth because it was so dry.

I tried to suck in a breath through my nose, but the pressure was too intense, and my lungs didn't want to receive the air as they fought against me. My hand reflexively tried to grasp my neck and my chest, but I couldn't move.

My wrists were bound and rubbing at my nearly raw skin based on the burning ache.

My eyelids fluttered, but I couldn't force them open. It didn't feel like anything was hindering me from opening them besides my own exhausted body.

I was so tired.

With as much force as I could muster, I tried to move my legs, but as I thought, they were also bound. Even in my partially conscious state, I knew I was tied to a metal chair. I could feel the cold metal beneath me and through my jeans.

I groaned as the pounding in my head intensified and that's when I realized my mouth was taped closed.

If it was possible in the moment, I would have begun panicking, but a thick fog was clouding every thought besides the pain. It was an all-consuming, mind-numbing pain that meant there wasn't room for much else.

Nearby, I heard shuffling as I tried once again to fill my lungs with air. Just as I had comprehended the sound, the tape on my mouth was unceremoniously ripped from my face.

I'm not sure what sound left my mouth, but it was enough to make the person chuckle.

"You were out for a while, sweetie. I'm so glad you could join us." I could feel the heat of the person—a woman based on the voice—standing right up against me, but her voice sounded like it was emanating from across the room, bouncing off the walls to reach me.

The room was spinning as I was able to open my eyes.

"I'll give you a second to wake up."

And she did. I could feel her warmth and the brush of her fingers was soft against my heated skin. She pushed my hair out of my face and gave me a few sips of water which did little to quench my miserable thirst.

My eyes opened wider this time, and the woman instructed someone else to turn down the lights. Without the brightness, it was easier to focus, but then, it was almost too dark to see anything that wasn't a few feet in front of me.

It was hard to move my head at all without the excruciating pain, so all I could see of the woman right in front of me were her black jeans and belt. She brushed my hair back again and gave me another sip of water before she kneeled in front of me.

The black hair was familiar and so was the perfect symmetry of her heart-shaped face. Once my eyes focused, I realized who it was.

"Le—Lexi?" A simple name took more effort than had ever been necessary to croak from my dry lips.

Her mouth curled into a smile, and she barked a quick laugh. "Oh sweetie, you're so close and so fucking stupid."

FIFTY-FIVE

Luke

"That makes sense," Josh said after I explained my thought process, beginning with how the night at Murphy's happened years before, how she mentioned it in her letter and everything in between.

The closer we got to Murphy's, the more of a pull I felt. Maybe it was all in my head—actually, it was definitely all in my head—but it was like I felt closer to Hazel.

It had been three hours since Hazel had been taken when we pulled up to the bar. Nothing seemed out of place as the sun set behind the dark building, and I hoped I hadn't made a severe misjudgment. There weren't any cars in the quiet lot, but as I knew all too well, there was a back door and a parking lot on the opposite side with employee-only parking.

With absolutely no fucks left to give, I parked in a front-row spot right by the door.

"Do you think we should call the police?" Josh asked, staring at his place of work in concern.

"We don't have time for them to get here, and we don't know

if Hazel is actually here. Stay here and call them. If anything happens besides the police getting here, then call me."

"You seriously want me to sit here while you go inside by yourself?"

I nodded, pulling my gun from the holster and double-checking that it was loaded. "Yes, because whether you fucking like it or not, you're my little brother and I'm not letting you go in there. I also need someone to watch my back, and I wouldn't want anyone else but you doing that."

Josh contemplated it for a moment but swallowed and nodded. "Fine, but if anything goes south, I'm coming in after you. Also, Rhonda probably has the back door unlocked for the reno. That way, you don't have to kick the door in."

"Yeah, okay. Thanks, man," I said and closed the door.

I crouched low and carefully observed my surroundings as I made my way to the front door. The gravel of the parking lot crunched beneath my boots, giving away my approach to anyone within hearing distance. When I made it to the door, I stayed low and tried the handle. Like Josh said, it was fucking locked. Plan *B*.

Staying close to the building, I rounded the corner with my gun drawn. I was officially out of sight of Josh and on my own as I continued down the side street. There were several dumpsters full of trash that made the smell nearly unbearable. I quickened my pace.

I approached the next corner, which should have taken me directly to the back of the building. It had been a while since I'd been back behind our favorite bar, but if my memory was correct, the door was only a few feet away from the corner where I stood.

With a deep breath, I poked my head around the corner and even with a quick glance, I didn't notice anyone or anything out of place. I chanced one more look just to be sure and ended with the same result.

It was entirely possible that Valerie had left both entrances unattended—especially if she wanted to give me easy access to find her. But as the thought crossed my mind, two large arms gripped me from behind. Taken by surprise and out of practice, the man easily forced the gun from my grip in only a few seconds.

How the fuck I had missed him, I wasn't sure, but I didn't have time to contemplate my errors. I couldn't see the guy behind me, but he had to be at least my size, maybe taller. And damn, he was fucking strong.

I stumbled forward, his arms grappling to tighten around my neck, and then slammed him backward into the brick wall behind us. His back hit it with a thud, and his arms loosened just enough for me to elbow him in the ribs and throw my head back. It connected perfectly with his nose, producing a satisfying crunch.

I freed myself, and I turned to face him just as his fist came centimeters from my nose. He wasn't letting up even after being shoved into a brick wall by a two-hundred-and-fifty-pound man and being headbutted in the face. Blood was pouring from his nose, but he didn't seem to care as he lunged at me again.

It only took a few seconds to realize he was big, but he was also sloppy.

I spotted my gun several feet away, but I didn't have the time to grab it before he came at me again.

That time it was a right hook that I predicted immediately as he dipped his shoulders lower. As he moved forward, I caught him with a check hook, stepping backward as he moved forward and landing it square on his jaw. He was too aggressive for his own good, and the spray of blood from his mouth was glorious and wide.

There was a sense of relief in my muscles at releasing stress and anger upon someone who deserved it. He tripped over his own feet and landed on the ground, clutching his jaw and cursing. I could have gone for my gun, but I didn't. I wanted to feel the bones in his face break beneath my knuckles.

With a few final hits to the face, and blood covering his gnarled features, he was out cold and possibly dead. I had an ache in my hands that I hadn't felt in years, but the relief I'd felt only moments before evaporated as I grabbed my gun and headed toward the back door, not sparing a glance back at the mangled guy on the ground.

Inside Murphy's, it smelled like a mixture of liquor, paint, and cleaning supplies. The back door of the building opened directly to the hallway with the bathrooms and a door with a sign labeled Employees Only. It was the door Valerie and I had slipped through years ago, which took you to the second floor and the storage areas.

If they were there, I expected them to be up on the second floor, but I checked out the first level before heading up there. With my gun poised in front of me, I swept the first floor. I searched behind the bar, the bathrooms, and the poolroom and found nothing besides materials for the renovations Josh mentioned.

With the first floor clear, I headed through the employees-only door and up the steep, dark staircase. It was so narrow that my shoulders barely fit, and although I'd never been claustrophobic, the illusion that the walls were closing in on me was intense. Once I stepped onto the first landing, my steps as quiet as possible, I expected to find another attack waiting. But there wasn't anyone there.

I climbed the rest of the steps, sure there would be another ambush at the top, but again, nothing. Had she really placed the protection of the entire building on the shoulders of one man?

It was so eerily quiet that even my soft steps and heavy breathing seemed loud in the dense silence. The entire second floor was nearly pitch black. The only light came from the gaps between the boarded-up windows around the entire space. Boxes and boxes of liquor and beer and bar supplies were piled in every corner. Up there, it was easier to recognize that the bar was a renovated house based on the layout of the space. There was the main room right off the stairs, with a hallway leading to several smaller rooms immediately to my right.

I thought maybe I'd been wrong, and the man downstairs was just a decoy based on the silence and lack of movement until I heard a laugh from the end of the hallway.

It was a laugh I knew all too well, but it wasn't Hazel's. That laugh was dark and filled with cruelty few would likely ever know, so I walked toward it.

My heart thundered in my chest, and I tightened my grip on my gun. I battled with myself, both hoping Hazel was there and praying she wasn't.

Another laugh erupted from the last room on the right, and I let my gun lead me through the doorway. It took everything in me, all of the control I could muster, to not shoot Valerie on sight.

She was poised behind Hazel, who was slumped back in a chair in the middle of the room. Seeing the state she was in felt like my heart was being ripped out of my chest. Her hair was tangled and falling behind the metal chair that was screwed into the ground. Her hands and legs were bound to the chair and the duct tape was still over her mouth. Her nose was likely broken based on the amount of blood running down her face.

What I wouldn't have done to take all her pain away, to trade places with her or go back even a few hours before and stop her from leaving me at all.

"I'm so glad you could join us," Valerie said as she moved slightly to the left so I could clearly see the gun I figured she had. It was pressed against Hazel's head.

I opened my mouth, about to tell her to put down the gun when she raised her hand in warning. "No, don't start, Bear. This is how this is going to go: I'm going to talk, and you're going to listen. You will only speak when I ask you a direct question, otherwise, I will shoot your little Angel. Got it?"

I seethed and I could feel my pulse quickening.

"That was a question, Bear. You should answer it."

"Got it," I said through clenched teeth. I didn't want to take my eyes off Valerie, but I did a quick scan of the room. It was practically empty save for a few boxes stacked in the far-left corner and a few more in the opposite corner against a door that led to the room next to us.

But there was no one else there.

"Great," she said, the tone of her voice rising a bit with her approval that I was listening. "Now, gently place your gun on the floor and kick it to me."

"You can't be fucking serious," I said. There was no fucking way I was dropping my gun when she had one pointed at Hazel's head.

"Oh, but I am, Bear. What part of all of this makes you think that I'm not fucking serious? Now, I'll give you a pass for talking out of turn just this once, but next time, I'm going to hurt Hazel. So, kick the gun to me, otherwise, I will ensure she is in a significant amount of pain."

I wanted to just shoot Valerie right then and there, but that meant gambling with Hazel's safety. I'd figure out another way to get us both out of it; there had to be another way.

Without another viable option, I flicked the safety on and placed my gun on the floor before kicking it until it came to rest directly under the chair Hazel was bound to.

"Good job. I knew you'd make the right decision. Now, we can talk without the pesky issue of pointing guns at one another getting in the way." She smiled a saccharine smile, and I bit my tongue.

Hazel's head fell from one side to the other, and a pained groan forced its way through the silver tape. Every muscle in my body tensed. The red marks on her wrists where the rope had rubbed and burned were raw and looked painful. Her ankles were partially covered by her jeans, but the rope was flush with her skin there and was sure to look the same as her wrists. Her hair, in its tangled mess, fell behind her shoulder as she rolled her head to the opposite side, exposing her neck and another irritated mark right below her jawline.

And those, along with her nose, were only the injuries I could see. There was no telling what else Valerie had subjected her to.

"Don't worry about her, Bear," Valerie said, noticing my thoughtful examination of Hazel. "She'll be with us shortly. I couldn't leave her out of all the fun completely, but for now, I want just you and I to talk. It's been too long since we've had a real conversation, and if you actually participate—when prompted, of course—then this will end up a whole hell of a lot better for your Angel."

My Angel. The way she said it was repulsive, and for once, I didn't think of the scared yet incredible magnetic woman with the halo headband. No, I remembered the photograph Valerie had taken of Hazel with angel wings, a halo.

"It appears," she said, glancing out the window over her shoulder. "That you enjoyed the little gift I left you."

If it weren't for her peeking over her shoulder and the man who likely still lay on the ground outside, I wouldn't have known what she was referring to. Her eyes flitted down to my hands fisted at my side like she was looking to see how bloody and bruised they already were.

"That was honestly a twofold gift. On the one hand, I really wanted to watch you beat the shit out of someone again and then come up here extra pissed and worked up. But it was really a gift for you, too. I know how much you like to let out all that aggression that's likely pent up. Don't you feel better now?"

My fingers twitched and nervous energy pulsed through me. It used to work—making someone submit, hearing their bones fracture under my fists or anything in between. But it was also the pain I was subjected to that kept me grounded. And at least in the few minutes I was in the makeshift ring, I felt *something* instead of the nothing I had become used to.

I craved that release like it was a high. I was angry at my father for killing my mother; I was angry at my mother for not seeking help, and I was mad at myself for letting it happen. I was mad at the entire fucking world.

Fighting was easy and convenient—that's all there was to it. It was a convenient and easy crutch, and one that I had to learn wasn't necessary. But just because I didn't fight anymore—didn't need to—didn't mean I wasn't going to fight for *her*.

I would never stop fighting for her.

"Answer me, Bear," Valerie said.

"Not necessarily."

She sighed. "Well, that's a shame. To be honest, I did think he would be a more formidable opponent, but it appears that even in your retirement, you're a force to be reckoned with."

I stood in front of her silently, not giving her any reason to hurt Hazel more than she already had.

"I know your patience is probably wearing thin—I can see the vein in your forehead pulsing as well as your eye twitching from here. So, I'll try to speed things along the best I can." As she spoke, she shifted the barrel of the gun in front of Hazel's face and used it to push all of her hair over her shoulders.

"Do you know how much I love you?" she asked and then glanced up at me expectantly.

"I guess I don't."

Valerie shuffled her weight on her feet and continued running the muzzle of the gun over Hazel's shoulders.

"Your answer doesn't surprise me because I think if you did know how much I love you, then we wouldn't be in this situation. We'd still be married, happily in love. I might be pregnant, maybe even with our second child. Our life would be beautiful, but instead, we're standing in here. You forced me to kidnap this innocent woman and—"

"I didn't force you to do jack shit."

Without hesitation, Valerie tossed the gun in her hand and slammed the back of it against Hazel's finger. The sickening crunch made me lunge forward and quicker than I gave her credit for, Valerie had the gun pointed at me.

Hazel gasped with the pain and groaned against the tape. Her finger was broken, and it had pulled her from her unconscious state for at least a moment. Valerie's other hand was twisted in Hazel's hair, forcing her head back at an awkward angle. I was vibrating with anger. Hazel's pained noises were the worst sounds I'd ever heard.

"What did I fucking say, Luke?" Valerie questioned over Hazel's muffled groans. The transition from the pet name—whether I liked it or not—to my actual name was a difference I noted.

Hazel's eyes were unfocused as she stared at the ceiling. She kept trying to force her eyes open, but it wasn't working. Her face was contorted in severe pain, and all I could do was stand there and watch it happen.

"Now that you see I'm very fucking serious, let me continue."

FIFTY-SIX

Luke

Like nothing had happened, she switched her tone from foaming at the mouth to casual conversation.

"I knew I loved you the day I met you. Even when we were just friends, I loved you like no one else has ever loved another person, and I knew we were meant to be together, to put it simply. Although it's not really simple. See, I love you for all of who you are. There isn't one thing that I don't love about you, but what really fascinated me at the beginning was the darkness I saw inside of you. It was almost otherworldly the way it swallowed you," she said, lost in thought and memories.

"And most women, hell most people in general, would have run the other direction when faced with what you could turn into—such a beautiful monster full of beautifully explosive rage. But *I* wanted to drown in it, and you let me. We were such a good pair, and we still can be. We *will* be a good pair again once you stop lying to yourself and listening to all of the outsiders' opinions."

She took a deep breath and narrowed her eyes at me.

"When I found out that you were seeing this one," she said,

tugging on Hazel's hair once again. "I was so disappointed. We were a good team because I could handle your darkness. But she can't. She's too broken for that. I mean, can you imagine how hard that's going to be on her—being with you when her fiancé beat the shit out of her? She needs someone that's more suited for the light, and you, well, you just need me. She's going to make you miserable. She won't challenge you the way I do, and she—"

Valerie's monologue was cut short by a louder, broken sob. I hadn't taken my eyes off the gun Valerie pressed into the base of Hazel's neck. Every once in a while, Hazel's eyes would open slightly and nearly focus on me just to fall closed again. After several attempts, they stayed open long enough for her to register me, and that's when she sobbed. There weren't any tears, but there was enough sadness in her eyes that she didn't need them. I could see the weight of the pain as her chest heaved labored breaths that rocked her entire body.

Valerie leaned forward and smiled when she saw Hazel was conscious. "Perfect timing, sweetie," Valerie said, patting the top of Hazel's head. She lurched forward at the contact and shouted in pain. I was going to break my teeth with the force I was clenching them.

"So, while I have both of your attention, I would like to explain why I chose this location. It holds a special place in my heart, and I'm sure it holds a special place in your heart, too, Bear." As she spoke, her sickly sweet voice crawling over my skin, she stepped around Hazel for the first time since I'd walked into the room. "Hazel, let me tell you about my favorite memory in this little bar. Bear and I, we spent a lot of time at this place with our so-called friends. Of course, this is long before they turned him against me and made him question the love of his life, but that's neither here nor there."

Valerie's steps were slow and measured as she positioned herself between us. Hazel was only about six feet away from me, but with Valerie between us, it seemed like miles. The gun was still trained on Hazel, taunting me with the possibility that Valerie could snap at any moment, but Hazel's eyes were glued to me. In the dim light of the room, it was difficult to see anything as the sun set outside. But through my eyes, I tried to show her everything I was feeling. I hoped she could see the pain, sorrow, disappointment, and the love.

I hoped she knew I loved her because the possibility of both of us leaving that room alive seemed to disappear the longer Valerie spoke. Hazel wouldn't die; I'd do anything to make sure that didn't happen. But I didn't want to die without her knowing how much I loved her.

Even if she would only ever be able to see it in my eyes, that would have to be enough.

"My favorite night was actually almost four years ago to this day. We'd just celebrated Thanksgiving with all of our friends, and everything was so good. It was probably the happiest I'd ever been. Well, we came here as we always did, but that night was special. You see, Hazel," Valerie said, turning slightly in Hazel's direction but making sure I stayed in her peripheral. "Bear and I were on the dance floor, which was our favorite place to be back then, when this man bumped into me. He'd been watching me all night, taunting and teasing me, really. Bear even saw it, didn't you?"

Valerie didn't take her eyes from Hazel and neither did I. As I said, "Yes," I shook my head no. She was embellishing like she always did with every story she told. She was a pathological liar and a raging narcissist. The guy that bumped into her did nothing but accidentally brush against her as he tried to squeeze past us on the crowded floor, but back then, when Valerie spoke, I listened. She had manipulated me to the point of believing anything that came out of her mouth because no one else would ever love me the way she did.

"And finally, when he almost ran me over, knocking me to the ground, Bear lost it. He hauled me up, pushed me behind him and tore into the man. It took all of the bouncers in the place to pull him from the bar. We were thrown out of the back, and God, you should have seen him. He was covered in blood, there was blood all over the dance floor, and there was a fire in his eyes that I just wanted to burn in." Valerie glanced back at me and licked her lips. "The man didn't press charges because he himself had warrants out for his arrest, but my Bear could have killed him. And the thought of that..." She trailed off, glancing back over at Hazel, who was more awake now. "Sex was always best when you were pissed, and that night was no different. We came up to this exact room and fucked like it was the only thing that would keep us alive."

Valerie, in her high-heeled black boots, closed the distance between us and, with the gun still trained on Hazel, ran her manicured nails down my chest, over my stomach until she cupped me through my jeans. Her touch was revolting and made me want to shed my skin as I felt the warmth of her palm through the denim. I tried to back away, but she just gripped me harder. My stomach rolled and I made the mistake of looking at Hazel over Valerie's shoulder.

A single tear fell down her already bruised cheek and mixed with the dried blood just below her nose.

"And the entire time you were fucking me up against the boxes, all I could think was that I would love you for my entire life. We even had a conversation while you were *inside* of me." She gritted her teeth, pushed closer to me, and squeezed me harder, digging her nails into the fabric. "Do you remember what I told you?"

Fuming, I shook my head, knowing it would only upset her more if I didn't feed into her story and go along with her lies.

"I do, of course, but I remember all of it. I told you that you could have killed that fucking guy, and you said you would kill someone for the people you love, for me. And I felt it, Bear. I knew you meant it, and I told you that killing someone for the person you love is the most romantic gesture I could think of; it shows a certain amount of devotion and bravery that nothing else can compare to. And you agreed, Bear," she said, removing her hand from my pants to drag her nails down my face. "You told me that that was your version of real, true love."

She was so close I could feel her breath on my skin, and even in the cold room, I was sweating through my clothes.

"Do you still think that, Bear? That killing someone is a way of showing your love for someone else? And don't hold back this time, I want to hear what you have to say."

I heaved a momentary sigh of relief when she stepped back. I had a minimal recollection of that conversation, and it was probably because I was in the throes of sex. It was too easy to get lost in my head when I was high off the adrenaline of beating the shit out of someone combined with sex hormones. During our relationship, Valerie learned that the best way to get me to do something or agree to something was during sex, although, she had no issue manipulating me outside of the bedroom either. Back then, nothing I said during that act should have been used against me.

But I vaguely remembered her mumbling those words.

Valerie cleared her throat, drawing my attention back to her, and looked at me expectantly.

"I think it's all subjective," I said, unable to think of anything else in the moment.

She shook her head like that was not what she wanted to hear. "Don't lie to me. I know you would kill someone for the person you love. To protect the person you love most in this world, you would kill someone," she stated, not questioning that I would still do it, and I would.

"Yes," I said, locking eyes with Hazel. There were more tears now, and I was about to expand on my answer when something to the right of the room caught my eye. The door between our room and the next barely moved on its hinges, but it did.

I'm not sure how he did it, but Josh managed to open the door just enough to peek through the small opening without making a sound. He was lucky—as were we all—that Valerie's back was to the door. Her right hand held the gun steady, still pointing it at Hazel, while she watched me to her left.

Once I noticed Josh, I quickly averted my eyes back to Valerie. I didn't know what he had planned, but I hoped my little brother had something up his sleeve.

"I knew you would. That's so good—" As Valerie began speaking once more, Josh attempted to swing the door even wider. But his second attempt wasn't as silent as the first. The distinctive sound of movement behind her made Valerie whip her head toward Hazel.

The last thing we needed was Valerie opening fire at Hazel or Josh or anyone, so I pulled her attention back to me the only way I knew how.

"Princess, look at me." The words were sour on my tongue, and I had a hard time believing that I managed to get them out without puking up the contents of my stomach. The old pet name was one I swore to never fucking say again, and I told Valerie as much, but seeing her face, you wouldn't know that.

Her head turned on a dime, and she inhaled a sharp breath. In a turn I wasn't expecting, her eyes grew wide, and she appeared more like the woman I met so many years ago. There was hope in her eyes and less anger and tension in her jaw and the rest of her features.

She was delusional, and the way she flipped from murderous to innocent in an instant just proved it further. The last thing I wanted to do was pretend for even a second that there was something more than feelings of disdain and complete hatred between us, but to give Josh an opportunity to do whatever the fuck he was planning on doing, I'd do it.

"This doesn't need to be complicated, right?"

My eyes briefly connected with Josh's on the other side of the door, and he nodded. He knew what I was doing or at least knew it was as a diversion for him.

"No, Bear, it doesn't," Valerie said, taking a small step toward me but keeping the gun trained on Hazel.

I chanced a glance at Hazel while Valerie shifted her eyes to her as well. If I never saw her cry again, it would be too soon. The tears were streaming down her face, and her cheeks were flushed, probably from the pain.

And I knew I'd do anything for her, even pretend to understand what my delusional ex-wife was talking about. It was the only way I'd be able to ensure that she wouldn't hurt Hazel and Josh would have the opportunity to open the damn door.

"You look good, Valerie."

She was vain, and she loved compliments about her appearance. She craved knowing that she was the best-looking person in a room, bar none. She grinned like I knew she would.

"Why the theatrics, Princess? Did you really want my attention that bad? Do you still need me? We grew out of each other. That's why we had to part ways; you know all of this. So, why did you have to take it this far? I don't understand the point of all of this," I waved my hands, motioning at the room around us. "Pretending to be someone else, the fake social media accounts, taking those photos of us, following me."

I had talked long enough that Josh was able to push the door open a few more inches but not enough to move the boxes that were in front of it. Whatever he had in mind likely required a clear path and those boxes had to move at least a few more inches.

"You still don't get it, Bear. I knew you wouldn't believe my words." Her voice was pleading and panicked, but she gave Josh the opportunity to make some noise without her noticing. She was too focused on making me understand. She lowered the gun still trained on Hazel a few inches and took another step toward me. "So, I had to show you with my actions. And how do you know someone truly loves you? What's the most romantic and brave gesture of that love? Spilling someone's blood. *Killing someone for them.*"

I almost didn't register Valerie's words as I watched Josh

push the door open the rest of the way and step into the room on nearly silent feet.

What happened next wasn't like it's portrayed in the movies. When chaos erupts and a million things happen at once, the editors slow down the speed of the film so the viewer doesn't miss a single bit of the action. They cut from one viewpoint to the other.

Without an ounce of hesitation, Valerie spun away from me and raised the gun toward Hazel once more. In the same breath, Josh stepped farther into the room and raised his own weapon aimed at Valerie. Both of them fired as I leaped for Valerie's arm, hoping Josh's aim was true and I wouldn't get caught in the cross fire.

Then there was a bang. Then blood and sirens and screaming.

Josh was gripping a Taser that had hit Valerie on the back of the thigh with the live prongs. But he was a fraction of a second too late. The moment Josh tased Valerie, she pulled the trigger, missing Hazel's head, which seemed to be the original target, but hitting her left shoulder before she collapsed to the floor.

Valerie twitched and groaned on the ground as Josh continued tasing her, never letting up on the voltage whipping through her body.

Hazel was screaming, but every other sound in the room was muffled by the sound of blood pumping wildly in my ears. I jumped over Valerie and immediately began untying Hazel's wrists. My hands were shaking, and the rope kept slipping through my fingers, but I managed to get her free. I worked quickly untying her ankles and cursed when I saw the raw skin beneath her jeans.

I reached to remove the duct tape on her mouth, but between the tears and the blood, the tape over her mouth peeled back.

The screaming had stopped—she'd lost consciousness—and the lack of sound coming from her was so much worse.

Her entire body had gone limp and there was blood pouring from the bullet wound on her shoulder and soaking the green material of her sweater. There was so much blood. Being a vet, I saw blood every day, but there was something different about seeing the blood of the person you love. It seemed thicker and harder to stop. The smell was noxious, like I could taste it.

As gently as I could manage, I lifted Hazel out of the chair and grabbed the gun that I slid underneath it. I stepped over Valerie, who was being held at gunpoint by Josh. The murderous look in his eyes was one I had never seen before and could go my whole life without seeing again. In his right hand, Josh held the gun steadily pointed at Valerie's head, while in his left, he still gripped the Taser and shocked her each time she tried to move at all.

The sun was gone, and it was too dark in the upstairs of the bar to perform any sort of first aid on Hazel.

"You got this?" I asked Josh while carrying Hazel through the doorway and into the hallway.

"Yes, take care of Hazel." He didn't tear his eyes away from Valerie, who was watching me with wide, surprised eyes. She attempted to move, so Josh hit her again with the Taser. "Stay the fuck down, you psycho bitch!"

The sirens were close. They had to be close because I didn't know how much blood Hazel had lost or what else Valerie had done to her. The narrow stairway was even more difficult to descend with Hazel in my arms, but I tucked her close and barreled down. All the while, I told her that it would be okay.

I told her that she would make it because she didn't survive years of abuse at the hands of Michael to leave the world so soon after she'd gotten her life back.

As I ran through the empty bar, I told her that the world was a better place with her light in it.

I kicked the front door open, and I told her again that she had to hang on.

The police pulled into the parking lot first with their sirens at full volume as soon as we hit the cold winter air. I turned to protect Hazel from the gravel shooting in every direction. The cars stopped in front of the bar but left enough room for the ambulance that had just turned the corner.

The stupid sign at the top of the door mocked me as they came to a stop. And my relief was short lived at seeing the ambulance as I glanced down at Hazel after I directed the cops upstairs and told them it was the woman on the ground that had kidnapped and tortured Hazel. And that the man wielding the gun was my brother and helped me save her. She was growing paler by the second, and her breaths were coming in short, shallow gasps.

Both of us were covered in her blood, and I couldn't tell which one of us was shaking.

The ambulance stopped in the spot the police had left, and when the doors swung open, I hopped up and placed her on the gurney. Over the noise of the sirens, I explained to them all of the injuries I knew of to the best of my ability.

"Are you hurt, too?" one of the paramedics asked. I shook my head. "If you're riding with us, get up front so we can take care of her."

Helplessly, I jogged around to the front and slipped into the seat as they tended to her. The paramedic that spoke to me before alerted the driver that we were ready to go. He sped out of the parking lot and narrowly missed a car that refused to yield.

Through the small window between the front cabin and the back, I heard them talking and discussing Hazel's condition. I peeked back, and it didn't look like the oxygen mask did much to help her breathing. In the few seconds we'd been on the road, they'd already cut off her sweater, exposing her skin to the cool air.

I lifted a hand to wipe the sweat collecting on my brow but stopped. My hands were covered in Hazel's blood. It was already drying, and it was the smell that reminded me of my parents' bedroom—finding my mother on the bathroom floor, it smelled the same. And I fended off the panic again, just barely.

"Five minutes out," the driver said, wailing on his horn as we sped through a red light.

Without anything else to do and willing to try anything, I began to pray for the second time in so many hours.

I hoped that God, or whoever was listening, could hear the desperation in my prayer and would have mercy on me—on Hazel. We hadn't had enough time together, and I already knew I couldn't live without her. I was powerless. I'd gotten her in that situation, and I couldn't do a damn thing to get her out.

I prayed until the ambulance came to a stop at the emergency room entrance. I hurried out of the passenger seat. They already had Hazel out and were pushing the gurney through the doors.

For a split second, and just before the paramedic told me to wait in a room around the corner, I reached out and touched Hazel's hand. There was no warmth radiating from her fingers that still hung limply over the edge of the gurney. The sheets had been stained red as well. Everything was red with her blood.

But as I touched her hand, I fought the urge to panic about the lack of warmth and told her that she had no choice but to stay.

FIFTY-SEVEN

Luke

For the second time in my life, I spent the third day of December standing in a cemetery. For the second time in my life, Josh stood next to me as we stared at the brand-new headstone. Although the two days were separated by fifteen years, it seemed like the first day hadn't happened all that long ago. I found myself comparing them in silence.

It was cooler the second time, but the air seemed thicker. More people attended the service the second time, too. My parents' service had taken place in the morning on a Wednesday. Most people had to work, but it was less expensive than waiting for the weekend. There were only a few people—namely neighbors, coworkers, and my uncle that attended along with Josh and me.

People also didn't want to celebrate the life of a man who killed his wife. And a wife who killed her husband in self-defense.

There weren't any flowers because that cost was a luxury, and honestly, flowers made it seem like a celebration—I wanted it to be anything but a celebration. They both lived miserable existences and died in just as miserable circumstances. There wasn't much to celebrate—their deaths had left Josh and me orphans. We were also the worst kind of orphans; we were poor, homeless orphans.

They were both cremated. But after Josh and my uncle insisted on having a place to visit them—a place to visit our mom, at least—I managed to scrounge up enough money from my minimum wage job to afford to buy them two footstones. Mom's included the epitaph, "Loving Mother," along with her name and the date she died. But Dad's was blank but for his name, his date of birth, and the date he died. It was also across the cemetery.

I wish I could've given her more. But more words meant more money, and I had no more to give.

The second service was full of people. Although it was a Thursday afternoon, most of them felt it was enough of an occasion to take off work. I hadn't even gone back to work after spending most of my time in the hospital.

There were also flowers everywhere—her favorite were red and white roses, and they were ordered in abundance. The family's personal pastor flew down to conduct the funeral and called it a celebration of life as each person stood to talk and share stories.

Not knowing whether I should attend or not, I decided it was best to say my goodbyes and put an end to that chapter of my life. Although I didn't know if closure would ever really be an option. I arrived halfway through the service and stood in the back while Josh waited in the car. Away from the knowing eyes of her family, I tried to listen to the pastor, tried to comprehend the stories her family and friends told, but it was all muffled like I wasn't there. I knew I was a ghost of a person—too much had happened.

I didn't attend the graveside part of the service, but when everyone else left, Josh and I walked over to the freshly dug grave and just stared. We'd been staring for a while when Josh muttered, "Good fucking riddance."

I nearly laughed, and I probably would have laughed had I not been replaying all the times I had wished Valerie dead. Every time she reentered my life and hurt someone I cared about, I may not have wished her dead, but I hoped she would disappear at least.

The way Valerie lived her life, I knew one day she would likely piss off the wrong person and wind up on the wrong side of a gun. I just never imagined it would be Josh's gun.

After I hurried Hazel out of the bar and sent the police upstairs, the Taser Josh was keeping on Valerie gave out. The way he described it was that in the split second that she realized that he no longer had control, Valerie lurched for the gun in his opposite hand. They struggled for several seconds, hearing the police pounding up the stairs and into the dark hallway, before her finger slipped on the trigger, sending the bullet straight through her head.

One of the officers saw the ending and vouched for Josh's side of the story. The police questioned him for a while, but after talking to me and the thug she hired to pick a fight with me outside of the bar, they let him go.

Her death felt unceremonious. I was expecting there'd be more to it, but what I was most concerned about was Josh. Whether it was unintentional or not, he'd had a hand—literally—in ending her life. But not to my surprise, Josh had come to terms with it rather quickly and hadn't let it weigh on his conscience too much. At least not at that point.

After the police released him and he'd joined me in Hazel's hospital room, he'd said what we were all thinking: "The world is better off without her."

"Let's head back. I'm done here," I said, walking away without waiting for Josh to respond. His footfalls on the grass behind me let me know he was following, but I didn't glance back. I didn't want to see her name or think about her one more time.

The car ride back to the hospital was quiet. There was too much to think about.

Valerie was dead, and Hazel was alive. That was the most important thing: Hazel was *alive*.

The wound in her upper chest could have been fatal had the bullet been only an inch or two lower. After hours of surgery to remove the bullet and repair the damage, she'd been unconscious for an entire day. It was one of the worst days of my life, knowing that any number of post-op issues could arise, especially while she was unconscious.

They also reset her broken nose and fingers and tended to the raw skin around her ankles and wrists from the restraints. After she finally woke up, they diagnosed her with a severe concussion, but having to be laid up in a hospital bed made it easier to recover from.

Almost thirty-six hours to the second after we entered the hospital through the emergency bay, Hazel woke up. It was like the world had stopped spinning when she was unconscious, but when her hazel eyes—although swollen and black and bruised—found mine, the earth had resumed its dance around the sun. Because goddamn, that woman was my sun.

I'd sat next to her every second she was asleep. The only time I moved was to use the restroom or find a coffee refill because I wanted to be there when she woke up. I'd felt utterly helpless watching her and hoped to God she would wake up. Her dark hair fanned across the white pillowcase, and I hoped one day I'd get to tangle my fingers through it. I hoped I'd be able to feel her kiss me back with the same urgency and heat I'd once felt. I hoped I'd one day be able to hear those three little words fall from her lips. The same words I had been chanting in my head every time I looked at her.

Staring at her while she was unconscious, I remembered something she'd said that morning after Halloween. Sitting in my kitchen, hungover as hell on her birthday and as beautiful as ever, she told me that not all unexpected things were bad. I hadn't believed her then—my pessimism about it bone deep. But after everything, I had begun to believe her.

The first time she opened her eyes, it was only for a few seconds, but it was enough. She saw me, registered my face and then smiled before sighing my name and letting her eyes fall back closed. It kept me going for the next hour before she woke up again, that time for slightly longer.

I was terrified she was going to hate me. I'd failed her in the worst possible way and spent hours after she'd woken up apologizing. That was until she all but yelled at me to stop saying I was sorry because it was making her headache worse.

She claimed there was nothing to forgive, but I didn't argue. I wasn't in a place to argue, nor was I in a place to not give her whatever the fuck she wanted. She told me that I was never allowed to apologize again, so I promised myself I'd spend my life apologizing and making up for it with my actions.

"Luke, you coming?" Josh asked. He'd parked in the visitor lot of the hospital, and I hadn't even noticed. We'd all become used to the routine of staying with Hazel. Every day it was the same parking lot, riding the elevator to the third floor and waving at the nurses at the station just outside the elevator before heading down the hallway to the right and into the farthest possible room.

Once Hazel had been transferred out of the ICU, one of us stayed with her at all times. Between me, her parents, her sister, and Amanda, someone was always with her, but I was eager to get her home.

Josh and I took the same route, but when we approached Hazel's room, the monotony of the routine came to a grinding halt. At the sound of raised voices, Josh and I both turned to look at each other in disbelief before breaking out into a sprint the rest of the way.

I pounded through the open door to find Becky sobbing. She

was beside herself, trying to calm a belligerent Chris who was yelling at Hazel. She was sitting in her hospital bed with her arms crossed to the best of her ability.

"The fuck is going on here?" I asked in an authoritative tone that silenced everyone.

"We're leaving. Right, Chris?" Becky said between sniffles.

He scoffed and nudged her out of the way. "Like hell am I going anywhere before I get some fucking answers."

"Everyone, calm down. What are you babbling about?" I stepped between Chris and Becky, blocking him from a direct path to either woman. Although I wasn't surprised to find Becky in Hazel's room, I would have been surprised if she'd brought Chris along with her.

After Hazel woke up in the hospital, and once I finally located her purse and phone underneath the passenger seat of my car, Hazel had several missed calls and urgent texts from Becky. Even recovering from being shot, Hazel responded to Becky and let her know she could use her apartment for anything if needed, and Amanda offered up her time to watch Emmy. Hazel still hadn't figured out exactly what was going on, but it seemed like she was preparing to leave Chris. Which was why I was surprised to see him.

"She's the one that put ideas into my wife's head," Chris spat as he looked around my large frame to glare at Hazel. "She's the reason Becky's leaving me and taking my kid. Hazel left her fucking fiancé, so now Becky thinks she can do the same thing to me."

"If Becky's leaving you, then it's no one's fault but your own, Chris," Hazel chimed in from behind me. I peered over my shoulder and gave her an incredulous look. Her eyes were still rimmed with darkness and her arm was hanging in a sling, but she was still ready to fight.

"Now look, Chris. I don't think you're going—" I began, trying to keep my tone calm in the hopes of diffusing the situation, but I watched the rage tear apart his features and his face reddened.

"Luke, don't start throwing your weight around like you can do something with it. I'm going to figure out what that bitch told my wife to make her decide to move back in with her damn parents and take my fucking money and my kid."

Bitch. The word lit my very short fuse.

"I know you probably won't understand this because you like to yell and talk down to your wife, but the last thing you're going to do is call the woman I love a bitch. *Especially* when she's lying in a hospital bed. Now, you can leave on your own, or I can make you leave. Which one would you prefer? Because honestly"—I shrugged—"I would be fine with either."

He gulped and sucked in a long breath through his nose but didn't let his angry expression waver for a minute. By the way his hands were fisted at his sides and his jaw clenched, I knew he would fight me on it. He was a man scorned and needed an outlet.

His closed fist reared back, and a smile crept across my face.

I think I heard Hazel, or maybe it was Josh, mutter a curse under their breath before Chris's fist flew through the air, not connecting with anything. His expression dropped as I pushed my forearm underneath his chin and pinned him to the wall. The TV hanging above us bounced when his back thudded against the wall and he expelled a tiny grunt at the impact.

Just as I was about to begin my threatening well-rehearsed speech, hospital security darted into the room, looking more frazzled than I expected.

"Fucking finally," Hazel sighed, slumping against the bed. "I've been pushing this damn button for the past ten minutes." In her right hand, between the fingers that were not broken and bandaged, Hazel was holding the remote to her bed that also had several necessary buttons that could call the nurse or security.

They were both large men that had trouble catching their

breath even as they stepped up to Chris and me. They each grabbed one of Chris's arms, gripping them tightly around the thick material of his jacket and escorted him out of the room as he muttered curses and other things I didn't hear.

"Now that that's sorted, Becky," Hazel said, turning as much as she could to the woman who had become her friend. "Are you okay?"

"Yeah, yeah, I'll be fine. Honestly, it's nothing new. I need to go pick up Emmy from my parents, though. Can we talk later, Hazel? Let me know when you're out of here."

Hazel's brow furrowed, and she eyed Becky skeptically but ended up agreeing.

"I'll walk you down," Josh said as Becky tried to slip past him. She mumbled a "thanks" and waved to Hazel and me one last time before she rounded the corner.

"I swear, these fucking crazy men and—"

"The woman you love, huh?" Hazel said abruptly. I whipped my head to her, mouth agape.

For a moment, I didn't know what she was asking, but I realized I had said those exact words out loud only minutes prior.

Hazel sat expectantly, tapping her good fingers against her sling with her eyebrows raised.

"I just—you know it was—sometimes—" I fumbled hopelessly for the right words. Giving up entirely, I scrubbed my hands over my face and massaged the sudden tension in the back of my neck as I waited for her to begin her verbal undressing. But she just stared with the same look on her face like she expected me to say something.

"Angel, this is not—why are you looking at me like that?"

She quirked an eyebrow, but a hint of a smile brushed over her lips, pulling at one corner of her mouth.

"Now, why are you smiling?" I asked, genuinely dumbfounded.

She shrugged. "I don't know, maybe I just think you're *cute* when you're flustered."

I tipped my head back and laughed. It had taken her over a month, but she'd finally used the damn word against me. And I understood why she didn't find it to be the compliment I always meant it as. The grin on her face told me she was proud of herself, and I couldn't stand it. I had to kiss her.

I crossed the room in two strides and gingerly grasped her face in my hands. Her eyes widened like she didn't expect my reaction, but there wasn't a second that went by that I didn't want to kiss her or touch her.

Her lips were soft and supple beneath my own and when she sighed into my mouth, it was like coming home. She tasted like coffee and faintly of her mint toothpaste from that morning. When my tongue flattened against her lips, she was already letting me in and shifting to wrap her arm around my shoulders and tugging her fingers into my hair.

It went against everything stoking inside of me to pull away, but I did. And Hazel groaned at the loss.

"I love you, Angel," I said with confidence, still cupping her face as we sat only inches apart. In that moment, I watched her eyes gloss over, her lips part on a gasp and the rise and fall of her chest grow quicker as the words fell over her. Nothing else mattered, nothing existed beyond our connection. Her gaze never faltered, and once the gravity of my confession settled over her, her lips tilted in a sweet, promising smile.

"That's good because I love you too."

And then I kissed her again because every second her lips weren't on mine felt like I was lost. It was the first time she'd said it, but I knew I'd never tire of hearing those words from her. She said them with the same conviction I did, and I could feel her confidence radiating through me.

I loved her with every dark, bruised, and damaged part of myself, and it seemed to be enough for her. She was so easy to love. I knew if I got to love her forever, and if she honored me by returning the favor, it wouldn't be long enough.

"God, I need you, Luke. I need to get out of here," she

murmured against my lips, breaking our kiss for only a moment before gripping my hair tighter and pushing us back together.

"Who's ready to get the heck out of—" The doctor walked into the room, peering up from his clipboard to see us in an intimate yet significant moment. "Here. Are you ready to go home, Hazel?"

She didn't even have to say anything—words were inconsequential to her bright eyes and her sunshine smile that lit up the room and my entire world.

EPILOGUE

Hazel

Eight months later

"Okay, and this is the bedroom. I've already cleaned the sheets and the towels in the bathroom are clean as well. But there are extras in the closet if you need any. And I—"

"Hazel, seriously, this is incredible, but we've been here before. I know where everything is." Becky laughed. "Thank you for dropping everything and letting us in early."

"What are friends for? I just want to make sure you feel comfortable and have everything you need."

The day Chris followed Becky to the hospital and accused me of having something to do with the reason she was leaving was the day she left. She'd spent the previous seven months living in her parents' spare room with Emmy. It worked for the time she spent there, but it was affecting her relationship with her parents. So, she decided to get the hell out, which is where I came in. I offered up my little one-bedroom apartment that I only spent a total of two weeks in.

She was supposed to move in the following week, but after a

particularly nasty argument between her and her parents, she wanted the keys as soon as possible.

Even being in the apartment for that short time, the memories came hard and fast and were more overwhelming than I expected. Most of them didn't center around the apartment, but just knowing that on the other side of the dining room and bathroom wall was the place where Valerie lived for weeks was enough to keep me from the place.

The police had searched the apartment just after I was admitted to the hospital and to no one's surprise, her shrine to Luke was expansive. One wall was littered with photos from the previous few weeks—photos taken from right outside his windows, right outside my windows, from the clinic, near my apartment. They went on and on, and as time elapsed, the creepier they became with photos of us in the middle of sex and one where we forgot to close the blinds completely when I was on my knees in front of him.

They were collaged on the wall in chronological order with notes jotted down in the corner of each. Most of them depicted what stage she thought we were in in our relationship and where the photo was taken. She drew things like angel wings, halos, and sometimes horns on my photos, and sometimes her notes referred to me as a bitch or a whore, but Luke was always referred to as Bear.

Knowing the other types of activities that may have been going on over there, I couldn't stand to stay in my apartment. With the help I needed from just getting out of the hospital, it made sense to either go back to Nashville in the interim or move in with Luke.

I pretended like I had a decision, but I knew better. Luke, in his brazenly possessive way, was not going to let me go. And secretly, I loved it.

I'd kept the apartment for this exact scenario– as a sanctuary for anyone in need. I knew it would be useful one day.

"Mommy, do I have my own room?" Emmy sprinted into the

room, blonde hair flowing behind her and shoes clicking against the wood floor.

Becky sighed and pulled Emmy into a tight embrace. "Not yet, baby, but someday soon you will."

The details of her exact situation with Chris were still a mystery, but it was easy to assume it was pretty bad if she felt the need to flee to her parents'. It wasn't that her parents were bad people, they were just the type of people that always required something in return.

And although my situation with Michael—along with being kidnapped by Valerie—was the worst thing I would ever have to go through, I was eternally thankful that I didn't have a child with him. Watching Becky navigate leaving her marriage while trying to provide for her daughter—especially after being a stay-at-home mom—was enough to make me grateful it was just myself that I had to get out of that house.

Michael tried to contact me a few times when I was fresh out of the hospital and had just begun physical therapy. He ended up moving back to Nashville and working for a law firm there, but he flew all the way to Austin to try one last time with me. He claimed he wanted a chance to make amends and Luke dutifully stepped in when I was too shocked to slam the door in his face.

I hadn't spoken to him since then, but my mom told me that he was miserable, which was only a slight consolation. He moved back in with his parents, and his mom *always* kept a keenly watchful eye on him. He couldn't do anything without her knowing.

He deserved to be miserable for a long time. But maybe Luke was right, and I was too forgiving because a part of me didn't exactly want Michael to be miserable forever. Maybe just for the same amount of time he had controlled my life.

And extra miserable for the year he hit me.

But in some twisted way, I had Michael to thank for leading me to Luke and that softened me a bit.

My phone vibrating in my pocket released me from my

thoughts. I was late, I knew I was late, but getting Becky settled was also important.

"Are you sure there's nothing y'all need then?"

Becky waved me off. "We'll be fine, Hazel. Go live your own life, but if we do end up needing something, I'm sure I can handle it."

"You're right, you can," I said with a smile and stooped to Emmy's level. "Bye, Emmy. I'll see you soon, okay?"

She released her death grip on Becky's legs to throw herself into my arms. God, I wished I had her energy.

"Bye, Hazellll!" She pressed her little mouth to my cheek, and I couldn't help but smile. She would be okay; they both would be. "Also," she whispered into my ear. "Thank you for helping my mommy."

Her unsolicited gratitude pulled at my heartstrings. "You're so welcome, sweet girl."

Turning out of the parking lot of the apartment complex, my phone rang again, and I cringed.

"I know I'm late, I'm sorry, but everything with Becky took a little longer than expected. I'm on my way right now. I'll be there in like twenty minutes tops. I'll break speed limits and overall drive recklessly if it means I get there sooner," I said upon answering the phone.

"You will not drive recklessly. And you're already late, so what difference will twenty more minutes really make?"

"I'm really sorry. I just wanted to—"

"Angel, it's okay. There's no need to continue apologizing, especially when you were busy helping other people. I will see you when you get here, okay?" Luke said, calming the rest of my nerves.

I hated being late, especially for big, important events, and this was one of them.

"Thanks for being so understanding. I'll see you soon."

"I love you."

"I love you, too," I said with a cheesy grin he likely heard in my voice.

It was unlikely I would ever get tired of hearing him say that he loved me. Luke loved me big; he loved me so thoroughly sometimes it was hard to reconcile that men like Michael and Luke even existed at the same time.

But after witnessing and experiencing the worst of the worst, it was easier to identify the good. And Luke was my good. The very real possibility that everything could have ended so much worse also made that good so much sweeter.

That's not to say, though, that the months after Valerie died were any walk in the park. I had newfound issues with confined spaces and had become overly paranoid about keeping track of my surroundings. Restaurants continued to be difficult or any space where there were a lot of people in close proximity.

We planned to fly up to Nashville just after the new year, but it only took thinking about getting on the plane to send me spiraling into a full-blown panic attack. And then, I would begin panicking even harder because I assumed Luke would be upset that I was panicking. Michael would have been upset, but like I said, Luke loved me big.

Only a month earlier did I finally get on the damn plane. It took a lot of work to get there, but baby steps were still steps in the right direction. And we both celebrated the little wins.

Writing also helped me cope, and after scrapping the entire first draft I'd been working on the year prior, I decided to go in a new direction and write what I knew best—us. Luke and I—or a version of us—would be the main characters, and I would write our story. It seemed bookworthy at least, but I was keeping it a surprise. It was cathartic to get it all out onto the page and see it from as much of an outsider's perspective as I ever would be able to.

Luke hadn't had the best time either and was less inclined to find an outlet. His night terrors had returned with a vengeance.

Many nights for several months following my release from the hospital, I'd be woken up by the sounds of his yelling. Luke choking and crying my name was my own version of hell.

Oftentimes he dreamed of finding his parents dead, which was a dream he'd had for quite some time, but the new one was a graphic depiction of what that night in the little room above the bar could have looked like if neither Luke nor I made it out. He said Valerie would kill me while he watched, then from outside of my body, he could see me witnessing her kill him and then herself.

Watching the person you loved struggle was heartbreaking. Especially when there wasn't much you could do to fix it.

But with time, patience, therapy, and a ton of really good sex, we made it through. We even made it through living with his brother for almost six months which was nearly a nightmare in and of itself.

Everyone involved in that day had lingering issues they were still fighting months later. Me, Luke, Josh—we all had our demons. I would have assumed Blakely was also reeling, but she'd disappeared. The night I was admitted to the hospital, her phone had turned off and hadn't turned back on since. She hadn't gone to see her parents as she told Amanda. Her parents didn't even know where she was, save for sporadic phone calls from different locations each time.

The likelihood we would ever find out her motivations for aiding in my kidnapping dwindled the longer she was missing.

Josh decided the best way to deal with being a part of Valerie's death was to drown himself in women. His room became a revolving door of hookups and one-night stands. Luke and I had both walked in on him in the kitchen, the living room and even on the back patio with new women, and although I was not going to say anything since I was a guest in their home, I think the day he moved in with Reed we both were relieved.

That's also when we realized that Luke's house couldn't be our home. The family that moved into the house next door—the house Michael and I once lived in together—was a cute younger couple with a new baby. They seemed happy and were almost identical to what I, at one point, imagined my life would look like with Michael.

I kept as far away from them as I could.

But Luke and I both agreed it was time for a fresh start. It was time to distance ourselves from the painful memories. We wanted a place that wasn't haunted by our pasts as we tried to move forward.

And the perfect place happened to be just north of the city, near the neighborhood where Luke and Josh grew up. The house, though, was a far cry from the childhood home Luke described to me.

When I pulled into the driveway, a smile I had no control of broke across my face, and an overwhelming sense of calm washed over me. At the sight of the light-brown brick and spacious, white porch that wrapped around the side of the house opposite the garage, it all felt right in a way it hadn't before. Like that was the place we were meant to be.

I parked my car next to Luke's truck and noted that our realtor's car was gone since she probably wasn't going to wait all day for me to get there. We'd closed on the house that morning and after signing the never-ending pile of papers, we were supposed to meet at our new home to celebrate when Becky called.

Luke dropped me at the old house to retrieve my car, and I kissed him and Sadie goodbye with the promise to be as quick as I could.

It was a blazing hot summer day. The Texas heat and humidity immediately made my skin sticky with sweat, but I didn't want to rush into the house. It would be the only time I'd walk into our home for the first time, and I wanted to cherish it. So, when I stepped out of the car, I paused to scan the landscaping and marvel at the tall trees planted throughout the yard.

They cast shadows across the lawn and over the house, sparing it from the scorching sun.

Our home sat on a huge lot set far off the road, and it ticked all of our boxes. It wasn't too far of a drive to the clinic for Luke and had a huge kitchen, a living room with a fireplace along with enough bedrooms for our future, including an office for me. The backyard was also massive and fenced so Sadie could run between her naps.

It was perfect.

Standing in the middle of the yard, staring up at the house, I probably looked insane. Our neighbors were likely peeking out their windows, wondering who the hell had moved in next door, but I couldn't care.

A sound in front of me pulled my attention from my survey of the house, but it was a welcome interruption.

Luke's large frame occupied the entire doorway into the house. He casually leaned against the wooden doorframe, and his arms crossed over his broad chest. His dark tattoos were on full display, peeking out beneath his short-sleeved T-shirt that curved around his biceps. A knowing smirk tugged at one corner of his lips, and the effect it had on me was the same every time—my heart raced, the stupid butterflies erupted in my stomach, and I had to adjust how I was standing to relieve some of the pressure that built between my legs.

It was a similar smirk to the one he'd given me when we'd realized they'd miswritten my name on most of the paperwork. Instead of "Luke Shepherd and Hazel Cooper," it was "Luke Shepherd and Hazel Shepherd." His smirk was one that said he thoroughly enjoyed the sight of his last name attached to my first name.

His dark hair was mussed from running his fingers through it too many times at the closing. That, combined with his smirk and relaxed stance, screamed casual dominance and confidence. Like he was the king of his fucking castle.

"Are you going to come inside our house, or are you just going to stare at it all day?"

I rolled my eyes, shook my head, and hurried across the lawn and up the porch stairs. Once my feet hit the porch, Luke opened his arms just in time for me to jump into them. I buried my face into the crook of his neck and inhaled his spicy, manly scent as he grasped under my ass and kicked the door closed with his foot.

Before setting me down, he pressed his lips to mine in a hungry, possessive kiss that I had begun to crave. His tongue licked at my lips, hoping for entrance, which I conceded, but only for a moment. It was a challenge, but I pulled away with one final peck to his plump lips.

"I want to see the house," I requested while wiggling in his arms. With a sigh, he let me down but didn't let me go far before he could slap my ass.

I pretended to be affronted by the gesture, my hand defensively covering my ass.

Luke laughed and pulled me into his side. "I'm not sorry. Those damn jean shorts are a tease," he said with a kiss to the top of my head.

"Yeah, yeah. Now, let's go," I urged him forward.

"We've already seen the house several times. What's so different about it now?"

I smiled up at him as we stepped from the open entryway into the spacious living room. "Now, it's ours."

The floors were a rich-brown hardwood that continued throughout the entire house and warmed up the space. It was hard to discern what my favorite aspects of the house were. It was between the vaulted ceilings in the living room with exposed wood beams, the massive brick fireplace, or the windows that spanned the back wall of the space with a perfect view into the expansive backyard.

"Is Sadie back there?" I asked, my voice bouncing off the walls in the empty room as I walked closer to the back windows.

"Yup, she was back in the corner a few minutes ago," Luke said as he stepped up behind me. His steady fingers smoothed down the sides of my arms and the warmth of him pressed against my back.

Sure enough, Sadie was tucked into one corner of the yard in a shady spot. She was hidden beneath trees, rolling in the grass with her tongue hanging out the side of her mouth.

"She seems to be enjoying her new backyard."

"Yeah, she saw the grass when we got here and wanted to go straight outside." We watched Sadie for another moment before Luke spun me around to face him.

With his hands cradling my face, he kissed my lips gently. I melted into him, and we got lost for a minute, standing in the middle of our new living room. "I have something for you," he said when he pulled away, but there was something odd in his voice. His tone was slightly off, and my heart began racing in response.

He threaded his fingers through my own and began leading me through the empty living room until I spotted something to our right. I stopped in the middle of the room, removed my hand from Luke's and stood in front of the fireplace. On the mantel were photographs I assumed Luke had placed there.

The first one was in a delicate white frame with flowers carved into it. It was of my entire family—Mom, Dad, Delilah, Tony, my niece, nephew, and me—sitting in front of the Christmas tree. Miles, my nephew, was in my lap, eating a cookie with icing smeared across his mouth, and Amber, my niece, was cradled in my sister's arms. It was several years ago, yet we all looked relatively the same.

It was a photo I'd long forgotten about.

The second photo was in a dark metal frame. The photo inside was one we had taken at Friendsgiving the year before, right before everything went downhill. We set the automatic timer on Amanda's phone and squished onto and behind the couch. Everyone—even Blakely—was smiling.

The third photo was one I'd only seen a few times before. It was in a wooden frame that appeared much older than the rest, but the photo fit it well. It was of Josh and Luke at a lake they used to go to as children with their parents. Their mom is tucked between them with a huge smile on her face, her dirty-blonde hair wet from the water and the three of them are squinting at the sun directly behind the camera.

It's the picture Luke kept by his bed.

"It feels like home," I said to Luke, who was standing next to me, his hands in his pockets.

He shifted, tugging me into his side and running a hand over my back. "You feel like home," he murmured into my hair. "Come on," he said, leading me into the kitchen. My heart began thumping in my chest once again, realizing the photos weren't the *"something"* he had for me. The kitchen was bathed in the afternoon sun that soaked the white cabinets and the dark floors in warm light.

In the middle of the room, though, on the butcher block island, were two bottles of champagne and two glasses. The sun reflected through the window above the sink and glinted off the champagne glasses.

"This is a big moment, I figured champagne was good for the occasion," Luke said, slowly releasing my hand as he rounded the island.

"That's a fantastic idea." My heart rate was slowly going back down as I glanced around the kitchen to see if he'd hidden any other surprises. We were at the point in our relationship where every time Luke said he had a *"surprise"* or *"something to show me,"* I assumed he was about to drop to one knee and whip out the second-best thing that he could have stuffed into his pants.

We'd had the conversation and agreed that after we closed on the house, we would discuss it again. I was trying to enjoy the part of our relationship we were in rather than rushing toward the next step. The ring would come, and if it didn't happen immediately, that wouldn't delay our future.

"But this is... umm..." He stopped with his hand hovering over one of the bottles. He pushed it to me, sliding it across the counter slowly and as it got closer, the easier it was to read the label and the note I had written on it in a gold pen.

"Saved for Michael and Hazel's wedding day!"

My throat tightened and emotions I hadn't been vulnerable to in a long time bubbled to the surface. I could feel the sting of tears behind my eyes, but I willed them not to spill. My first reaction was, *How could Luke do something like this to ruin what was supposed to be an amazing day?* But I thought better of it. He had to have had a reason.

"Okay, see, I knew you'd react one of two ways, so it looks like that, based on the look on your face, option number two was the correct reaction." Luke hurried out as he came back around the island. With his hands on my hips, he turned me to face him and trapped me between his arms with his hands braced on the counter on either side of me.

He leaned down until we were nearly eye level, and I had no choice but to look at him or my shoes. His eyes were much more intriguing, and, in the sunlight, they were a startling, vivid green.

"This wasn't supposed to bring shit up, I swear. I found the bottle while packing and just thought that it would be a good way to end that chapter. Start fresh and move forward by either drinking the very expensive champagne the fuckface bought for us *or* smashing it on the ground outside. I'm up for either, that's why we have the second bottle. I've come prepared." He smoothed my hair out of my face and gripped the back of my neck while his thumb and forefinger on his other hand tilted my chin higher. "I love you, Angel. And I was only thinking of you when I grabbed that bottle this morning."

I could feel the honesty and truth in his words radiate through me. That part of my life was over, and I was so far removed from it that I was a completely different person than I was that same time the year before. Hazel of the year before would have been doing her best to keep the peace in an ugly, toxic and terrifying relationship. She would have been putting her needs second only to anyone around her, and she was utterly miserable and constantly in pain.

That Hazel would have gawked at the idea of drinking the champagne on any other day than her wedding day. But that Hazel was as dead as the relationship she'd been in.

"It's supposed to be really good champagne," I said with a deep breath, and the smile on Luke's face made the stress in my shoulders dissipate. He kissed my forehead and offered the bottle to me to open.

I shook my head and pushed it back to him. He shrugged and opened the bottle with a satisfying pop. I watched over the counter and through the backyard to Sadie still rolling in the grass as Luke poured our glasses behind me.

He said something that I didn't catch as I daydreamed about what it would be like when we got all of our furniture—both new and old—into the space. As I imagined which angle the couch would best fit, a glass of bubbly champagne appeared in front of my face. I retrieved my glass from Luke's hand and caught sight of the fresh ink on his forearm. It was a tattoo Devon had drawn up for him.

It was my silhouette—my hair, my back, the curve of my hips—but nestled between my shoulder blades and shaping around my sides were feathery angel wings that complemented the halo hovering above my head.

When Luke first approached me with the idea for the tattoo, I immediately told him it was a bad idea. It was loosely based on the photograph Valerie had taken of us in an unsuspecting position.

But I guess it was Luke's own version of the champagne—he'd taken something awful and stained with terrible memories and turned it into something beautiful. It was oddly cathartic.

And it has become my favorite tattoo. He'd inked himself onto my heart, so it was only fair I am inked on him, too.

I ran my nails over the smooth skin and over the tattoo. Goose bumps erupted over his tanned skin and around his dark hair. I covered my smile by taking a sip of my champagne.

Since we'd walked into the house, my phone hadn't stopped buzzing, so I ripped it from my shorts pocket and set it on the counter in front of us. I had almost a dozen missed text messages from Amanda.

Luke laughed, peering over my shoulder and seeing yet another message come through.

"Can she not be away from you for half an hour?" he asked.

I bit my lip and contemplated telling him the truth, not that it would hurt at that point. "She thinks you bought a ring and, for some reason, believes that today, right now, is the time you'd propose. She's been crazy about it lately, but I think it's just because she's *so* single that she wants to live vicariously through everyone else."

I took another long sip of champagne, enjoying the bubbles, as Luke shuffled behind me and chuckled. I finished my glass and his hand brushed against my stomach. "Bought a ring, maybe like that one?" he whispered into my ear, and it was all I could do not to drop my glass.

He caught the glass as I fumbled with it but kept one arm banded around me. I gasped at the oval-shaped stone that was comfortably tucked into the black velvet box he'd placed on the counter. My hands covered my mouth and the tears I'd nearly cried before—the regretful, sorrowful tears—morphed into tears of pure, unadulterated happiness.

I thought I was going to go into cardiac arrest with the way the organ in my chest pounded and based on how difficult it suddenly was to suck in air.

For the second time that day, Luke spun me around to face him, retrieved the ring from the counter, and dropped to one knee. My eyes flitted back and forth between Luke and the ring but finally settled on his face, although the tears in my eyes made it hard to see anything.

"You have made me happier than I ever imagined I could be. I feel like I've been looking for you for forever, and you were literally right next door. For most of my life, I believed the unexpected was a bad thing. But you changed that. You were so perfectly unexpected in all the best ways. I know the way things happened wasn't ideal, but at least it led me to you, Angel. So, with that, I want to promise you that I will always be honest, I will love you every day like it's the last day I will do so, and I will make sure that we continue to make new memories together. Hazel Cooper, will you marry me?"

"*Yes.*" The word flooded out of me like I'd been holding it in for a lifetime. As Luke tried to stand, I flung my arms around him, somehow knocking the large man off balance for just a moment. But he quickly righted himself and wrapped his arms around me like he'd never let me go.

"Okay, let's hope this sucker fits," Luke quipped, pulling back to wiggle the ring free from the box and slide it onto my finger.

It fit perfectly.

The diamond was even more brilliant in its rightful place on my finger, and the platinum band was thin and cool against my skin.

"I don't know what to say right now," I said honestly. It was the last thing I was expecting from the day, but my cheeks already hurt from smiling.

"No need to say anything because I need to kiss you now." And that he did. He kissed me thoroughly and until I felt it in my toes. His lips and tongue were urgent against mine, like it was the last piece of the proposal puzzle.

"We have to break in this house," he muttered against my lips, both of us equally out of breath.

"Oh, we absolutely will, with or without a bed." I smirked.

"Pour me more champagne and you can tell me if you think the kitchen island or up against the wall is the best place."

"Both. I'm going to make love to my fiancé on every surface of our house." With that dirty promise and a wink in my direction, he turned away and began refilling our glasses. I took the opportunity to shamelessly stare down at my hand like it was a foreign object, like it had been replaced with an unfamiliar version of my hand.

Luke reapproached with my champagne glass in his hand but paused before he gave it to me. He clasped my fingers in his and kissed my new ring. "It looks good."

"Yeah, I'll give you that one: you did damn good," I said, mimicking his motion and raising my glass. As was his usual, his free hand found its way around to the back of my neck and tangled into my hair. I understood what he meant in that moment, when he said I felt like home to him, because he felt like home to me.

Sometimes home isn't a place, it's a person.

"I love you," I whispered once I realized I hadn't yet told him since he'd proposed. "A life with you is worth going through everything we've been through. And I'd do it all again and again if it meant that we ended up here, together, every single time."

We both smiled, and the happiness flowed between us freely and easily.

"To the memories we'll make, Angel," he said, tapping his glass against mine. We sipped the expensive champagne and when he kissed me again, it tasted like forever.

THE END

ACKNOWLEDGMENTS

First book, done! Wow, I never thought I would actually get here. I've been writing my entire life, and one day dreamed of being a published author. But as so many dreams do, it felt like a far off, unattainable goal. Then Luke and Hazel barged into my head and set up camp there. There wasn't much I could do besides tell their story.

I lived and breathed these characters for nearly two years until I felt I'd done them justice. Luke and Hazel will forever hold a special place in my heart as the first characters I truly shared with others. I'm fiercely protective of them, and I hope you love them as much as I do.

And with that, there are so many people to thank:

My husband, thank you for putting up with the numerous late nights and days of writing. You handled my several breakdowns and bouts of self-doubt with patience and kindness, and I will be forever thankful. Your unwavering support was key to getting this book finished.

My Alpha reader, and Mom, you're my greatest cheerleader, and your honest feedback and support is a guiding light. Thank you for listening, and participating in, hours of brainstorming, which most of the time consisted of me ranting and babbling. Your patience is also remarkable. I probably would've told myself to just shut up by now.

My other Alpha reader, and best friend, I'm lucky to have found a lifelong friend that appreciates reading and writing as much as I do. And who will read my really sucky first draft

three times to make sure she does not miss a single detail before giving feedback. I feel confident in saying that there wouldn't be a book without you.

Ellie and everyone at My Brother's Editor, thank you for taking my manuscript and making it shiny and pretty. I'm eternally grateful.

Mayhem Cover Creations, thank you for taking my chaotic and nonsensical cover design ideas and crafting the cover of my dreams!

And anyone else who told me I could do it, and actually, everyone who also told me I couldn't, thank you.

ABOUT THE AUTHOR

Grace Turner lives in Houston, Texas with her husband and two rambunctious pups and has a revolving door full of friends and family always visiting. By day, she works as a lowly paralegal, and by night she reads, writes, and breathes contemporary romance. *Unexpected* is just the beginning for Grace, so keep a lookout for the rest of Murphy's Law series.

Made in the USA
Coppell, TX
24 February 2026

72256443R00331